The Tea Merchant

The Tea Merchant

Part 1 of a two-book series

JACKIE PHAMOTSE

PENGUIN BOOKS

The Tea Merchant

Published by Penguin Books
an imprint of Penguin Random House South Africa (Pty) Ltd
Reg. No. 1953/000441/07
The Estuaries No. 4, Oxbow Crescent, Century Avenue, Century City, 7441
PO Box 1144, Cape Town, 8000, South Africa
www.penguinrandomhouse.co.za

Penguin
Random House
South Africa

First published 2024

1 3 5 7 9 10 8 6 4 2

Publication © Penguin Random House 2024
Text © Jackie Phamotse 2024

Cover images: Fire background © THINGDSGN – stock.adobe.com;
Couple silhouette © TRAVELARIUM – stock.adobe.com;
Green tea leaves © Elegant Solution – stock.adobe.com;
Child and man silhouette © orfeev – stock.adobe.com

Editor: Thembi Mazibuko

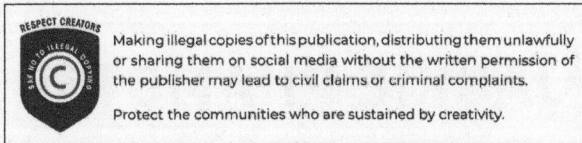

Set in 11.5 pt on 15.5 pt Palatino Linotype

Printed by **novus print**, a division of Novus Holdings

MIX
Paper | Supporting
responsible forestry
FSC
www.fsc.org FSC® C022948

ISBN 978 1 77639 191 2 (print)
ISBN 978 1 77639 192 9 (ePub)

The Author

Jackie Phamotse is a writer, businesswoman, social activist and philanthropist. Her debut novel, *BARE I: The Blesser's Game*, was published in 2017 and was awarded the African Icon Literary Award in Lagos, Nigeria, in 2018. Her second book, *I Tweet What I Like*, was inspired by the late struggle icon Steve Biko, *I Write What I Like*. Her second novel, *BARE II: The Cradle of The Hockey Club*, was released in June 2019. Jackie won the SA Book Awards 2020 for best fiction for her novel *BARE II: The Cradle of The Hockey Club*. The awards are powered by Nielsen BookScan and SAPnet. She was also nominated for a bestselling award by Nielsen BookScan and SAPnet in 2023 for her book *BARE IV: Mercy*.

Google listed Jackie as one of the most searched personalities in South Africa in 2020, the same year she won an award for her Social Activism at the Women of Wonder Awards ceremony, and the Generational Wealth Foundation listed her as one of the most influential educators.

Jackie's work revolves around the narrative of women and children in Africa. Her stories are raw, well-researched and highly thought-provoking.

Jackie's main objective is to create awareness and find long-term solutions to eradicate social ills. Her books aim to educate and empower young people to make better life choices, especially with the fast-growing rate of femicide, rape and many other social ills. Her work encompasses creating awareness around rape culture, mental illness and human trafficking. She currently lives in Sandton, South Africa.

To my mother,
Calextina Makatleho Phamotse

May your type of love continue to lead us.

Prologue

To survive, we create and take lives

7 NOVEMBER 2002, Belville, Cape Town

S peak with assurance. Be firm. You're educated and dedicated to this profession.

Luna Parks was desperate for this job. Finding a nursing job in the current economic climate was difficult; she had just graduated. She had been studying for so long that she didn't have a social life. Her mother had told her to take a gap year and find something fun to do. Apart from surfing the waves on Sundays and walking along the beach, she preferred living in isolation. She also wanted to follow in her mother's footsteps and become a nurse. Luna would not sit idly at the Muizenberg flat her mother still owed money on and watch her slave away, returning exhausted from her twelve-hour shifts. She wanted to help her mother pay off the bond so she could retire comfortably.

Julie Parks had gone through a lot of painful experiences in her life. Her husband had left her without warning years ago. Love was wicked, and Luna wasn't sure if she wanted a part of it. Her parents had never fought in front of her, so she grew up oblivious to living in a broken home. Everything seemed fine until the day her father woke up early, cleaned the house, made lunch, and shared a meal with them, afterwards smiling and dancing with her. Her father loved Luna and worshipped the ground she walked on. Luna was his little princess. Her father taught her how to surf, which they did on Sundays. On that day, Julie was getting ready for a night shift, and Luna's father dropped her off as he always did.

When Julie returned in the morning, all his belongings were gone. He'd even taken down the pictures on the wall and replaced them with Luna's baby pictures. He'd burnt all the photos in which he was featured and made sure that nothing that resembled his existence was left in their lives. Luna was woken up by a hysterical mother. Julie cried like a woman whose husband had just died. But he was just gone. He'd only left a note, in which he thanked Julie for the good years and asked her to take care of Luna. Everything that had brought them together twenty years ago was gone. Luna learnt a valuable lesson that day: men always left.

Get out of your head, Luna. Focus on why you're here.

There were quite a few candidates attending the interviews, and only two posts were open. The advertisement had not stated a specific age or gender. In the last seven months, Luna had been to eight interviews; this was the last one of the year. Two rows of chairs seated the hopefuls, but Luna didn't see anyone around her age. Only certain people made it onto the short list; black people rarely received attention at this clinic, as if it were designed only for the white elites. Luna felt out of place because no one there shared her skin colour. It was also unlikely that she would get the job without any experience.

You want this job, but don't appear too black or too desperate. You are more than your skin colour. Speak well, and they will overlook any other factor that makes you inferior.

As Luna surveyed the row of candidates sitting quietly in the clinic's hallway, waiting to be interviewed, she noticed that the woman beside her seemed prepared and calm, but she had visible creases in her clothing. The man to her left already had wet patches on his shirt and fiddled with his papers the entire time. They had all risen early to make the 08:00 a.m. appointment.

Luna's eyes roved over her own outfit for the umpteenth time that morning: a white shirt, a flowing skirt paired with flat, black, formal shoes – they were a Christmas gift from her mother. Luna was confident that she was the perfect representation of an educated, well-mannered young nurse. Some of the other candidates were dressed in stylish suits and stunning dresses. Luna wished that she owned a suit, something that hinted at being in control. She had never felt as unsettled. She took a deep breath, fortifying her wall of composure, not letting her anxiety creep in. As she sat on the unyielding plastic chair, nothing escaped her gaze.

Where did I study? What are the responsibilities of a nurse? Where do I see myself in five years' time? Why do I want to work here?

The corridors were clean, and the clinic lacked any colour or decoration. There were only the stark white walls enhanced by bright, fluorescent lights. The pungent smell of bleach and sanitiser tickled Luna's nose. It looked like a mental institution instead of a clinic. The nurses were also clean, sleek and well-poised, as if they'd been hand-picked from a magazine. Their backs were ramrod straight, and they hardly spoke to anyone, presenting cold faces of indifference.

'They always get us all here and never give us feedback,' the man to her left said. 'I have been here three times already. It costs money to come here. I don't think I even want this job any more. I mean, what type of clinic is this?'

'It's going to work out, sir. You have worked for years, and this is just an interview. You should be fine,' Luna said and returned to her notes; this was no time to babysit an adult. She needed a distraction, so she pulled a fashion magazine from her bag. Luna loved browsing through outfits and accessories that she knew she would never wear. The styles were bold and designed for confident people, and Luna was too shy to carry off any of the looks as the designers had intended. Her wardrobe consisted mainly of black clothing, no colour. She didn't need to draw attention to herself. The row of candidates moved quickly as they all inched closer to the interview room. She noticed that the candidates came out of the interview with frustrated or teary faces. Something was amiss. No one looked happy when they came out of that office.

'Oh, you old dog, get a damn life!' one lady cursed as she left the interview room. Everyone lifted their eyes in shock at the outburst. A man in a doctor's white coat was standing at the door, seemingly unaffected by the lady's insult. Luna panicked and tried to calm her rapidly beating heart. Shortly afterwards, a female nurse told them that the doctor was taking a lunch break. Luna decided to remain seated, not wanting to miss her turn.

Hours went by, and her name had not yet been called. The candidates' bright optimism in the morning had dwindled to fatigue and restlessness. It was already 7 p.m., and Luna felt her energy reserves slipping. She knew she had to wait, but she had not brought food or money to buy it with. She had filled her stomach with water from the cooler.

Remember to make eye contact, don't bite your nails, and don't smile like a fool; that man won't take you seriously. Sit up straight and make him understand your circumstances.

'Are you seriously leaving without dealing with my complaint?' A loud voice jarred Luna from her musings. She spotted a thickset black girl with big curly red hair near the reception area. She was dressed in a puffy pink dress with big, round glasses framing her eyes. The girl seemed frantic, and the receptionist was trying to calm her down. The newspaper with the job advertisement was clutched tightly in her hand. She must have been here for the interview, but there had been so many people that Luna could've missed her.

With all that colour, she doesn't look like a nurse! Who comes to an interview dressed like they are attending a high-school dance? I mean, the red lipstick is just so out there. It's too much!

The man in the white coat summoned the sweaty man who was sitting next to Luna. She decided to ignore the girl's hysterics and focus on her notes one last time. She bowed her head and studied what she had written. She had an answer for every question and had been reciting the answers in her head like a parrot.

'That man doesn't know what he wants. Good luck, missy.' The sweaty man walked past her, shoving his documents into the nearby wastebasket as he left.

'Luna Parks, you may come in. You are the last one, lucky fish. Thank you for waiting.' The woman with the creased attire had given up hours ago and gone home.

As Luna stood up and smoothed down her skirt, she noticed

the red-haired girl skulking in the corridor. The reception area was deserted, and Luna's footsteps echoed in the empty corridor as she walked towards the office. The doctor in the white coat looked exhausted, and Luna wasn't sure whether this bode well for her.

'The day is gone, young lady, so let's not waste each other's time. Let's see what you have.' His flirtatious tone immediately made her uncomfortable, especially when he then winked at her. The man was tall and thin with an odd-looking moustache and a bald head.

How could I let this happen? Did I even have a choice?

It was 10 p.m., and Luna was huffing alongside the red-haired girl as they jogged back to the interview room. It was weird that the girl knew the layout of the clinic and could access the security systems. They had just shoved a dead body into a compartment in the cold room. The chill that was racing down Luna's spine was not just from the icy temperature in that room – there was also the dread of being caught for what she and the red-haired girl had done. Her eyes scanned each door and window along the way to ensure nobody had seen what they had done.

Who is this girl, and why is she so familiar with the clinic? I have just committed a crime with a complete stranger! Is this a trap?

'You came here for a job, right?' the red-head said, looking at Luna from behind the doctor's laptop. 'Well, welcome to your new work-place, Miss Luna Parks!'

'W-what do you mean?' Luna's voice was barely a whisper, and she struggled to hear her words over her thundering heart.

'I've just processed our job applications, and we've been approved to report for duty at the beginning of next month. I'm Amora Groot-boom, by the way. I'll be taking the other vacant position. Thank you very much!' She handed Luna the documents she had just printed out on the nearby printer.

'D-do you know what we've just done? How can you be so calm?' Luna's hands trembled as she took the employment papers she had to complete.

What have I done?

An interview had turned into a murder and a job! Two young nurses from different backgrounds, who had met by chance, were now forever tied together by their deadly secret. That day, they swore an oath to each other and vowed to always stay together. From that night on, the one could not do anything without the other.

Chapter 1

And so it begins

9 FEBRUARY 2005, Belville, Cape Town

I am going mad; this place is eating at my life. I can't live in isolation any more. There's no harmony in my soul; I might as well jump into the ocean and get eaten by a shark. How do I get out?

Luna's heart was heavy with guilt over what she and Amora had done three years ago, and thoughts of her mother also kept her on edge. It had been ten years since her father's departure. She wanted to call Julie, but couldn't let herself do it. Luna could already picture what she was doing because it was the same each year. Her mother journaled her broken love story and cried all day.

It was Luna's day off. She worked non-stop and hardly took weekends off. She was trying so hard to portray the image of a dedicated nurse who was caring and helpful. Luna had built great relationships with the local fire department and paramedics, as she processed their patients quickly. There were always bad cases over weekends: physical assaults, car accidents and drug overdoses.

Work was hell; she couldn't bear the environment any more. Each time she had an opportunity for a promotion at work, a white person would always take it with no explanation.

'Luna, you are still young. The position is for someone older with more experience. Your time will come,' Dr Rivers always said. Mark Rivers was the new CEO at Charles and Robertson Private Hospital, which also owned the clinic. The staff were required to work in both places with no wage increases or bonuses during the holidays.

Dr Mark seemed suspicious of Luna and Amora's positions in the clinic. He had only been there for a short time, but he was already making Luna uncomfortable. He always took shifts that corresponded with theirs and had recently become too friendly with Amora. He also kept asking questions about them and where they came from. It didn't help that Amora was attracted to him and would often forget herself in her interactions with him.

Luna decided to visit the Iziko South African Museum to escape her chaotic thoughts. She loved to spend time in the city centre, marvelling at the old architectural style of the buildings. The vibrance of the city made it feel like a constant carnival. She could feel the energy as she walked off the street and into the museum. The State of the Nation address was due to be delivered in the nearby Parliament buildings in a few days' time, and the city was bustling with activity. She'd had to take a few detours to arrive at the museum because some roads had already been blocked off. There were signs all over the city in preparation for President Thabo Mbeki's speech. The president always spoke about the economy as if he genuinely owned the country. Still, Luna didn't care much for politics.

Her mother always made Luna watch the news when she visited her home. Luna often visited Julie in Muizenberg since she moved into the nursing boarding house after she started working with Amora. The drive from Muizenberg to Belville had strained her in the first year. On the television news, Luna could see how the cities around the country had changed since South Africa had been declared a democracy. But Cape Town was slow to change the tide. The white people made it known that they ruled the Western Cape, and nothing would be taken from them. The Cape was still as cold to its people of colour as its oceans.

'You can't just rely on your education; you must know your identity. That's when your spirit will settle, Luna.' Her mother's words echoed in her mind, though she didn't really know what they meant. Julie Parks made her daughter study her heritage, as it meant a lot to her. History was imperative; the truth had to be known. After three long years of attending nursing school, working at a private clinic as a young Khoisan girl was hard. Luna wasn't seen. No language honoured her heritage, though the Xhosa and Zulu people were referenced in everything. Did South Africans truly think that this land was only built by the Nguni, Tswana and Pedi tribes?

That was always the story, the documented history, aided by the praise songs blasted out on television and radio. The Khoisan were the forgotten race, although, at times, their presence would be remembered and celebrated. Their identity had been melded and categorised under the Coloured umbrella. This was the reason Luna had wanted to visit the museum. She was there to learn about the rock art exhibition and to appreciate and understand her identity and history.

No radio station spoke her language; few newspapers wrote about her people. These were all the things that made her mother sick to her stomach. Could Luna even openly refer to herself as a proud Khoisan South African? Her mother refused to talk about the sudden transition from an apartheid to a democratic South Africa and still carried her identity document as if she would be asked to furnish it on the streets after curfew. Luna had lost her great-grandparents through the vines of slavery. It was a topic that was too painful for her mother to discuss. People wanted to move on from the brutality that wiped away their history. Julie obsessed over every archived article about the Khoi and San people.

How many families didn't have fathers or mothers because of the apartheid regime? How many had lost their identity by changing their names and surnames to fit in better – just like her great-grandparents had done? How could all these people just vanish? Why were they not seen?

'Luna, you are not just black, you are part of a people who created humanity. You are the seed of all black people. You can't just live like you are a lost sheep. Know your customs and share them.' These were her mother's famous last words after each birthday celebration.

Luna's phone vibrated, nudging her from her ruminations. There was a message from Amora: Let's meet for drinks when I knock off at 7.

You turned me into a killer, Amora.

Amora had a larger-than-life personality and could talk her way out of any situation. Even with their different personalities, she had become Luna's safety net. Life had given Luna a friend she hadn't asked for. Amora had a thick Xhosa accent and was entertaining and stylish. She could always find a good bargain and often tried pilfering from stores, one of her favourite pastimes. A shirt or a pair of shorts could fit between her large boobs. Nothing about life was serious to her. Even when Luna spoke against larceny, Amora always said that no one would believe that a hot girl like her would steal. It was true; no one ever checked if she stole anything. Their eyes would always be on Luna, the cream-coloured Khoisan girl with the bony hands and tiny feet.

Luna's phone started ringing incessantly as Amora tried to get hold of her, probably to chat to her about her text. Once Amora had come into her life, everything had become malformed in minutes. How would Luna's life ever be normal again? Amora drank excessively and would come to work intoxicated. Those were the days on which Luna hated their connection the most and felt that the only thing holding them together was their deadly secret.

But it was pointless to brood over what they had done three years ago; the authorities hadn't found anything that could lead them to Luna. What Luna struggled with was keeping the secret buried. The dead man haunted her dreams. She saw his pale face in her sleep and remembered how pronounced each emotion had been that night. His body was discovered before Luna and Amora started working at the clinic. Staff at the clinic still spoke about the dead man often, but Luna dared not include herself in those conversations. She kept to herself most of the time, and Amora became her pillar at work. They rarely hung out after hours, and Luna was happy about that. Even though she had got used to having Amora around, she didn't want to be seen anywhere near her after work, especially when Amora went on one of her drunken escapades with men. Luna fired off a quick text, declining the drinks invite; she was in no mood for Amora's exuberance.

We vowed to stay together until everything ends, but will it ever end?

Luna was filled with wonder and awe as she toured the museum; she felt as if she had picked up a piece of her identity within the rock art she saw. After the tour, she walked towards Parliament and witnessed preparations for the president's address. Luna noticed the South African Navy practising their formations in the distance. They were so well-coordinated, moving together as a unit. She got as close as she could to marvel at their precision. A crowd had gathered to watch. She appreciated the sailors' lean forms and handsome faces in their uniforms and wondered whether love would ever be on the cards for her. But there was no hope of her ever finding love. How would she ever tell a man that she had killed someone?

Her phone beeped. Dr Mark Rivers: Hey, Luna, sorry to bug you on your day off. Can you come to the clinic anytime this afternoon? I have some things I'd like to discuss with you.

Luna frowned as she read the text. Despite the cool weather, her palms began sweating, and she was startled when the phone rang in her hand.

'Loyiso, what's up?' She answered after the first ring.

'Luna, I just got fired. Remember that report we filed last weekend? My supervisor picked up the discrepancies.'

'Oh my God! Loyiso, that's horrible.'

'I'm just giving you a heads-up; I'll find another paramedic job, so don't stress. You might want to cover your tracks at the clinic.'

Luna had enough to worry about without wondering whether she still had a job. It was probably the reason why Dr Mark wanted to talk to her. There and then, Luna decided that she had to escape Cape Town; a lot had already happened that could land her in jail. She loved her job, yet there was always something missing. She walked to her car and drove to the clinic.

Later, as she closed the door to Dr Mark's office and quickly walked away, a grim smile played upon her lips as she went to find Amora.

'Luna, if this is a sick joke, you better tell me quickly. What do you mean we're leaving? My shift is still not done!' Amora protested and struggled in Luna's hold as she dragged her down the corridor towards the car park. Some patients and nurses gave them curious looks as they passed.

Once they got to the car park, Amora wrestled her arm from Luna's deathly grip.

'You have much explaining to do, like what the hell? You've become quite the spontaneous one lately. What's the rush, Miss Parks? You look like you've seen a ghost. And you weren't even answering my calls earlier.' Luna started pacing in front of her car.

'Amora, we must leave this afternoon. My car is small, so we can't pack all our belongings, but we must leave here as soon as possible. I thought we could take the bus, but that won't work.' Luna's mind raced with all the permutations of the quickest exit out of Cape Town.

'You are not serious! Today? Why the rush? Besides, the boys at radiology said they want to have a braai later,' Amora shouted in frustration. 'I at least have to grab my belongings from the nurse's quarters. Why the big rush? Are you okay?' The smell of alcohol wafted between them; Amora was drinking on the job again.

'You have ten minutes. We can't afford to lose more time. This is serious, Amora; I need you to trust me. Do not say goodbye to any-one. Okay?'

Amora's gait was unsteady as she walked back to the clinic's rear entrance. Luna went to sit in the car, biting her nails and waiting for Amora to return.

Amora had detected Luna's distress, although she didn't under-stand what had happened. Luna had a wild look in her eyes, like the night three years ago, after which Amora had started drowning her memories in alcohol.

Luna had bought them some time, but it depended on Amora fol-lowing her orders. It would be another hour at least before anyone noticed something amiss. Luna glanced at the envelope on the pas-senger seat that held their transfer documents. It was going to be a drastic change, and there was no time for self-pity. No one could bail her out or give her affirmative courage. Running away was the only way to forget what she had just done.

How will I outrun my actions?

Luna couldn't bear to think of what would happen if people found out. She could not put her mother through all the dishonour and mortification. No one knew Luna well enough at the clinic to bail her out except for her partner in crime, Amora. Even Amora couldn't know about this; she wouldn't understand. Luna's circumstances wouldn't let her be what she has always wanted to be – an excellent, law-abiding nurse.

The decision had been made, and she was fleeing. Luna glanced at her friend as she ran towards the car with her belongings; she was just in her own world. Luna envied the happy ignorance on Amora's face.

Luna and Amora were finally leaving the city. Luna fervently hoped that the nightmares would also remain behind.

Chapter 2

Kisses from the mountains

06:30 p.m., 9 FEBRUARY 2005, Clanwilliam, Western Cape

'That man you like, Dr Mark, is not what you think he is, Amora,' Luna warned as they drove past Piketberg on the N7.

Amora was gazing out the window, admiring the landscape. It was as if the distant mountains were rising to kiss the heavens, the wind was rubbing the clear skies, and the red soil rising in the heat as the blue Tazz drove along the freeway. This environment was so different from the busy city; it was isolated and dusty, and the land looked parched.

'Are you thinking about Dr Mark? He is a hottie, right? Did you do all of this because of Mark? You must be joking!' Amora giggled, clapping her hands together. She was surprised that Luna was talking to her because there had only been silence in the car since they'd left Bellville. It did not seem as if Luna wanted to explain herself, and she was clearly tired and worn out. Amora cranked up the volume on the car radio, enjoying the music and imagining her new life.

'This is much bigger than Mark, but we are not safe any more, Amora.'

Understanding the paranoia that had crept into Luna's psyche earlier that afternoon was challenging for Amora. What had happened to bring about such a dramatic change in the space of a few hours?

'We were just fine,' Amora said. 'It's been three years, but you are still scared. That entire situation is over. We have moved on; look at us. Who would have thought we would be friends? I mean, you are the odd, idiosyncratic type, and I am extraordinary and fun.'

'So you think. I can be open and outgoing. I mean, I like fun. I go out.'

'You call sitting alone by the beach or surfing with sharks in that icy water fun? You might as well become a nun. Have you ever been with a guy? You know what that is, right?' Amora stared at her; she didn't believe Luna had ever been intimate with a man.

'I don't have to; I have seen enough dicks to last me a lifetime.'

'Oh, hell, you are a dirty little virgin! My dearest Luna, you are going straight to hell. Like, come on, who is still a virgin in this day and age? You probably have spider webs lining your thighs.'

'I don't believe in sex before marriage.'

'Yet, you live in Cape Town. I am pleased we are going to the villages; maybe you will lighten up and run back to Cape Town. I give you six weeks, because you will hate it.'

'Come on, forget about that. All I am saying is, don't try calling Dr Mark. Leave that man alone.'

'Fine, but it's clear that you did something. Maybe those late nights at work got you into his bed, and now we are on the run. Either way, we could have shared him.'

Luna stared at Amora in disbelief, especially when she noticed that Amora had meant it. She was insane. There was no way Luna would ever sleep with a married man, let alone share him with a colleague. What nonsense was that?

Amora sensed the tension within Luna, but the wine in her system calmed her nerves. Luna was her friend, and she trusted her. It's not like they were running away to some small town without jobs; Luna had taken care of that. It was an honour to be a working nurse. They were both super bright and had passed their exams with flying colours.

'Don't look at me like that,' Amora said.' I told you that you are no fun. But I don't care right now. Just get us to this dodgy town and we will take it from there. As for Mark! Whatever.' Amora rolled her eyes and looked out the window.

Changing from a milieu that was still blooming and going to a small town would be hard for Amora, but she would learn to embrace it. Luna said the plan was to be there for a year and then move to Port Elizabeth. Amora had to trust her judgement. What had happened between them in that clinic three years ago had to stay dead and buried. That may be the point of leaving everything in the city and starting anew. Who knew, perhaps they could even find love and open their own hospital in this town.

'Do you see that? It's massive!' Luna broke the silence , pointing to her right.

'Is that the Clanwilliam Dam? It's so scenic.' The water was placid compared to the ocean views they were used to in Cape Town, but it was picturesque and calming. 'It's such a marvel! It's not the ocean, but it will have to do.' Amora attempted a smile but couldn't shake off the feeling that something was very wrong. Luna had done something, and now she was part of it. But the majestic Cederberg mountains and the fresh air gave her a sense of ease. Sometimes, it was better not knowing and just accepting things as they were. Amora wanted all the adventures she could get. Luna was kind, thoughtful, funny and generous; she wouldn't lead her astray. Yet all Luna could see in Amora's eyes was the life she had stolen from her, but Luna still needed her. Luna drove on, heading into the wild mountains.

'This timeworn car won't get us there on time, friend. It looks like we will be driving on a dirt road soon; turn right. You drive like an old lady,' Amora said teasingly.

'We will get there; you shouldn't have packed the entire shop. You don't need all those clothes.' The Tazz couldn't carry its load. The back wheels were close to the ground, almost lifting the front of the car. And there was more luggage tied to the top of the roof. If they got pulled over by the traffic police, they would undoubtedly get a fine. But that was the least of Luna's concerns.

'You made me leave my CDs at work, and there is a jacket in your office that we left behind,' Amora said accusingly. 'But you really did some magic with our new jobs. The transfer papers confirm our positions and accommodation. Getting a job is hard, so you must know some important people. I thought this kind of process would take months. Also, what do you really know about the Cederberg?' Keeping up with Amora's chatter was always an imposition.

'We have what we need here,' Luna said convincingly. 'We will be fine; you packed for the both of us. Anyway, we don't have to know a place to begin our lives there. That clinic was holding you back. You have so much to offer, Amora. You were at the top of your class in nursing school, and now you can use your brain to help me change things in this little town called Clanwilliam. We will be joining three other nurses. It's a small clinic, but the community needs us.

'They have been without a local doctor for months now. Even though there is one who comes once a week, it's not enough. We have a far more meaningful role to play now. In Cape Town, we were just numbers; those people didn't see or value us. And I enjoyed wearing your winter jackets,' Luna joked. 'They felt like a big hug.'

'I am still wondering about you wearing my clothes – as if my clothes will fit you, Luna. You are a walking street pole. Okay, I'm on board with this new adventure; let's hope the community will receive us well. From what I've read in the travel guide I bought at our pitstop, it sounds like this Cederberg place is a historical gem. It's more of your people – I mean, Khoisan and all.'

'This is not the 1970s; everyone has moved on. There will be mostly farmers, and whatever else we get will be fine. Besides, no place now has only one ethnicity. You need to cut this junk you consume,' Luna laughed out loud.

'Do you even know your Khoisan culture? Or have you lived too long in the city?'

'My father spoke about it, but he is long gone now. My mother shares things sometimes. I went to the museum this morning to learn about the history of our art; I found it quite enlightening. It's hard to talk to my mother about our people's history, as these are dark, painful stories.' Luna accelerated, trying to dispel the discomfort that had crept up on her.

'Does she even know you have left Cape Town, Luna?' Amora gazed at her with concern as she sipped on a bottle of water. Luna was always so secretive. Even after working with her for so long, Amora knew little about her family. She had never met any of Luna's relatives and didn't even know where her mother lived. Amora had been much more open about her family and their whereabouts. It was like Luna was born in the streets with no family tree.

After three long hours in the summer heat, Luna and Amora arrived in the small town of Clanwilliam. It was just as Luna had imagined, the picture perfection of crusty mountains, clear blue skies and lots of nature. There was no evening traffic or the smell of the sea hovering in the air. Luna had been planning this move for a while because she knew it would always be impossible to stay in one place forever. Still, for Amora, it was an immediate work transfer.

'Hang on, I didn't know the road would be this bad,' Luna called out as they flew over a bump and Amora spilt water all over her dress.

'I wanted to make a good impression! Now, you have me all wet!' Amora laughed out loud. She was always lighthearted, warm and generous, and Luna enjoyed that about her.

As they approached an intersection, Luna drove nervously, hoping not to get lost. Amora sat unobtrusively in the passenger seat and continued reading the travel guide.

'How did you find this place, Luna? I mean, we could have gone to Port Elizabeth or George. This small little town seems like a reject campsite. We are in our mid-twenties, friend. We are too young to work in a village,' Amora joked.

It certainly was different. It looked like something out of a wild cowboy film. People were selling fruit and vegetables along the main road and they had passed a majestic church building that seemed to tower over the town and keep vigil over evil. There were a few cafés and cottages lining the street. It was a small community with a population that could fit into a small stadium.

'It's not a village; it's a town full of tradition and culture,' Luna said. 'Many people say it's beautiful, and just look around – it's a holiday in the fields. I got the post through a mutual friend. She said we would like it here; we will be stationed here only for a year. That's enough to get us through. We still need to pay our student loans; we are not here for fun. I bet you are thinking of hiking and swimming in the dam. You enjoy a good time.' Luna winked at Amora. The heat gave way to the sun, just perfectly peeking out behind the mountains. It was a view they could appreciate.

'Now, look at that,' Amora said. 'Such perfection! I think I will enjoy waking up to this. But you won't survive in this desert heat. We will be back in the city in two months.'

'I doubt it; I feel we will have much to do here. Let's just say the farm life can bite you hard, and maybe you will finally learn how to drive and cook.'

'I don't need all of that! I just want to marry a good man and nurse my people,'

'Marriage?'

'Yes, Luna, I want a family.'

'Let's give it ten years, and we will revisit this conversation. You have a wonderful family back in Franschhoek. Your mother seems happy; she loves you, and you live a free and wild life, my friend.' Amora just sighed at the mention of her family's wealth. Luna knew that was not her plan; marriage at twenty-five was not the answer to their problem.

'Luna, I think something happened to me—' she whispered under her breath.

'Yeah, sure. Wine happened to you.' Luna laughed as she brushed off Amora's statement. It was a lost opportunity to hear her friend's heart. Amora nodded in disappointment and returned to the travel guide, hiding her tears. Discovering the secrets that the Cederberg had to offer was far better than sharing her own with Luna.

'I don't see any buildings or restaurants here. Are you sure we will find this place?' Amora glanced out the window; all she could see was a long, badly tarred road and a few small houses on the side of it in the middle of nowhere.

'From what I read earlier, this is the only main road. We should be at the nurses' quarters in a few more minutes. Just keep looking.

I know there is a farm up there too, and if you look closely, you can see people in the fields.'

'I need more water; the dust is getting to me. I can't believe you talked me into leaving my stable job for *this*. I don't think there's a local playhouse or a cinema. How are we supposed to entertain ourselves over the weekends? It's just dry land from what I can see.'

A long road lay in front of them. Animal and vehicle tracks across the arid land showed signs of life while birds were chirping in the surrounding trees.

'Look up there!' Luna pointed to the top of a hill. She'd noticed several homes and felt instantly safer. She drove up and surveyed each building through the windscreen. Even though there was an immense line of trees on her right, the houses were situated within a few metres of each other. She was overcome with the tranquillity of the evening.

A trickle of perspiration slid down her forehead; sweat covered her small, thin hands at every turn. She was looking at her friend with pity and sorrow. Even though her heart was racing, Luna didn't want to alarm Amora. Everything about this small town spoke of family, stability and decorum. This was exactly what she needed – a clean break from the rush that was Cape Town.

The map led them to an old double-storey boarding house. The walls were sun-beaten, and cracks snaked up the peeling walls while others slithered down from the faded roof. An old man stood outside, flagging their car down. He wore an old brown shirt and a pair of jeans.

'I think we are here. That should be Mr Sly Fourie.'

'Let's just hope everything is ready; I feel like taking a long shower and a nap,' Amora complained. 'My phone is dying. Please make sure that your camera saves all our pictures. We must make time to visit that cave that we saw earlier. We should have stopped at many places along the way, but Miss Timekeeper, Luna, kept us from all that exquisiteness. This man doesn't look like what I had imagined; he looks like he is a heavy junkie.'

'Don't say another word, Amora. Be nice! He must have been waiting for us all day. I told him that we would get here before dark.' The Tazz pulled up in front of the old man. The dust had gathered on top of the car. A school was on the far right, within walking distance but slightly up the mountain.

'At least we won't be sleeping in a stable. Imagine that! We aren't as holy as Jesus was,' Amora said facetiously.

'You are wicked!' Luna called out. She wanted to kick her, but instead she collapsed with laughter.

The man spoke softly as they approached him, as if he were talking to himself. Amora looked at Luna and shook her head in disapproval. 'You see, he has bees in his head,' Amora whispered.

'Mr Fourie, thank you for waiting for us. We are happy to be here.'

'Ladies, I am glad you could make it. I know it's a long, uncomfortable drive, but you made it in one piece. Coffee and cornbread are waiting for you.'

He was a tall man with white hair, but the sun had burnt parts of his face and hands. He reminded Luna of a shepherd. The old man came to the car to assist them with their luggage. Amora held her purse and walked behind them like a teenager without a care in the world. Luna just looked at her, pulled her bags from the boot and followed the old man.

'Your friend doesn't carry bags?' the man asked, realising the car still had bags on top of it. He seemed bewildered.

'She is a special case, don't worry. She will get her hands dirty soon.'

'I don't do that sort of thing, sir,' Amora responded.

'You will suffer greatly in life if that's your attitude.'

'Oh, what the hell!' Amora ran back and pulled off a small bag.

'Is this good enough, Moses?' she called out contemptuously. Luna turned and found her swinging the bag like a cowboy.

'Stop, Amora!' she chortled. When the man noticed this, he couldn't help but accept her humour. She was lively and warm-hearted.

'You see, sir, we are from the city. You will love us. This place needs some vibrance! Will you show us around; we need drinks, loud music and hot boys. Do you have a son?' Amora said as she came running up behind them.

'No, Amora. Stop! I am so sorry, sir. We don't need all of that.' Luna pointed at Amora and shook her head.

'To answer your question, yes, I have a son.' Mr Fourie frowned and squinted at Amora. She wore a big pink dress and had red lips and big hair. The smirk on her face said it all: Amora was trouble.

'We have lived in the city all our lives and the drive here was so majestic. I haven't seen scenery like this except in the picture-perfect winelands. We are so happy to be here.' Luna's voice shone with optimism.

'You will soon meet your housemates, but they went to the community centre for a meeting. We have been struggling to get clean water to the farms. They also need some medical supplies. The school down the road had a health day today, and we couldn't even leave them any essentials; the teens need your help. Our town is warm and welcoming; you will feel right at home in no time. Get settled in, and I will show you around in the morning. Did you spot the clinic on your way up?'

'Clinic?' Luna turned to see if Amora had noticed anything, but she just pulled her face in confusion.

'It's less than two kilometres down the same road you used to get here. You will see it in the morning.'

They waited patiently as Mr Fourie opened the door. To the left of the entryway was a shared laundry room with a kitchen on the right. The wooden stairs creaked with each step they took. Luna tried looking outside for hope. The homes up the hill looked so welcoming. She thought of the families that lived there, their horses and pets, when she noticed three farmhouses close together on the far left of the hill.

'Who lives there?' She pointed at the distant buildings.

'Some old man and his blind granddaughter; we hardly ever see his son. He comes and goes. They own the tea farm behind that mountain in the west. You shouldn't worry too much about those people. They must stay up there. We have had enough of them.'

'Oh, you clearly don't like them very much,' Luna probed.

'That man up there has taken too much from us. All we need from that family is the tea they make. Otherwise, they could die for all I care.'

'Tea?'

'You ladies are nurses, right?' Mr Fourie dismissed Luna's question. He knew the Coals well. They were a different breed of people.

'That's why we are here. I don't see myself coming here for anything else,' Amora said contemptuously.

Mr Fourie gestured to the first room on the right.

'Are we sharing a room?' Amora whispered.

'Well, we don't have much space here; I hope you don't mind. You don't pay rent; that's a bonus, right?' Mr Fourie pushed the door open. On the far right, there were two old single beds with no bedding or sheets, steel cases and lockers. The room smelt musty, as if it had not had any fresh air recently.

'And where is the bedding, sir?' Luna asked softly.

'Didn't they tell you? You have to bring your own. We are a boarding house, not a hotel. We run this place through community donations.' Mr Fourie placed their bags on the floor and stared at them in disappointment.

Luna felt her stomach clench into a knot. This could be a house of horror or even an old prison. The windowsill by the one small window was covered in a layer of dust and the window was so small that they would have to keep it open most of the time to get any oxygen.

Amora instantly detested it. This was the gutter; her room in Cape Town was way better and cleaner. The discomfiture on the women's faces said it all. This wasn't what they'd hoped they would get.

'And bathrooms? Do we at least get that?'

'It's at the end of the passage. It's not much, but looking at you, you might want to step outside in the fields …' He was body-shaming Amora. His tone was sleek, and his eyes roved over her body.

'Right, Moses. You can keep your opinions on that one to yourself.' Amora rolled her eyes; she had been bullied so many times that it didn't hurt any more. Luna just looked at the man and felt repugnance overcome her.

Mr Fourie pointed down the hall and Luna quickly went to inspect the bathroom. When she returned, she wasn't impressed. Amora didn't care to look; she knew the standard was way below par.

'I guess you could help us renovate this place once you've settled in. Young people are the cornerstone here.'

'We're nurses, not builders, sir,' Amora retorted incredulously. She was not here to build anything.

'We are a community; we help each other around here. That's the culture. As you can see, we all live to serve each family. We don't do things in isolation. I will speak to the community leaders and see how we can fix this place. We will start with the roof over the weekend. After we were hit by floods last year, we haven't had time to recover. You will see evidence of that in town tomorrow. For now, rest, and I will bring your coffee.'

'No thanks. I am not a coffee person,' Amora said rudely. She was so irritated by Luna that she couldn't force any eagerness. Amora left the room and went outside to smoke.

Luna looked out the window, pondering. She could see a part of the tea farm from there and wondered why Mr Fourie did not like the family who lived there. In small towns, everyone knew everyone else's business, which would be a real challenge.

There was so much noise in Luna's head and in the country of her birth. A second black president, wars in the townships and Cape Town still had hate in the air. Was her life any different to all the people who were still enslaved? This small town seemed like a dried husk where hopes came to die; everything was so backward. It sounded like the community relied on itself to make things happen. Being a nurse wouldn't change anything in this environment. And all she'd wanted was to start a new life.

'Miss, are you okay? Do you need anything else? I need to get back to my wife.' Mr Fourie inwardly scoffed at them. The wilderness was no place for spoilt, self-governed, idiotic females. To him, they were fastidious, uppity spinsters from Cape Town – too stubborn and worldly.

'You may go to your wife. I am fine; I just didn't expect all of this. We have nothing at this point. We have our clothes and no other supplies.' Luna felt so dejected; this was supposed to be a break, a new start. She hadn't imagined that they would be living in such a dump. Maybe Amora was right – they should have gone to Port Elizabeth.

'As I told you before, we survive on community donations, and the farmers play a big role here.'

'We don't want to inconvenience anyone. We will get by with what we have.'

'Over the weekend, I will mend the fence and roof and get someone to help repaint your room.'

'Thank you, that will help.'

'Is your friend always this demonstrative?'

'She can be a little animated, but as you can see, she had good reason to burst a blood vessel.'

'At least she is striking; with hips like that, the farmers will do anything she wants in no time. I mean, those red curls frame her face well.'

Luna was taken aback. What was Mr Fourie implying?

'Please let us rest, Mr Fourie. You have said and done enough. We will find our way from here.' She showed him the door and slammed it behind him in anger.

'The nerve! Old creep!'

She heard Mr Fourie stumble down the flight of creaky stairs. Luna was not inclined to push him over but she needed some sort of release. She took one of her bath towels from the bag to beat the dust from the mattress before she sat down on it. It helped release some of the pent-up frustration of finding herself in this environment. However, the dust motes tickling her nose triggered a coughing fit. Luna thought wistfully of the comfortable apartment she had left behind in Bellville. She dangled her feet over the edge of the bed and began planning how they would set up the room. She needed to go in search of linen.

Amora wanted to go for a walk to ease her mind, but it was getting dark, so she lit a cigarette instead. The sun had fallen behind the big mountains and a cold breeze was heading their way. Some of the houses on the hill lit up and cars drove by in a rush. The rest of Luna's car still had to be unpacked and Amora needed more cigarettes. She didn't know where she was going to get her next fix.

Amora thought she would prefer something other than this rural life. As peaceful as it seemed, it wasn't home. Two ladies in nursing uniforms walked past her. They were so busy chatting that neither of them bothered to greet her.

'Elitists,' she murmured. 'What do people do around here?'

Come on, Amora. Don't let that old fuck play with your mind like that.

Amora had had a weight issue since childhood and school had made it worse. Long hours in the library and junk food paired with alcohol had worsened the problem. It was all her father's fault; he was a wicked man. Her skin crawled from the sudden fear that shot through her. She pulled deeply on her cigarette as she stood by the fence, observing her surroundings.

A wagon passed by quickly; three more came past carrying crops and small water tanks. It boggled her mind that people still used horse-drawn wagons in the 2000s. She waved at the men and they lifted their hats in acknowledgement as they passed by. Those small gestures made her feel seen. Maybe there was a reason she had to leave the city. Amora drank so much most days that she often couldn't make her morning shifts. She had lost so much, but she didn't want to revisit those childhood memories. Self-pity wasn't going to bring her family back, so she kept those thoughts at bay. Eventually, she killed her cigarette and went inside.

'I can't believe you made me do this, Luna! Like, the Cederberg, of all places in the Western Cape! The beach is so far from here and I was beginning to like Dr Mark and it felt like it could've gone somewhere. He was so helpful and kind; and the staff were beginning to enjoy working with us. Now we have to deal with this filthy place. Just look around; there is no life here! I bet the lights don't even work. We don't know anyone here. How are we going to survive?'

Amora pushed her bags under her bed and lay down on top, like a bag of potatoes.

'I'm glad you're back. How long were you going to stand out there for?'

'As long as you find us a better place to stay, Luna. I don't think I want to be here.'

'Well, we have no choice. Just calm down and help me clean up. I've already tried to remove the dust from the mattresses and found some buckets and cleaning supplies in the kitchen. I even met Lucy and Bree, who also work at the clinic. They are in the room next to the bathroom. Lucy shared her old sheets with us. Isn't that nice of her? We are sorted for now.'

'Nice? Those girls didn't even greet me.' Amora rolled her eyes.

'Did you introduce yourself, or were you busy burning your lungs?'

'I didn't care. Tell them I said I would pay them back as soon as I get my first pay cheque. That's if we even get to work at this clinic. I don't know what the big deal is with this place. I see why you might like it. It's beautiful in its own way. However, I don't know what's in it for us. I need to send money to my mother, and I haven't seen her in three months and now we are here. I don't know how to tell her that I am here. This was a big move for us. Now I owe these girls because you just took these sheets without talking to me.'

'Your parents are rich, Amora. You can't still be slaving for them. They don't need your money. I still can't believe they refused to pay for your nursing fees. Like, they own a wine farm!'

'You don't know my mother well, Luna. Let's just say I must pay her for being alive.'

'That's ridiculous!'

'How much do we owe those girls?'

'Nothing, I guess. I don't think that's what they want. They were just being kind. Let it go now.'

'I'm sorry, friend. Maybe I'm a little tired and I have a lot on my mind.'

'You are shaking; are you okay?' Amora's face was sweaty and her skin flushed.

'I'm tired. I need food or something.' Amora tried sitting up but stumbled.

'Let me help you.' Luna rushed and placed her back on the bed.

'What were we going to do in Cape Town?' Luna asked. 'We had been at that clinic for three years and you know how nurses get moved around. We were not growing in that place, and the city is great, but we had done all we could for that clinic.'

'I get that, but this place, Luna!'

'We are here now, and I hear the locals are good people. You need to calm down and stop thinking about that man. He is not all that. You were not raised to be a doormat. I just think you don't like change, Amora. Your enigmatic doctor was married, and I am glad we can start the year on a clean slate. You don't need the drama. Besides, there is far more freedom here and this clinic needs us. As nurses, we are here to help this community.'

'Well, I hear all that, but couldn't you negotiate a better place for us to stay in? This little dumpster won't hold up all of me.' She looked at Luna with a big smile, hoping they could find some joy in the moment.

'You know what? We have all that we need now. I had packed food for us; there is bread and milk on the back seat of the car, and I have leftover muffins somewhere. That will carry us through the night. One of the girls said they would be chilling in the lounge. We can quickly fix our room, head downstairs and go and meet everyone properly. Will that make you feel better?'

'That sounds like a plan. But let me tell you, I saw people up the hill – a family.'

'Amora, we are surrounded by people's homes here. Where were you looking when we drove here?' Luna laughed and shook her head.

'At least we are not on the moon.'

'There is safety in numbers; we will be fine. We need to check you out as soon as we get to work in the morning. That flushed skin doesn't look good.'

'Are you my doctor now? I don't need all that. Just keep that old man away from me and get us some food.'

Luna kissed Amora's forehead and rushed downstairs to fetch the last of their bags. As soon as she left, Amora took a small bottle of gin out of her bag and drank it like pure water. She hid the bottle under the mattress.

The two women packed their clothes away in the rickety cupboards, fixed the beds, hung their favourite pictures on the walls and then shared some coffee in old cups. Amora hated the smell of coffee, but she didn't show it. Then they joined the other ladies in the lounge and returned a few hours later to prepare for bed.

Chapter 3

To live a full life, we have to outlive our past

An acrid smell filtered in from the open window and irritated Luna's nostrils. She lay in bed attempting to sleep, grateful for the linen they had received from the other girls she had met earlier. Although her body was weary from travel, her mind would not settle.

'Can you smell that?' Luna called out. Amora stood up and peered through the window. An overwhelming flash of heat and smoke covered most of her view.

'It's coming from up there! The houses on the hill, Luna!' Luna rushed to look. An angry inferno of flames licked up the mountain, quickly consuming most of the land. The town was blanketed by smoke and they couldn't see much. Then, the piercing screams of women and children erupted.

'The houses are on fire, Amora. Wake the ladies up; I will check downstairs. I don't even know if we are safe here. Let me call Mr Fourie and see what's going on. He said he lives down by the dam.'

'Do you know where that is?'

'No, I didn't see it earlier. Hurry, wake up everyone!'

'Get up! There's a fire! Lucy, where is Bree? Get her.' Amora ran to each room, screaming at the top of her lungs. Although the girls did not greet Amora in the afternoon when they passed her outside the house smoking, Luna had insisted that they needed to be cordial.

When they gathered outside, there was a flurry of activity. The community had been alerted to the fire and some men were racing up the hill. The local police rushed past them, and, as more people came out of their homes, the police requested that they bring water buckets and whatever else could be useful. Luna, Amora and Lucy followed while the others stayed put. They wandered the streets, trying to figure out where they could go. People were running amok.

'Go up there!' Bree called out. Luna heard her and began running.

Luna tried to stop a lady with two children but couldn't find the words. Terror and panic were etched in each wrinkle on the lady's face. The girls ran towards the hill, but Amora lagged behind. She was unfit and complained that her feet felt heavy with every step.

'We don't have to go up there, Luna. We don't know if it's safe. Let's wait and see if we can't be stationed at the clinic. Maybe that's where we should go. That old creep said it's down this road, not up there.' She was bent over, trying to catch her breath. Her top was already drenched in sweat.

'We have to go help; we haven't been to the clinic and we don't know how things work around here. Our best bet is to follow the police. I can see their lights up there. Just keep walking,' Luna called out.

Amora started gasping for air. The smoke was billowing around them, reducing visibility as the minutes ticked by. They wouldn't have enough oxygen if they went straight into the smoke. Amora, Lucy and Bree pulled their tops over their noses to reduce the smoke inhalation. Luna always insisted on wearing her long nightgown; this time, it gave her the extra material to cover her mouth and nose.

'Walk on the side of the road; you don't want to be run over,' Luna told everyone on the way. She was still trying to get answers, but talking to people in that state was pointless. The cacophony of sounds created a very charged atmosphere.

'Go back inside! Get inside!' a man called out in the dark. Luna panicked when the smell of burning flesh assailed her senses. People were burning to death, and she felt helpless. How many burn victims would need to be treated? Would anyone survive the fire? Was the clinic adequately resourced to handle the influx of patients?

'Jump in!' said a white man with dark stubble who had come by in a wagon and was heading towards the fire. It was disorientating having so many people shouting and not knowing who they were addressing. Luna turned towards the wagon and was rendered speechless. The man was breathtaking.

How could a man in the dark be so alluring?

Luna looked at the girls for approval, but Amora was already trying to jump in. She would waste no time getting a free lift and would not spend another minute in the smoke, walking on a dirt road. The women were all shivering from the chill in the air.

'Ladies, are you getting in, or should *we* accept this man's offer?' asked a wily-looking man wearing overalls covered in soot. He wanted to push the women out of the way, but the bearded man gave him one long stare, and the man scurried away.

The bearded man wore a Navy uniform: dark blue pants, a sky-blue shirt with black epaulettes on the shoulders, and a black cap. He was alone in the wagon except for crates of vegetables and some chopped firewood. He would be a great help and looked like he knew what needed to be done. Luna figured he'd be specially trained in emergency evacuation procedures. And besides, it wasn't safe being in the choking smoke without any sense of direction.

'Will you ladies be able to help? I hope you'll survive the smoke.' The bearded man felt a warm rush as he glanced at Luna. He took off his black cap as a sign of respect when he spoke to her. She quickly noticed his gaze and moved closer to the wagon.

'We can help, please, sir,' Luna beseeched.

'Well, then, jump in. You have to be careful out there; this fire is beginning to burn out of control. Hold onto your seats. We have some way to go. I was at the market earlier. Apologies, my lady,' he said as he pushed a bag of apples from the seat.

Amora was struggling to get into the wagon; it was too high, and her body mass too heavy. Lucy tried pulling her up, but Amora kept falling back. The bearded man turned to see what the problem was. His eyes softened as he saw what the hold-up was.

'Hold these. Don't let these boys overpower you,' he commanded with ease and shoved the horses' reins into Luna's hands. Luna stopped staring at him as he got off; his features were so pleasant, even in the murky darkness. He rushed to help Amora, lifting her quickly and helping her get onto the wagon.

Luna giggled, the horror happening around them momentarily forgotten. She admired the man's kindness and willingness to help anyone in distress. He rushed back, and Luna handed him the reins. The fleeting touch of his hand sent tingles through her fingertips. Her reaction surprised her, considering they were all in a precarious situation. The bearded man steered the wagon onto the road and ushered the horses towards the hill. Violent flames were dancing in people's homes and wails filled the area. Despite attempts to extinguish the fire with water buckets, it was not enough to contain it. The fire department was nowhere in sight. It did not seem like the fire could be extinguished in time to save lives.

The wind whipped their faces as the wagon raced up the hill. The foul stench of burnt vegetation and flesh clung to the air. Most of the town's buildings were made of wood, which did not bode well if the fire could not be contained. It was an old country town with few streets and limited resources. Desperation coloured the eyes Luna looked into. These were traumatised people, staring death in the face.

'Sir, you need to cover your face with a wet cloth. I can't even breathe and you are heading straight for the fire. Do you know where you are going?' Luna called out nervously, trying to hold on as tightly as possible. The wagon was moving too fast.

'Field fires are common around here, especially because the weather's been hot and dry with the coastal winds blowing into the mountains. Don't worry about me.'

Luna noticed a flash of teeth in the darkness and realised he had smiled at her.

'Look at the house on the hilltop!' Lucy pointed, straightening up in the wagon. Smoke plumes were escaping from the broken windows and open door. It would be difficult to get up there on foot or with the wagon; a helicopter would've been more efficient.

'Hold on, ladies. The wagon will tip you over if you don't stay in your seats,' the bearded man called out.

'We will need gloves; how will we handle the burn victims?' Luna's mind was sharp amidst the chaos and was already in problem-solving mode. The man pointed at his brown leather bag at her feet. Luna snatched it and rifled through it. It had everything, from heat protectors and gloves to water packs. She glanced at him with gratitude and kept the bag with her; he nodded.

'There is no way these horses can get up there. You are sending them to their slaughter,' Luna called out apprehensively. There had already been carnage at the bottom of the hill, where some horses had succumbed to burn injuries. It broke Luna's heart to witness so much pain, suffering and death in a single night. It was so much worse than the Bellville clinic at its busiest.

Amora and Lucy had already covered themselves with coverlets they found on board. They sat side by side, observing the crowds as they raced past.

'They are well trained, Miss ...'

'Luna Parks.' She turned to look at the man. There was insufficient light to make out his facial features, but his deep, resonant voice lingered on her skin.

'Well, no time for introductions. Do you need a hand with those?'

Luna shook her head. 'I am a nurse; we are all nurses here.' She glanced around at the girls. 'We live at the nursing boarding house. I hope and pray it hasn't burnt to the ground.'

'The fire is up there; it won't reach your home. Just prepare yourselves. These people will need you. Stay close to each other; we can't afford to lose more people.'

'What do you mean? Are people dead? How do you know?' Amora asked, shaking violently. She held onto Lucy for comfort. Despite being a qualified nurse, Amora was squeamish. Whenever she was allocated to triage, she always swapped with another nurse.

'Unfortunately, we have lost seven people already. I was just at the clinic when I came across you ladies. There's a doctor from the Navy attending to them. I am surprised you didn't know this. We have been trying to kill this blaze for an hour now.'

'Oh no, sir, we were not aware.'

'I will have to leave you by the side of the road. Do you have family up here? I mean, in one of those houses?'

'We just got here, so we don't have family around. I have seen this uniform before. I was supposed to work in Simon's Town, but I couldn't change ...' He cut her off with one look.

'Then you will help these people. I have a few necessities in the back and have called for help. Our officers will be here in no time. The smoke will block the trails soon. I have guys on the other side of the mountain working on bringing us soil from the farms. That will kill the fires faster than water. The water tanks won't help much in this situation. If you look to your left, three homes are already gone.' Her eyes roamed over the villagers using buckets to put out the flames.

'I don't see any medics here,' Luna murmured.

'Everyone in this situation is a medic; we don't have time to waste.'

'You sure know a lot about fires,' Amora chimed in.

The man didn't respond; his eyes were stuck on the danger they were approaching. The fire had moved from the top of the hill; the houses near it were built far apart. If they had any chance of stopping it, they would have to work together and pile up sand near Mr Rassie's house, the headmaster of the school, the bearded man explained. This would save the other houses, but how many other lives could be in danger? There were no streetlights so high up; people walked with handheld torches and paraffin lamps. This was incredibly dangerous due to the flammable nature of paraffin.

The man got off the wagon and assessed the damage. Two men came and joined him; they blocked off the roads and began to work. Lucy and Luna rushed from house to house to see if anyone was injured. It was hard to move around, but Luna helped the police separate those who were dead and those who needed medical care. The local school bus transported the injured to the clinic and those without shelter to the nearby school for the night.

The fire was still creeping closer to the houses, consuming everything in its path. Luna knew this could end their lives, but when she heard the piercing scream of a little child, she could not ignore it. The dense smoke compromised her visibility, but she crouched low and tried to follow the sound.

Although the community fought valiantly, the fire was consuming most of the hilltop homes. Most people stood by silently, watching the roofs of their houses cave in, resignation etched deeply on their faces. All they could do was watch their entire lives die in the flames. The bearded man and his friends worked tirelessly, saving more people, animals and valuable items. They moved fast and as a pack.

'That girl will burn to death; get her out of there!' one of the men called out. More people rushed to help, but flames danced wildly all over the back of the house. The wind exacerbated the fire and made the smoke denser. It felt like everyone was in the middle of an erupting volcano. With faces covered in soot and seared hands and feet, exhaustion was evident in their gait and faces. The fire had a life of its own; it was impossible to contain. They gasped for breath, trying to find oxygen amid the pungent and suffocating smoke.

Two men managed to pull the three-year-old from the Wendy house behind the main house, where she had been trapped. Luna rushed to the girl's side and felt her pulse. Luna sighed in relief as she felt a faint tap against her fingers.

'She's still alive but is unconscious from smoke inhalation. Let me see if I can revive her!' Luna said to the two men. She started performing CPR on the child, praying while she did so. After a while, the child's chest inflated, and Luna lay her on her side and she started coughing and crying. Her breathing was rapid and shallow.

'Get her to the medics!' One of the men picked the girl up and ran towards the medics stationed inside the school bus that Mr Rassie had lent to the rescue team. As some men fought the inferno surrounding the house with buckets of soil and water, Luna started looking inside the house through the broken windows and doors. It was carnage inside, with charred furniture and melted plastic. There was a bitter smell and Luna covered herself more fully with her gown. In one room, which seemed like a bedroom, she saw a crib, and although the curtain railing had fallen across it, there was a wrapped bundle inside it.

'Guys, quickly! Is it safe to go in? I've spotted a baby in a crib!' Luna ran around the front of the house to alert the men putting out the fires. One man, wearing fire-resistant clothing, volunteered to go in. Luna ran back to the window so that he could hand her the bundle from the inside.

'It is a baby, and unfortunately it's dead.' Sadness coloured his words as he handed over the bundle. The blanket the baby was wrapped in disintegrated in Luna's hands while parts of it were burnt into the baby's skin. Its tiny limbs were curled inward, and the skin had split on most of its body. It was a horrific sight, so Luna took off the coverlet she'd found on the wagon and wrapped the burnt bundle in it, then held the bundle to her chest. Despite her eyes burning from the smoke, they clouded over anew at the loss of such a young life.

When Luna joined the rest of the community on the road, she noticed that two additional bodies had been pulled from the house and were covered in blankets – the parents. No one moved as they watched Luna emerge from the smoke. Lucy was holding the baby and its bottle and shoes with her head bowed. The bearded man came running; he moved everyone out of the way and cleared the path for them to get through. Everyone was shattered; men and women bowed their heads in silent prayer as Luna passed by with the baby.

'Lord, Your will hurts. Lord, if You have called her, take her kindly. Let her rest in her mother's womb as she came. Let her feel her mother's skin and hold her protector's hand. Let them come to You in the light of Your mercy and grace. May You handle them with care. Amen.'

Luna laid the child on her mother's burnt body, settling her right on her chest. Lucy approached, quivering with grief. She opened her hand, took the child's belongings from Luna, and placed them in the dead father's hand.

'This is your baby girl. She is with you now,' she whispered to the father.

The bearded man stood next to Luna in silence. She appreciated his comforting presence at such a tumultuous time. Luna had dealt with many injured patients at the clinic in Cape Town, but nothing could compare with the horror and devastation that was happening in this village. His friends came and stood next to the bearded man. They all looked bedraggled, covered in soot and surrounded by the melancholy of loss that hovered around them.

There was a moment of complete quiet as the mourners stood in silent vigil. The wind had ceased, and stillness descended over the charred lands. Mothers pulled their kids closer, covering their eyes. Death was a thief; it stole more than the souls of the dead. Even those who stood there felt as if their hearts had been ripped to shreds.

Their faces were gaunt in the shadows cast by the torches and lamps they carried.

Luna's anguished cry pierced the silence. She was on her knees, holding onto the dead woman's feet. Amora broke through the crowd to offer her comfort. Luna was utterly broken. Lucy and Bree led her away from the scene while the men helped remove the bodies and loaded them onto the bus. Amora kept her eyes on the men left behind; they were moving like a well-oiled machine. She handed out water and then started checking on the bystanders.

As she rushed from one person to the next, she made sure to clean their wounds and that they drank some water. The helicopters had finally arrived and were emptying their water buckets from above, while more water trucks had arrived from nearby towns. After an hour, the embers of the fire that remained were dying. Lucy and Luna headed back to the boarding house with the aid of the police. Amora had asked to stay a little longer to clear the roads with the group of people who still wanted to help.

When they got home, Luna, Bree and Lucy stood at the window by the stairs, watching the broken souls pass by. The small town was headed for a dark time. Many cried as they had lost someone dear to them; it was hard to witness the first moments of dawn. They walked to their homes down the street in complete silence. No one dared speak; the night had said it all. Even in the darkness, they saw tears shower the ground.

'Welcome to our small town,' Bree softly said as she tapped Luna's shoulder.

'I don't know what these poor people will go through in the next couple of days. However, this is not the welcome I had wished for.'

Chapter 4

I cast a spell on you, my love

There had been no time to do his morning chores, nor did Cameron Coal have time to sleep. He thought about the nurse more than anyone else he had seen the night before. Her kind nature and shy persona. Even in the heat of a firestorm, she had taken charge and helped people. He recalled her face and her sad eyes. Her piercing cries the night before had touched even his icy heart. He needed to head back to town to meet with his team and assess the damage. The community leaders would have to unite to bury everyone in the local cemetery. This would have to be done in a day or two.

Cam looked out of his bedroom window. Everything here seemed so unfamiliar; the sky was darkening and grey clouds were forming. The Coal family farm was more than dry land and dying fruit trees; the land was big enough for all kinds of vegetation. The barn contained a few goats, some sheep and seven cows. Certainly not enough to be regarded as a commercial farm any more. Things had taken a turn for the worse since Cam joined the Navy. The porch sagged, the stairs were unsteady and the water tanks needed repairs. There were two old chickens with countable feathers that Cam loathed but his daughter Mia loved.

As Cam took stock of the farm, he noted his slim and malnourished horses tethered outside the barn. They had not been at peak performance while pulling the wagon the previous night. The fields were covered in weeds and long grass due to the lack of recent rain; that's why they carried the fire so quickly. John, Cameron's father, had not prepared for spring. He had done nothing at all. The duck pond was dry. Cameron just couldn't understand how things had got this bad.

Just as his thoughts ran wild, he heard Mia singing to herself. She was always singing; it was her way of telling everyone she was awake. Now, she was singing a song he liked. He tip-toed to her door and just listened for a while.

'I can hear you, Father,' Mia said underneath her blanket.

'I am not here,' he whispered through the keyhole.

'I can smell you ...'

'Oh, that's how far you are taking it.'

'I heard you come in hours ago. What were you doing outside for that long?'

Cam walked in, opened her curtains and settled at the foot of the bed.

'I was cleaning the yard; the gate was also broken.' These were pebbles of lies. He didn't want to share what he had witnessed when he rode home; it would make her feel unsafe. The fire had got close to their farm, but the saving grace had been that the gate was several metres away from the house.

Cam couldn't believe no one had seen the fire coming onto his property. He tried not to think about it, but it niggled him. Most community leaders did not stay too far from his farm; how could they just go into their homes without seeing the fire? Perhaps there had been too much smoke? Maybe he had been the first to notice? Or was it that the farm was cursed since his wife died? No excuses could take away his disappointment. When everyone was back in their own homes, his yard had caught fire near the gates. He had spent most of the dawn putting it out and no one was there to save his little girl. He had got there just in time once again.

'You were at the water well, running around, coughing and praying. I could hear you, Father.'

'When you work hard, you also pray. I just wanted you to wake up to a clean yard. I have made you some porridge because there's no time to bake bread. I didn't really see you when I got home yesterday. I took the wagon to the market; I thought we would ride to town together.'

'I was taking a walk. I didn't know you would arrive yesterday, but you didn't sleep here.' She rolled over and got out of bed.

'I had a small job to do, but I am home now.'

Cam made tea and settled down with her. The kitchen only had one small coal stove, a table and a few chairs. The house was just big enough for a family of four.

'Father, was there a fire again?' Mia sat quietly at the kitchen table. She was trying to mask the fear that heated her body.

Cam was silent, unable to formulate words as flashbacks from the previous night assaulted him – people running, the howling and whimpering sounds from dogs searching for their owners in the deep heat of the mountains, shoes drenched in mud and blood, the smoke that covered each home like a shroud, the dead bodies. The shrill voice of a little girl running in the dark echoed in his ears. He never wanted to carry his work cases on his shoulders but last night had brought him unsolicited thoughts.

'Father, the fire took more of them again. The people of this land,' Mia said softly, rubbing her nightgown with her tiny hands. She often did this to keep anxiety at bay. Cam noticed her hands and hung his head in grief, knowing that she couldn't see the pain in his eyes.

'Mia. Please, just eat your breakfast. You will hurt yourself. Remove your hands from your body. It's rude to touch oneself at the table. I told you this many times.' He pushed the porridge bowl in front of her.

'I was in my room; I felt the heat. I smelt the smoke. I waited for you.' The words sliced through him; her small voice trembled as she held out her hands. Waiting for him to touch her. Her bottom lip quivered as she suppressed whimpers from escaping her lips.

'You are safe, Mia. Just eat.'

Cam watched Mia play with her food. She kept on mumbling and sagging deeper into her chair. Mia had a lot to say but she didn't want to speak. He had missed all her birthdays and didn't even pitch on Christmas Day, but now he had returned like nothing had happened.

'I can smell the smoke on you. You didn't come to my room! I waited ...' Tears came from the night of her blind eyes. She pushed her hands out, waiting for him to touch them in comfort. He looked at his little girl with weary sadness. A fire had taken her eyesight when she was only two. She had been seeing doctors for years, but no one could help her recover fully. And here they were, ten years later, and a fire had almost taken her again.

'Father! Father!' Her small hands were still dangling in front of her.

'Baby ...' He touched her gently, then came around the table and held her. Picking her up from her seat and placing her onto his chest. She was all that he had now. The pain in his daughter's body escaped her and filled him up.

'The fire is gone, baby. Daddy got rid of it.' Her tears trickled onto his soot-covered body. Mia rubbed his back and felt the blisters rise from his skin. Cam winced when he realised that he was injured.

'The fire, Father, has eaten you.' Mia touched him gently, but his blisters felt raw and painful. He moved slightly from discomfort but didn't want to alarm her. His face was tense; his eyes sparkled with tears.

'Your hands, Father. Why are they covered?' Mia rubbed him soothingly, trying to figure out what must have happened to him.

'I'm fine; they are just a little cold.' He pulled away, trying to conceal the burnt skin.

'The fire ate you just like it ate my eyes!'

'Just in passing. I will be fine. All of this will go away; don't be scared.'

'But it took Mama and Grandma. Is it coming for you?' Mia took a deep breath and swallowed the sob she felt lodged in her throat. She hated crying, especially in front of her father, because he rarely knew what to do.

'Mia, not in this house. We don't speak like that!' His harsh tone shook her straight into her seat. Cam saw what he had done but wouldn't let her dwell in grief again. There was no better way of saying it, but there was no room to mention Summer any more. Her memory had to be far more than just a fire.

'Papa John left me here. He said he was going to get my medication and milk.'

'He is sleeping.' It was another white lie. His father was a drunk who disappeared and only resurfaced when all his money was gone. Cam knew how much his daughter loved her grandfather and he wouldn't hurt her with unnecessary information.

'Should I give him my food? He must be hungry. He wasn't home all day yesterday.'

'No, Peanut, leave him to rest. We will check on him later.'

'Father, there is a strange smell in his room. He hangs out his sheets unwashed every morning, and the smell is sour and odd.' Cam knew what it was; he was wetting himself again. This only happened when he was in a drunken state.

'Well, I will speak to him about that … maybe it's the milk he drinks. You know adults shouldn't drink milk.'

'But I drink milk. Will my bed also smell like that?' Her innocence pleased him; she was still a child.

'You are certainly not an adult, Peanut,' Cam sighed.

'Father, will you be leaving again?'

'Not for a week or so. I am taking time off. I promised to build you a better bed; you are growing quickly. I also need to trim your hair. You can't have hair that comes down to your bottom.'

'My hair follows the wind, Father,' Mia chuckled, wiping the tears away.

'Right, eat up.' Cam pushed down the nervous qualms. Ever since his mother and wife had died, he had tried to pick up the pieces. His wife, Summer, was the only woman he had ever loved. Her grave was not too far away from the farmstead. It was hard for Cam to confront the truth, so he just didn't go to that side of the farm. Mia wasn't allowed to go there alone. The area was infested with scorpions and snakes. He didn't want to risk having her stung alone in the wild.

There were other pressing issues Cam needed to attend to. He had completed his training in the Navy and his father had asked him to return permanently, but his answer was always no. There was no way he could take over the running of the farm; he didn't have the heart for it. He enjoyed being part of the Navy and had no other reason to return, even though Mia was there. His life wasn't going to be about the farm. His father had promised to stop drinking, but from what Mia had just told him, he would have to find his father in town and bring him home. It was always an embarrassing affair. Clearly, John was still struggling to run the farm by himself. Cam's father was a weak but cold man. When his wife died, he'd lost all control over who he was. The farm just became a bitter reminder of the great love he had lost.

Cam had just been promoted to be the captain of the submarine fleet. Three submarines had been commissioned from Germany to replace the current fleet. As part of his new responsibilities, he had been tasked to oversee the project and ensure a seamless delivery over the next two years. Cam would not turn down the promotion. Mia would have to leave the farm and attend a school in Cape Town that could accommodate her needs. Running a farm had never been Cam's passion; that was Sole's dream. When they buried Cam's wife and his mother, Sole left right after the funeral and had not been back since. The rumour in town was that he was in Cape Town.

'Father, what does the ocean look like? The one at your job?'

Cam stood up and cleaned the table.

'Peanut, the ocean is picturesque. It is a huge, rippling blanket of water. You will love it.'

'Do you like it? What do you really do there? Can you swim, Father?' Mia had never seen the ocean; she had only heard about it on the radio. She was inquisitive about why the ocean had taken away her father. She was lonely but refused to say so.

'Yes, Mia. My job is to protect our ocean resources from harm; just as the army people protect the land, we protect the waters.'

'You protect the fish too?'

'That's right, but it's a little more complicated than that.'

Cam noticed Mia's bare feet and that she was still in her night-gown, which she had outgrown. He sighed and looked away. She was growing up too fast. It felt like he had just blinked and Mia was no longer in nappies. She was becoming a young lady. Cam worried about her education and safety. He would have to begin teaching her certain things so that she was aware of her surroundings. His father was not fit to care for her any more; he also needed supervision. The more Cam looked at Mia, the more she resembled Summer, his darling wife. The long brown hair, the creamy skin that melted the sun. Her sweet and calm demeanour. He loved her profoundly, but he also loved being in the Navy.

'Can you bring me some water from the ocean?'

The question raised Cam's eyebrows. He stepped closer to his daughter to lead her outside. He quickly thought of a plan to cheer her up.

'Come with me, Peanut. Ocean water is very salty and can make you sick.' He gently touched her hand, not wanting to direct her entirely. He had taught her how to move around by following her senses. How a person's shadow fell and where the light hit. She could use her hands to feel objects and her feet to sense the type of surface she was walking on.

'Father, did you also eat?' Mia stepped down, feeling the wooden floors. She put her right foot down first and checked if anything was there before putting down her left foot. There was a sigh of relief when she navigated her way safely. Mia didn't want to disappoint her father. She knew his eagle eye was on her.

'Easy … don't rush your steps. I just made enough food for you; I am fine. I still have to cultivate the land and feed the animals. Let's hope the chickens have given us eggs for lunch.'

Cam would never eat if Mia was not fed. He had often gone to sleep hungry so that she and John could eat something. When the floods had come last summer, all their crops were washed away just after they'd planted the seeds. They'd missed the harvest season and there was nothing. Then came the wildfires that ended it all. The farm was making little money and Cam had to send what he earned home. With John's alcohol habit, it was clear he didn't take care of anything in Cam's absence.

Seeing his daughter stand and move on her own gave him hope. Year after year she had got her bearings right. When Summer died,

Mia hadn't wanted to leave the house. She felt every ounce of grief her father and grandfather carried, the emptiness in them, and bore it like a grey cloud. Summer had been their anchor; she'd always brought so much light and joy into the home, but now, no one wanted to talk about her. The deaths of the Coal women had ripped the family apart.

John hadn't stocked up on food; Cam only saw some rice and a few other items in the pantry. John had not cared to ensure that Mia had food before he went on his drunken spree. Cam hated the man his father had become; they fought each time he visited. This was the first time Cam would spend more than two days at a time at home. The house had lost a mother's touch; the windows and doors had to be fixed, everything was covered in dust and the bedding was so old he didn't even remember the last time it was changed. He stood by the door and watched his little girl feel her way around.

'You see, one step at a time.'

'Father, I live here. I know my way around. You don't have to wait for me.'

'Evidently, you don't need me any more.'

'I do, but I have grown, Father. I know this land better than you. Did you see the tea I planted? I have my own field. Grandpa John said I could do as I wished. He said he had tried to plant the tea many times but didn't have time to nurse it. I have made sure that it's in the right place. He used too much water and never allowed it to taste the sun.'

'Tea? Where? What do you know about tea?' Mia's revelations surprised him. Summer and his mother were the only people who knew how to farm tea; that's how the farm had survived for years.

'I can taste the soil; you must taste it first and feel the temperature. Grandpa was using the wrong side of the field. Tea needs a little bit of love and freedom.'

Mia walked past him and stepped outside. She searched for her walking stick on the side of the wall. Cam observed her with awe. She had placed it right by the door and he hadn't even noticed it. He smiled proudly at her efficiency. His little girl was not so little any more. He had missed so many milestones. How on earth would he make up for all this lost time?

It pained him when he thought of how disappointed Summer would be. She never wanted him to join the Navy. The plan had been for him to take over and they would make the farm what his mother had always wanted it to be. Before she died, they had drawn up plans to expand the land, maybe even sell off some areas. They couldn't use all the land they now had. It would require money to cultivate it, and they would have to employ labourers. This was not Cam's plan; he had Mia to care for and little to his name.

'You can't eat soil, Mia! You will get sick.'

'I don't eat it; I taste it. Did you know that soil has textures, and tea only likes harsh, solid conditions? Soft soil is good. If it's sandy, then it has good drainage.' Cam was shocked by how much Mia knew.

'Father, I will show you, but first tell me, what do you see? Is it a beautiful day today? I can't feel the sun's warmth so it must be cloudy.' Mia turned her face towards the sky, seeking the warmth she had spoken about.

For a moment, Cam just breathed. The simple things sometimes made him want to weep, so he did not like coming home. His musings were always wistful and filled with longing for what could've been if the fire hadn't consumed his Summer. Cam took Mia's hand and walked towards the back of the farmhouse.

'So, what do you see?'

'Well, you're right. It's cloudy today. The sky is grey but the sun's rays keep shining through in some areas of the sky.'

'You are sharing the wrong thing, Father,' Mia giggled, unconvinced.

'What am I missing?' Cam turned his gaze towards the burnt side of the hill.

'Tell me about the colour of the soil, the texture, and the shades. The grass around it and the wildflowers. Tell me about the footpath and the ants on it. When the sky is grey, does the soil change colour?'

Cam didn't think of it that way. Whenever he thought of anything, his eyes always went towards the heavens. The soil or its colour were not his priorities.

'Well, Miss Mia, the soil is dry. I see no ants.'

'Oh, Father, you still have a lot to learn.'

Mia ran towards the stables. Cam came chasing after her, the air filled with laughter as he caught her by the waist and placed her on his shoulders while running and tickling her. She laughed so loud that she had tears running down her face. He was reluctant to admit that he missed the priceless sounds of joy and peace.

When they'd tired of walking around the yard with Cam describing what he was seeing, Mia showed him her tea crop. He was surprised to note that the crop was in the area where the fire had stopped. There were perfect rows of plantations. The beauty of living on a farm was having access to hectares of land. Each section had the potential for all kinds of vegetation. As they got closer, from a distance, he noticed the border that the fire had created on the land. The left side was burnt and the right untouched. He couldn't understand how that had happened; the fire hadn't touched a single seed Mia had planted. It was so perfect that you would think it had been done on purpose.

He couldn't believe it! How could a child do all of this by herself? The work she had done would have taken weeks, if not months. It was far more than John had sowed in years. They stood side by side and Cam told Mia what he saw. The tea had grown so much that it only needed two more months, right on time for harvesting season. Mia stilled, feeling the wind; she could tell it would rain soon. Cam just stood there in wonder. Pride filled him, and he held her hand. Mia felt his appreciation even though he said nothing.

'And you say you did all this by yourself, Mia?' Disbelief marked Cam's question.

'I was born here, Father. My mother and grandma worked this land. This tea is part of our heritage. I have taken the time to learn more about it. I wanted to show you all this the last time you were here, but you didn't stay long enough.'

'But how?'

'I take care of the land most of the time; I can take care of myself too, Father.'

'When do you get the time? School must be busy now; it's the beginning of the year. Don't you have friends? Is Papa John a good tutor?'

'I have the animals; I don't need friends.' Cam felt sorry for her; most people didn't know how to deal with Mia's condition. He wanted her to be more social, to learn and to enjoy her youth. No child should be this isolated.

'Animals won't teach you about life, Mia. You have to be with other people.'

'I am with you and Papa John. When he is around, he takes me to the fields and we have a good time there. Last summer he showed me the mountain river and the big dam. I can catch my own fish now.'

'You will drown, Mia! That's not safe.' All Cam could think about was the creepy men who lurked around town; she was too young to be in the mountains with a drunk.

'What books are you reading now? Can you read?'

'No, I can't. Papa John said books will make me lazy and that I have to work the farm with him.'

Mia used her toes to draw in the soil, trying to mask her embarrassment. The school in town had kicked her out because they couldn't find a teacher to teach her. She didn't want to tell her father it had been three years since she attended school. Papa John said that girls didn't need all that education. He said all she needed to know was right here on the farm.

'What do you mean? I have been sending Papa money for your schooling. You need to tell me the truth, Mia Coal!'

'He said the farm needed that money. I am telling the truth.' Mia started to tremble with fear; her father never got this angry at her. Based on where his body heat came from, he was kneeling in front of her. Cam gripped her shoulders and breathed heavily.

'Who was your last teacher?' Cam's anger increased the more she spoke. He had the pressing urge to go and find his father. How could he have allowed this to happen?

'Mrs Walker. She was nice. She tried to help me but fell ill. And ever since then, I have been told to stay home.' Mia was tearing up. She loved school but felt like she didn't belong there.

'Well, you are going back!' Cam marched off, racing towards the house. He washed himself while consumed by thoughts of where he would begin searching for John. The man had wrecked his grand-daughter's education; this farm was close to ruin and there was no way Cam could let it slide.

Mia knew she was in trouble; she could feel her father's rage even though he was in the house. The banging inside stopped her from coming closer. She heard him on the phone, followed by a string of curses. Mia sat down outside and tried to keep calm. Had she said too much? Papa John was in trouble. She sat behind the house for a while, hoping her father would calm down and fetch her, but then she heard the wagon pull away. It raced past her moments later, and the dust hit her face.

'Get back inside! I will see you later,' Cam yelled from a distance.

'Father, what about the eggs?'

'Just do as I say! Don't wander off again. Don't go to the fields by yourself. I will be back.'

Cam felt a burning rush of adrenaline mingled with rage as he raced towards town. Even though he was going to search for his father, the nurse interrupted his thoughts. There was only one way to thank her for helping them the previous night, but he was unsure how appropriate it would be to show up at her workplace. He couldn't bring himself to see her; what would he say? It would have to wait. Mia needed to get back to school and he had to take care of her affairs first.

Chapter 5

Sometimes peace comes with death

Luna was lethargic as she got out of bed; she had not slept much after the trauma of the night before. As she peeked into the hallway, she heard the shower running. Amora was already outside smoking, which was part of her daily routine. Luna searched for a bucket and filled it with water to clean herself. She could smell the smoke in her hair. On her day off, she would undo her cornrows and wash them.

'Thank goodness for our nursing caps,' she whispered. Just as she was getting dressed, Amora returned. She noticed the bucket and cracked up.

'There is no way I can do that; you will have to wait for me. I won't be kneeling on this dirty floor and wiping my ass in a damn bucket. Hell will first have to freeze over.'

'Amora, just admit that you don't know the technique. Haven't you camped before?'

'I hate camping for this very reason. I won't fit in a bucket.'

'You don't have to get inside it; just wipe yourself. We don't have time. I think Bree is in the shower, but I heard Lucy's voice there too.' Just the sound of that made her uneasy, almost uncomfortable to say it out loud.

'What do you mean?'

'Bree was showering but Lucy was talking ...' She chose her words carefully, but they already sounded wrong.

'You need sleep, friend; I don't understand what you are saying.'

'I mean, they are showering … I guess.'

'No, you mean fucking! I heard the noises. Come on, you can't pretend you didn't hear the moaning. Let's just say this small town has wild things indeed.'

Luna was shocked. Was that what she heard? It was impossible. Lucy and Bree? They are nurses. She tried not to imagine it. Why would they do that? Didn't they fear God? She shook her head and quickly finished getting dressed. Amora tried joking with her, but Luna didn't want to hear it.

'Go shower; I think they are done. Don't say a word about this; it's rude. Let's mind our own business for once. I don't want any drama, Amora. Keep your damn lips shut.'

Amora took her towel and stared at Luna. 'Take the bucket out before anyone sees you. You don't have to be so primitive; you will not be using that around me. I don't want to see your private parts each morning.' Amora laughed so hard she had tears in her eyes. Luna didn't care much; she had grown up like this. It was no big deal to her. She wiped the floor and removed her little bar of soap. Her tiny body looked so fragile, but she was more than capable.

'You have seen far worse; now go shower. I don't want to be late. Don't forget to make your bed.'

'Yes, Mother. I bet you will fix it while I wash my fat ass. You also need to tell me more about that Navy hunk. I saw how he looked at you. All that heat around couldn't stop him from playing bodyguard. The man worked all night and just disappeared. I mean, what a waste. I asked around; people seem to fear him. They say he began his career in the army or something. All I can say is, he better marry one of us.'

Luna busied herself making her bed to hide the smile on her face at the mention of the bearded man. He had been so hands-on with helping, and his quiet presence next to her when she was devastated by the baby's death had soothed her frayed nerves. It was silly to keep thinking about him when she didn't even know his name. It was probably futile because he wouldn't even tell her what it was.

'Come on, Amora, men like him are always married. Is that why you decided to stay behind? You were stalking the boys?' Amora was always hunting down men. She wanted them but no one chose her.

'What do you think I am?' Amora's wide smirk said it all. Luna just shook her head.

'I thought people's lives meant far more to you.'

'I saved those I could. I had to make sure everyone was safe.'

'When you say "they", do you mean the Navy guys?'

'Of course! Did you see how hot they were in that navy-blue uniform?'

'I saw guys who were at work like all of us. Get that nonsense out of your head. We are running late. I have to warm up the car and ensure we have unpacked everything.'

'While you are at it, find me something to wear. My uniform might need some ironing. You know I don't know how to do that.' Amora winked and left, passing Bree and Lucy in the corridor. They were wearing T-shirts and nothing else. Lucy and Bree giggled like school kids and disappeared into their room.

Luna went to the balcony off the lounge after cleaning her bedroom. Amora was still in the shower. She had a magical singing voice but never wanted to sing in front of people. Luna struggled to open the double doors; they looked like they hadn't been used in years. The handle looked like it could fall off at any moment. She stepped outside and observed the people on the street. Devastation greeted her as she surveyed the carnage up the hill. A lot of rebuilding and repairing would likely happen in the coming weeks.

She saw people rushing to work and spotted the school bus stopping to pick up some students. Life went on regardless of the tragedies that happened. The sky was grey, reflecting the sombre mood of the community. The mountains were covered in clouds and smog. Luna was grateful that she was there and had a job. The fire had not affected their boarding house, and Mr Fourie had promised some renovations. But he hadn't come to see them as promised and he wasn't answering his landline phone. Luna didn't know whether he had a car or drove a wagon, as some of the people in the area still did.

The car's battery was flat, so she and Amora had to walk the two kilometres to the clinic, following Lucy's directions. The stench of the fire still lingered in the air. They spotted a police van and some people near the burnt-out houses. The helicopter with the Navy insignia was parked nearby.

'I guess the investigations have begun.'

'Do you think they found more bodies? It was dark; we might have missed people.'

'Let's hope not, Amora.' The horror they had faced could never be repeated. Luna had never before seen so much pain in people's eyes.

'How many do you think got fried?' Amora spoke recklessly, walking behind Luna.

'What? Please watch your tongue, young lady! We don't speak like that!' Luna strode away, irritated.

'You know what I mean. You don't have to leave me behind. Wait!' Amora couldn't keep up with Luna's pace; she was moving so fast that Amora could hardly catch her breath.

'You need to really change how you speak about people. We are new here and people will get offended. They don't know us; I don't want to be ostracised because of your behaviour. Can we just get to work in peace? You'll have to keep up, mind your step and watch out for potholes,' Luna said as they walked down the street.

'I know all of that, but you were the hero of the town last night, Luna.'

'I wouldn't say that. We were all trying to do what we knew how to do. You also did your part; I didn't hear you come in this morning.'

'I didn't do half of the things you did, Luna. That poor baby you held. I must applaud you. I wasn't going to be able to hold a dead baby like that. It was like it was your own. I feel bad for the families who had to witness their family members die like that.'

'I doubt it was the first time, as painful as it is. People die every year because of wildfires. The community must find ways to protect their homes and create some form of barrier around them. I don't know, but a plan must be made. That child didn't deserve to die like that.'

They passed an old, rundown petrol garage with only one person servicing cars on their left. On the opposite side was a bookstore and a café with a motel up the road.

I could probably spend my Sundays at the café.

The town was undeniably timeworn, but a sense of concord centred Luna. After a few more metres, they saw a long queue of people snaking around a brick building and out of the yard; there was no gate. Some people were lying on the grass, others sat on chairs and many just stood around. Luna noticed a man covering his face with a blood-stained towel; another's burnt leg was exposed through his trousers that had been cut open.

'I guess we have a long day ahead of us,' Amora sighed. She felt tired already. Amora pulled something from her bag and turned around.

Luna's attention was on the people. It would rain soon and with the type of wounds these people had, they had to receive immediate attention. A lot of time had already passed. She hurried along, looking for another nurse to help her.

'We were told you would help us,' someone called out.

'My child, look! My child,' another lady said as she followed Luna. She pointed at a young boy, pulling the boy's top up and exposing his badly burnt stomach.

'We have run out of ice; our power has been cut off. The mayor hasn't even come to see us. We don't have water in our homes and depend on river water. We live behind that hill. More people are in their homes without the means to get here. Please help us. We have been here since early morning; no one has eaten and that old hog won't open the doors.'

Luna glanced at the front door of the clinic while the lady shouted at her. She was clearly frustrated and drained.

'All that old hog knows is to run her seedy motel that the cops don't even bat an eyelid at. This clinic is not her house; she can't treat us like trespassers!' an old man yelled from the queue.

'I will be with you shortly; I am deeply sorry we are late. We are new in town, but I will be with you shortly.' Luna searched for Amora.

She was walking past the patients as if she were going to a hair salon, not a clinic with needy patients. Luna tried calling her, but Amora held her head high and kept moving.

'Is this the clinic?' Amora had no limits; she always said the wildest things with no sensitivity. Luna was appalled.

'Where did all these people come from?'

'They are all casualties from the fire!'

'Maybe we just have to dress the minor injuries.'

Luna tried to speak to each person, introducing herself and assessing their injuries. She needed help, but Amora had already opened the door and gone into the clinic. Luna sighed and looked around. Everyone wanted her attention; she couldn't do this alone.

She entered the clinic, where she and Amora were introduced to the head nurse, Eve Russel, who was old enough to be their grandmother. Eve had a large round face and red hair tied into a neat ponytail in the nape of her neck. She had worked at the clinic all her life and didn't care who came and went.

'Ladies, get settled in. I want all those people away from here before the rain comes. You are young; you can work speedier. And you are three minutes late. We can't have that here; you knew how busy we would be this morning. I want these people out of here as soon as possible. I have made name tags for you; grab them at our reception area.' Luna couldn't stop staring at Eve's yellow teeth. She spoke with her entire body as if explaining their roles to a classroom. Sweat was running down her face but she was not even running.

Amora rolled her eyes. Was Eve complaining about them being three minutes late? Was she crazy? No one had slept a wink in this town because of the fire and she moaned about three minutes! Amora wanted to laugh in Eve's face, but Luna caught her eye. It was the best discipline Luna could give Amora then. The reception area had a small wooden table in the corner. Amora took the name tags and handed Luna hers.

'Young lady, learn to say thank you. I slaved over those,' Eve said.

Luna couldn't believe what she was hearing. The tags just had their names written on them, with no branding, and they were held by a string.

'I have to meet important people,' Eve chided them. 'This clinic services the entire community. There is no time to waste. Move along!'

Luna couldn't hide her smirk.

Wasn't she sipping tea like no one was outside when we found her?

The clinic was right next to a pharmacy, a small yet welcoming building right in town on the Main Street. The pub across the street had men coming and going. Amora's head ached; she couldn't keep up with Eve's directions about what they had to do for the day. All she heard was that there would be no lunch break for them. Lucy and Bree had the afternoon shift after lunch. There was no doctor, as expected, and the nurses did not have an office. They had to share a room to do their admin in.

Luna took some medical supplies and began to work; she didn't bother to talk to Eve and her enormous ego. Amora took forever with each patient. Luna worked for hours, hoping she could treat everyone.

'You need to eat something; you look flushed,' Amora said to Luna much later, as they collected more supplies from inside the clinic.

'It's getting hot. I am glad that half of the people we found here are gone. That old eagle is going to give us a problem.' Luna looked around to see where Eve was. She had said she was going to the post office, which gave them a couple of minutes to take a break. However, they didn't have any food and were very tired.

'I thought you said I should watch my tongue.' Amora came to sit with Luna underneath the tree on the front lawn so that they could catch their breath. The cloudy skies kept the sun's warmth at bay, which worked in their favour. They could see right into Main Street. It was almost evening and everyone in the village was preparing for it. A lot of people were carrying big bottles of water and large buckets.

'I've earned the right to be incredulous!' Luna exclaimed. 'We can't even eat; Eve even monitors how often I use the bathroom. I thought we could go to the supermarket on our lunch break and get what we needed for dinner. I mean, how will we settle in here without everything we need? I tried talking to Eve earlier, but she wouldn't listen. It's like she already hates us because we come from the city. Can you believe that she turned people away, saying they could self-medicate at home? I mean, she didn't even look at their injuries. I just stood there and watched her like a fool. She was so mean and ruthless, and she smokes like a chimney – worse than you, Amora.'

Luna was speaking softly, but her brown eyes looked sad. It felt like she just could not catch a break. Life always had other plans and she was never in control of what happened around her. She thought of the mess she had left behind in Cape Town and resolved to suck all of this up. It was her only chance to attain some peace. There was no sense in packing up and leaving; she didn't have enough money to go elsewhere.

'You should have told me to sit on her damn face!' Amora said. 'What a rude old woman; she probably doesn't have kids. No wonder no one wants to work here. Like, did you see what we found here? She needs us, she won't survive without us.' Amora always admired Luna's work ethic; there was never a day she didn't do her job well.

'She is always on the phone and didn't even assist with one person,' Luna complained. 'However, I heard something. Well, some people were talking about the tea plantation on the other side of town. They say it's the biggest tea farm in the Western Cape. They also said that the people working there are never seen or returned to their families. What type of work do they truly do?'

'That sounds like a slave plantation,' Amora said worriedly. 'Do you think they still allow that with this newfound freedom?'

She knew it was a possibility, but something inside her told her to keep quiet. She thought of her mother and how she treated her farm workers. She didn't want Luna stepping on the wrong toes. Amora was happier away from that entire family. Being in Clanwilliam gave her back her free will. Luna still didn't notice the look in Amora's eyes; something was eating her alive. Each of them had secrets, but neither was willing to share them to protect the other.

'I don't know, Amora. From what I could gather, it's owned by a ruthless family and they own most of the businesses here in town.'

'What businesses? I mean, this place has one long street with maybe twenty businesses. I saw a butchery, a garage, that dry café, and a grill house restaurant. Oh, and the motel. I don't know, I haven't seen much but I can count all these establishments in ten seconds.'

'One man said that his brother was taken to that farm seven years ago. They tried to see him, but they were chased away by men with guns. Another added that his sister worked there as a domestic and three months after she started there, the farmer told this man's family that she'd died from influenza. She was only seventeen. The family didn't even get to see her body; that's even worse. When we left the boarding house, did you notice that we don't have any neighbours. It's a stand-alone building and a few metres away is the school. There is no one on the right. Then it's the open field and, in the distance, the houses that burnt down. It's like we live in a forgotten area of the town. I don't know what to think; I've heard many stories now.' Luna was scared but also curious.

'Luna, don't believe everything you hear; these people fight against each other for whatever reason. It's a small town; they don't have much to do but chatter. I don't want you to stress your little heart about such things. I know you; don't even think about going there. You are here to be a nurse and that's all you will be. I told you about that dodgy boarding house and that Mr Fourie. Where was he last night? Was he hoping we would all be asleep and die in the fire? Why didn't he come and see if we were safe? Isn't he hosting us? Like, come on. We don't have food and this bulldog won't allow us to do anything.'

'The man I spoke to said he had some kind of evidence, Amora. He wasn't playing. And about Mr Fourie, I think he is just old; he wouldn't be fighting a fire anyway.'

'All I am saying is, even if it's true, stay out of it. It's not your place.'

'Fine. Let's do our work and then get out of here.'

'Oh, look at that – Bree and Lucy are at that pub in full uniform!' Amora said and pointed in the direction of the motel.

'Yes, Amora. They were supposed to take over from us but they are an hour late and galivanting with some random men! Where is evil Eve when you need her?'

'I don't even know who they are talking to. Look over there, the wagon. It might be those Navy guys we saw last night.'

Amora quickly stood up from the lawn and fixed her hair. She needed to be perfect because there was no way she would meet her heroes looking like a cooked, oily, fat cake.

Luna looked around and saw the bearded man's wagon was parked near the motel. She also saw what looked like a brawl taking place outside the bar at the motel. People were shouting, but she couldn't hear much. The two men standing near Bree and Lucy ran towards the ruckus.

'There is a fight there at the motel. I can't really see what's happening.'

'There he is. That guy! Your guy!'

Luna strained her eyes to see him but couldn't identify him in the crowd. She was unsure if she'd recognise him if they met again. Meeting under the cloak of darkness and in the light of day were two different things. Luna squashed the hope in her chest that she would see the bearded guy again – it had just been a passing fancy.

Chapter 6

Forgiveness can be an ugly dance

'If you were not my father, I would rip you to shreds. Is this the life you promised my mother? Is this how you lead us? You keep breaking this family every chance you get. Is this the life you are living for your granddaughter?' Cam's hands were clutching his father's shirt and the seams were nearly bursting. None of his friends had ever seen him this way. John was so drunk that he didn't even recognise Cam fully, but he heard his son's voice. He found it odd that he could be here; from what John knew, Cam was supposed to be away on a mission for the Navy.

Cam bubbled with the anger that was spilling hot and poisonous onto his father. His tongue felt like a serpent's, striking his father repeatedly with words. Cam couldn't believe that instead of helping the people in this broken town, his father chose to drink. People had lost so much overnight and yet John wasn't even bothered. The home he was supposed to care for was rotting with Mia inside. No land had been prepared for farming except for what Mia had done; there was so much to do and yet here the man was – wasted. The town needed men who could aid those who had lost their homes, but John had given his life to alcohol. Cam had dragged him out of the motel bar in full view of his concubines.

'You must be my son, the proud Navy seal. Always at the service of us commoners. So noble. Care for a drink?' John sneered. His emphatic pronouncement made Cam boil.

'If you don't snap out of this, I will kill you myself.' Cam trembled, feeling the rage he had kept bottled in for so many years rise and threaten to choke him. He hated seeing his father among the local prostitutes and the environment made him sick. There was no respect or holiness here. Where was God when he needed him? He had never imagined that he would hold his father like this. He wanted to break John free from his demons, but how could he do that when his father revelled in it?

'Why don't you just do it? Just save us a lifetime of suffering. Then I can join my wife in the forever life.' John was swaying and struggling to remain standing.

'With the life you lead, you do not deserve to share the afterlife with my mother! All you had to do was take care of Mia. Why are you here?'

'A man needs a break, a drink and a little excitement.'

'This can't be all that you have become. You have been here for how long? My child was almost killed last night and that's all you can say? You needed a break?'

'Come on, Cam. When will you drop the act? You know why I am here. My darling Emily is gone. What did you expect me to do? Sit and watch flowers grow? I am glad you are back. Come in and have a drink with me.'

'Let him go,' Seth Fourie said. Cam was trying to breathe but his chest felt too heavy. He had picked up his friends, Seth and Ryan Adams, from the school prior to coming to the motel to fetch his father, as John was always a handful when he was drunk. Cam, Seth and Ryan had grown up together and were colleagues in the Navy, but coming home this time was not an exuberant celebration for them. They were three childhood friends who had become the backbone of the small town.

'Just look at him!' Cam said to Seth.

'He is still your father; let him go. You need to let him be. Just get him home.'

Seth wanted to help the community, but he could only do so much with what he'd found at the local school. He'd called in favours from his network of friends in the Navy, who would arrive in the afternoon to deliver some supplies; however, Cam always came first with them. He was like the big brother they never had.

Seth pulled Cam away and Ryan, the Navy doctor who had assisted with the casualties the previous night, came to break John free. Cam's grip was so tight that as soon as Ryan pushed him, John stumbled and dropped to the ground; the people working in the nearby shops stood at a distance and watched the men tussle.

'Father!' Cam called. His insides clenched in frustration. Ryan led Cam back to his wagon; his friends felt bad for the two men. The Coal family had been held in high esteem over the years, when they'd had the most successful farm in the area.

Over the years, twice a year, the three friends would visit each house in the town to see how the community was doing. They also offered all kinds of skills to the kids who needed extra help at school and provided various services to the families that had lost their sons in wars. They fixed roofs, gates and did any household chores that required a man's touch. This is how the three of them would spend their holidays so their families would have support on their farms. But things had changed in the last three years. The locals had begun talking about working on the other side of the mountain for another family who was employing most of the youth in the area.

A woman who had chatted with John inside the pub came running out, demanding that he pay for the drinks he'd consumed, but saw him lying on the ground. Cam felt sick to his stomach. Ryan and Seth picked John up and placed him in the back of the wagon. Cam looked at his father in shame.

'Get him home, Cam,' Seth said. He was a stout, short man with lots of facial hair. A Navy sniper with ten years of service, he was a man of few words. Cam respected him, especially because Seth had repeatedly covered his back on their missions.

'We will take care of the people here,' Seth told Cam. 'The clean-up team will secure the mountain and ensure that we don't have another flare-up. We have found some kind handymen who have offered to help rebuild the few homes that have burnt down. We've also managed to get water tanks up there and blocked off the burnt fields. Just go take care of your father. We will come around later.'

'Did you manage to get some food for the people? Our farm is a wasteland; it pains me that I can't assist with that.' Cam glanced at his drunken father.

'Don't worry, the other farmers will help us. I also have a friend in Lambert's Bay who will donate some food. His truck will arrive in the next two hours.'

'I spoke briefly to Seth's dad, Mr Fourie,' Ryan chimed in. 'All the burials will be done tomorrow night. We can't keep the bodies for too long. I will gather the community tonight to prepare them.'

'I don't know what we would become without you, gentlemen,' Cam said. 'Give me an hour or two and I will join you.'

'We serve and protect, brother. Keep cool with the old man; we all have bad days,' Seth sighed as the wagon drove off.

Cam didn't want to waste more time; there was so much he had to do. Mia was alone and the food he had bought from the market the previous night had been ruined by all the commotion during the fire. He stopped by a local store and picked up a few things. Mia needed new shoes, but Cam's father was so wasted that he couldn't advise him and Cam couldn't guess what size she wore. He would have to return to town with Mia once things had settled down. It hurt Cam to see his father plonked down in the wagon like a sack of potatoes.

Luna and Amora observed the commotion from a distance but couldn't determine what was happening. Amora wanted to run across the road to take a better look, but Luna held her back, cautioning her about Eve's return.

'You need to learn to stay out of people's business, Amora.'

'We live here now; we should know what the local hunks get up to.'

'We still have work to do, and you are worried about drunk men.'

'Didn't you see him? That's the hero guy!'

'Everyone is a hero; we all did what we could.'

'I have always wanted to see those men in action. Navy men mixed with army soldiers; last night was a movie! Those men came in like angels, strong, bold and damn fearless. I have never seen men sweat like that.'

'Do you have no shame? People lost their lives and here you are thinking about bagging a man.'

'I don't care what you think. We are alive and those who died are at peace now. There was nothing more we could do. Did you want me to jump into the fire and kill myself? Now, I can't just admire God's creatures without you playing the Virgin Mary! What's wrong with you? Like, who hurt you? If you want us to live here, you better act like it. How will we create a new life in isolation? We need to be around people and what would it hurt if we loved these people! You need to get over your shit. I don't want to be as bitter and cold as you are towards men. I am here now, and you made us move here. You need to try to act normal. Take your ass out of the darkness.' With that, Amora stormed off.

Luna felt the impact of Amora's words. She didn't want to fall in love; she couldn't let herself look at a man that way. There was no chance that anyone would love her after what she had done. Amora could always shirk off the past and move on, but Luna couldn't; her mind wouldn't allow her to find peace. This job was the only thing she had now. But Amora was right; she had to relax a tad.

Luna's mother had got burnt by love. Growing up without a father had been a challenge for Luna; her mother always held on to him as if he would return one day. But it had been ten years and he had never called or checked up on them. Luna hated what that did to her mother. Her father's abandonment had reduced Julie to a workaholic stuck in the past, sitting around, waiting for a man to come back. Luna had promised herself that her life would never turn out that way. She thought about the room she shared with Amora; there was so much to fix and she wasn't about to call her mother and ask for money. Luna had to wait to tell her that she had left the city until she was settled.

She watched as the commotion outside the motel died down and sighed heavily. She took a moment to look around. They were in a valley surrounded by mountains that placed them in the centre and covered them like a warm blanket. There was so much to see and learn about the Cederberg region. The land was beautiful, not all was lost, and this new life would be happier than if she just sat around and waited for the worst to happen. Luna would have to force herself to live again.

It was different here; she had to embrace a simpler life. Though some people had cars, others still preferred to use horses and wagons. Luna also wouldn't use her car every day, which would save costs. Everything was within walking distance anyway; she and Amora would have to do what the locals did. Thinking about the roads and flat battery in her car, Luna realised she had no money to pay someone to help her replace it. She and Amora would need food and other essentials to carry them through the month.

Just before the clinic closed for the day, Eve returned with Seth and Ryan. They stayed in her office for a while, where Seth remained standing while Ryan sat down. Amora had noticed that Eve excluded her and Luna in all her conversations, but she eavesdropped unashamedly. She could see through the window that Eve's laughter and endless compliments were making Seth uncomfortable. Amora watched as Eve flirted with the two men. She had no shame, and at her age! Amora found the guys to be profoundly striking now that she could see them clearly in the light of day.

Luna decided it was time to leave, as she had managed to clear everything off her list. It had been a good day, with no mortalities, at least. She needed a break and, hopefully, a night with no emergencies. Working with Eve was going to be challenging; she was controlling and rude. Eve didn't even bother to check if she and Amora were settling in well. All she cared about was being a socialite. She only spoke to people of a certain class and only helped those with whom she had a personal relationship. Luna didn't understand why Eve was a nurse; she didn't care about helping those in need.

As Luna and Amora packed up their stuff, Eve came out of her office. Bree and Lucy were already gone. Some people had needed help at the school, so Eve had let them go an hour earlier.

'I guess your first day was momentous. I expect you back at 8 a.m. and not a second later. The wonderful men in my office will be working with us to assist the community. I don't want them to need anything; ensure that everything is clean and accessible. I am expecting you to only give them what they need. Nothing more. They won't be around for long and don't think I won't be watching. Do what you are told and keep clear of them.' She looked pointedly at the girls. Her eyes moved from Luna's old flats up to her fatigued face. Amora didn't bother to look at Eve. Her attention was directed at the men in the office.

'You mean clean toilets?' Amora asked in repugnance, her eyes still stuck on Ryan. Eve followed her eyes and placed her entire plump body before Amora to obscure her view. Amora stood on her toes, unfazed. Luna pulled her back. It was not the time for Amora to force things.

'Whatever you use, you clean. Who do you think will clean up after you?'

'Everything is done, Ms Eve; we are done for the day,' Luna murmured, trying to relieve the tension in the room.

'Good. Take the spare key; I won't be here in the morning. You will have to open.' As Eve spoke, the men came out and removed their caps. Luna found the gesture heartening and reverential. It reminded her of the bearded man, but she quashed the thought as soon as it arose.

'Good evening, ladies. We will be on our—' Amora interrupted Seth's farewell by stepping forward and offering her hand.

'Are you stupid!' Eve slapped away her hand. 'That's no way to greet these gentlemen. I told you to go and finish your jobs before you make fools out of us!'

The men were already uncomfortable; they quickly nodded their goodbyes and left. Eve was still mumbling something under her breath but Amora was equally boiling. How could Eve do that?

'Wash the floors before you leave. Just look at this; this is a health centre. We can't live like pigs around here.'

'I am sorry, but that's not my job. I am a nurse; I don't clean floors.' Amora stood at attention, not changing her stance. Eve's eyes widened.

'Where do you think the cleaner will come from? Should I do it?'

'We are nurses and that's why we are employed here,' Luna said firmly. 'As I said earlier, we have done what we could for the day and will return tomorrow. Have a pleasant night.' Luna gracefully picked up her things and Amora followed.

'You are the only pig around here, Eve!' Amora mumbled under her breath as they walked away. Luna wanted to laugh because she finally agreed with Amora. How dare Eve treat them like slaves?

On their way back to the boarding house, they picked up some food from the café; Amora sneaked in a bottle of whisky without Luna noticing. When they arrived, Bree had left them a note.

> If you find this note, it means we are still helping at the school. If you have the energy, you are more than welcome to join us. We will be having a prayer session and handing out food packs. If you ladies can't make it, that's still fine. See you later.

When Amora saw the note, she clarified that she would not be attending. Luna, though, decided to join Bree and Lucy and quickly changed into more comfortable clothes.

Chapter 7

Time waits for no man

G*oodness, this place is peaceful.*
Luna needed the break and the transitory walk to the school helped clear her mind. So much had happened in such a short period of time and here she was, stepping into her new life. For the first time in quite a while, she felt calm. Luna wore a long black dress, which helped to give her confidence. A group of people were cleaning the school grounds. It only took Luna ten minutes to get to the main gate. Several horses grazed on the grass on the other side of the gate. At first glance, the school looked old but well-maintained.

The place seemed busy; Luna wasn't sure where to go, until the bearded white man from the previous night approached her. She fought down her queasiness as her heart stuttered. The flash of recognition paralysed her. She instantly remembered his piercing, warm brown eyes.

'You don't sleep much, do you?' he said with a gigantic beam. He had some tools in his hands and a cloth over his left shoulder. He looked busy yet unperturbed and there was an ease in his step.

'I would love to, but there is so much to do around here,' Luna said as she strolled towards him. He was in different clothes this time: a pair of khaki shorts and a loose-fitting T-shirt. Brown hair covered his arms and legs. This was the first time she could clearly see his five o'clock shadow and dark-brown crew cut. When Luna stopped about a metre away from him, Cam came closer still. He stood so close to her that she could hardly breathe; his scent of the sea and burnt leather assaulted her senses.

'We seem to bump into each other at odd hours, my lady.' Luna knew he wasn't making any ownership claims but was being respectful, as when he took off his cap when he spoke to her the night before, but her heart still accelerated.

I'm freaking out here; I should've stayed with Amora.

'I guess we are on the same undertaking.'

'Things have calmed down; there isn't much to do now.'

'I thought I could lend a hand.'

'You are a nurse, right?'

'Yes, sir. I am.'

'Care to look at my burns?' He raised his left hand and showed her the blisters; Luna hesitated momentarily. She was unsure of the protocol for treating Navy guys, especially after Eve's earlier reaction. She looked around, concerned about who could see them, but people passed them without a second glance.

'Is everything all right?' Cam noticed the panic in Luna's eyes. She pulled him closer, which threw him off balance. Her presence seemed to drown out the noise around him until it felt like they existed in a bubble – just the two of them. What would happen if he touched her face? He was close enough to do it.

'Your hand seems fine to me. You will be all right.' Luna looked away and took a step back. Why did he suddenly feel so bereft?

'You didn't even look at it,' Cam said accusingly. The truth was, he had thought about her all day. Seeing her hold the dead baby had made him curious about who she was. Within the fibre of her tiny, delicate body, strength, grit and courage were wrapped in empathy and care. The flutter of his feelings scared him. There was no room for her in his life. He thought about Summer for a moment, but this girl has captured him. Her smile and the tiny wrinkle he noticed on her nose enchanted him. She was shy, just like Summer. This could not happen; he wanted to step away, but his body felt glued in place. He noticed her lips moving; she was saying something.

'Sir, can you hear me? I have seen enough; you will heal. Just stay away from hot water or steam and don't break the blisters. If they do break, wash them with mild soap and water. With the influx of patients today, the clinic is low on antibiotic ointments. Maybe your friend, Doctor Ryan, can assist you.' Luna folded her arms, trying to break free from his gaze.

'My name is Cameron Coal, but everyone calls me Cam,' he murmured, bridging the gap she had created between them.

'I'm pleased to make your acquaintance, Mr Coal.' A slow smile formed and lingered for far too long on Cam's face. She finally knew his name. He was tall; he towered over her just like the surrounding mountains. His shadow felt warm and inviting. Luna didn't know if this was the time to run away or to continue staring at him. His eyes danced with mirth, and she clenched her hands to restrain the urge to run a hand down his beard.

How would his bristles feel against my hand? My mother would be scandalised if she knew my wayward thoughts about this white man.

'If you insist on being formal, Miss Parks, it's actually Captain Coal.'

Cam turned abruptly at the sound of Mia's tiny voice. Her small feet emerged from the shadows.

'Peanut, I told you to stay in the car.'

'I got thirsty.' Cam dropped his tools and went to her. Luna stood frozen, amazed.

'Okay, I will sort that out for you. Where is Uncle Seth?'

'He said he was going into the hall.'

'You should have stayed in the car,' Cam said again. He picked Mia up, turned around and walked back towards Luna.

'I'm sorry, Miss Parks. I have to attend to my daughter. It was lovely to meet you.'

Luna wondered if it was sensible to ask him about the blind child, but Cam's body language had changed; he was protective, almost using his body to cover that of the little girl.

'I guess I will see you around. This little lady needs to get home.'

'Oh, you are leaving?'

'Yes, of course.' An image of a wife, a needy child and maybe three more kids flashed before Luna's eyes. She looked away.

Cam noticed her withdrawal, yet there was nothing he could say.

Now was not the time to lay his dirty laundry out; he didn't even know how she felt about him. However, he did have to attend to Mia and her needs. She had to come first.

'I have stolen your time,' Cam said apologetically. 'If you are looking for your colleagues, they are packing food in the main hall. They seem to be delightful people. This little town of ours needs the extra help. We will lay the deceased to rest tomorrow, and hopefully things will slowly get back to normal.' Cam was still holding Mia, her face turned towards him.

'Thank you. Take care of the little lady and your hand. I don't think I will attend the service; the clinic needs us,' Luna said politely, resisting the urge to ask Cam if he would need any help with his little girl.

Her mind gave her a million answers she didn't require. Soldiers in the army and sailors in the Navy never stayed in one place for too long. He would have to leave Clanwilliam and this little thing he may be feeling would die and leave her broken-hearted.

'This lady just needs her bed. Have a good evening, Miss Parks.'

'Do you live around here?' Luna was desperate to prolong the conversation. The words tumbled out of her mouth before she could reel them back in. He turned his gaze to Luna with a smile.

'Yes, we have a farm on the other side of the hill. It's a family business.' Hearing of him say those words made her feel numb.

He has a family.

'So, you're in the Navy...'

Let it go, Luna!

'Yes, have you seen us around besides last night?'

'I lived in Cape Town and actually witnessed you guys practising for the SONA a few days ago. But your profession seems taxing; I am surprised you have time to come home.'

Even though Luna wanted to stay and talk to him, she suddenly also had an overwhelming urge to escape from the conversation. Cam was too close and she was talking way too much. She didn't know why this made her so anxious; it was as if he could see right through her. Two people lived inside her: one good, peaceful gem, and the sad, lonely monster. Besides, she had no business talking to this man while the other nurses were hard at work. Luna didn't have a personality like Amora's; standing there suddenly felt incredibly awkward.

'My friends and I were excused from duty because of the fire; the SONA is happening tomorrow,' Cam explained. 'Besides, there is always a good reason to come home. However, many programmes and camps require us to be on base. This country won't survive if we all stay home.'

'What do you mean?' Asking this made Luna feel like she'd failed an exam, but it was the only way she could continue talking to him. The way he was gently rubbing his daughter's back to comfort her and standing close to Luna to keep her in his circle of attention made Luna's heart beat faster.

'We have open seas; many people have tried encroaching it from all over. So, we protect our marine environment and run anti-piracy operations. If our marines sleep, our waters will be invaded. It would be like sleeping with your doors open.'

Luna thought about her ancestral history and what her mother had tried to teach her. Her people's land had been invaded many times, and the natives of the Cape had not had a naval team to protect their borders. The South African borders had been porous, and the colonialists had taken full advantage. She didn't want to think of Cam Coal like that.

Could he also be to blame for my ancestors' dark history?

Cam's eyes locked with those of the child he carried; she seemed disorientated.

'Father, how does night look? Where does the sun go at night?' Cam whispered something in Mia's ear, and she giggled.

'That's a good question. I hope your father told you it plays hide and seek.'

'He said the moon eats the sun. Do you believe him?' the little girl asked, her body turning to locate Luna's voice. She held out her tiny hand to greet her.

'My name is Mia Coal; this is my father. Did he tell you he is my mother's husband? And he is a very important man. He works under the big ocean and sometimes he is a farmer.'

'That's not true, Mia,' Cam laughed and pulled her back safely into his chest.

'Well, you know many things,' Mia said softly.

'She has a smart mouth.' Cam tried to obscure a yawn.

'She must be the best student in class. Does she go to this school? I haven't seen any other schools around here.' Luna wanted to find a way to ask about Mia's condition but the look on Cam's face made her want to run.

'She is smart.' He didn't want to bring up his issues, but he feared Mia would say something that would spill all his problems on this young lady.

'I see. Well, let me not take up too much more of your time. I think the ladies might be looking for me.'

'I doubt it. Either way, don't put too much on your shoulders. The men will handle all the hard labour.' Cam sounded concerned. Mia was becoming restless.

'Just going to do my job, sir.'

Cam nodded and cleared the path for her.

Luna gathered her dress and walked off in search of the hall. She felt hot from the exchange with Cam.

Cam watched her go from one classroom to another. He found it funny that she wasn't asking for directions. When she finally disappeared into a room, he walked towards his waiting wagon. The thought of going back home drained him. He didn't know what to expect and could not fight his father in front of Mia. He had to pull himself together.

Cam cleaned the house while Mia and John slept. He was surprised at the burst of energy that surged through him. He packed away all the food he had bought, swept the dust from each room and fed the animals in the barn. The wood he would use to build Mia's new bed was stacked outside.

While Cam was doing all this, he thought about Luna's kind eyes, her petite frame and her gentle heart. He didn't want to compare them, but Luna was just like Summer. She had also wanted to serve and give, never putting herself first. The pain of losing his mother and wife always reminded Cam that love was a dangerous game. Not a day went by when he didn't think of their catastrophic deaths. Now, he was left alone to raise a child, and his father was falling back into his grief.

It was almost midnight when Cam took a break. He sat outside and gazed at the mountains. He needed to rest, but he had to think about what Mia needed. She had to return to school; Mia needed a parent but instead he'd taken on more responsibilities at work. He had been so happy once; distant memories of Summer registered in him like the wind on his face. Summer had liked the farm; she knew everything about this land, and here he was, struggling to raise a child. How could things have turned out this way? The truth was, he had buried all his pain by going to the Navy. He didn't even remember when it was time to plough or harvest.

He knelt to touch the soil, but what was the point? Whether dry, wet or sandy, how would he get over the fact that he wasn't made for all of this? He was no farmer. From a distance, he saw the Robinson family land and, further up, the Jacobs'. The men both had wives and, from what he could tell, solid families. That was the one thing he didn't have.

'Lord, I know nothing of this land. How will I feed this child? My hands don't sow as they should; I have tried but Summer died for this land, and I have nothing to give it,' Cam whispered to the heavens, hoping for an answer.

Before Mia was born, Summer had harvested the tea and the crop would always sell out. So many bags were harvested from this very land and the tea was so good that every store in town stocked only their tea. Sole, his brother, was the family lawyer. He drew up contracts with every shop and restaurant in the area. They were planning to expand and also export overseas. Their business was going so well that some hotels had even requested personalised labels on the teabags to fit in with their brand.

The farm also produced crops that fed their livestock. But now all they had was dry land and burnt yields. Cam couldn't do anything now; there was so much he didn't know because his mother and father had farmed the land and handled its affairs. He felt helpless; there was no time to rebuild their reputation. No millions in the bank to hire people with the necessary skills, and the land now seemed dead. He walked towards Mia's crops. How had she done all this alone? How did she know what to do and where?

He walked between the rows and looked at each plant. It was just as Summer had left it – each stem in perfect condition. Mia was special. Her little hands had accomplished far more than he could ever have imagined. But he knew it wouldn't be enough to save the farm. Cam had to retreat; there was no reason to wander the fields at night.

Chapter 8

For a child shall restore even the coldest heart

15 MARCH 2005, Clanwilliam, Western Cape

Mr Fourie kept his word and repainted their rooms and fixed the fencing around the boarding house. There was a nice set-up under the trees where the ladies could have Sunday afternoon tea. They took turns to clean the area and mostly used it on their individual rest days. The spot quickly became Amora's drinking nook and Luna's reading daybed. Lucy and Bree were no longer hiding their relationship from Luna and Amora, though Luna always steered clear of their public-affection displays. Amora found it entertaining and didn't care much. Lucy and Bree had gone from hiding their sneaky ways in the shower to openly holding hands while sitting together in the garden.

The community had moved on from the vicious fire and homes were being rebuilt with donations and insurance money. Luna hadn't seen Cam again after that evening at the school. She didn't bother telling Amora about their encounter out of dread that Amora would call her a hypocrite. Cam awoke feelings Luna didn't know she could have for a man and it frightened her. Her visceral reaction to his nearness the last time they'd met still confused her.

From what Amora knew, they had left Cape Town because of Dr Mark and his calculating ways. The most thrilling part of keeping a secret was disassociating with its reality. Luna savoured her new life and nothing was going to change that. She would not pay Cam any attention and give Amora something to talk about. His friends continued the work they had said they would do at the clinic, but Cam was nowhere to be seen in those weeks.

Bree and Lucy had invited Luna countless times to join them at the local bar, but she stayed away from them because of their unconventional love affair. That was just not the type of entertainment she cared about; Luna was a traditionalist in relationships. She didn't even bother wanting to learn about their ways. Even though she remained respectful and kind, seeing two women kiss made her feel awkward. Amora had got used to going out with Bree and Lucy; they bar-hopped and drank all weekend. Luna felt less pressure to fit in. They had settled in well, and Eve remained the dog they all disliked. However, they knew their way around and found solace in their peace.

There were a few silver linings. Luna spent her time exploring the town and took solo trips to the dam, went hiking with the locals and hosted first-aid classes on Saturday mornings. Many of the locals had begun warming up to her because she was welcoming, kind and vibrant; she was a nurse who sincerely cared about her community. It was a freeing feeling not to have to look over her shoulder the entire time. There were weekly Sunday chats with her mother, but she had not yet disclosed her departure from the city even though Clanwilliam was now her home, and she cared for the people who needed her. She worked over the weekends when there were emergencies and was always willing to help, from doing home visits to assisting pregnant women to deliver safely at home.

Luna enjoyed what she was creating; it gave her life more purpose. The relative quiet of life was comforting, even though she still felt like a fraudulent Capetonian. And she was still wary of people and their intentions; it was good that Amora also kept her distance. After all, they were not real friends. Luna didn't need her any more. All they shared was a dead man and a job. The sensory input of village life was far more than she had expected. No vehicle exhaust fumes, heavy traffic or hawkers at every turn to disturb the peace – certainly, no loud music.

Ryan worked at the clinic twice a week, which was all he could do while juggling the demands of his role in the Navy. Just before Luna got ready to lock up one evening, he came rushing through the door with Mia in his arms. She was unconscious. When Cam had showed up a week ago, Luna thought that he was working on the farm, but the way Ryan now spoke about him alarmed her.

'The man is a captain; he has many responsibilities. Kids get sick all the time, but Mia will be fine. She spends all her time in the river; that water can get cold. She will get over it in a day or two. It's just flu.' Luna tended to the child as best she could and thought of it no more. Even though she didn't appreciate Ryan's icy tone and was concerned about the child's condition, she wondered what else was happening on the farm. Luna noted that Ryan was wearing his uniform throughout his visit. That alone made his appearance more formal.

Luna was the only nurse on duty that day; Amora also had flu. Ryan didn't speak about Cam, although Eve asked him about Cam's well-being countless times. Mia also appeared a little reticent, certainly not as talkative as the last time Luna had seen her. She presumed Mia's weak immune system held her back and let her be. But Luna was surprised when Ryan brought Mia back again the following day. She had got worse; still, Cam didn't accompany her.

'She will have to stay the night for observation; I don't know how we will do this but there are no hospitals nearby.' Luna turned a concerned eye on the child.

'I don't think that will be possible, Miss Parks,' Ryan said. 'I was given strict instructions to have her back home before sunset.'

'Well, I have my own instructions, sir. This child needs medical care, and seeing that you have brought her back here, I will have to make sure that she is okay. You're a qualified doctor and you know she's not well.'

Ryan clenched his jaw in frustration. 'Just give her a shot.'

'It won't help in her condition. I will have to bring her temperature down.'

'Like I said, she still needs to go home.' Ryan seemed antsy and jumpy.

'Where is her father?' Luna looked at him with antipathy.

'Captain Coal has other urgent matters to attend to. I am her official guardian for now.' Ryan's throat felt parched. His emotions had no place here.

'Well, that's a pity because I need to know what her living conditions are. She looks like she has lost a lot of weight and is not dressed properly. Has she been eating? Three meals a day at least?' Unimaginable stories percolated in Luna's mind.

'I can assure you that she is in excellent hands. It's just a fever. Give us the medication and we will be on our way.'

Ryan sat down with Mia passed out on top of him; she looked weak and listless. Luna wanted to take the child and lay her on the bed but Ryan would not let her. Cam would get a piece of her mind; Ryan didn't even smile once or give her the impression that he was willing to compromise. At that moment Luna wished Amora was there, but now she would have to stand up for the child. Mia was damp with sweat and looked like she could fall into a coma at any minute. It seemed paramount to Luna that she yell at Ryan, but it would also scare Mia. Fear entered her mind, sending cold, quivery chills to her knees.

'She will have to stay here tonight. Go back home and tell the family that there is no way I am letting her go,' Luna said in a voice that would brook no dissent.

'Like you said, this is a clinic, not a hospital. We will administer anything you give us,' Ryan said.

'If she dies, her blood is on your hands. How can you do this? You are a doctor, or are you so used to killing people in wars that a child's life means nothing?'

'Well, that's your delusion, Miss Parks. I don't mind how you see me; just take care of this child or close up shop.' Ryan was no ordinary doctor; he had served in the army for ten years before the Navy had headhunted him. He had worked in conditions that no commonplace nurse would frequent.

'I will leave the child, but you must give me your number.' Ryan stood up and pulled out his phone. Luna was like a dog with a bone and Ryan knew that Mia would receive the best care with Luna. She had a reputation for helpfulness in the town.

Luna looked at the cracked screen and wanted to reject the phone with a snotty comment but begrudgingly took it from him.

'Miss Parks, cellphone number!' Luna glanced at Mia; she felt a deep compassion towards her. Luna punched her number into Ryan's phone and handed it back to him. She would have to be mentally prepared to confront Cam; this child was in a terrible state. Someone was going to have to answer for her pain.

Sounds of scuffling outside drew her attention. Ryan looked out the window and left without saying anything or looking at Mia. Luna seethed with suppressed anger. All this time, she had thought Cam was a responsible father who cared for his daughter, but now the signs suggested otherwise.

Why are you not here, Captain Coal?

'You're not even going to tell her you're leaving?' she called out after Ryan. He raised his hand in disapproval and jumped into a Navy truck.

Luna returned, picked Mia up, placed her in a bed and checked her pulse. It was horrifically low; she couldn't take her home with her. There was no equipment to stabilise her at the boarding house, and Eve would skin her alive if she took anything out of the clinic. Luna had no choice but to sleep there herself.

'I guess it's just you and me, little one. What did they do to you?' She tucked Mia in and sat quietly beside her. Mia shivered in her sleep and Luna put her on a drip. It was unlikely that Eve would come back that evening. For some odd reason, Luna was relieved. She asked Amora to bring her a change of clothes and some soap. Bree also stopped by and brought her some books.

Ryan called once before midnight, but he cut the call short when Luna enquired about Cam's whereabouts. Something was amiss and she would find out what.

Chapter 9

The gift of sorrow is the memory of their love

Cam would have to return to Simon's Town soon. He'd be stationed there as the new captain. The farm visit was supposed to have been a short stay – three to four weeks – yet so much had happened. He had had too little time to repair everything. There had to be more to life than just fixing things and then rushing back to work. He slaved away day and night at the Navy base only to return and do the same at home. His father had disappointed him.

Sweat dripped from all parts of Cam's body as he toiled. There was nothing he could do but continue working on the house. Winter would come soon and with Mia getting sick, he didn't want to leave without securing her safety. Cam was grateful for the promotion bonus he'd received because at least there were some funds for the most pressing repairs.

There was nothing more he could do for John and Mia; it felt as if he was a visitor in his own home. He asked Ryan to take care of Mia because seeing her so sick broke him. It resurrected painful memories that he'd rather keep deeply buried. The last time he'd gone to the clinic with someone, they had died in his arms. He couldn't bring himself to experience that again, not with his only child. Death seemed to follow him like a skunk smell.

Cam's stomach was in knots. He spent most of his time trying to repair the house, but he needed supplies; he had already depleted the funds he had. So, he would have to do without new doors and windows, and certainly no new kitchen ware. He wanted to get started on Mia's bed. Maybe that would make her feel better when she returned. Ryan kept him updated; he often spoke about the feisty nurse caring for Mia. Cam smiled, picturing petite Luna standing up to a tower like Ryan. Luna was constantly on his mind; he had repeatedly replayed their conversations in the past weeks. It had not been the content of the discussion; they could've discussed the weather and he still would've found it riveting.

'That girl knows how to get under my skin, but Mia is in good hands,' Ryan told Cam over the phone.

'I don't know how to care for my child, Ryan. I've tried but I don't know how to cater to her needs. Each time she gets sick, I run away from her side like she has leprosy. What type of father am I?' Self-loathing dripped from Cam's words.

'I hear you, but you need help, buddy. You can't live like this. Mia is your child and she will withdraw from you equally if you continue like this.' Ryan felt Cam's pain; it had been like this for years. Ryan and Seth always stepped in and helped where possible, but Cam had to overcome his loss this time. Mia needed him.

'I love my child, Ryan. You know I do, but I don't know how to be a father. John wrecked me. You know our family history. Who do I model my father behaviour on? You know how John is. Sole and I practically learnt to be men on the streets from your and Seth's father and the Navy. John was never present with us – all he cared about then was the farm. All those workers we had on the farm twenty years ago … we had everything then.

'But my father was a ruthless taskmaster, brutal and heartless. He treated his workers like shit. Even as a child, I was powerless to fight for them; he'd push me aside and continue whipping the wayward workers. So much blood spilt on this land, no wonder it's barren now.'

'You know what it was like back then, Cam. You're not responsible for your father's actions. Cruelty was prevalent on many farms in the Western Cape.'

'It's a dark history that haunts me still. As if I don't already have enough on my plate,' Cam said, wiping the sweat off his face. He was bare-chested and working in the oppressive heat.

'Mia is your child, Cam. You must find a way to do this. That nurse can't take care of her forever. Mia has a bad fever; it's been two days, but she should come home any day now. You need to pull yourself together and stop hiding in that house. Seth and I will be leaving tonight for camp. I would have loved to stay longer, but duty calls.'

'I know.' Cam raked his hand through his hair.

'You took this break to make things right; use the time wisely. You can't possibly hold on to the past; you are not your father. What happened is long gone and has no bearing on what you can become. Let history stay where it belongs. You can still change the narrative, buddy.'

'Regrettably, it lives in all of us. We are products of each soul that died on this land. We can't escape that, and you know it. My mother and wife died on this land, and I can't seem to find my feet here. It's like people see through my uniform. I can hear their whispers and can't accept or live with them.'

'So, what can you do now? Can you wake up the deceased? Your wife is gone; let her rest. You know how much Aunt Emily cherished that farm; you can't just sit there and wither away with it.'

Nothing could bring Summer back; not even Cam's earnest heart-ache would change the dead feeling inside him. He missed her. This would have been the perfect time to take a trip to the Garden Route. The sight of blooming flowers, ocean views and campsites would have delighted them. Mia had always wanted to see the ocean but it scared him to take her there. It was the last thing he he had done with his late wife; he couldn't bring himself to do the same with Mia.

'If I were to tell you what I have found here, you wouldn't speak like this,' Cam said. 'I came upon some inexplicable documents when I cleaned Mia's room last night. There is much more to this land that I can't fix.' Cam sounded defeated and shattered.

'Whatever it is, bury it,' Ryan said. 'Let sleeping dogs lie, Cam. You have a farm to save, and the Navy still needs your expertise.'

'John sold most of our crops and drank the profits. This farm needs capital, and I can't raise it when I am at the base. I don't even know how to contact Sole. It's like he doesn't want to be found.'

'Your brother has probably found a good life in the city or outside the country. You don't need him, Cam.'

'He is family and still my mother's child. I care deeply about his well-being. I can't make decisions about this land without him. He knows this land better than me.'

'You have Mia and John; she knows that land like the back of her hand.'

Cam exhaled and thought about Ryan's comment. Mia knew everything, from how the soil felt and tasted to which land was more fruitful. By just standing in the fields, she could tell if it would rain or not. Yet, Mia was so young and fragile. Her abilities were remarkable; even without her eyesight, she was the anchor in the soil.

'Mia is special, Cam. There is something there that you refuse to see. Your daughter will change everything around you if you let her in. Just take the time to see who she is.'

Cam didn't know Mia as well as he should have. And now she was with a nurse he barely knew. He wanted to help her, but his heart contracted at the idea of being in the same room as Luna. She was the reason why he couldn't sleep; he struggled to breathe around her, and enjoying her company brought on the guilt. He was still mourning Summer. It had been a decade of grief and loneliness but going on missions and keeping busy helped.

His thoughts about Luna terrified him. She was young, driven and had golden brown eyes that shook him to his knees. Every afternoon he secretly drove to town and parked at a safe distance to watch her close the clinic and walk to the boarding house. He had done this since the night after their school encounter. Cam knew her schedule off by heart, but it was his best-kept secret. It was a clandestine indulgence he afforded himself as a reprieve from the taxing demands of his life. Luna had a relaxed and calm gait, her smile traced the mountains and her soft laughter the wind. He longed to wrap himself around her like the white uniform that made her look so smart.

'Did you at least spend some time with Martha?' Cam asked Ryan, referring to Ryan's wife. Martha Adams was a teacher at the local school. Ryan and Martha had been childhood sweethearts who got married five years earlier. 'What you have done for this community is noteworthy. The people here need a doctor, but we also need you in the camp.'

'Yes, Martha is fine. My duty is in the Navy; I will serve as needed. Things have been tough for her; however, that fire didn't kill people's hopes. It will take time to rebuild, but Seth has that side covered. He managed to get donors for building materials and food. The school has been our saving grace; some people still use it for accommodation after the learners have gone home. Luna visits from time to time to check on the health and safety of every civilian. She has been the backbone of this community since that fateful night. I don't know much about her, but people here like her. They call her the *night angel*.' Ryan sounded happier. Cam squashed the stab of jealousy he felt. Just hearing about Luna sent a frisson of warmth through his body.

'Martha must have enjoyed seeing you more frequently than usual.' Cam needed to move away from hearing anything about Luna.

'She is well fed; that's all I can say for now,' Ryan said, sounding sure and satisfied.

'Is it what I am thinking?' Cam asked outright.

'Indeed. Martha is pregnant.'

'Well, good job. Congratulations! That is wonderful news.'

'The little one should be here in the spring,' Ryan said.

'You must be in love. I mean, with the baby.' Cam paused in between every word like he was choking on regret.

'Cam, I am in love with my wife. Who happens to be carrying my child. Is that good enough?' Ryan fired back at him.

'I didn't mean it like that.'

'Well, some of us try to live harmoniously with our words. A man's word speaks louder when it's coupled with actions.' Ryan knew that the words stung but he was tired of nursing Cam. Ryan was the captain of his life; Cam had no authority in it.

'I apologise, Ryan. I am a fool, I know.'

'Go and be a fool at your daughter's bedside.' The line went dead.

Cam felt despondent; his friends' lives seemed to bloom and flourish while he languished in the wasteland masquerading as a farm.

Where was his happiness? Why was he robbed of his happy family? Contrition followed hot on the heels of his pitiful musings. How could he be so envious of his best friend?

He knew Mia would be safe with Luna. From what he had seen, she was one hell of a combatant herself. There was no need to rush things; Cam would wait. Even though Ryan's words hung over him like a death knell, he had to focus on John's health and fixing the farm.

Just before midday, Cam took a break and helped his father to bathe and eat. John was getting old, and the alcohol intake was beginning to cause dementia. Cam helped his father move into the bathroom; he seemed better. He could talk and cooperate with Cam's requests.

'How can I dress you if you refuse to dry yourself?' Cam was trying to accommodate his father, but he was losing his patience.

'I didn't ask you to do this, Cam. Why are you here anyway? We don't need you,' John said, sitting in the bathtub and pulling his legs towards his chest.

'I live here; my child lives here.'

'Maybe you must move. Be your own man. It's my and Emily's house,' John mumbled. Cam stood next to the door and looked at his father's fragile frame. Over the years, John had lost his muscle definition, and his skin was sallow. He was eating less and drinking more.

'Now you want to talk about Mom. All these years, you made us forget her, and now this is her house?'

'Forget all that you want. I want you out of here. And if you dare change my house, I will shoot you myself. Don't you dare think you will leave with Mia.'

'You must have lost your mind. If I leave, my child comes with me.'

'Then be a good boy and get me a beer and chips. I'll forget all this. If you dare embarrass me again in front of people, you will sleep in the streets!' John's gnarled finger wagged towards Cam.

'Father, you still cannot see what you have done to this family. Sole is nowhere to be found; my child is close to anorexic, and you are an alcoholic. We are months away from losing this farm. The tea plantation is dead; we have no crops and are in serious debt. We owe so many people in this community and you drank away my child's trust fund. When was I going to be told that Mia is not going to school any more? She has been sitting here without care or education because of your selfish ways. You promised me this would never happen.' Cam spat the words at his father.

'That child needs special care, Cam. People here refuse to teach her. You should have thought about that; I had to fight to keep her in that school. No one wants a child who's blind and hardly speaks. Mia only speaks to you, haven't you noticed? She hates people and that school is not for kids like her. None of this would have happened if you had stayed and cared for her and the farm. I am an old man; I shouldn't be raising your child. Especially a child that needs so much. We ran out of ways to survive; I am too old to plough these fields. If you care about the farm, leave the Navy and assume your duties here.'

'You know I don't know anything about farming, Father!'

'Whose fault is that? You wanted to live in Cape Town and be around your boys. It's what you get for disobedience. Do you not read your Bible?'

'I have to work!'

'Work this land, Cam.'

'I have to get Mia back to school. You should consider selling this farm.'

'Over my dead body! You are useless and selfish, yet you want to compare yourself to Sole. He left because you failed to protect your mother from that damn fire! You hid in this house when the fields burnt her flesh. You killed all those people and now this farm is cursed.'

'I am not like you; I did no such thing!' His father's words bludgeoned Cam's heart to mush. He couldn't believe that John would utter such bitterness towards him. He couldn't remember everything that had happened that night, but for John to bring it up after all these years hurt like hell.

'Mia is your curse! That's what you will live with. Get the hell out of my sight, foolish boy!'

Cam felt powerless to say anything; rage boiled beneath his skin, torching his rationale. He wanted to strangle John, but something held him back. His body vibrated from its core and shattered him. He felt at odds with himself. Cam had been young; how could he have helped all those people? He didn't want to remember; all he knew was that he loved his daughter with everything he had.

He entered Mia's room and gazed at pictures of her and Summer. The thought of his little girl not speaking to anyone eviscerated him. How could he not have noticed? Cam didn't want to be this type of man. Mia was increasingly isolated and had begun withdrawing from the world. How could he be a good father when he was away for most of the year? At that moment, all he saw was Summer's disappointed eyes staring at him. Shame drowned him as his vision blurred with tears. Cam had failed all of them. Grief was his constant companion as it descended on the room and permeated his soul.

He was trembling with every passing memory while he delved through Mia's cupboard. He noticed then that she didn't seem to have any clothes that would fit her properly. He sat down on the floor and silently wept. Suppressed sobs shuddered through his body. He hadn't noticed anything about her in all these years. Yet she never grumbled or asked anything of him. What type of father was he? How could he do this to his only child?

The springs visible in the mattress could have easily ripped into her skin, yet she'd said nothing but just slept on the floor most nights. And the dust and bedbugs were stealing all the oxygen in the room. It hurt Cam deeply.

Rain clouds gathered as he packed away his tools for the day; he was almost done with the house repairs. The weather matched his mood perfectly because he felt broody, angry and thunderous. Cam needed to release the pent-up energy, so he rode his horse into town. His mind was a wild whir of fragmented thoughts that wouldn't form anything coherent. Halfway to town, the heavens stopped holding back. Fat raindrops landed on him as he tried to outrun the downpour. There was no point in turning back, and he deeply yearned to see Mia.

There was no better time to start being a father to her. He still felt the sting of his father's words on his skin. He had fresh bread and jam in his rucksack for Mia.

John had watched his son ride away; he was finally in a more lucid state. Cam was so broken and bewildered. John wanted to stop Cam from riding out as a storm was brewing in the heavens, but too much had been said. He couldn't bear to tell Cam everything; the truth would have to find its way to him. He wasn't ready to destroy his son. Cam already struggled; he had been for years.

John remained by the window as the horse disappeared across the fields; he was gazing towards the graveyard where his wife slept. In just the little time Cam had been home, he had repainted the house and cleaned all the rooms. John had noticed the small changes Cam had made to the kitchen table to better accommodate Mia. He had smoothed out the edges and given it a fresh layer of paint. The wooden floors and door handles were as good as new. From the looks of it, Cam must've had help from Seth and Ryan.

How long had John been out of it? Did he sleep through this entire process? Alcohol had stolen most of his life now. Cam had done so much in such a short space of time. John hung his head in shame and headed for bed. As he wrapped the blanket around his frail bones, he heard the raindrops splatter on the roof. Without the tell-tale sound of water dripping in the bathroom, John knew that Cam had fixed the leaks in the roof. Even though remorse filled him, the pride in his son settled more comfortably. The only thing John wished for was for his son to truly love Mia. Maybe one day, he'd move on with a good girl and start his own family.

'I'm sorry, my dear Emily. I should've done better for our two boys.'

Chapter 10

It's in the storm where we find peace

Luna managed to keep Eve away from the clinic so that she could spend the nights caring for Mia. Over weekends, only a few people needed assistance in case of emergencies, but there were none that particular weekend. Most of the locals spent their weekends at the beach resorts on the West Coast, fishing at the dam or helping the community rebuild the razed homes. Mia had come at the right time; Luna needed a distraction. She redirected all her energy into caring for the little girl. Mia's fever broke on the second night.

The clinic had been a house before it was repurposed as a clinic – there were three bedrooms or wards, a kitchenette and a lounge, which had been converted into a reception area. It was not as fancy as Luna's previous place of work, but she didn't mind. She found purpose in being useful. This weekend was about Mia. Luna worried deeply about Mia's weight and how soft-spoken she was. Luna had tried to feed her, but she'd hardly eaten.

On the third day, Eve called in and told Luna that she was attending a wedding. She instructed Luna to keep the clinic closed for two more days. Luna was happy to follow her orders; she passed the message on to Amora and the girls and placed the information on a notice board near the gate.

The clinic is closed due to maintenance work.

That morning, she watched as Mia slept in the narrow single bed. Luna worried that the sheets covering her were not warm enough. Mia had shivered intermittently but the night sweats were gone. Some colour had returned to her skin. Luna noticed cuts and calluses on Mia's feet, as if she hadn't worn any shoes in years.

'Little one, what have they done to you?' she whispered, trying not to startle Mia awake.

'I know you are there.' A faint voice disturbed the silence.

Luna held her breath. Although the sun crested over the mountains, the news had forecast afternoon rain. She had thought Mia was asleep, as it was too early for her to wake up.

'How are you feeling?' she asked, pulling a chair closer to the bed.

'I am thirsty,' Mia responded.

'There is water next to you,' Luna said without thinking. She realised her error when Mia raised her hand and felt around the bed sheet. Luna grabbed the glass and placed it in Mia's searching hand.

'Did you sleep well?'

'Yes, thank you. Has my father come for me? I need to get back home.' Since Mia's arrival, she had called for her father morning and night. Luna didn't know what to say because, in her experience, fathers came and went as they pleased without thinking or caring for anyone but themselves.

'I believe he will be here soon; try to get some rest.'

'He will be leaving again soon. I need to get back home.'

'Leaving?' Her question came fast; Cam couldn't leave town without coming for his daughter. She needed to see him.

'He works in the Navy; he never stays long,' Mia murmured. Luna checked her phone. Ryan hadn't called her. She wanted to text him, but his icy indifference made any contact awkward.

'Let's get you back to good health and we will worry about everything else later. Deal?' Mia didn't respond.

'I will make you something to eat and we can read something together; what do you say?'

'I am fine. Thank you.'

'Can we at least read together? Some good people left us books that I think you will enjoy.'

'I can't! Do I have to? Is this a school?' Mia said, clearly uncomfortable. Luna wasn't sure what to say; entertaining a child wasn't her best skill.

'Oh no,' Luna said in answer to Mia's question. 'This is a clinic; I am sorry we didn't tell you. Dr Ryan dropped you off here.'

'I know, but when can I go home? My grandpa, Papa John, needs me.' Mia sat up and squared her shoulders to show how serious she was.

'You have a grandfather?'

'Yes. I live with him when my father is away.' Mia rubbed her nose.

'And where is your mother?' Luna knew where she was going with her questions, but Mia just shook her head and said nothing.

'You have a mother, right?' Luna's question was met with more silence from Mia. 'That's fine; you don't know me. I understand.' Luna came closer and took Mia's hand in hers. Her body felt warm, and Luna wondered whether it was caused by disappointment in her father or the fever.

Luna took Mia's glass and pulled the sheets over her shoulders as she lay down again.

'I will read to you.' Luna tried to give her a charming smile but belatedly remembered that Mia couldn't see her.

'Who are you, lady?'

I'm the lady your hot father spoke to weeks ago ... he takes my breath away.

Luna delayed her response to rein in her wayward thoughts. She wanted to comfort Mia but was unsure what answer would achieve that.

'Well, I am a nurse. My name is Luna Parks. I am twenty-four years old and—' She didn't know what else to add. She couldn't even think of a rehearsed speech that her mother had taught her. It wasn't an interview or a school test.

'You don't sound like my father; are you from here?' Mia tried hard to imagine what the nurse looked like. There was something familiar about her, but Mia couldn't solve the puzzle – she wasn't any good with puzzles, even at school.

'I was born in Cape Town; I went to Queen's Park High School before I went to nursing school.'

'Did you finish all the grades?'

'Yes.' Luna noticed the slight shock on her face.

'I miss school, Miss Luna.' Mia wrapped her hands around her tiny frame in shame.

'You will be back in no time. This illness will be gone in a couple of days, and then you will be reunited with your teachers and friends. You have friends, right?'

'I am not allowed to go back there,' Mia mumbled. Luna was bewildered.

'And why is that?'

'Papa John told my principal that we have no money. Money is for the farm.' Luna heard the desolation in Mia's voice.

'And what does your father say about that, Mia?'

'I don't know.' Mia found it hard to talk about her father; she loved him and didn't want people to know anything that could hurt him.

'When last did you go to school?'

'Two summers ago … I think … I don't know.'

'Would you like to go back?' Mia nodded but Luna sensed fear in her answer.

'Who lives with you at the farm?'

'It's just my grandfather and I.'

'Does he treat you well?' Luna recalled the state of Mia's feet. She could tell no one properly cared for this little girl. She was too young to have feet like that.

'Well, I will have to talk to Dr Ryan and see what can be done.'

'Please don't! I don't want to get into trouble!' Mia's body vibrated with fear.

'You have to go back to school, Mia; you can't just sit around. Kids your age go to school and learn a lot there.'

'I learn more at home.'

'Well, you still need school. A farm is no place for a child.'

'I take care of it.'

'That shouldn't be your job.'

'I'm growing our tea; I know a lot about the land and the animals.'
Luna just brushed off what Mia was saying.

As Luna tucked Mia into bed, Mia could finally smell her. Luna smelt like sweet cream and berries; it was a clean, non-invasive smell, and Mia held onto it. Luna's smell made Mia feel comfortable and safe and her hands were soft and warm; all Mia wanted at that moment was to feel her touch again, but she held back. The nurse wasn't her mother. Mia had blurred images of her mother rocking her to sleep while singing a lullaby. Her mother was gone, and her father refused to speak about her. Mia tried hard not to cry but her broken soul needed release. She felt her eyelids prickle and she cleared her throat.

'Miss Luna, are you the lady my father was with after the fire?'

'I believe so, Mia. I wouldn't say I was with him; we met at the gate. I was going to help the people inside the school.'

Mia smiled, chuffed that she had solved the puzzle.

'So, you are the lady he laughs about! He said you are pretty and caring. Is that true, Miss Luna?' Luna felt a warmth in her belly. She felt giddy knowing that Cam was somewhat affected by her presence too.

'I don't know if that's true.'

He thinks I'm pretty …

'Each time I asked him about you, he said I would be blessed if I were to see you.' Mia sounded genuine and calm. Luna didn't know what to make of this.

'Well, I am happy you are here, and that I can care for you. Your father seems like a good man.'

Luna tried to believe what she was saying, but fear crippled her. She didn't want to feel anything for Cam. She had never had a man's affection or attention; even worse, a man of Cam's stature frightened her. He was a virtual stranger with whom she had made minimal conversation. It made her nervous that people seemed to steer clear of his farm. Mr Fourie's warning also niggled at her. No one wanted to talk about the Coals; people in town abruptly stopped engaging when the family name was mentioned.

'Miss Luna, have you seen the beach?'

'You have so many questions today, so you must be feeling better. Yes, I grew up right next to it. Have you not seen it?' Luna smiled at Mia. Although Mia could not see her, Luna hoped she could hear the smile in her voice.

'My father said he will take me when I am old enough.'

'I think you are old enough. Let me get you food so you are strong enough to swim in the sea. The ocean is a powerful force of nature.' Luna didn't understand why Cam kept life away from his daughter.

'My father works in the water; he says it's dark and has a lot of dangerous animals.'

'That's true, but it's also gorgeous; you will enjoy it.'

'Can you take me there? Cape Town. Is it far?'

The question startled Luna.

There's no way I'm going back to Cape Town.

'Let's focus on getting you better so that you can return to school.'

After they had eaten breakfast and Luna had bathed Mia, they sat outside under the shade of a tree and Luna read to her. She had not realised quite how inquisitive Mia was. The story took longer than anticipated, as Mia peppered Luna with questions. The pub nearby was still quiet, but Luna knew that the rowdiness would start later in the afternoon.

As Mia regaled Luna with stories about how she grew tea on their farm, Luna was amazed by how much the little girl knew about farming, but she still felt a pang of sadness because Mia should have been at school. How could her grandfather and father let her work so hard?

Isn't it illegal to keep a child at home when they can go to school?

They eventually went back inside the clinic when Mia started yawning. The sun felt great in the morning, but the heat became oppressive by midday, and storm clouds were now gathering. After Mia finished the vegetable soup Luna had prepared for her, she read to her until Mia fell asleep. She must've been feeling much better, as her appetite had also returned. Cam's daughter seemed full of life, but it didn't seem as if the elders in her family let her live. Luna's conscience would not let her ignore the situation. She tried texting Ryan, but he still wasn't responding to her messages.

Luna went to the shops and the boarding house to gather a few essentials. Dr Ryan eventually called, but he didn't stay on the line long; he told Luna he wasn't in town and said nothing about fetching Mia.

What kind of father would let his friend dump his child at a damn clinic and not bother to check on her well-being?

Luna thought about how she'd felt the day her father disappeared; she hated that feeling. Years of pain, unspoken trust issues and neglect rose from their tombs to confront her. She remembered all the nights her mother had cried herself to sleep. Luna saw the same pain in Mia – the silent screams and consistent disillusionment. No child deserved to be abandoned like this, especially when her father was still somewhere around Clanwilliam. Mia was just a little girl, longing and praying to be seen; not even her eyesight mattered in the face of her shattering heartache. Once the rain started falling, it mirrored the tears Luna wished she could cry to purge her pain. She switched on the lights and stood by the window, watching the raindrops slide down the glass pane.

Cam was standing across the road, bleeding in dishonour and repentance as the rain failed to wash away his sins. He was watching Luna; she was the light in his doom. Luna was so gentle and at ease with herself. He wanted to walk into the clinic, grab her and thank her with pulses of gratitude. He couldn't believe how he felt. Just the sight of her made him tremble with hidden desire. No woman had come this close to Mia, not since her mother died, or burrowed as deep into his heart as Luna had. What woman would sacrifice herself to aid the lamb he had forsaken?

Mia joined Luna at the window and seemed to be standing on a chair, as if she, too, could look outside. Cam didn't know how to react; they were laughing, and Luna was holding Mia's hand. That was always what Mia requested of him when she got anxious or sad. He watched in awe; it was so easy for Luna to take in the child he had neglected to heal.

Joy transformed Mia's face, and, for a moment, Cam felt out of place. Mia didn't need him; she had found grace and mercy with Luna. Jealousy twisted his stomach like a knife, and even that brought him shame. The rain washed his tears away and any doubt that he would ever feel such intense emotions for anyone else. No one had come close to breaking his walls down like Luna had. Even the heavens couldn't wash away the uneasiness that hovered over him, like a dove to the sky. He felt cracked open and knew he would never be the same again.

Cam could walk towards the back of the clinic without anyone noticing and the rain helped to muffle his horse's unease. He left the horse in the nearby garage and returned to the place near the window where he could see his daughter and her carer. Mia looked so slim up close; he had never noticed it before. Luna must have bought her a new set of sleepwear. He should have done that; he was Mia's father. The thought momentarily angered him, but he sighed loudly and humbled himself.

'Lord, please give me strength. Make me see what you desire for me and my child.'

Peace settled on his shoulders once he opened his eyes. Cam continued watching Luna and Mia, but his attention was focused only on Luna. She seemed so tender and kind towards his little girl. Only the room they were in was lit up. The moderate lighting made her glow in places only he could see. His heart swelled in pockets of joy and admiration. Luna was perfect with Mia. John had said Mia only spoke to him, but she giggled and responded to Luna. It astonished him; Mia must feel comfortable around her.

Cam was soaked to the skin, but he didn't even feel the chill. The view of his daughter and Luna laughing warmed him right through. Luna's attentiveness towards Mia had taken him to a place he had longed for: a home filled with peace and love flashed before his eyes. It was a mirage created by his yearning. Her softness gave him peace, but how would he get closer to her with all the mess around him? Who would want a father-in-law like John and a home mired in a horrific curse? Would she be able to bear the weight of being a mother to a blind child? Luna was still so young; he didn't want to cheat her of her youth.

Was that what God wanted him to see? Could he forgive himself for his past transgressions? Could Cam break down the fear in his heart and love his child without feeling sorry for her? Thoughts competed for prominence in his mind so that he didn't even notice Luna approaching him.

'Captain Coal, what on earth are you doing in the rain? You scared me.'

'Forgive me, my heart fails me.'

'Come inside; you'll catch a cold.'

Luna caught his heated gaze and held it. His laboured breathing was the only sound in the clinic's silence. The world stopped and the night gave way to a spark that only Mother Nature could create. Amid the storm and the cracking thunder, two heartbeats danced in accord.

Chapter 11

To love we have to surrender

'So, we meet again, Miss Parks.' His deep voice fluttered on her skin. Luna was still recovering from the shock of seeing Cam there. She snatched a few towels and handed them to him and tried not to make eye contact or breathe in his direction.

'If I knew where you lived, you wouldn't have to lurk outside like a creep, sir.' She wanted to kick herself; that was not what she wanted to say.

'So, you want my home address?' Luna's eyes tracked his movements as he wiped the excess water from his hair and face. Her appreciative yet demure gaze made him feel ten metres tall. He suppressed the urge to preen, puff out his chest and beat on it with his fists. How did Luna manage to tap into his primal side?

'Are we back to "sir" again?' Cam knew that his unannounced visit frazzled her. He admired how she tried to keep her composure. He narrowed the space between them despite his soaked boots. The tension that had coiled in his stomach faded. He was where he needed to be.

'You're also using my surname, sir— uhm, Captain Coal…' Luna craned her neck to maintain eye contact because she was so much shorter than him. She couldn't think straight with Cam standing so close, especially when his unique scent tickled her nose. As per the norm, warmth suffused her at their closeness. He was even closer to her than he had been at the school. Raindrops still clung to the tips of his hair, made even curlier by the water. She fought the urge to run her hand through it.

'You have my daughter; I know you know me now.' His voice was barely a whisper and Luna was entranced by his lips.

'I don't have her; she is a patient in the clinic. Do you really think she wants to be here?' Luna maintained her muted tone. She was reluctant to break the spell surrounding them. It felt so intimate to be alone with him in this room with the storm raging outside. Mia slept peacefully in the ward with the light casting a glow on the reception area where they stood.

'Mia's in your care and from where I am standing, she is doing just fine. Thank you for taking care of my daughter,' Cam murmured, raising his hand as if to touch her face but lowering it just as quickly.

'I was just doing my job ...' Luna's heart accelerated.

Is he about to touch me?

She squared her shoulders and turned away from him. She couldn't afford to be distracted by Cam's charms. He had left his daughter in a stranger's care for days without calling to check on how she was doing. There were so many questions Luna needed answers to. She inhaled deeply and tried to compose herself.

'We are all honoured and pleased that you have revived this clinic,' Cam said. 'The community speaks highly of you. Ryan told me that all was well and that my daughter would fully recover. My daughter is a strong young lady; we live on a farm and such things will happen.'

Luna didn't know how it was possible, but she still felt his warm gaze on her.

'You should have come to see her; she needed you. No child should be left in the hands of strangers.' Luna rubbed her arms, suddenly feeling the chill of turning away from Cam's warmth.

'Do you mind turning around? I promise I won't bite. I knew Mia was safe and you're hardly a stranger, Luna.' He wanted to get close to her but restricted himself to a chair nearby. The atmosphere couldn't have been more pleasant. Cam felt seen and free; shame had momentarily left him.

Luna turned around slowly, hoping he wouldn't ask to leave. Her mind failed her as she scrambled for words. His presence filled the room; it was so potent and desirable, even from a distance.

'Why are you here at this ungodly hour?' she asked. 'Why would you come here at this time? The clinic is closed, and this is not a hospital unless you have an emergency I'm unaware of. Mia needs rest and better nutrition. Have you noticed how small she is for her age? She needs a break.' Cam chuckled and his eyes lit up with laughter. She had never seen him so carefree.

He needs to laugh more; he's gorgeous when he does.

'You just chastised me for not checking up on Mia. When I do, you still ask me twenty-one questions. Do you want me to leave?'

'I said no such thing, Captain Coal.' She fidgeted with her T-shirt, smoothing out non-existing creases.

'If Mia is fine, I will stand guard until sunrise. The roads are wet; I don't think my horse will be happy out there.' He continued to wipe down his arms. Luna's eyes strayed to his biceps, which contracted as he folded his arms.

Stop ogling him!

'We don't need security, Captain Coal.'

He seemed so different tonight – calm and gentle, with an air of mystery lingering around him. His hair had grown and was pushed back, and his beard was fuller than when Luna had last seen him. His rugged look made him even more attractive to her.

'You like to keep things formal, Luna, but it's just you and me here. My full name is Cameron Coal. However, you can call me your husband from now on, or Cam.' He winked at her, hoping she wouldn't be offended. Something in his spirit was assured. He couldn't believe what he had just said, but it felt right. It was too late to take it back.

'Husband? Sir, you must be sick or confused.'

'Are we back to "sir" again? Do you have a problem with me becoming your husband?' Cam asked, his gaze unwavering. The longer they spoke about this, the more it settled within him.

'That's a little forward, don't you think?'

'I don't see a ring on your finger. You've been at the clinic for days and you mentioned you live at the nurse's boarding house. Why would a lady like you be here all alone?'

'That is none of your business. I am not looking for a husband. You probably have a wife waiting back home; Mia must have a mother. Direct all that energy towards your sick child and listen to her. She has a lot to say.' Luna was still trying to probe into his life. She needed to know more about him, but he said nothing.

Cam stood up and rubbed his head in discontent. She wasn't letting him in. He tried to control the sadness brought on by the sudden mental image of Summer smiling up at him as he twirled her around in the barn. Luna was not the type of woman he would let go of. He had to try again and let his heart lead him. Cam checked his phone and unlocked it to read the message that flashed on the screen from his neighbour, Jeremy Robinson.

Mr Robinson: Hi son, your father left the farm. We tried to stop him, but he wouldn't be deterred. Just thought you should know.

Cam swallowed the curse scratching his throat. He needed to make a quick call, but Luna looked like a deer caught in the headlights. He should not have revealed his heart so quickly.

'My family will be eternally grateful for what you have done for us. So, how is my little girl?' He shivered from the wet clothes clinging to him.

Luna noticed how cold he was and offered him a bath sheet, but Cam declined. She was so drawn to him, but it left her feeling off-kilter. She would only admit to herself that she had feelings for him, but now wasn't the time to explore them. Luna felt out of her depth; she had never encountered such an intense man before. He seemed to want to clarify his intentions towards her, but she would not entertain them.

'Mia is medicated but that doesn't mean she doesn't need her parents. Come see her.'

Cam slowly followed Luna into the room where Mia slept peacefully. The shame he carried like a mantle settled back on his shoulders. He wished things were different, but his gaze returned to Luna. The compassion in her eyes made him want her even more. Her skin tone reminded him of strong tea with a dash of milk and he itched to touch her; it dragged him into the belly of desire. He extended his arm toward her, losing the battle with his reflexes, but she stepped away.

The rain was pelting down on the roof and slid in rivulets down the window; it would not let up. Luna worried that they would have to call it a night soon.

Where will Cam sleep?

He was drenched and needed a shower and a change of clothes. As he stood looking at his daughter, Luna voraciously took him in. She noticed his youthful eyes; his hair was trimmed on the sides and back but needed to be reshaped. She couldn't really tell how old he was, but he must be several years older than her.

'Shall we step out and let her rest? Will you be taking her home in the morning?'

'Is that your professional advice, or are you tired of having us here?' He flashed his charming smile.

'She is much better,' Luna said. 'I think you are more than capable of caring for her.'

Cam allowed Luna to step out first and he followed her to the kitchenette.

'Tea or coffee? You look so cold.'

'I don't drink coffee; it's poison. A man like me would never drink that. And I don't think you should either. You've come to the land of tea farms.'

Luna just shook her head and smiled.

'Mia told me a little about the tea, but what strikes me the most is how much she knows about farming. We took a walk today; I have never seen a child so passionate. She didn't want to talk about music, toys or books. I don't know how she has all this comprehension, but she loves farming.'

'Mia is astute for her age. We just don't know what to do with her.'

Cam filled the kettle with water and Luna showed him where he could find the tea bags – she had brought her own container. Her mom had given her an antique wooden box with carved flowers and brass handles when she turned twenty-one. There was an inscription and a logo underneath the container that Luna couldn't decipher. The box was a family heirloom, but her mom could not explain the inscription either.

Cam glanced at the tea bags in great surprise. It was their last consignment of tea, which they had produced a year ago. Even though it didn't have any branding, he identified the label. He looked at Luna in wonder; it gave him the courage of his convictions.

'You have good taste,' he said. Luna didn't know what Cam meant, but he seemed impressed with her.

'It's just tea, Captain Coal.'

'That's what you think. You mentioned that Mia knows so much about tea; she should have told you how she makes it.'

'Yes, she said she can feel everything. She said nature talks to her, Captain Coal.'

'If you call me that again, I will be forced to marry you. Maybe then you can call me by name.'

Luna felt her stomach turn and heat covered her face.

'I am serious, Cameron.'

'Cam.'

'Cameron. That's your name, right?' She smiled.

'Mia is like her mother; Summer was good with her hands.'

'Was?'

'Yes. Summer died ten years ago. In a field fire.' Cam felt the pang of loss clench his stomach.

'I am so sorry for your loss.' Luna was relieved that Cam didn't have a wife, but not at the expense of the grief etched on his face. Her heart bled for Mia, who didn't have a motherly touch in her life.

'Summer knew more about Mia than I ever could. I keep failing Mia. Luna, being in the Navy takes so much from you. We have an entire country to serve; there is limited time for family. Raising a child with so many challenges has proven to be harder than I had envisioned. Summer was supposed to be here for her, and John is another problem.' Cam sighed and got up from the chair.

'You can't leave!' She touched his hand as he walked past her, and their fingers intertwined momentarily. He regarded her closely with a smile. Luna looked down, embarrassed by her reaction.

'I am not leaving you, Miss Parks. I have brought some bread for Mia. It's in my pack on my horse.' Cam touched Luna's chin so he could meet her gaze again. His finger gently touched her cheek and he winked.

'Where is the horse? It's raining, Cam!' she called out after him as he left.

'In the garage!' he chuckled out loud.

Luna waited by the door, watching him check if his horse was fine. Ever so attentive and caring, he ensured that no water had come into the garage and then took the bag and ran back to the clinic. He seemed excited and unaffected by the rain.

'Ta-da! Fresh bread! I baked it for Mia, but I have more reasons to bake now that you are here.'

Even though his visit was unplanned, Cam was happy just to be around Luna without any prying eyes. She was a black woman, after all, and this little town wasn't used to interracial couples. Even though he knew that it should no longer be an issue in democratic South Africa, the stigma had a ripple effect on the perception and traditions of many people. Cam had seen death more times than he cared to count but he knew that all people were inherently the same. They all bled the same colour and their organs were all in the same place.

'We are not allowed visitors here, so I doubt you will see me after this,' Luna said. 'Will you leave with Mia in the morning or when the rain stops?'

'I don't plan to leave anyone here, Miss Parks. My mission would not be complete.'

Cam wanted to see love and desire colour Luna's eyes.

'Mission?'

'I always complete what I start; but for now, I have to make you eat this bread.'

'It's so late to eat.' She blushed.

'With me, you will never go hungry. If you ever wake me up one day and request bread, I will fulfil your wish. I am good at many things, and tonight, I will be your watchman. I hope that won't be a problem.'

'Captain Coal, I think we should be talking about Mia,' Luna said shyly, trying hard to restrain her feelings.

'Mia is fine; you're here and her father is here. I don't see what there is to talk about.'

Luna wanted to ask Cam about his wife but talking about Mia was far better than listening to his love story. From what she now knew, his wife was dead, and that was enough for now.

'Tell me more about you,' Cam said while he started slicing the bread 'How did you end up in this small little town? There is nothing here. I mean, every young professional wants to work in the city. You look smart and resourceful. You have done so much around here and I wonder what type of woman raised you. I don't want to offend you, but I am curious. I have taken time to watch you, maybe even study you. I know that sounds crazy, but when you want something, you desire to know its origins.'

'I don't like the city; I am fine here.' Luna shifted uncomfortably. 'I was born in Cape Town; my mother still lives there. There is not much to know, Cameron. We all go to school and find jobs after, and that's why I am here.'

'Where did you work before?'

'At another small clinic in Cape Town.'

'Cape Town is just down the road, Luna. You are getting defensive; why is that? Maybe you have a crackhead ex-boyfriend or an irrational former boss?' Cam stopped slicing the bread and looked at her.

Luna could not meet his eyes. 'Can you please stop!'

Cam watched her squirm and decided to change tactics. He didn't want them to lose the camaraderie that they had built since he arrived.

'Do you want kids?'

'I don't know, I am not there yet. I've just started working and I am fine here. I want to settle into what I do and then continue studying.'

'It sounds like a lonely life.'

'My life is enough; I don't want distractions.'

'Would getting married be a distraction?' Cam passed her a slice of bread slathered in apricot jam and poured the tea.

'Marriage! That thing destroyed my mother. It's not a goal in my life. Can we talk about something else? I don't think this is an appropriate time; I don't know you well enough.'

'I guess we will have to spend more time together then.' Cam sat down at the reception table and invited Luna to do the same. There was an uncomfortable silence as they ate.

'So, tell me, have you ever done something you deeply regretted but had to hide it?'

The words felt like a serrated knife in Luna's back and Cam held the handle, twisting it. She couldn't look him in the eyes; her bones felt like melted butter.

Why is he asking me this? Does he know something about my past? Is he spying on me?

Luna felt as if her heart was lodged in her throat.

Where is Amora? I haven't spoken to her in days. Has she already been arrested?

Luna wanted to pick up her phone, but Cam's eyes glued her back when she shifted in her seat.

'Luna! Did you hear me?' Something he'd said had upset her and it made him wary to push further. He pulled his chair closer to hers and held her palms in his. Cam's hands dwarfed hers.

'Luna!'

She snatched her hands away and fled to the bathroom. As she sat on the toilet seat trembling with nerves, tears clouded her vision.

Will I ever find peace?

Chapter 12

In the dark the light emerges

When Amora, Bree and Lucy heard that Luna would be at the clinic with Mia again, they dressed in their best outfits and walked to the motel. They laughed and chattered among themselves and made small talk with the locals along the way.

'Can you imagine riding a horse with Luke?' Bree called out.

'The bus driver? There is no way he can handle all of this; he is too young and skinny for me,' Amora chuckled.

'What kind of man do you like? Maybe tonight we can help you scout through these farm boys,' Lucy said, holding hands with Bree as they walked.

'I don't think so, Lucy.'

'Amora, you are so much fun! With a personality like yours you could get any man or woman you want.' Lucy winked at her.

'What has changed? We party like crazy and dance like teens. You can't be alone all the time,' Bree agreed.

'Who said I am?' Amora joked, faking being a girl about town. She was struggling to find her place in Clanwilliam. There was so little to do, and Luna had chosen community service over having fun, which made Amora realise that Luna didn't want her friendship.

'So, while we burn our heels at the clinic, are you warming the sheets with someone? Is that why you left Luna alone in that room? Does she even know you're out?' Bree asked.

'I do my thing here and there and that's all you need to know. I don't have to tell Luna everything; she is as good as a nun. Why bother her with such?'

Two days earlier, Amora had moved out of the shared room with
Luna and taken a rundown room downstairs. Mr Fourie had tried to
stop her, but she'd insisted on staying there, even though the room
had no lights and the door needed replacing. Amora felt disorientated, in limbo and isolated.

'I have always wondered why you two are so different. Luna is
the town miracle and saviour and you are just a—'

'You have no fuckin' clue who Luna is!' Amora snapped.

Bree was startled when Amora turned on them and tightened
her jaw.

'Then tell us,' Bree implored as she pushed her blonde hair out of
her face in the evening breeze. It was getting colder, and the clouds
were concealing the moon. It would rain soon if they didn't hurry.

'Luna is Luna. That's all I can say.'

'Oh, it must be that man!'

'What man?' Amora was confused. Luna wasn't interested in men;
she didn't want anyone near her cherry.

'I spoke to the good Doctor Ryan,' Lucy said. 'He told me that Cam
is deeply in love with Luna. I am not surprised that she is the one
nursing that little girl. Cam is a catch; everyone in town fears him
but loves him too. He is one of those used-to-be-rich boys who has
transitioned to serving his country. They could make a wonderful
match, seeing that Luna is a Godly servant.'

'Well, I don't think Luna likes him back.' Amora's tone came across
as distant and spiteful.

'Some friends you guys are,' Bree said, rolling her eyes.

Lucy's eyes widened. Something didn't add up. Amora didn't
seem to like Luna much, but Lucy didn't want to waste the night on
Amora's insecurities. She just wanted to enjoy the evening and get
roaring drunk.

The rain caught them when they were only steps away from the
entrance to the motel. It was a busy night; farmers and tourists had
flocked to the space as if it were carnival time. This gave the place
a buzz and created a heady atmosphere. A crowd had gathered outside, waiting to be let in. The girls stood at the outer edge of the crowd.

Bree waved at someone at the door, and he waved them in. She walked ahead of the girls and pushed through the crowd. They quickly found seats at the bar and watched as people chatted and danced in the open space between the tables. Bree didn't waste any time; she ordered a round of beers and started the party. Amora took a beer, guzzled it in one go and ordered another one.

'Take it easy, Amora. We just got here,' Lucy chuckled, looking over her shoulder as Amora started moving around on the dance floor. There was laughter and a jovial atmosphere among the young crowd.

'We are here to have fun and that's what I am going to do,' Amora shouted so that she could be heard above the music. Bree stood up and joined Amora on the dance floor; finally, the room felt like a party.

Amora was starting to rely more on Bree and Lucy for entertainment. They were more open to bar hopping and having a good time. Amora also found ways of entertaining herself with alcohol – her most trusted friend. Every weekend had become a drinking marathon and tonight was no exception.

A man on Lucy's left had just finished his meal and now his eyes were fixated on Amora on the dance floor; the look on his face made Lucy nervous. She had noticed him when they'd arrived but didn't want to pay him any attention. Lucy got up and pulled Bree aside and spoke to her briefly, but when Lucy turned around again, the man was dancing with Amora. She wanted to warn Amora, but it was too late.

'A nurse who dances like you should be on that pole, dancing for all of us. You just missed a good penny.' The man pointed at the stripper pole at the back of the room, centred on a dimly lit small stage. Amora turned to see what he was referring to, and what she saw didn't please her.

'Excuse me?' She straightened up but the man was big in stature and almost as heavy as a rugby player.

'Amora Grootboom, right?' He roughly pulled her into his arms and brushed her face with his thick, greasy hands.

'Seth Fourie!'

'Wonderful! I am glad we don't have to waste time with introductions. I have never seen a nurse dance like that.' He grabbed her ass and squeezed.

Amora felt dizzy, sick and irritated. It seemed as if the apple didn't fall far from the tree. Seth was a pervert just like his father. She had seen him around with Cam and Ryan, but he was not in uniform this time. He seemed bulkier than she remembered from the night of the fire.

'Let me go at once, Seth!' Her ribcage felt as if it was being inverted in his arms.

'There's no need to struggle. You know me and I know you. I could say we are friends.' His voice revolted and annoyed her, especially when the stale smell of fried onion rings suffocated her nose.

'I said, leave me alone at once.' Amora's voice didn't lend itself well to gentleness, but she had to find a way to push him away. Yet, she felt helpless. The man was like a beast, hungry in every way. She had foolishly hoped that her big body would deter him, but he stood firm. The more she struggled, the more he kept digging his nails into her.

The two girls at the bar were watching the scene unfold, but Lucy pulled Bree back when she was about to say something. 'Stay out of it; we don't know what they are discussing. Remember, Amora has been busy in this town. I wouldn't put it past her if they had met up before. Can we just let her have fun? They are just dancing, and we can't see much from where we are.'

'But look at her face, Lucy! She looks awkward.'

'If you don't sit down and eat these fries, I will have to take you home. I don't know why you can't stop talking about people.' Lucy gently kissed Bree and they continued with their meal.

'So, what do you say? A lap dance or a warm kiss?' Seth kissed Amora in her neck, and she shuddered in revulsion. How could he touch her so freely without her consent?

'If you don't leave me alone, I will scream.' She tried pushing him away, but he grabbed her so tightly that the lace on her dress ripped. Amora felt the fabric around her waist tear, exposing parts of her underwear for all to see. Instead of trying to free herself, she now had to hold her dress together.

'You can scream all you want when I pump you full of my seed,' Seth leered, sniffing Amora's neck.

'You smell like yesterday's beer, and you are not my type,' Amora sneered. 'Besides, my friends are waiting for me, you filthy dog. What type of man are you? Have you no respect for women? If you continue, I will have to report you to the police!' She wanted to spit on him when he licked her face belligerently.

'Are you going to let her talk to you like that?' The men around them had noticed that Amora was rejecting Seth's advances.

'All she's good for is being on her back and taking it like the slut she is,' another called out.

'Just look at that fat ass. She belongs in a museum, like her ancestor, Sara Baartman. She should be locked up in a cage for entertainment,' another man added.

Amora tried to locate Bree and Lucy, but they had their backs to the dance floor.

'You see, you are nothing around here. I'm doing you a favour by talking or even touching you. No sane man around here would ever make *you* his wife. You look like an abomination. With all that face paint, you still think you are desirable,' Seth said disparagingly.

'I am a nurse, a respected woman!' Amora's voice wavered as she tried to suppress her emotions. She would not let Seth win; she had sworn that no man would ever make her feel worthless. It was challenging to remain stoic as the men's words pummelled her, so she bit her trembling lower lip.

'You're as respectable as a whore on the street. Can't you see I'm doing you a favour by giving you attention? What did you think was going to happen when you came in here dressed in that tight dress with your balloon tits out. Let me suckle, Mama Africa!' Seth continued his verbal abuse. Howls of laughter from the old men watching the show rang in Amora's ears.

'Go suckle on your mother's tits, asshole!' Amora said through gritted teeth.

Seth's beefy arms tightened vice-like around her. Then he pushed her to the ground and poured his beer over her. Everyone stood around and clapped and lifted their glasses in celebration. Amora held her hands over her head and sobbed irrepressibly. She had never experienced such humiliation, not even in her younger years. Would she always be haunted by scorn and insults?

'I am sorry, young lady. Please take my hand,' an elderly man said and extended his arm. Amora continued to sob on the floor; she couldn't trust his sincerity. 'I mean you no harm, I promise.' He spoke softly to her as he helped her up.

Amora noticed that Bree and Lucy had slipped out of the bar. She felt desolate and alone.

'Don't get involved, old man. She is mine!' Seth said.

'I don't belong to you! I am not yours. You are a dog; you don't deserve to protect us in the Navy! I pray you die at camp. You are not worthy of the uniform you wear! I bet your mother hated you as you hate women.'

'You keep referring to my mother; I will show you your mother, slut!' Seth charged at her, trying to grab her from the old man. He was boiling with antagonism; how could she embarrass him like that in front of everyone?

'Let her be, Seth; you were not raised like this. What would your father say? You shouldn't be here! You better go before I put my hands on you.'

Seth hesitated, then clicked his tongue and stormed out.

John Coal guided Amora to the bar area. Her gaze didn't leave Seth's back. She had noticed his service pistol and was tempted to run after him, grab it and shoot him in his filthy mouth. But she couldn't get over the shame in her heart. She had always been strong and good at protecting herself, but it had just taken a few minutes for a stranger to strip away her self-respect and dignity and feed it to the sailors.

'Forgive that young man; he was never like this.'

John pulled out a barstool for Amora. His hands shook with anger at what Seth had done. Something had touched and pulled at his heart; he had horrendous flashbacks of what the environment on his farm used to be like. The black women's heartrending cries for their husbands and children. The blood on his soil screaming in the darkness of death. The beatings he had given the men, year after year. John saw the shadows of the many souls tortured on his land reflected in Amora's eyes. In John's mind, Amora embodied all of them. It was as if they had finally found a body to inhabit to shame him in his old age. John passed Amora a glass of water and patted her back as if all the evil his family had done could be rubbed off in a single motion.

Amora looked at her dress, which was ripped in several places. She couldn't believe what a monster Seth was. Why did she decide to wear a new dress on a night like this? Amora had thought she would make a good impression, that people here would see her beyond her white nursing uniform. She had hoped they would see a proper, genteel lady who fit into their world. Amora longed for something to fan her face with as she seethed with rage. Wearing such an impractical item of clothing had made her seem like a clown, something to be laughed at and mocked. How could one man be so evil to her and yet so giving to his country?

'Well, pardon me,' the old man said to Amora. 'My name is John Coal. I live on a tea farm in a valley near here. I don't know how you know that man, but I suggest that you avoid him. He has a strong temper.'

'He came to me,' Amora said cautiously.

'Men like that don't have boundaries. I am sorry, young lady. Did you come here alone? Where are you from?' John took a swig from his beer bottle.

'I came here alone. I work down the street at the clinic.' The question stung; Amora looked around, but Bree and Lucy hadn't returned. They had left her here to be eaten by lions. This was the moment she realised, once again, that loyalty was like a berry tree – bears only approached it when the fruit was ripe.

'Secretary?'

'No, I am a nurse, sir.' Amora felt icy inside and her wet dress clung uncomfortably to her. The loud music was back on, and she could feel the eyes on her from behind.

'Well, damn, who would have thought!' John snorted loudly. 'Don't mind those people; they are drunks. This is what they do. Now tell me about yourself, Miss Nurse.'

'My name is Amora Grootboom.'

'Come on, you can give me far more than that. Are you married, kids, parents?'

'No. None of that. My name is Amora; please address me as such,' she said as her temper flared in a decidedly unchristian manner. John gave her a searching look.

'I can respect that, Amora. You are just like my son, Cam, cold and reserved. It's probably not your fault, but you need to watch how you react to people. Not everyone is your enemy.'

'Thank you for helping me. I should be on my way.'

'Leaving so early? Don't let that pig drive you out of here. Have a good night like all of us; let me grab you a beer.' Amora's ears perked up.

'I can't drink any more. I have been trying to quit but it's been so hard. So much has happened. Look what took place today. But I have to stop drinking. This has probably been a sign.'

'A sign? You don't look like a heavy drinker. One beer with an old man won't hurt.' John gifted her with an odd grin and winked at her.

'My father died from kidney failure a decade ago and my mother has been sucking the life out of me ever since,' Amora said glumly. She couldn't stop thinking about her father and Seth; they were evil men who had no love inside of them.

'In what way? Grief can manifest in different forms. Maybe that's what's happening.'

'It's just who my mother is; she destroyed my father after he inherited our wine farm. It's not a big piece of land but it was good enough for all of us to enjoy a promising future. But my mother kept sending all the proceeds to the Eastern Cape; we never knew what she did with the money, but she kept taking it. I can never enjoy my salary. Even today, she asked for half of it. Can you imagine what that does to a child starting her own life? I have nothing but alcohol going for me at this point.'

'Was your father a good man?'

'I don't know if I would use that adjective. The family that gave us the land truly valued him. My mother was a cleaner for the family, and my father was a groundsman. He had worked for the family for fifty years. He'd had a hard life, but he esteemed his master. I thought I would have a good life after we got the land ten years ago, but my mother cut me off when I went to nursing school. I wanted to be a neurosurgeon but now I am just a nurse in a small town.'

'Cam and Sole became enemies because of all the years I pitted them against each other,' John said, referring to his two sons. 'I think I always valued Sole more and Cam never wanted to take over the farm, as I'd planned. Sole left soon after his mother's funeral.'

John thought about what he had done to his sons after as his wife died. It was the first time he felt comfortable talking about his pain; he had spent all these years drinking himself into a grave to numb his sense of failure. Amora was giving him what he'd always wanted, a non-judgemental ear. The effects of grief had stayed with him all these years and history had stolen his retirement. He couldn't escape what his family had done in the 70s and 80s. He could neither forget nor forgive himself. Everyone knew of his evil deeds, but he hadn't been able to stop himself. It had been their way of living, and the law, back then.

'You have to get your kids back, sir.' Amora turned to look at John.

She spotted Seth smoking by the door as she and John talked late into the night. Seth was now looking at her in disgust, plotting his next move, and Amora knew it. This was the same look the man in the interview room had given her a few years ago. It was dark and deadly. She turned around but John's head was hovering over his beer. Seth kept on staring, puffing and spitting, and from what she could see, the rain was not letting up. She was in serious trouble.

How was she going to leave this place in one piece?

Chapter 13

To love even when sin is the melody

13 APRIL 2005, Clanwilliam, Western Cape

Eve observed Luna from a distance; she was her best nurse. Luna always worked diligently and made the clinic a home for many. Everyone spoke about her warmth and kindness, and Eve had come to respect her.

Eve was getting on in years and would likely need to appoint a head nurse in the coming weeks. She was heading to Cape Town for a training workshop on a quiet day at the clinic. Watching Luna swooning on the phone reminded her of her marriage. The love she and her husband had shared, and their bitter divorce, had sent her straight into ICU two years ago. She could only hope Luna would be happy for as long as she possibly could. Eve knew that a man phoned Luna several times a week, and that packages were regularly delivered to the clinic for her. Luna's smile would transform her face with happiness whenever she received these parcels.

'You really don't have to do this, Luna,' Cam said over the phone one evening just before Luna's shift was going to end at the clinic. He and Luna had established cellphone contact after spending the entire night talking in the clinic when he had vowed to be her watchman. A few days after Mia returned home, Cam went back to Simon's Town to assume his new role as captain. Every free minute he had, he called Luna. He sent her packages of tea from all over the world to try out.

'Mia needs us; school is very intimidating,' Luna told Cam. 'I know how it feels. Kids can be mean, and she doesn't have siblings to lean on. I really don't mind, Cam.'

Luna had promised Cam that she would ensure that Mia was settled at school. John put her on the school bus every morning and Luna checked in during lunch break to make sure she was okay. Mia struggled to make friends and reading was her biggest hurdle. After Amora left their shared bedroom, Luna used the extra space to create reading materials for Mia. She didn't know what she was doing, but Luna had read up on blind children and their needs. Each time Cam called, she shared new articles with him and felt she had found her purpose.

'Mia has to find her own feet; school can't be that hard for a twelve-year-old.'

Things had gone well for a few weeks until Luna received a call from the school. Mia was not talking any more; she had begun having panic attacks and it was hard for the teachers to get through to her. So, Luna took it upon herself to teach her at the boarding house on certain days when she was off duty.

'She has only been back for a week or so after the teacher's complaint; we have to give her time. Besides, she is just like you: stubborn and cautious. It will take time for her to trust people. I have given her some stuff to help with learning. We are making progress. I have tried getting her books written in Braille, but they are expensive and can only be found in private schools and big cities. I don't know how we are going to access them from here. Nevertheless, I have good news: I found audiobooks that she can listen to.'

'You see why I love you?' Cam was more convinced than ever that his feelings for Luna were real. After her weird response to his questions that night at the clinic, he had scaled back on interrogating her but instead had shared more about himself and his life. Luna had been like a frightened foal, and he had worked hard ever since to gain her trust.

'Love me? You just like nurses in general.' Luna felt as if her heart would beat out of her chest at his love declaration. She giggled into the receiver.

'When I return, I plan on making you my wife, Miss Parks.' Cam had not yet tasted her lips but was ready to make Luna his bride. Just thinking about her coloured his cheeks and his flush bled down his throat. They had come close to kissing many times that night as they moved from the sturdy chairs to the softer couch, but Luna kept pulling back.

'Let's get Mia back on track and then we will have to talk to your mother,' Cam continued. Luna was startled.

How will I face my mother? So much has happened; will she accept my move and pending nuptials so quickly? Is Cam even serious?

Luna had promised to stay pure for as long as possible, but Cam seemed like a good man. He did have a child and a broken family structure, though, and her mother was never going to approve.

What did Luna know about raising kids, especially blind ones? She also shared a big secret with Amora. They had left Cape Town to avoid all men, and now she was breaking the rules. It was good that Amora was not clingy; she had no inkling that things had got this serious with Cameron. What was holding Amora and Luna together now was the clinic, and soon they would just grow out of their shared secret. That's what Luna hoped for; it just had to go away.

'There is no way you are speaking with my mother until you woo me, Cam Coal! You still owe me a proper date, so we are not even close to involving our parents. My family is unlike yours; you must send my mother a formal letter. Maybe even a cow or two.'

The talk about cows caught Cam off guard. The farm was going to waste; he couldn't afford to send cows to Luna's family. They were a hair's breadth away from losing the farm. Most of his salary went to property taxes and the debt his father had accumulated over the years. Luna continued talking, and all he could think about was not being homeless when he returned. This would be hard, but he loved her; he knew it. It was time to move on – she was the woman he had chosen.

'I thought feeding you bread and giving you my shoulder to sleep on could be considered a date,' Cam laughed.

'I think I deserve a proper date, Cameron.' Waking up with her head on his chest the morning after they had spent the night at the clinic had felt surreal. As the night had progressed, Luna insisted that he change into some scrubs that they kept for patients who did not have clean clothes with them. When she'd started nodding off on his shoulder, he'd offered to put his arm around her so that she could settle on his muscled chest.

'Well, good news from my side: I will be home for a weekend in three weeks. I hear John is doing much better; your presence must have changed something in him. At some point, I thought he was going to kill himself. I don't know, but I pray he doesn't fall off the wagon again. Mia needs him so much; it pains me that I am not there, but at least she is in school now.'

'The teachers say she misses the farm; she talks about her kitchen and that damn horse you refuse to let go of.'

'We will see how things go. I have to come back and prepare the land for winter. I think we can also sell Mia's tea; it might help with her school fees.'

'Her tea tastes amazing; she shared a few cups with me. It's the best tea I have ever tasted. You should really think about investing in it.'

'That land is special. I just don't know what to do with it right now.'

'You are not thinking of selling, are you?'

'I don't know, Luna. Let me come home and see what's left of it.'

'I have been seeing your friend in town lately. Shouldn't you all be in Simon's Town?'

'Which friend? Ryan is with me; we will leave for Namibia in two days. From there, we sail to Madagascar.'

'Seth Fourie.'

'Something atrocious happened here at work and we had to discharge him.'

'He was fired?' Luna was shocked.

'He is struggling with a few issues; anger-management issues. We think he killed three people, and we just couldn't take the risk of having him around. The police are investigating. That was one of the reasons I had to return to work so quickly. I had to change my team. I have worked closely with Seth for seven years, but he has turned into someone else. I am not one to talk badly of any man; however, Seth needs help, and we couldn't help him. We did all we could. But he was supposed to be in Cape Town; I am shocked that he is there. He was in the army before he joined the Navy, and it hasn't been easy for us to control him.'

'I think he has things to do here in town. I spoke to Eve, and she said he'd been a troubled child.'

'His father is Mr Fourie from your boarding house. They don't stay far from the school. Mr Fourie is a nice man, but he was never any good with women. His wife left him a couple of times but always comes back. So, Seth has always been an odd child, but he is extremely loyal. He was my dearest friend and I feel horrible that I can't care for him now. He has to stay away until he can get over his issues. He is a brilliant sniper; he knows what to do when the time is right.'

'A man with a mental illness and a gun. That doesn't sound good, Cam. Does he have his service weapons with him?'

'My darling, Seth's been handling guns ever since he could walk. We were all born into them; his family owns the gun shop in town. He certainly doesn't need anything from us. He has everything he needs right there.'

'Well, apparently, he was so drunk that something bad happened at the pub at the motel: a fight or something. It was the night that you were at the clinic with me.'

'Men in bars fight; don't pay too much attention to town gossip. Rather tell me what you want from me.' She felt his tone change and his smile filled the receiver.

'How about you take me for a ride on your old wagon? I want to see the mountains. Maybe I can ride with Mia in the back. I will prepare a picnic basket. It would be wonderful. Winter is upon us; maybe this will be our last warm month.'

'Consider it done, Luna. I'm here to fulfil all your desires. Meet me at the bus stop three Saturdays from now. Don't forget, I am travelling and cannot call until then.'

'So, I am just supposed to wait, like that?'

'You are not just waiting; you are preparing to receive the man that chose you.'

'I'm going to miss talking to you,' Luna said shyly. It was challenging for her to be so explicit about how she felt.

'I'll think of you each day until you're in my arms again. Do you know how special it was to hold you so that you could sleep a little in the early hours of the morning?'

Luna blushed. 'So you keep telling me. Actually, don't worry. Mia will keep me company if you don't mind.' She had to change the subject because her body always felt funny when Cam mentioned her being in his arms.

'As long as she doesn't misbehave and prevents you from working, I am fine with it. Please keep an eye on John; my daughter doesn't trust him much any more. I can't say more now; I have to go.'

Luna wanted to ask Cam what he meant, but the phone went dead. She assumed that John wasn't feeding Mia or couldn't cope with her condition. So, she would make it her mission to master it while Mia taught her about farming. The thought of spending time with Mia thrilled her. Mia was a child, but it gave Luna the sense that she had a sister. Mia filled the gaps Luna so desperately needed. She wasn't alone any more, which felt so good. She had someone to love and care for, a pure person who had no intention of using her.

Luna attended to a few more patients and then briefly met with Eve to discuss the work schedule, before Eve set off for Cape Town.

Luna arrived at the boarding house just before sunset. Bree and Lucy were sitting outside studying for an exam. It was getting a little nippy, so Luna, dressed in her white uniform, went to sit under the tree with them. There was no sign of Amora.

'I thought we were all done with school.'

'We decided to take a short course, nothing serious,' Bree said, highlighting something in her notes.

'I only see you ladies at breakfast most days. What's been happening with you?'

'What's there to do in this town?' Lucy replied.

'It's not that bad.'

'Look who's talking! Just a while ago, you hated this place. You couldn't bear walking the streets, but now everyone knows you by name. You have done well as a nurse. Many come here and leave in two weeks. It's not easy working with the dragon lady.'

'Eve is okay. You have to do your work and get out of her way. That's all. I find this place charming and peaceful.'

'I bet you have found someone,' Bree whispered.

'Someone? Me? Not at all. I am working with the school, which takes up most of my time.'

'If you say so.'

'I am working with a smart child. She is blind but has so much potential.'

'You must be talking about the Coal reject. Parents are nowhere to be seen. They say her mother died in a fire or something. You need to be careful, Luna.'

'She is not a reject; some would say you are a reject yourself.'

The words fell right into Bree's gut. Being gay was not the coolest thing in town and many of the locals wanted to drive her and Lucy out. Luna wanted to take the words back, but she would not let Bree talk about Mia like that.

'Oh! That's how you feel! Now we know.'

'I feel nothing; your relationship has nothing to do with me. You need to watch how you speak about children. Mia was probably born blind.'

'And Cam told you that, Miss Know-it-all?' Lucy chimed in. She gave Luna a cold, challenging look.

'I didn't come here to talk about a child,' Luna said.

Lucy's comment made her nervous. She and Cam had never discussed how Mia became blind. Was she born blind?

'Then what *do* you want to talk about, Luna? Do you think that child just woke up like that? Just like you rocked up here with your web of secrets?'

'What are you talking about?'

Luna felt panic rise inside her. Lucy's look told her far more than she wanted to hear. She was unsure what they knew about the Coal family, but whatever Amora might have said had given them some ammunition.

'You better check yourself; you are getting too close to that family,' Bree warned.

'I know what I am doing; stay away from my personal life.'

'Or what, Luna? Tell us what you will do, princess,' Lucy laughed.

Luna stood up; she could feel her blood boil. Her anxiety felt like a knock on the chest and a kick simultaneously.

'Go find your blind girl and, while you are at it, check on your crazy friend,' Bree said snidely. 'She may have slept with the wrong bull. You two need to be checked in the head before you get killed or kill others.' Bree just couldn't help herself.

Luna's reaction was comical, but Bree and Lucy knew she was hiding something.

Chapter 14

For a son to take a life, life must mean far less

'Seth, what on earth were you thinking? I saw the dismissal letter. Do you have any idea what this means for our family? What this will do to our relationship with the Fletchers?'

The Fletcher family owned the biggest tea farm in the area; through the years, they had taken over the market the Coals had dominated. Many feared the family, who still followed the old, traditional ways of dealing with their staff. For them, a person's word counted more than any contract. Their staff were worked to the bone, and no one was ever allowed on their property without an invitation from the patriarch, Joshua Fletcher. Sly Fourie and his family supplied them with guns and other questionable items. They needed to tread carefully when it came to that family.

Sly stood at the top of an unstable ladder handing Reece, his assistant, some plumbing supplies. Sly didn't care to know the reasons why his son had been discharged from the Navy, but he did want him to return to Simon's Town to beg for his job back.

'Those people are not on my level,' Seth said. 'I am a sniper, not some flimsy shooter they found in the bushes.'

'You must follow commands, son.' Sly gave his son a rueful smile.

'Those dogs made Cam captain when I have given them everything. I know far more than he could ever imagine.'

'But they deemed him to be more qualified for the role, and you two are a team. Everyone has a role, and you have to play along. This gun shop has been in our family for years and people from all over come here to buy these babies, but if people find out you have been dismissed, our business' reputation will be damaged.

Swallow your pride, go back to your friends and fix it. Cam is a reasonable man, but you need to watch your drinking. I can smell the beer oozing from your pores just from where I'm standing.'

Sly glanced at Seth and saw a man who had become a shadow of his former self in a very short time. He was wearing a white shirt that looked like it had been pulled from a mud bath and jeans so tight, they looked like they would rip from all sides. With his bald head, he looked like an ex-convict. Sly could see the rage in his son's eyes. Seth couldn't stand still; his pacing made Sly anxious. Seth didn't hear his father's plea. Sly simply could not get through to him. Seth's hands twitched uncontrollably as he surveyed the guns in their locked cabinets.

'Boss, I am going to call it a day soon. Will you still be around, or should I lock the store?' Reece called out as he packed away some hunting knives.

'I think I will stay today to keep an eye on things,' Sly said as he glanced at Seth.

'You better get those wayward thoughts out of your system, boy,' Sly warned his son.

'What do you know about my thoughts? You are an old man stuck in this forsaken town and all you do is hurl insults and make demands. You couldn't even get into the army and are stuck in this little shop. If I were you, I would start selling everything and stay home like everyone else.'

'Your arrogance got you fired.' Sly came down the ladder and put it away. 'You can come and work here; we have shelves that need repairing, and the chimney at home needs to be fixed. If you stop staring at those guns, you will also see that the ceiling needs some repairs as well.'

'I am a sniper, not a handyman,' Seth said after hauling a big shotgun from the glass cabinet. He smelt it and kissed the barrel.

'I wouldn't do that if I were you.'

'I will do as I please – this place is my inheritance. Father, you seem to have forgotten that I still pay the bills around here. This shop stopped making money years ago. You depend on Joshua Fletcher;

I know you have been slacking on your commitments. I am here to set things right.'

'You will not work for that man, Seth!' Sly's tone had changed.

'I will work wherever I please.'

'That man enslaves people, and I will have no son of mine working for a killer.'

'And you are not? All these guns you sell don't kill? Or do you think you are so clean that none of these has spilt blood before? Have you forgotten how blood tastes, old man?'

Seth took the gun and thudded towards his father like a man possessed while Reece panicked and ducked behind the counter. Seth's steps echoed on the wooden floors; the cracks that came with every footstep made Sly take a few steps back.

'You need to put that thing down. Why do you have to be such a black sheep? You have always been a loser – just a lost cause. Seth, the Navy was the only place that would take you from the army. You are trigger happy and no one can fix you.'

'You are no father to me! Look at you slobber like a dog, begging at my feet.'

'Lower the gun, Seth.'

'What will you do? I can kill you both and burn down this store.'

'Your mother will be disappointed; just stop this nonsense.'

'That thing you call a wife is no mother to me. You've lied to me all these years. I really thought you would tell me the truth eventually. You are a vile, evil man who deserves to burn in hell for eternity. Even my sister could not stand to live because of you. I know how rotten you are; that's the kind of blood flowing through my veins. How could you expect that I would turn out better than this?'

'You have no idea what you're talking about, son! Just put the gun down!' Sly commanded.

As he came closer, Seth pointed the gun at his father and then placed the barrel right on Sly's nose. Sly stumbled back into the counter behind him; there was no room for him to take another step and he was pushed against the cabinets. He knew then that Seth was not his son any more.

Seth's arm was steady and the murderous look inspired panic and fear in his father.

'Seth!' Reece called out his name, but it was like the man had zoned out. A customer entered the shop and instantly ran out once he comprehended the scene.

'Listen here, old man. I am going to take what I need and leave. If you dare stop me, then you've chosen your grave,' Seth said to Sly's face. Sly nodded, terror draining the colour from his face.

'You see, that wasn't hard. It's still better than the unspeakable and debased acts that you've committed. You should learn to mind your own business and be at peace. Nonetheless, you will never have peace from tonight onwards. I shouldn't have to do this, but you made me.' Seth was speaking softly but without any remorse. He didn't care that his father had just passed water down his legs.

Seth pushed his father down with one hand until Sly's face touched his boots. Seth barked out an order to Reece, who immediately began packing a bag for him. Reece was so frightened that he added more items than Seth had requested. He filled the bags with bullets, guns and a pair of binoculars, as instructed. Two men at war, but who was the real beast?

'I guess Christmas has come early for me. Have a good day, gentlemen. Oh, and Father, we will braai later today. Don't be late; I'll be serving you the best meal you have ever had, fresh from the slaughterhouse. You like a good time, don't you? Let's celebrate; it's been a good day,' he sniggered as he pushed the door open. The bags were slung over both his shoulders.

'Boss, I am deeply sorry, sir.' Reece rushed to aid Sly.

'Lock up. It's not your fault. That boy has turned into a manic. I fear for the person that he is after; those guns have a target. I just don't know what to do. A man full of so much rage and hate always has a deadly plan. This is a small town, and his target could be anyone. All we can do is watch our own backs.'

'Should we call the police?' Would he be reporting a potential rape or a murder, Reece wondered?

'No, son, his ways will catch up with him. His mother and I had tried to raise him well, but as you can see, we have failed. I thought

Cam and Ryan's influence would help but his dismissal has set him off.' Sly shook his head. He wasn't sure whether Seth had uncovered the family secret Sly had tried to keep buried for over thirty years. If Seth had found out the truth, there would be no telling what he would do with the information. It would utterly ruin the Fourie name in the town and destroy his family.

'He mentioned something about Cam. Do you think he will kill him for his position in the Navy?' Reece asked.

'At this point, I wouldn't put it past him; he is remorseless.'

'Is your family safe?' Reece was still very young. He worked at the gun shop after school and used his salary to pay for his sports trips. Sly trusted him, as Reece was a loyal boy – certainly nothing like Seth.

'I have to speak to my wife; she should be at school. Her classes end in an hour.'

'I still think we should alert the police,' Reece insisted. 'Someone's life is in danger, and from what he did to you, I don't think any of us are safe. He took a lot of stock; now we have to close the shop prematurely.' Reece locked the doors and placed a closed sign on them.

'Let's catch our breath first; I will think of a plan. The police won't stop Seth. Most of those boys who work at the station have been friends with him for years; they won't believe us. And he hasn't committed a crime yet. It's pointless.'

'Then I think you should call Cam and tell him; he would know what to do.'

'Let's not bother him, son. We will be all right.'

Sly knew things would turn out for the worse, but he felt helpless. He loved his son; he had lost so much already, and he wasn't willing to lose him too. Sly decided to clean and prepare the store for his customers, as going home made him feel anxious. He would not enjoy a braai with his son tonight and pretend that Seth had not just assaulted him. So, he decided that he would stay at the shop that night.

Alone in the gun shop, Sly paced the floor, praying that Seth wouldn't return. He left the shop in darkness and read his newspaper in the kitchenette at the back of the store. Sly needed food, but he could not risk going out the door. His gut told him to stay put and wait, especially when he spotted Seth's truck at the garage across the street. Seth had stepped out of the vehicle and was speaking to the petrol attendant; he was still in his old clothes but had a can of beer in his hand.

Sly couldn't hear what they were discussing, but Seth seemed very agitated. The next moment, Seth grabbed the attendant and shoved him to the concrete floor, kicking him a few times. Sly wanted to scream in shock but held his hands over his mouth; tears poured from his eyes in disbelief. His child had turned into a monster! Sly watched as Seth took the petrol pump, helped himself to some petrol and then raced off without paying. The attendant gingerly stood up, his arms clutching his sides as he stumbled to the toilet.

Sly was shaking, the faint pain in his chest intensifying. He was ashamed that a part of him was praying that Seth would not stop at the shop. But Seth was driving right past him, in the direction of the clinic. First the army, then the Navy, had destroyed his son, taken away his innocence, and now no one was safe. Sly sat down on the cold floor and cried. Once he managed to pull himself together, he tried calling Cam and Ryan, but their phones were off. He pulled his whisky bottle out from under the reception desk and drained the contents. He had to warn his wife. All those guns in a drunk, deranged man's hand were like a nuclear bomb waiting to explode. He tried reaching Edna, but she didn't answer.

'Okay, maybe she's bathing, or she's cooking or at the church,' Sly reasoned. His chest was tightening, and he rubbed his fist over it. The images of Seth on top of him was not allowing him any peace. Seth had never done anything like this before, but he did have a dreadful history with guns. Sly kept on trying to reach his wife, and at last she answered.

'Edna, pack your things and go to your sister! Seth is in town and things don't look good,' Sly warned. He told her what had happened and reminded her of Seth's past, but to a mother, Sly's story just didn't hold water.

'You want me to leave our home and go to Lambert's Bay at this hour? Where are you? Seth won't harm us; he is our son. Yes, he is devastated about losing his job, but he won't touch me. You have lost your mind if you think I will leave my house.' Edna could hear Sly's desperation, but she refused to believe what he was saying.

'So, he's told you?' Tears were running unchecked down Sly's leathery, wrinkled cheeks.

'Yes, I *am* his mother,' Edna said. 'Sly, get a grip on yourself and just come home. I made dinner for us, but neither of you showed up. I hoped we could all talk about this as a family. I don't think what happened will happen again. Maybe you just pushed him too far, like you always do. He wouldn't shove a gun in your face for no reason.'

'You didn't see what I saw in that boy, Edna. He is not our son right now! He is demon-possessed, and you are to leave that house at once!'

'You saw a man who is going through something, and he just needs to vent. Why are you like this? You like exaggerating; you need to calm down and come home. If my son is in pain, I won't just leave him. Yes, he has problems, but he is just like you. Don't you see that?'

'Leave that house now! I have no son. If he comes close to you, you better call the police.'

'I am not moving; he can slaughter me if he wants to.'

'Edna—' As Sly tried to speak, the line went dead.

There were no screams, yet no life remained. Wrath and wickedness had descended on the Fourie home.

Chapter 15

The Vow

7 MAY 2005, Clanwilliam, Western Cape

Winter was slowly creeping in, and the mountain landscapes were flourishing due to some persistent rainfall. The mornings and evenings got icier. Sly and Seth Fourie dug a grave and buried Edna, concealing Seth's evil deed in their backyard. Sly's heart bled with pain and grief. How much more would he have to endure at Seth's hands? The morning after Edna was killed, he called the school and fabricated a story of Edna's sudden departure to Lambert's Bay to take care of her ailing sister. Another secret to keep; no questions were asked. A good old family tragedy covered in mud. No one spoke of that night again, yet the animal was relentless in his hunt.

Seth was like an eagle in the sky, homing in on its prey. Every day, he watched and observed, his grief always accompanying him. The truth was inside of him: the real reason his sister had killed herself was the burden he carried along with his guns. He did not eat or speak to anyone; all he did was drink. His anger and hate towards Amora simmered and grew as time passed. Her big mouth, her free spirit and, most of all, her rejection had chafed his nerves raw. She had moved on like nothing had happened, yet no one had checked on his well-being after the incident at the motel. He felt betrayed, ashamed and embarrassed. It was always the Coals getting in his way – father *and* son.

Amora was his trigger. Something about her made Seth hate women even more. She was an easy target, as she limited her movements between the clinic and the boarding house. Late in the evenings, she went to bars and readily accepted the advances of other men. Why had he not been good enough to touch her? Did she think he was beneath her? Seth plotted and planned as he followed Amora around town. He was waiting for the right moment to execute his plan. When Amora spotted him observing her, her hurried steps and frantic looks just empowered him. He lurked like a sinister presence, coiled and ready to strike.

'Bree, this man is stalking me,' a terrified Amora confided at the dinner table one evening. 'He knows what I eat and watches me when I go to work and come home every day. He once called out my name in the street and came to the clinic to ask for water.'

'Well, maybe you gave him what he wanted. Now he can't get enough. Just talk to him.'

'I gave this man nothing. You know what happened that night when you guys left me in the pub. This man is crazy! Do you even believe that his mother just left town in the way they say? I see him watching me all the time. Does he not have a job? I can't even walk home from work any more. He and his truck are always somewhere on the main street, watching and waiting.'

'I think you enjoy the attention. Just talk to Seth and hear what his story is. You can't run away each time you see him. This is a small town; you're going to see him around. Come on! We left you to your business that night because you've always enjoyed male attention when we go out.'

Amora tried many times to talk to Lucy and Bree about Seth, but they would not believe that he was stalking her. He was too well respected in the community, along with Cameron, Ryan and other local men who served in the Navy. No one would believe an alcoholic like Amora. She was considered a tease and that she philandered with every good-looking man in town. But how else could she numb the feelings of worthlessness that plagued her daily? At night, in bed, she would hear the crunching footsteps outside her window. Seth probably had keys to the boarding house and could invade her space whenever he felt like it; the thought of it made her sick. It became difficult for her to concentrate at work; she was always exhausted from trying to stay awake at night in an effort to protect herself if he decided to come into her room.

The next morning, Amora walked to work with Luna. It was one of those rare days when they happened to leave the boarding house simultaneously. Luna seemed happier and lighter, without a care in the world. Amora tried talking to her as they walked along, but Luna's head seemed to be in the clouds. Why had Luna decided that they needed to come to this forsaken town, and why had she abandoned her?

'You are preoccupied these days, Luna. You come and go, and no one knows what you are doing.'

They hurried along down the street, past the gun shop. Amora couldn't bear to look at the place, but she tried not to panic. The clinic was not too far away, and she hoped they could reach it without seeing Seth.

'We each have our private lives, and I am enjoying mine,' Luna replied. 'We were not joined at the hip in Cape Town, so why would you want that here? Try to do something fun; drinking is not my thing, and you seem to thrive in that space.'

'I thought coming here would be good for both of us, but I was mistaken. Luna, I don't like drinking, but I have to.' Amora glanced around the street, but this time she couldn't see Seth's truck. The morning was a little foggy and cold and the mountains were surrounded by a halo of clouds, while the streets were still awakening from their slumber.

'Amora, we are two very different people; what did you expect? I am not here to babysit you. We are adults, and we deserve our own space. You are building your life and so am I. I didn't question you when you decided to move out of our room without warning. I don't see why there should be a problem now. I think you're doing well; Bree and Lucy have you running these streets. I am honestly fine with that. I plan to work closely with the school and the community. Since arriving here, I feel as if I have a greater purpose; this community needs a doctor and I think I could fulfil that role if I return to my studies. I am happy that things finally feel lighter, and work is perfect too.'

Luna checked her phone; Cam was due to arrive that morning and she didn't want to miss his text or call. She tucked her phone back into her bag.

'Are you seeing someone?' Amora gasped.

'What do you care? I told you, we have different lives. Focus on yours. I am expecting a call from my mother, and she might come to visit in a couple of weeks.'

'So, you finally told her that you've moved here?' Amora sounded both shocked and disappointed. Luna constantly called the shots and Amora couldn't do anything without Luna's approval; she was moving on like salt in water. Amora watched as Luna scrambled for words.

'She is my mother; she was going to find out anyway. Maybe you should just go see your mom too. Take a break from this place and reconnect with her. The worst is over now.'

Luna glanced at Amora and smiled, but it felt as if she were kicking Amora out of her life.

'So, we are just colleagues, right?' Amora's eyes were swimming in tears.

'That's right. You finally get it. Amora, I am not your sister, but I care about you. However, I don't think we want the same thing. I'm happy that you moved out; now I can finally see that I am an individual with my own goals and dreams. You will be fine; I don't know why you have become so irritable. If you don't run your mouth off, we should be safe. It's been a few months, and we haven't heard anything from Cape Town. I had my friend Loyiso keep an ear out as well.' Luna turned away from Amora; guilt still ate at her when she thought of Dr Mark.

Amora shook her head. She couldn't understand why Luna was turning against her. She had not mentioned anything about the interview-day incident to anyone. She went over her conversations with the girls and couldn't remember telling them anything.

'What has happened to us?' Amora asked Luna. 'I really don't understand. It's like you are becoming a different person, Luna.'

She felt lost, swimming in a sea of confusion, terror and loneliness. Luna had uprooted their lives in the city, leaving Amora out in the cold.

'If you have anything to disclose, this would be the best time,' Luna said.

'What do you mean?' Amora extended her arm in front of Luna and stopped her in her tracks. Luna stiffened at Amora's icy tone.

'Bree and Lucy mentioned something about death and killing the other day. You better watch what you say, Amora! You can't trust anyone here.'

Luna seemed calm, almost condescendingly so.

'I said nothing! Why don't you believe anything I tell you?' Amora growled.

'I don't have to; I just watch your behaviour. That's all.' Luna stalked off, pulling out her phone. Amora couldn't stand how Luna had changed. She treated Amora like a juvenile that had no place in her world.

'You are doing all this because Eve gave you some power! Is that it? You are still a nurse, Luna! You are no better than us!' Amora screamed after her as they walked through the clinic gates. The only response Amora got from Luna was the sharp tapping of her heels as she walked away.

Amora checked the notice board and saw that Luna was working a three-hour shift that day. She would be off the entire weekend, including Monday. She had never had so many days off.

'Why does Luna have so many days off?' Amora asked Eve, who was sitting in the reception area, enjoying her morning coffee.

'If you worked as hard as Luna and came to work on time, you would get some free time too. Luna has proven herself. Everyone loves her because she is always here! You see, my girl, free time is earned.'

'But... I am also always here, Eve!' Amora's mouth curved ruefully.

'The difference between you and Luna is respect for your work. You are still standing here, and she is already with a patient. Don't think I haven't seen you sneak out to nap in the toilet. Hanging out at bars and drinking every night will not get you far in life. Luna is up for a promotion soon because of her work ethic.'

'I rue the day I met Luna,' Amora murmured.

Amora got to work and said nothing until she noticed Luna packing her belongings, taking a call on her phone and speaking briefly to Eve. Before Amora could say anything, Luna was out the door. Luna hurried down the road to the bus stop nearby. The bus from the Navy that came around to drop the locals off had just pulled up. A uniformed man stepped out of the bus, carrying a backpack, and embraced Luna. Amora couldn't identify him from a distance but suspected who it could be. She watched as the laughing couple embraced like teenagers.

'Aren't they just stunning? She found herself a good one,' Eve said as she stood by the door watching Luna and Cam.

Amora couldn't respond. All she knew was Luna had stopped her from dating Dr Mark, and now she had moved on and left Amora hanging. How selfish could one person be? Amora was left with nothing yet again. She couldn't believe that this was Luna – the virgin girl who did no wrong in people's eyes. If only they knew the truth, those rose-coloured glasses would come off very quickly.

As an infuriated Amora watched the couple in disbelief, a lone figure was observing her closely, his cigarette smoke spiralling into the clear sky.

Chapter 16

This love can be ours

'If there was anything under the sun that has beauty like yours, I would capture it so that I could give it to you daily.' Cam cupped Luna's face and kissed her on the cheek, then lifted her into his arms. She tried to pull back – people were watching – but the delight of his lips on her face excited her.

'My heart is under siege!' Luna giggled as Cam set her back on the ground. She held on to him, not wanting to leave the comfort of his arms. Her heart raced like a thoroughbred horse because of seeing Cam after so many weeks.

'There are worse wars than my love for you.'

'I didn't think you would be back on time.'

'I am a man of my word and time allows me to keep my promises to you. I was not going to waste a second getting back to you.' Cam brushed his lips against Luna's. It was a sweet first kiss; the brief pressure of his warm lips against hers left a lingering tingle.

'People are looking at us!' She glanced at the passengers on the bus, who were observing them with smiles on their faces.

'Now they know that I have finally found my rose.' Cam waved at the driver as the bus pulled away.

Luna hid her face in his chest while reacquainting herself with his scent; it felt so familiar and comforting. His arms circled her waist and she had never felt such firmness and power from one gesture. Cam was perfect, a man filled with light and grace. He was admired by his peers and feared by his enemies. Relief settled in her bones;

she could let go and just accept his love. He ensured that she felt his presence every second he was away with late-night calls and text messages. Luna couldn't believe that he was there, holding her and worshipping every inch of her. He was hers to keep.

'If home feels like this, then it was imperative to return at once,' Cam whispered. His hot breath coated her ear and warmed her.

'It's so good to see you; I missed you, Captain Coal.' Shyness overtook Luna, and she was unsure how to handle the emotions swirling within her. Happiness intertwined with overwhelming affection.

'Are we back to "Captain Coal" again?' Cam's flirtatious gaze travelled over her entire body.

'I bet Mia is dying to see you. We should get going.'

'I came here for you – Mia can wait. You said she was doing well now, so I have no reason to see her immediately.'

'So, where are you going to sleep?' Luna glanced at all his luggage.

'Don't you know by now? Where you lie, I will lie.'

Luna was startled. 'At the boarding house? With all those girls? No way, you must be joking.' She backed out of his arms so that she could look at him properly. Worry and discomfort coloured her face. How would they fit on her narrow bed?

'Well, if you can stay there, so can I.' Cam seemed adamant, and she didn't have the heart to deny him.

Cam pulled her closer again and searched her soul with his eyes. She felt powerless against his magnetic pull. His touch felt like a warm blanket and Luna was ravenous for it. They stood there silently, wrapped in each other's gaze and embrace. The world seemed to carry on around them, but they were suspended in time. Recommitting each other's face to memory, relearning each other's curves and edges. Cam had created a need within her, a longing for heat and surrender. It superseded the joining of the skin or the locking of eyes; it was an internal vow. He was staying for her; he was here for her. Luna saw a promise, an entreaty and a benediction in his eyes. Love had finally found her.

'Luna Parks,' he said gently.

'Captain Cameron Coal.'

'Will you start a new life with me?' The question felt sacred. His plea carried an indulgent and warm tone.

'A life with you will fulfil me, Captain Coal.' Luna was finally taking a leap of faith; she knew that Cam would catch her in the warmth of his arms.

'There are no sweeter words than those you utter to me.' He hugged her, savouring the feel of her body against his for a beat before he reluctantly pulled away from her.

'Would you like to have lunch at the café? They make the best cheese sandwich. No bread is better than mine, but it may be adequate to convince you to stay with me for a lifetime.'

'Everything you touch, Cameron, succumbs to your wiles – including me.'

He smiled as he picked up his bags and they threaded their fingers together as they walked past the clinic. Luna melted beside him; they spoke to a couple of gentlemen along the way and greeted some of the locals. Cam was dressed in his Navy uniform, his shoulders were broad, and his face was filled with pride and delight.

While Cam moved gracefully along the sidewalk and commanded respect, others sneered and tsked, muttering under their breath as they became aware of Cam and Luna's interracial relationship. It was a love that either pulled crowds and had the heavens whisper in song, or it hardened others' hearts.

'Cam! Cameron. Son!' a man called out.

'It's Mr Fourie, Cam.'

'Oh, Mr Fourie, how are you? Are you well?'

'Things haven't been good for us, but we are happy you are back. My wife is away at the moment and will be for quite some time, so I have to fend for myself.'

Sly and Cam spoke briefly. He was still holding Luna's hand when she was distracted by her phone.

'You crazy bitch! You walk around like royalty, yet you have blood on your hands! How could you do this to me!' Amora's text message was raging with bitterness and fury; how could Luna have started up with Cam when she kept on denying any attraction? On the night of the fire, this man had helped Amora and saved so many. How had Luna ended up with him?

Luna was rattled after she read Amora's text. She was panicking as she looked around to see if Amora was in sight. They had passed the clinic but hadn't seen her. It irked Amora that she had suddenly become invisible.

'Can we catch up a little later, Mr Fourie? My lady needs to eat, and we are running late.'

'Indeed. Will you be staying at the farm?' Sly asked politely, still keen to talk. But he could tell Cam had other things on his mind, and he was still carrying his luggage.

'I will come around to the shop, don't worry. Please prepare hunting gear for me and my lady. I will pick it up tomorrow.'

Sly bid them farewell and rushed back into his shop. Cam noticed that he locked the door behind him; he found it odd but carried on walking.

'Is everything okay with him?' Luna asked.

'It's probably family politics. It can't be easy with Seth unemployed. So, do you know what you feel like eating?'

'Anything is fine; just make sure the meal has eggs.'

'Eggs? Mia has rubbed off on you, I see.'

'She eats like a farmer's child,' Luna giggled, still trying to hide the panic she was feeling.

'I am pleased you two are getting along,' Cam said. 'My child has been through so much. I want her to find her feet and live like other kids. We have a lot to overcome as a family and her being with other kids will heal her. Your presence will make a huge difference in her life. We all need you, Miss Parks.'

'And I need you, Cameron. You and Mia have been a revelation in my life. You mentioned hunting! I don't know how to do that. Do we get to kill actual animals?'

Cam laughed, amusement lighting up his eyes.

'You will see. When I came to the clinic that night, I waited, unable to move. I watched you pray over my child.' He stood still and turned towards her. Luna hadn't realised he had observed her for so long.

'No one has ever done that for us. You held Mia like she was your own. People in this town have always avoided her; they treated her like a pariah. My father made it worse and forced her out of school so that he didn't have the responsibility of handling the backlash from the school. Having a blind child can be a curse when the world doesn't value them or treat them like other kids. She is just a child but the fear she carries kills my heart.

'When her mother died, we all died. I don't know how to be a father; I don't want you to feel like you have to replace her mother. You don't have to do anything that you can't. Your being here is enough. Mia speaks to you and that's enough for me. She had stopped eating and talking for a long time and spent her time in the fields with her animals and the land. Getting through to her had become a battle. I blame myself for not stepping up and taking full responsibility. I fear I can't be what she needs.'

'Cameron, you are a father, and no one can judge you. We can all learn; we can ask for help. You don't have to do this alone.' Cam closed the gap between them and embraced Luna.

'Thank you, Luna. Shall we eat before I carry you on my shoulders? How can I appease you?' He winked. It was a bittersweet moment. Cam was still hurting but this was neither the time nor the place to bleed out.

Luna put her small hands on his chest and lay her head there. His heartbeat was strong, but she felt his pain despite his attempts to cover it with bravery and humour. Just knowing that Cam was giving himself to her caused her nerves to skitter along her skin.

Am I worthy to love and be loved by a man like him?

'If it's not the woman of the moment!' Ryan Adams approached them with a big smile.

'My brother!' Cam called out in surprise. 'I was wondering what had happened to you!'

'You left me on the bus; I was fast asleep. The bus had to turn around to drop me off. You obviously had only one thing on your mind!' Ryan grinned mischievously.

Luna stepped behind Cam; she wasn't used to so much attention.

This would be the first time Cam introduced her to his friend as his girlfriend. The look on Cam's face spoke of great respect and adoration; Ryan stood to attention and acknowledged Luna.

'My lady, when this brother of mine catches his breath, we hope you will become our in-law.' Ryan beamed as he extended his hand towards her. Luna smiled and shook his hand.

'Dr Adams, I wasn't aware that all of you were returning.'

'My love …' Cam said humorously. Luna's heart contracted at the endearment.

'Whenever our captain requests we descend to our homes, we follow his command,' Ryan said. 'I believe he has great news to share with us. I see now that the call to return home was worthwhile.' Luna felt a warmth in her cheeks; she felt seen and cherished. Cam squeezed her hand affectionately.

'Dr Ryan, this is my girl, Miss Luna Parks. Because of her work ethic, she will likely be the head nurse at the clinic soon.'

'How could I forget our very own Florence Nightingale! What you have done with our clinic and the school is noteworthy. You have given so many of our people a better life. The hygiene programmes at the school have been noble and remarkable. I also understand you help the kids with reading, and you provide aid during sports days. We haven't had that type of help here in years. We are truly honoured to have you, especially because you will become part of our family. I'm curious to see what else you've been doing when I lend a hand at the clinic during the Christmas holidays. Well, that's if my captain allows me to return home and permits me to work with you.'

'Miss Parks is her own person; I shall not stand in the way of her profession. However, I believe she will be with child or planning a wedding around that time.' Cam winked at Luna.

'Well, it looks like we will have to celebrate!' Ryan laughed. Luna pushed Cam playfully and shook her head.

'Dr Adams, my partner is jumping the gun! I would be happy to work with you. You'll find me at the clinic when you're ready.'

'We were just about to have lunch. Would you care to join us?'

'May I?' Ryan said. 'I would enjoy basking in the greatness of the couple before me for a while longer.'

Cam laughed as he placed his hand on his friend's shoulder. They were almost like twins in the way they walked and used their hands to express themselves. Luna enjoyed how at ease they were with each other.

'Most certainly! I would love to know more about you and your work,' Luna said as she led the way towards the café.

With darkness lingering in the recesses of his soul, Seth observed the friends' reunion with resentment and rage. His childhood friends, men he considered closer than his biological family, looked as if they didn't need him. They were walking the streets without caring to check on him since his discharge from the Navy. Out of sight, out of mind. Seth was parked at the petrol station, smoking and watching as they entered the café. His gaze collided with Cam's, but Cam just dismissed Seth as if he hadn't always had Cam's back! All those years, side by side, they had worked together like a brother and a shield. But Seth had become a nobody overnight. How could Cam just forget him?

Cam pulled out a chair for Luna and summoned a waiter. The café had an outside area, but they opted for a table inside due to the bite in the air.

'Brother, we are going hunting tomorrow night,' Cam told Ryan. 'Keep your phone on; my lady might be horrific with guns and shoot me by accident.' Cam kissed Luna on the cheek and sat down.

'With your experience as a hunter and hers as a nurse, you will live.'

'I don't plan on touching a gun, Ryan. This man is crazy.'

'He is a fantastic hunter; you will be fine.'

'In this cold?'

'This is the best time to hunt. If you wait for July, you won't enjoy the mountains.'

'I was thinking I'll take her to Hartebeestkraal because I haven't been there before, but they are full. As I got my dedicated hunter status through Kaapjag, I figured we'd go there instead. It's been a while, so I'm looking forward to sharing the experience with my lady.'

'Cameron, when did you plan all this?' Luna asked in amazement.

'I always have a plan; you will never need to wonder with me, my lady.'

Ryan smiled as he looked at the couple. Cam's eyes shone with joy and affection. He couldn't recall ever seeing Cam look at Summer in that way. Ryan was both pleased with and impressed by Luna. He knew how pleasant she was with people, and now, seeing her with his friend, gave him confidence that it was just what the Coals needed – a shining light in the darkness.

'Do you want to risk my life, Captain?'

'You will be one with nature, Miss Parks,' Ryan assured her. 'Try something new and see how it goes. However, please don't ask me to join you. I have something planned for my wife.' Ryan checked his watch; it was almost time to leave. He had something light to eat and then let Cam and Luna be.

Luna felt a sense of ease surround her and Cam; this would be her life now that he was beside her. They ate their food and spoke about their plans, dreams and wishes. Cam was encouraging Luna to study further, but he said that he wasn't willing to leave the Navy. He would only come home once a month, but Luna didn't feel comfortable with the idea.

'You won't even realise that I am not home when you are busy with your work and studies. I think you will be just fine. I want you to enjoy your life. With you in my life, things may change a little.'

'What do you mean?' Luna sipped her tea.

'Don't you want to be a farmer's wife and a mother?'

'I don't know; I haven't thought that far.'

'Well, I have; I know you will excel at it. Your patience and care with Mia are testament to that.' Cam felt happy and fulfilled. Their conversation was flowing as if they were already a married couple.

'I am too young to have kids, and I don't know anything about farming, Cam. Can we just get through this lunch before we talk about having kids?'

'As you wish, but think about it.'

How will I tell him that I've never been with a man?

Luna's mother didn't even know she was dating, yet Cam was already talking about kids and a farm. Luna had not even seen this farm. She liked Cam a lot, but could her feelings really have morphed into love so quickly? Amora's text had cast a shadow on the sunshine of her joy. Amora was bitter and enraged, and this time, Luna understood why.

The truth lies in Cape Town – the death of that man is going to come back to haunt me. How would I hold on to Cam then?

Cam gave her a moment to collect her thoughts; he touched her thigh, caressing it with warm fingers. She tried to calm her anxiety, but tears overwhelmed her.

'Oh no, love. Did I say something wrong?' Cam turned his chair to face her.

'I am happy, Cam, truly I am. I do want to be with—' But she failed to articulate her desires.

'I won't burden you; do you want us to skip the hunting?'

'It's not that at all.'

'Then tell me.' He cupped her face in his hands and kissed her gently. Luna felt cherished by him, especially with all the stomach-fluttering kisses she had received since he arrived. She felt an answering pull from within every time Cam put his lips on hers.

'You will be gone most of the time; how will I deal with that? I don't even know much about the Navy. Is it very dangerous, like in the army? Do people die?'

'You worry too much; I am here. I will always be here.' Cam felt the depth of her emotions and her concern about spending time together. Most sailors with partners struggled with this. But it didn't feel like the right time for Cam to change professions, not when he had just been promoted.

'Are you sure?'

'I am here, Luna. I don't plan to die. I am well-trained and we have the best team. I don't fear the waters. I will show you one day; there is nothing to fear.'

Cam pulled her into his arms to reassure her. Everything in that moment felt true and just. A promise she would have to hold on to.

I know I've done bad things, but please don't take Cam away from me when I've just found him?

Luna would be grateful to any deity that would heed her plea.

Chapter 17

For a touch could mean more than a word

Cam was the perfect gentleman, even though he was fighting the unthinkable. He was a wounded man who longed for his father's attention and validation in all respects. All Cam had ever done was work for his family, even though it never seemed enough for John. He had always said a man's true strength was the value of his legacy. Even though Cam was now a captain, it didn't bring in enough money to save the farm entirely. If they lost the farm, the legacy his grandfather had left them would be gone. This ate at Cam, as he knew little about the farm's operations. The last operations manager they'd had had left to work for the Fletchers. That was three years ago, and with John's addiction to alcohol, things had just got worse. Coming home was always bittersweet.

Cam had not given himself the right to grieve or confront the loss of Seth. They had been like brothers; Seth had taught Cam to hunt and fight in combat and had introduced him to the Navy years ago. The type of love he so effortlessly poured into Luna was the type of love Cam needed from his father. And the thought of Mia growing up empty, like him, broke him. Even though he held a powerful position at work, it didn't bring him any peace. Cam wanted more; he had to think about the farm and fixing his family. It could wait one more day, though.

For now, Luna was his priority. He couldn't run away from what he felt for her. This feeling was new and pure, and he deserved to fully embrace it. Luna was willing to have him, but he had to be gentle with her. She had a spark in her eyes that made him forget everything he had lost. She would be a fitting wife for him; he was a firm and decisive man. Every conversation with her felt like a promise, a commitment he knew he had to make. It was a privilege being with her; she lent him a more significant presence than just being a captain.

Luna didn't really cook, but she promised to make Cam dinner. Cam was still persistent about sleeping over at the boarding house. Bree and Lucy had left that afternoon for a weekend in Cape Town and Luna hoped that Amora wouldn't make a scene. It was all Luna could think about through the day, as well as worry about sleeping with Cam. As he paid for their meal, nervous energy flowed through her at the thought of lying with him.

After lunch, they went past Mia's school to check on her progress. Her teacher told them that Mia and a group of girls had gone horse-riding as a school activity. They would be taken home right afterwards. Luna and Cam then made their way to the bakery to buy fresh bread and other essentials. Luna was enjoying the process of learning about what type of person Cam was. It was in how he spoke to her; he was protective and firm but never angry. He complimented and encouraged her.

'What are you planning to cook?' Cam asked.

'Well, can I fry something?'

'Like what? Eggs?' Cam teased.

'I don't know, maybe steak or pork?' She grabbed Cam's hand.

'Let's get to the boarding house first and then we will see.' Cam walked ahead of her carrying his bags in one hand and the groceries in the other.

'Cameron Coal!' Luna called after him. He took giant steps as he walked because of his height. He purposefully walked faster, turning to check how far back she was, only to increase his pace.

'How dare you leave me!' She ran up behind him, quite out of breath.

'Young lady, you need to move those size-three feet!' Cam joked and raced up the hill towards the boarding-house gate.

'I should have allowed you to carry me on your shoulders.'

'If you can catch me, that's even better.' He pushed the gate open and ran towards the door.

'You don't have any keys and Amora is probably in there, naked, Cam!' Luna huffed and puffed trying to catch up with him. She paused to catch her breath. She had never been this happy. Everything was finally falling into place, and it felt so right. She looked up at the skies and inhaled deeply.

Thank you, Father. Thank you!

Luna let them into the boarding house, and Cam walked inside. It felt homely and lived in. The girls had placed fresh flowers on the kitchen table and the wall had a cleaning schedule with their names and pictures. Next to it on the walls were the pictures of nurses who had lived there before them. The history of each image, along with their arrival and departure dates, was documented underneath. Other pictures with more recent dates but no dates of departure also lined the wall. Cam wondered what had happened to these women, and whether they had been fired. He glanced around the space and noticed a common sitting area with a radio and a small TV. The president of the country's portrait hung next to those of a few nursing teachers. The national anthem was mounted on the other side of the wall, a reminder of Cam's duty to protect the Republic.

When Luna walked in, Cam had already packed away the groceries and was washing the fruit in the sink. 'You never cease to amaze me,' she said in a low, throaty voice. She glanced at his hands and back as he stood by the sink.

'It's going to be dark soon; I thought I should lead the way.' Cam's gaze was tracing her soft brown skin, wondering how it would feel under his body. He couldn't help but feel the stirring within his own body. Luna's cocoa-butter scent still lingered on him, driving him to insanity every time he inhaled a whiff.

'I am just shocked that you are in the kitchen.' Luna's gaze narrowed.

'Why are you shocked? Is the kitchen the garden of Eden?'

'Men don't cook, Cam, and what do you know about the great garden?'

'Well, I know a good man who found a wife there.' Cam approached her with an apple in hand.

'And the wife ate the same apple you're holding, right?'

Cam chuckled, thinking of the corny irony. Luna snorted and then covered her mouth.

He is so funny and charming!

'That's not the full story; she eats it and eats him too.' Cam came close enough to kiss her but instead took a bite of the apple and handed her the rest.

'Happy now?' Cam yearned to touch her. His shoulders stiffened as he tried not to grab and place her on the table. Luna felt the longing within Cam but couldn't let it be fulfilled. She wanted to rip off his shirt and run her hands over his chest, but what type of lady would that make her? She had thought about him for weeks during nights of wonder and lust. Now he was here, in her kitchen. It was such a simple pleasure: the longing, their eyes locking occasionally.

'See, the man bit into the apple and passed it on. The sin is for you to carry.'

'You are witty; continue with your foolishness, my lady. The night is young.' Cam walked to the kitchen table and started preparing the meat and vegetables. He continued as if she wasn't even there.

'I said I will cook; you can go rest and I will get dinner started,' Luna offered.

'I am not tired, and this will be good for us. You've never told me that you can cook.'

'Bree cooks for us; she does a better job than all of us.'

'So, I was right!'

'Who can blame me? I can clean and surf. That's enough.'

'You can what?' Cam turned to look at her.

'Ocean ... surfing.'

'Now that's something I need to see.'

'I grew up in the city. It's common for us. I've been surfing longer than I have been a nurse. I miss it.'

'You should teach Mia and me.' Cam gestured for Luna to come closer. As she drew close, he circled her waist, lifted her up and placed her on top on the table. He wedged in between her dangling legs and put his arms on either side.

'I am not good at teaching; you have to get someone else. It requires someone with experience. My father was an incredible teacher.' Luna felt breathless.

Cameron is so strong!

'You haven't spoken about your family much,' Cam said. 'Where are your parents?'

Whenever they drew close, they always spoke softly. It reminded Luna of their intimate moments at the clinic. She watched Cam's lips as he spoke and was tempted to lean forward and kiss him.

'Well,' she said instead, 'my father left my mother ten years ago. We don't know where he is now. My mother still misses him. I was fifteen when he left.'

'That will never be our situation.' Cam gently rubbed the back of her shoulders. Luna's skin tingled wherever Cam touched her. He was leaving a fiery trail of something she couldn't readily identify.

'I hope so. My mother has never got over it; she has been depressed all these years. My childhood quickly became a nightmare, but my mother did all she could for me.'

Luna wanted to believe Cam, but men left women all the time, and she wasn't going to turn out like her mother. The conversation soured the mood a little. Tight-lipped, Luna bowed her head and thought deeply.

'I guess we all carry the burden of family traumas, but I want to ease your burden, Luna. It's what a husband does for his wife.' Cam's warm hands cupped her face, staring into her tear-filled eyes. He wanted to comfort her, but he didn't know how to take the sadness away. His lips touched Luna's and he got swept away when she kissed him back. She put her arms around Cam's neck, and he pulled her closer.

'We need to finish cooking the food...' Luna cleared her throat as she stopped drinking from his lips. Cam's eyes were like slits in his handsome face as he gave her another peck and turned to the stove.

'You're right, love. I need to feed you.'

Luna offered to make tea as Cam continued to cook dinner. Then she took his things to her bedroom. Luna had started talking about her childhood, as had Cam. But he did not mention how he'd met Summer or how she and his mother had died. It was too soon to share the tragedy with her. It was still hard to accept that he had failed both his mother and his wife, which John had always held against him and was the reason his brother, Sole, had left.

'What happened to your mother?' Luna asked softly. She was back, sitting at the table, watching Cam move around comfortably in the kitchen. Mouth-watering aromas permeated the room, and sizzles and splats intermittently interrupted their conversation. The heat from the oven and the tea she had just finished drinking warmed her.

'She died.'

'Was she sick?'

'No. She is just dead. Nothing more.'

'And Mia's mother?'

'Dead!'

'Were you by her side?'

'We buried her.' Cam was getting irritated and feeling edgy; he walked off and started washing some of the pots.

'When was this?'

'Years ago, Luna. Let it be, please.'

'Why did you join the Navy?'

'It was work. We all need employment. The farm couldn't survive without the extra cash, and I had Mia to care for.'

'When did you get married? You must have been young—'

Cam turned his back on Luna. He didn't know why she was asking him so many questions. He fought the urge to walk out and take in some fresh air to calm down. The wound of loss had been prodded and was bleeding again. He was masking his grief with anger, which Luna didn't deserve. It wasn't her fault that these things had happened to his family. He opened the windows and looked out at the stars.

'And you said you don't want to work on the farm. How then will you save it?'

'I don't know yet, Luna.'

'You hardly speak about your brother; maybe he can help you.'

'He is a lawyer. I don't think he cares about farming. We don't even know where in the world he is. I don't really want to talk about this, Luna.'

'And yet you want to marry me, Cameron. How is this going to work?' Luna knew Cam was shutting down, but she wouldn't allow him to escape from telling the truth. Cam walked towards her and touched her face gently while looking searchingly into her eyes.

'We will get to all these things when the time is right. I don't want to mess up our evening with family drama.'

'Well, if you don't want the formality, get rid of this uniform and be the Cam I know.' Luna was right; they were both still in their work uniforms, and he hadn't even noticed.

'Care to show me the bedroom? I will certainly honour your request, my lady.'

Cam followed Luna up the stairs.

'While you change, I'm going to shower,' Luna said as Cam rifled through his bag. He nodded. Luna needed a moment to collect her thoughts.

He's not like your father. You can build your own little family provided no one finds out about what you did. I'll lose Cameron and go to jail. Mia would be destroyed. What will my mother think? So much is riding on this.

Cam seemed adamant about marriage; his wife's death had not deterred him from the institution, but the way he guarded Summer's memory scared Luna. He might still love her, which would take away so much peace and joy from their relationship. And even though Luna knew Mia, she didn't know Cam's father.

Despite all her misgivings, Luna felt an ache of desire she never thought she'd feel; she wanted Cam close and to feel every inch of his sensual energy. When he'd kissed her in the kitchen, his scent had surrounded her, and he had held her so close. She couldn't keep him at arm's length with the emotions he sparked in her, but she was a virgin. She felt vulnerable and exposed; talking about her mother's history had been tough. Luna dropped the towel and stepped into the steaming shower.

I've never been so close to a man. Do I tell him I'm a virgin? How do I handle this?

Cam was in her bedroom catching up on some phone calls. He was preparing for the hunting trip, and he also wanted to check in with his Navy team. They were planning a training session on the water for which he would leave in four days' time. Cam would not be able to make calls when he and his comrades were in the Atlantic Ocean.

He returned to the kitchen to lay the table. He had spotted some chopped wood as they'd entered the boarding house, so he went outside and fetched some of it to start a fire in the fireplace in the lounge. He needed this night and to be alone with the person he loved. When he returned some of the unused wood to the pile outside, he looked up and saw steam escape from the last window at the corner of the building.

He stood watching for a moment; the woman he loved was in that steam, naked. His heart raced as his body tightened with desire. Joy leapt inside him; he needed to affirm his love for Luna and let Summer go. He had been so scared to move on that he had never touched anyone since. It had been years since Cam had succumbed to the pleasures of the flesh. Would he be able to make love to Luna? Was he ready for that level of intimacy? The kiss in the kitchen had fanned embers into roaring flames of desire.

Steam had filled the bathroom, creating a cosy atmosphere. Music filtered through the confined space through a portable radio. Luna's back was turned to the door and her silhouette framed in the fogginess of the shower. Cam watched her lather her skin, from her legs to her breasts. He breathed heavily as he took in the sensual scene and then dropped his clothes by the bathroom door. Yearning ran hot in his veins, inflaming him to a roaring inferno.

'Cameron!' Luna felt a tentative touch on her wet back. She tried to turn and face him, but he took the soap from her hand and rubbed it down her back.

'You missed a spot.' His voice was deep and gravelly. He moved closer to her as a different kind of heat coasted down her naked back.

Their bodies were so close that she could feel his hardness in the small of her back. Luna tried to retreat, but Cam just came closer.

'Wherever you go, I'll follow.'

'You said you were working.'

'I got bored without you. Besides, you are in here alone. Why would I let you be lonely?' Hot water cascaded over them as Cam lathered her body with soap.

'I was almost done,' Luna panicked. She wanted to cover her petite body, but Cam had seen all of her already. He looked at her and touched her without barriers of modesty.

'Now, you can wash me.'

'Let me get your things and you can use the shower.'

'I will use what you have right here; no need to run away.'

'Who said I was?'

'Your trembling voice, but your body wants something different.' Cam pulled her towards him and cupped her breasts, rubbing them gently. Luna couldn't move or breathe as various sensations buffeted her. No one had touched her like this before. She felt a heaviness in her stomach that travelled towards her thighs.

'Have you washed a man before?'

Luna froze.

Is this a trick question? Is he asking if I know what to do?

Luna shook her head slowly.

'Well, you need to face me to be able to wash me, my lady.' Cam gently turned her around. Luna trembled; he felt her vibrations. He took her tiny hand in his and guided her from his chest down to his abs. Luna's eyes tracked every movement.

'Keep your eyes on me,' he said. Luna washed him, focusing on the contours of his body; his muscles flexed as her hands glided over his skin. They had long abandoned the pretence of washing each other. Luna explored Cam and he reciprocated. The music in the background created a gentle ambience in the steamy room. Enraptured by each other, their bodies moved together; they swayed and undulated in ways only lovers could. Her ardour consumed him as she kissed him passionately. Cam lifted her up and sunk into her, taking a first taste of his soon-to-be fiancée. She gasped from a flash of discomfort but didn't hold back to receive him.

Thoughts ceased to exist as moans and grunts echoed in the stall. His love came into her like a wave. In small, indulgent strokes, he moved her towards him. Luna writhed in wonder and delight. Pride swelled in his chest at being the first to breach her inner defences. She was safe, and as she cried out in ecstasy, his heat and love poured into her.

Cam wrapped her in a towel from the shower and carried her to the lounge. He placed her beside the fire on a blanket and pillows arranged on the floor. He laid her down, nuzzled her neck and watched himself slip in and out of her body. On the perfect night, he had taken Luna as his wife in the most primal way that mattered.

Chapter 18

Diverse people unite

Cam woke early to prepare for their long drive. He quickly dashed to the farm to fetch his bakkie. Luna was still sleeping when he returned. A police van was parked at the end of the street as he pulled up to the boarding house, and the policemen were talking to Mr Fourie. Cam waved, drove on and parked behind the Tazz. He didn't bother to investigate what it was about; he had a woman to please.

'You finally rise.'

Luna was ambling down the stairs wearing just his T-shirt. The smell of toast had enticed her from the bed. Cam looked comfortable in a pair of jeans and a black T-shirt.

'What time is it?'

'It's almost ten. We'll leave after I've fed you.'

Luna stretched her arms, ironing out the kinks in her body. Her muscles screamed from the previous night's activities; thinking about it brought a warm flush to her cheeks. Cam approached her and kissed her.

'Morning, love,' he said, folding her into his arms.

'Morning. When did you make all this food? We're unlikely to finish it.' Luna sat down and Cam placed an empty plate before her.

'I saw the pictures of the nurses on the wall; I need one of them for my office.'

'Which one?'

'The one in the lounge.'

'It's such an old picture; I didn't have a recent one when I arrived here.'

'That's the one I want.' Cam smiled.

'I will search for a copy for you.'

'I woke up early and spent most of my morning watching you, but that made me want you. So, I guess the kitchen calmed me.' Luna grabbed the teapot. She was embarrassed by Cam's overt attention, although she had welcomed his every touch the previous night. He had handled her with great care.

'Love, the car outside is yours, right?' Cam grabbed the bread and passed her the fried eggs and cheese.

'Yes, that old thing has given up on me. First it was the battery, then there were oil problems. I am lucky I can walk to work.' Luna shook her head at the thought.

'I will check it out before I leave. Winter is fast approaching, and you will need the car. Once it starts raining, how will you get to work?'

'I will be fine; I doubt you know anything about cars anyway.'

Cam smiled at her. 'I grew up fixing tractors on the farm. Your car won't be any bother.'

'If you have time, then you can check it. Let's just hope we don't get eaten in the wild.'

'I will ensure that you're back for our wedding. I need to meet your mother as soon as possible.' Cam squeezed Luna's hand. After the glow of their passion the previous night, Luna had finally agreed that Cam could meet Julie.

'I will give her a call on the road. Wait! How are we getting there?'

'My bakkie is right outside. You need to eat and go pack for us. I will save our leftovers for the road. We have a long drive ahead of us. I want to take you hiking tomorrow morning. There is so much to see in those mountains.'

'Will we have time for all these activities? I am not fit enough for the mountains.'

'I will carry you on my back; I will never let you fall.' Cam smiled;

Luna loved his warm smile and the poetic lines he used to charm her. She felt connected to him.

'I must say, you have a unique way of making tea,' Luna said. 'It reminds me of how my mother used to make it. You bring out additional flavour in it.' She sipped the tea.

'We have a long history with rooibos tea; it's been in our family for centuries. Our farm and the Fletcher farm produced most of the country's tea. At some point, we had big plans to export; however, the Fletchers took over most of our markets. History tells us the Khoisan people were the indigenous tribe who used the leaves for various purposes; they are the rightful owners of the tea. History has wiped them out.'

Luna watched him speak; his words cut her somehow. There was a sadness in his eyes that she couldn't explain. She didn't know whether it came from what happened to his family or if there was more to this story.

Where would my family be now if things had been different decades ago? Would we still have our original family name? Am I sleeping with the grandchild of the enemy?

'Everyone speaks of the Fletchers as if they are dragons.' Luna wanted to change the subject for selfish reasons. While still basking in the emotions of the previous night, she didn't want to recall her mother's stories about their dark history.

'Yes, they have taken over the Cederberg area like maggots on fresh meat. History tells us that a European explorer discovered rooibos, but that's not true. Throughout the Western Cape, the Khoisan people have their roots deeply entrenched in growing tea. Evidence of that remains throughout the Cederberg region. We have found ourselves in the middle somehow. They say this tea has no earlier ethnobotanical records, yet we all know the truth. My family has fought hard to keep our land, but what my father has done over the years is horrific.'

Why is Cam speaking about the tea so much? Is he also feeling weird after last night? All this talk about the Khoisan people?

'I never fully understood where they got their information, apart from what my mother has told me,' Luna said, mystified.

'Many people have different perspectives on the plant and its methods of use. You can make many things from that plant. Mia rubs her wounds and washes her hair with it. The Coals own land to the right side of the mountains and there are several eroded valleys where sandstone has accumulated; the tea grows on that shallow land.'

'Mia mentioned that your father told her about those areas but says it's too far to walk to,' Luna said.

'My daughter loves the outdoors, and it scares me that she wanders off alone; so much can happen to her. Mia has done what she can planting tea, but what you see on the farm now is nothing compared to what we could do if we had the capital to revive the land.'

'Cam, you can save your farm if what you're telling me is true. There are likely fields of untouched tea plants growing wildly that belong to your family.'

'I haven't surveyed the land in years.'

'Cameron! We must go see for ourselves. We cannot allow the Fletchers to keep stealing from you! Your father must fight this.'

'The problem is that we don't have the manpower to harvest and process the plants. We have so many challenges, including broken farm equipment.'

'You've been saying you know nothing about farming, but you know the process.'

'The theory of it is not the same as the practical.' Cam looked defeated.

'I've studied it, Cam. My great-great-grandparents apparently had a tea farm or something like that. I have a book that might help with the value chain!'

Luna's eyes lit up when she remembered the weathered book her mother had given her. It had been passed down from one generation to the next. Luna had received it at twenty-one in an antique wooden box.

She ran up the stairs and pulled the box from under her bed, where she spotted the bottles of alcohol that Amora had hidden from her. Amora had not come home yet, and Luna assumed that she had gone out partying and was probably passed out in some strange man's bed.

'You said your family was into rooibos tea?' Cam asked her when she returned to the kitchen.

'Yes! My mother has the full story … well, history. She gave me this book,' Luna said, setting it on the table.

The book was old and dusty, with a leather cover that carried the same inscription and logo that were on the bottom of the antique wooden box. When Cam flipped through the pages, he saw that handwritten notes and diagrams were drawn similarly to rock art. Splashes of black, yellows and reds covered the pages. He could follow the illustrations, but the words were in a language he couldn't read. Dates went back to the 1800s. There seemed to be letters wedged between some pages and something resembling a family tree.

'This is like a tea encyclopaedia! But I can't read the words; some word formations look like the motto on our coat of arms. The diagrams are clear, though.' Cam stood up in excitement, as if he had discovered a rough diamond.

'My mother made it her thing to learn |Xam – the language the book is written in – and she can decipher the stories contained in the book. She can help us. I never gave the book much thought since I got it. I guess being in a place that grows a lot of tea triggered my memory.'

'You are a godsend, Luna!' Cam pecked her on the lips. 'Well, I guess we have much studying to do.'

'You had a teacher all along in Mia. We have spent hours talking about rooibos; she knows more than you think. Cameron, you need to learn to accept who your daughter is.'

'I have.'

'No, you pity her. You treat her like an egg, not a human with a life, ideas and wisdom. Mia has so much in that heart of hers; her brain works like a machine. You just refuse to treat her like a human.'

'I love my child,' Cam said softly. Regret and shame hammered his heart; he had missed so many things about his daughter.

'Then treat her like your equal. Don't treat her like she knows nothing. She learnt how to walk independently, cook without you, and care for the farm without you and John. As young as she is, she is not stupid.'

'I am sorry.' Cam bowed his head. Luna hugged him, rubbing his back affectionately.

'Just let her be herself and you will see her magic. We still have to eat this stunning breakfast that you made. Remember, you promised to feed me, beloved. Stop thinking so much. There's still time to restore what you think is lost.'

'I am always at work; I don't know how to do this.'

'We will make it work. You have a farmer fiancée now with a book that can help!'

Before they left, Luna left a note on the fridge to alert Mr Fourie and the other nurses of her travels.

Chapter 19

Songs of death

A mora hid in the petrol-station bathroom for most of the night. Bree and Lucy were out of town and Luna's phone was off. There was no hope of seeking help from her after the text message Amora had sent her. Amora was entirely alone. Tears rolled down her cheeks as she sat on the toilet floor. She felt trapped, as if the walls were closing in. Nowhere was safe any more. Her blooming social life, her friends and her beautiful city were distant memories. This small town was not what she needed. Luna had established her own life in Clanwilliam, but Amora had not found peace. Her life felt like a constant echo because she herself felt so hollow.

Throughout the day, Amora had been aware of Seth watching her. His stalking had not stopped; instead, he'd got more brazen. It didn't matter where she went. He was at the gun shop, then at the café and he parked his car near the church shortly after. She spotted him smoking and talking to some of the locals from the clinic windows as if he were just passing the time. Amora knew what she was heading towards; Seth's eyes called for blood. All her life, she'd run from herself and her truths, and now, this man reminded her of who she was – a coward and a social reject. Even the make-up, the big red hair and a personality that filled the room were not enough. She was dead inside.

Bree picked up the phone after a few rings.

'Bree, he is still here.'

'We told you, just talk to him; that man has a good reputation. He won't do anything stupid. Besides, you must go home.'

'How do I just leave and walk the streets alone? It's almost eleven and my phone is about to give in.'

'Well, that's a sign that you should go home. We are in Cape Town; there is no transport to get us there. We had to take the local bus to get here. You will be fine. Go and have a drink at the bar; there are probably people there. I don't think this is a big deal.'

'I am thinking of quitting my job. I hate it here. I just can't be here any more!'

'If you hate it so much, just go to your mother. Leave if you are unhappy; make sure you tell Eve. You are too young to be living like this. For goodness's sake, get out of that toilet and just go home!' Bree sounded irritated. 'You have been off lately; this man cannot be the only reason you want to leave such a good job. We have been good to you and Luna. Did you guys have a fight?'

'We are on and off. I also tried to call Luna, but I don't think she wants to talk to me. Bree, things are not what they seem. It wasn't an easy journey to get to this town; a lot happened when we were at our previous job.'

Amora shuddered as she thought about what had happened in Cape Town. She could still see the blood on her hands, the scissors, the man on the floor. Amora had felt cornered that day. The lewd comments about her body and request for sexual favours had pushed her over the edge. Could people not see past her physical attributes to the person within? The thought of old men by the docks who had called her names and pulled down her pants, when all she had wanted to do was to be left alone. The countless times she had gone for interviews and the only request she'd got was to bend over. Man after man, interview after interview. That was what the man in the white coat had asked of Luna.

Her memories kept taking her back to the clinic fridge and Luna's cold, stony face. Amora wouldn't have had the guts to do that by herself but having an accomplice had made it easier for her to embed the scissors in that man's jugular vein. She had aced her anatomy class, so she knew where to aim for maximum effect. Rage had overtaken her, and a man had wound up dead.

But now was not the time to talk about the dead man. Luna didn't know that the police had come to the clinic in Clanwilliam after she'd left on her trip. Eve had spoken to them while Amora hid in the clinic bathroom. It appeared that people were asking questions back in Cape Town; calls were being made and Amora was the only one who knew the truth.

'Weren't you guys transferred as you said?' Bree teased.

'Something like that.' Amora held her tongue, remembering Luna's words. What they had done had come back to eat them alive, and here she was on the floor, scurrying like a rat from a man who didn't want to let her be. All Amora wanted was to be by the sea, her feet sunk in the sand.

'You are not saying much; Luna is happy, and you are a boiling pot. It doesn't make sense,' Bree said. Amora was about to respond when the door opened, and the petrol attendant asked her to leave. She tried brushing him off, but he held the door open.

'Bree, I have to go.'

'Lucy is also waiting for me; we just left the cinema.'

Amora's screen went blank. All her hope was gone. If that creepy man was outside, she was doomed. She slowly stood up and wiped away her tears. She was still in her uniform, hungry and cold.

When she stepped out, she scanned the area but saw nothing suspicious. She considered going to the boarding house, but it was a thirty-minute walk. She couldn't risk it; she returned to the clinic and locked herself in for the night.

As sunlight filtered through the windows at the clinic, she thought of packing up and going back home. How would her mother receive her? She had tried to be a good girl for many years, but it felt like her mother only hugged her with demands. Her mother always made it hard because she loved others more than she loved Amora. She gave so much of herself to the community, her siblings and their children that there was nothing left for Amora. It seemed that her mother was as starved for affection from others as Amora was of hers.

It felt like a never-ending cycle of broken women seeking external validation and never from within. Amora carried an ID photo of her mother in her purse, and she looked at it now as she contemplated calling her. A shaft of longing for a mother's tenderness spread through her.

'Oh, mother what did I ever do?' Tears ran unchecked down Amora's cheeks. 'Will I ever be enough? Shall I slave away until I die for you to see me? I am holding on for dear life. Why have you abandoned me?'

The suffocating silence in the clinic failed to provide the answers Amora so desperately sought. A deep darkness lay within her. In truth, she was just tired of life; her mother always took from Amora with no gratitude or acknowledgement for her sacrifices. When Amora's father died, her and her mother's roles reversed, and Amora became a parent to her mother. What did she know about caring for an adult at sixteen? Why did she have to bear the burden of wiping the tears from her mother's cheeks? When her mother eventually managed to gather up her broken pieces, she poured her love and attention onto others. Never on Amora. All her mother cared about was her bank statement at the end of each month.

With a scarf covering her head, Amora walked from the clinic to the boarding house as fast as possible. Why couldn't she just be like everyone else her age? All her plans had gone awry. She had no strength any more. Worse, all she had was the stupid job she hated. Her chest felt like a mountain of granite.

'What have you done to your life?' Amora whispered as she rushed up the road. Time was not on her side. She had to get to the boarding house. She just wanted to sit down with Luna and tell her everything. Fighting back the tears, she held her purse close to her chest.

Amora walked as fast as her feet would carry her. Her eyes were focused on each step she took as it led her closer to the boarding house. No one paid her any attention – always unseen.

'Keep going; you are safe. Just a few more steps.' When Amora saw the gate, a sense of reprieve assailed her. 'I am home.'

Amora had never had a proper home. For her, home had always been a place with a roof that she could sleep under. How could she have a home when her mother had never shared hers with Amora but everyone else was considered royalty?

Disappointment weighed Amora down as she found Luna's note on the fridge. The house smelt of freshly baked bread and ashes were smouldering in the fireplace. People had been there and not cleaned up after themselves.

Amora placed her belongings in her bedroom and went to Luna's room. The small single bed was neatly made up and her pink travel bag was gone. For some reason, it tore at Amora's heart like a knife. Things were not supposed to be like this. This had been their room. Amora sat down on the narrow mattress and thought of the first few nights they had spent together: the laughter, the memories they shared of their old jobs and how they had got here. Things were supposed to be fun now; this should have been their new life together. Luna had decorated the room and placed pictures of her community work on the walls. The books she was still reading were on the bed with notes.

Luna had carved out a life without Amora, yet another person who didn't see her. Tears pricked Amora's eyes and sadness choked her. Didn't anyone want to be with her? All she had left was the honour of wearing her uniform, even though it meant nothing to her now. For months, her self-loathing had grown like wildfire. Despite all her education, life seemed to keep her pressed to the wall.

'What's a girl like me to do?' Amora stomped around the boarding house in just her underwear and a vest. She needed to feel free, complete and unjudged. She desperately wanted to capture any feeling of home that she could. She went to the lounge, put fresh wood in the fireplace and lit it, then opened a bottle of wine and watched TV.

'Miss Luna hates the truth, but I saved her from that animal three years ago.'

Amora drank the wine straight from the bottle and lay down on the worn-out settee. All her feelings felt broken; she had no control over her life. She didn't feel the democratic freedom that

Mandela and his comrades had fought for. All she felt was utter desolation. She wanted to crush every inch of reasoning she had. What was the point of it all?

There was her childhood, a life with a mother who had sought praise only from others while her child stood in the rain, waiting. A mother who didn't care about homework but demanded outstanding academic results from her daughter, a mother who only cherished her in front of friends but shut the door in her face when they got home. Amora hated how her mother made her feel, even in her absence. Now, it was Luna and Seth.

'Who is the real animal here? I am always the bad guy, the big girl; men just grab me, and I should be okay with it. Oh, and why should I always try so hard to be human? One thing about me is that I'm loyal to a fault, but where has that got me? I noticed Cam first, yet Luna takes him like a trophy. She struts on the streets as if she is the mayor of this forsaken town. When will I get my joy? My happy ending? All I have done for these people, and I am still the black sheep no one wants to touch? Things in the city were much better.'

Bottle after bottle she drank, like a newborn, until the sun called the moon. She passed out on the couch until she was rudely awakened by someone grabbing the bottle of wine from her hand.

'You shouldn't sleep like you own this place,' a rough male voice said as Amora struggled to find her bearings.

'What is wrong with you?' She rubbed her eyes, suddenly aware of the man towering over her.

'I just came to see how this old place looks; I haven't been here for a while. You seem so comfortable. You didn't look like this in the bar, but you are consistent with the bottle.' He kicked one empty bottle towards the fireplace. Amora quickly sat up, still wobbly from the countless litres of wine. Her head ached, but the mockery in the man's voice unsettled her.

'How did you get in?'

'You live here? I didn't know that.' Sarcasm dripped from his statement.

'Leave! What is wrong with you?' Her voice broke in terror. She was alone and underdressed with a man who had made the past month a living nightmare for her.

'The fireplace is nice; I built it. After all, this boarding house belongs to my father, so you must be a good guest.'

'This is a women-only boarding house; no males are allowed here. You need to leave.'

'It doesn't look like you have company; the rooms are all empty. I thought I could keep you company. It's freezing at night and a woman like you needs to be kept warm.'

'I don't want trouble, Seth.'

'It's no trouble at all; I have lots of time. Would you like to share a drink with me? You look deep in your cups, but I like that. I was hoping we could chat, talk about life and alcohol, and maybe you will see that I am not such a bad guy.'

'You are a monster of a human! You should have been arrested for what you did to me. Then you stalk me like an animal for weeks on end!'

Seth's demeanour changed as he approached her on the couch.

'Women don't belong in bars except for whores. Are you a whore? Now that I look closer, you can be anything in our town.' He knelt on the couch next to Amora. She wanted to stand but he pushed her back. 'I didn't even get your name. Do you have a name, Miss Whore?'

'Fuck off!'

'Don't be rude; I told you I am a nice guy.' He squeezed her mouth, pressing her lips together firmly. 'Do you know where you are?' His eyes were angry slits in his face. 'Let me teach you. This old place used to be a small prison for farm slaves. People just like you, who stole from us. Do you not wonder why it's built like this? All these empty rooms that you now call home. Does it feel like home to you? Maybe it does because its foundation was built on the bones of many of your ancestors. There are mass graves all over this yard.'

'I don't care what this place was; you have no right to be here.'

'That's where you are wrong, Miss Whore! I own this place and all that's in it. When will you see that?' Seth's sweaty hands rubbed

Amora's thighs; she tried pushing him away, but he gripped her tightly, embedding his jagged nails into her skin. She screamed, but it only seemed to inflame him further. His hands became a living collar around her neck, squeezing tightly. Amora's mind was consumed by the aura of death that surrounded Seth. He was a python constricting her thoughts and slithering into her safety without a preamble.

'You will hold your tongue when you speak to me! Do you hear me?' Amora tried nodding, but he didn't let go until he'd composed himself.

'Fine, you are begging. I like that. We are having a good historical conversation and here you are messing up this beautiful moment. You are an attractive girl, but you are being mean and unwelcoming. I thought nurses were good, kind and gentle people. Listen to me like you would a therapist. Are you not going to offer me some of that cheap stuff you were drinking?'

Seth shook his head and sighed. Amora stood up, hoping to find an escape route as she walked to the kitchen, but Seth was hot on her heels.

'What do you want from me?' she asked softly while searching for another bottle in the fridge.

'You embarrassed me! What were you thinking?'

'I did no such thing.' Amora knew it was best to remain calm. Seth was already agitated, and she didn't know what could push him over the edge.

'You are stubborn. Do you think your protector will come and rescue you again? The mighty John Coal?' Seth was crowding her in the kitchen, breathing into her face. Amora fought the urge to show her disgust as his stale beer breath wafted over her.

'You need to keep your hands off me!'

She handed him the wine bottle and walked off, trying to compose herself. She would not give him what he wanted. He was trying to get to her; she needed to survive his stares. Seth noted her arrogant gait. This woman didn't care for him; the way she looked at him made him feel like dirt on her shoes. His roving eye followed the shape of her thick thighs; her peach floral underwear brought out something dark inside him. He had urges that came in flashes of rage and disgust.

'Do you think you're sexy?' he asked scornfully as he followed her upstairs. Amora's skin crawled under his gaze, and she wanted to cover up, but her gown was in the laundry basket in the bathroom.

'What do you care what I think of myself?'

'You parade your body for all to see like you are selling something.'

Amora wanted to respond but Seth was getting closer to her. 'I asked you a damn question!'

Seth pulled at her foot as she tried to climb the stairs; Amora tumbled down like a sack of potatoes, the edges of the stairs cutting into her face. Pain exploded through her face and body. She panicked; fear clawed at her and rendered her mute. Whimpers filled the space as she tried to control her reaction.

'What is wrong with you?' Amora spat out the words.

'My grandfather liked women like you. Goodness, he even married one of you! My father tried to stop him but there is something about your kind. You come and destroy. We have killed many of you, but you're like ants – consuming everything everywhere with gluttonous intent.'

Amora remembered how her siblings had been burnt to death in Cape Town and left on the streets like trash. From what she was told, the police had killed them because they had been part of a school protest. That was years ago; she had been young and had lacked understanding. The man in front of her didn't care about her pleas.

'Your kind broke my family; made my grandfather a dog sniffing after brown thighs. Now you are here on our land and in our homes. Why did you come here? To this town? What were you hoping to get here?' Seth knelt on the floor next to Amora's crumpled form, hurting her as he held tightly onto her arms.

'I came to work! I just want to work!' Amora beseeched.

'Shut up!' A slap slashed across Amora's face before Seth stood up and kicked her multiple times in her stomach. Amora finally let out a deep, painful cry.

'Stop! Stop! Please, sir! Please!'

'Call me by my name! You retarded monkey.'

'What?' Amora was dazed; her body was doubled over in pain and her head was pounding. She felt blood trickling from her nose; it was an effort to breathe. Were her ribs broken?

'Seth Fourie! That's your master. Seth Fourie.'

Amora couldn't understand what she had done to deserve this, but she had to beg for her life.

'You said my father let you stay here? The same man who raped his sister! She was raped by her own flesh and blood, and I was the product of that violent act! Can you imagine what my mother must have gone through? My aunt is my mother and I found out accidentally because of a blood transfusion I needed when I was on a mission. My history is coloured in pain and violence; that's why my soul called out to yours. You and I are kindred spirits.'

Seth had a wild look on his face. If Amora didn't escape from his clutches, she could only imagine what would happen to her.

'I am sorry, I am deeply sorry!' She crawled on the floor as Seth relived the horror of his biological parents.

'Sorry that my mother is also my aunt or sorry that you are a whore? Why would you walk around naked? You wanted me to see your filthy body? Do you want to turn me into my grandfather? I will not succumb to your charms!'

Amora tried running to her room, but he took the wine bottle and smashed it on her head. Amora slammed into the wall and dropped to the ground. Blood from her head splashed on the walls like melting lava. She cried to the heavens as Seth came crashing into her with full force. Amora begged him but he straddled her and rained fists onto her face. Black flowers started blooming in her vision.

'You will listen to me! You will respect me! You will ask for forgiveness!' Seth grabbed her and stared into her face; her eyelids were swollen shut.

Multiple personalities lived inside Seth – he was both a child and a man. Yet he remained calm while he dragged Amora down to the lounge.

'My roommates will be back soon.' Amora's voice was hardly

audible as he dropped her onto the cold floor. She heard his pacing footsteps and deranged laughter.

'You're a liar! Your sweet nurse has left you, whisked away by *my* best friend! That snake has your friend in the palm of his hand, and here you are, begging for your life. I saw that little note she left; she is not returning soon,' Seth chortled like a crazy person. Amora was trapped; tears streamed down her cheeks. She could no longer bear the horror of the situation.

'Tell me, when you are not lying, what else do you do?' Seth was crouching like a lion waiting to pounce on its prey. Amora was slowly pulling herself up, dangerously close to the fireplace. Seth noticed, and it excited him. Amora's hair was matted with blood and her vest looked like something from a horror movie.

'Do what you want with me; you are going to hell anyway. I am happy that you know you were born out of sin. That explains your corrupt DNA! You have no place in this world! You're an abomination!' Amora said as she turned her face in his direction.

'There she is! You are a whore!'

'No! I am your fucking worst nightmare!' Rage bubbled within as Amora drew breath from her painful chest. She was tired of being weak; she was tired of being agreeable! She was tired of hiding, of shrinking herself so that she could fit into spaces that did not want her. She was tired of pleasing people. She was tired of never being seen. She was tired of *being*!

Seth studied her bloodied face, her clenched fists and defiant stance; he stood up straight and walked towards her.

'Do you think you are a man! Do you know what I am?'

Amora said nothing.

'Have you ever looked into the eyes of a dead soul?'

'Many times,' she gasped. Breathing felt like the slice of a thousand knives.

'Have you ever seen a dead body?'

'Countless times.'

'Have you killed before, my little whore?' With each question, he came closer to her; she couldn't move. Terror kept her frozen.

'Many times!' The words slipped out; she had killed.

'My father killed his sister, yet she still lives in a catatonic state with vacant eyes. And here I am today, facing the demon I have chased for many years.'

All Seth could see was his father's face, his mother's hate, his grandfather's betrayal of his first wife and his dead sister! His father's depraved tentacles had even spread to Seth's sister, whom he had violated until she couldn't face life any more. Edna had known about her husband's nefarious acts and chosen to protect him. So, Seth made her pay for her participation in her husband's depravity. Seth had hidden the suicide note he'd found in his sister's room to conceal his knowledge of their acts so he could act on the information at the right time. The blood running through his veins filled him with shame and disgust. Was it possible for a person to hate who they were as much as he did? His anger and thirst to kill were a result of the foul seed from which he'd germinated; it had driven him to kill innocent people on one of his missions and lose his job.

Amora tried to feel around for something to hit Seth with, but he was faster, bigger and stronger than her. It was as if he could read her mind. With a single punch, she was on the floor. He dragged her body to the open fireplace and shoved her face and torso into the fire. The searing heat of the flames touched him briefly before he pulled his hands away.

Flesh to coal. Bones to ashes. Her screams eventually subsided as her face melted in the fire. Death hovered in the air, present to collect its debt. Amora Grootboom was nothing more than her ancestor's history. Ashes to ashes. Dust to dust.

Chapter 20

To find love and a curse

The bakkie sped up the mountains towards the Coal farm. The weekend had flown by with the many activities they'd enjoyed, from hunting and camping in the Cederberg mountains to hiking the trails. Cameron held onto the wheel with great contentment. After many weeks of constant work and training, this was the weekend he had dreamt of – peace and quiet and Luna's company. Cam could sense Luna's happiness; her face was suffused with joy and love.

Luna had never experienced such a thrilling and breathtaking getaway. It was like being on a constant roller-coaster ride. Cam had planned a perfect weekend full of surprises. With each passing moment he had held her close and showed her a whole new world. It was like nothing she had ever known, and she saw a side of him that she desired to keep only to herself. Sitting in the passenger seat, Luna kept her eyes on the scenery. The mountains were a marvel; the dirt road to the farm was long and bumpy.

'I can't believe you have all of this and still cry poverty,' Luna said. It was a massive property sheltered by mountains and trees.

'It's something else, isn't it?'

'You have what many desire; look at the trees, the land and fields of vegetation. This is probably worth millions, and you are thinking of just giving it away because you don't have time for it.'

'We have spoken about this, love.' Cam slowed the car down.

'Wait, where does that fence lead to? The one across that bridge.' Luna pointed at a fence on the far left of them.

'That's the beginning of the Fletchers' farm.' Cam's voice sounded sombre.

'Do you ever go there?'

'We are not friends.'

'That's a pity. It seems to be the best land in this area.'

'We have equal land sizes; the difference is that we haven't invested as much as they have over the years.'

'I've heard strange stories about how they manage their farm.'

'Keep your ears closed when it comes to that family, Luna. People may tell stories but they have no idea what they are saying.'

'Seems like you have a sour taste in your mouth, Captain Coal.' Luna turned to look at him; his handsome face gave nothing away.

'Some things are better left unsaid.'

'What do you think Mia is doing?' Luna had missed the girl.

'Probably chasing her chickens or watering her little garden. She always finds something to do. That little farmer never falls short of entertainment.' Cam smiled at the thought that he was going to see his baby girl.

'I am so glad she is who she is. Her laughter fills you up like music fills the soul.'

'I am indeed blessed,' Cam said. He drove on. A rickety wagon with a family of four passed by them. Several horses grazed the fields, and in the distance, shepherds guarded their animals. This was nothing like the city, and Luna loved it.

'What about your father? Do you think he is at home?'

'I pray he is, for my child's sake.' Worry crept in; John was unreliable, and the thought of him passing out on the floor or in the stables made Cam anxious. He was bringing Luna home for the first time and prayed that John was in good health.

'Have you ever drag-raced before?' Cam suddenly called out, raising his voice above the sound of the wind. Dust was gathering on the car; Luna tried asking him to slow down, but Cam was thrilled by the speed.

'Where on earth do you get this wild side? Surely a captain cannot do this!' Luna laughed.

'A captain who has had an eventful childhood can.'

'You are not dragging me into that life-threatening mess. I am not going to live on the edge. Having you in a submarine is enough for my poor heart.'

'You must live a little! You are quite the coward for a person that surfs in unpredictable waters full of sharks.'

'Says a man that stayed up all night hoping not to get bitten by snakes.'

'Oh, is that what you were thinking? I wanted to make sure that we were safe. Hunting is dangerous. We were sleeping in a small tent; anything could have happened.'

'So that's your lame excuse for quivering all night. You should have seen yourself. What were you thinking? Couldn't we have slept at the lodge?'

'Where is the fun in that? At least you were there with me.'

'I had to take a sleeping pill to get rid of my anxiety.' Luna had never slept in the wilderness before, and her mind had conjured up all sorts of horrific permutations.

'I don't remember that.'

'What do you remember?' She enjoyed Cam's laidback side. He was mischievous and had teased her endlessly on their trip. His laughter made her glow like a firefly. Luna was so happy; her cheeks hurt from smiling so much.

'Well, it depends ...' He raised his eyebrows in challenge.

'Come out with it, Cameron.'

'You in my arms, on top of me. Even better is the cold river bath and our morning activity that raised our body temperatures again.'

'You have a wicked mind!'

'That's the pleasures of having a woman. Look ahead, we are almost home.'

'With all these bumps, I am going to dislodge my kidneys,' Luna laughed joyously. She was finally going to meet Cam's family, officially, as his fiancée. Cam had made it clear that he didn't want to date indefinitely, and the only way forward was to get married. Luna felt as if she carried the whole world in her heart. She grabbed her hat as they went over another bump.

'Look at that! It's stunning; I can't believe you have all this.' In the distance, she could see horses and cattle around the house, vast fields of greenery and smoke coming from the chimney.

'It's not much but it's your home now.' Cam's eyes took her in briefly. Luna's natural hair was combed backwards, and the yellow shirt brightened her light skin. Her jeans moulded her body perfectly. His body tightened in desire as he thought of their time together. He never knew that so much joy could be found by opening himself to love again.

As the farmhouse came into view, he squashed the guilt of never having thought of Summer once during his time with Luna. Her exclamations as he raced over the bumps in the road put a smile on his face. Luna was very risk averse. During the weekend, he had to coax her to do the more daring activities, but she refused to handle the gun or shoot with it.

Luna took advantage of the next few metres to reminisce about their getaway. Where they had been, the mountains hugged the land in ways only the eye could appreciate. They call hunting an extreme sport, but she had felt warm inside; everything had been perfect, from rushing into the bushes to relieve herself to watching Cam shooting game and cooking it.

Cam had regaled her about the history of the Khoisan people in the Cederberg area, and they could see and appreciate their ancient paintings on their hike. Luna felt as if she had finally found a place she could call home. It was what she had desired all her life. It was odd that a white man was teaching her about her blackness, though she, in turn, was teaching him about farming. Reading about the Khoisan history was one thing, but actually seeing their art was mind-blowing for Luna. Cam had gone all-out in driving to remote areas in the Cederberg just to show her who she was. No one had ever taken so much interest in her, except for her mother.

The bakkie came to a halt by the side of the farmstead. It was sunny, with no signs of rain or heavy winds. Cam stepped out and came round to open the door for Luna. Even before her feet could touch the ground, Mia came crashing into Cam. The sound of her laughter raided his heart.

'Wait, young lady! What about me?' Luna called out. Mia moved so fast between his arms that he feared she would crash into the car.

'Mia! Watch your steps. You can't run like that,' he called after her.

'I can feel her father; I know where she is.' Mia moved around the car, touching each side to see which door was open.

'I can hear her voice. Miss Parks, it's you right? Miss Parks, you are truly here! I am so happy. Thank you, Father. Thank you so much.' She hugged Luna's legs.

'Yes! How are you, pretty girl?' Luna pulled Mia up and hugged her, twirling with her in her arms. Cam couldn't have asked for a better welcome.

'You smell like ash and flowers, Miss Parks.' Her soft voice was full of excitement.

'And you smell like honey.' Mia's lips were smeared with honey. They shared a laugh and then Cam grabbed Mia and kissed her wildly.

'Father! Stop. Put me in Miss Parks' arms. Father!' Mia chortled hysterically.

'If you are so sweet, then I have no choice. It looks like you had your way with my honey.'

'No. No. No.' She shoved her face into his chest to conceal the evidence.

'I have missed you dearly, Peanut. Are you well?'

'Father, I have missed you, but I have missed Miss Parks more. I have something to show her.' She tried jerking out of Cam's arms, but he continued kissing her.

'Cam! You are sucking the life out of her.' Luna came running to join in on the fun.

John observed them from the kitchen window. Luna had built a wonderful relationship with Mia and had helped a great deal in caring for her. The sound of happiness tore at his heart. His home had not sounded like this in years. He watched the three of them and marvelled at his son. Cam's deep voice sounded like music to John's ears. All these years, Cam had never laughed like this. It was so perfect that John wiped moisture from his eyes. The grief they all carried evaporated momentarily.

'She will learn not to miss you more than me!' Cam made Mia laugh so much that tears ran from her eyes. Joy shone on Mia's face like Cam had never seen.

'You are as short as a little honey jar,' Cam said, holding on to Mia and embracing Luna. Life didn't seem as harsh when he had his two favourite girls in his arms, laughing.

'Mr Coal, it's good to see you again.' John had come outside. 'Finally, you've released my son to come back home. I'd heard he was around, but he comes home days after the rumours.'

'My apologies,' Luna blushed. Cam was still holding Mia in his arms. Luna was anxious but seeing Mia happy settled her.

John took a step back to get a better perspective. Luna was beautiful, graceful and warm. He had not anticipated that Cam would develop a romantic interest in the friendly nurse. Their relationship would set tongues wagging. There were few interracial relationships in the community.

Remorse covered John like a blanket when he thought about how he used to treat black people on the land they stood on. It had been the expectation back then; how else would he have kept his workers in line? If a master was lenient, they'd take advantage. Ghosts from his past hovered around him and threatened to rob him of his moment of lucidity. His fists clenched from resisting the urge to drive to town and drown them in alcohol.

'Shall we go inside?' Cam suggested. 'We've had a long trip. Luna needs to soak her feet and I want to see what Mia has been up to. I believe all has been well? Ryan had said that he would pass by. Did he do so?'

'Yes, you just missed him. He dropped off some medical supplies for Mia and me. I have been struggling with a dry cough, and Mia has bad headaches at night. He also gave us some produce from his land – fresh fruit and vegetables from the market. And you should see the fish he brought; you will enjoy cleaning it.' He winked at Luna.

'I will start on that,' Cam said. 'We also came back with some game. I will bring in the rest of our luggage.'

John led the way into the house, and Luna followed behind him. Each step he took was laboured, and he seemed to run out of breath. He was dressed in an old shirt and a pair of shorts.

Luna inhaled deeply; this was Cameron's family home. It looked clean and smelt of fresh coffee and biscuits. The Coal history was evident in the pictures and knickknacks scattered around the house. Seeing Cam so happy had made it all worthwhile. She had prayed silently for a day like this; her mother would be gratified.

'Well, my dear, you must be exhausted. That bakkie has certainly seen better days. Did you two encounter rain?'

'Cam drives like a madman,' Luna giggled. 'We were very lucky with the weather. This is a stunning farm, Mr Coal. Thank you for having me here.'

'My son is stubborn; he wouldn't have had it any other way. You must tell me about your trip; Cam never takes time off work. You must be a special lady. He just works like an animal and doesn't even have time for us.'

John ushered her into the lounge, passing the old-style kitchen. The home felt lived-in and comfortable.

For a moment, Luna stared at the pictures on the walls. A blonde, blue-eyed woman dominated most of them. Luna looked closer at a portrait and saw that it was Cam and his wife on their wedding day. There were other candid shots of family gatherings, including one with Mia in her mother's arms. Cam's late wife, the woman she had dreaded to see! It felt as if she was watching Luna from every wall on which her image hung. Cam looked so happy with her. The family seemed intimate and loving. An older-looking woman stood by Cam's wife's side.

Luna's throat closed up from trying to keep her emotions in check; this was a rude awakening. Cam had kept his wife's pictures all over the house. Her beauty screamed back at Luna. Each picture held

Luna's mind hostage. She had wondered what it would be like to see Cam's wife. Apart from the blonde hair, Mia looked just like her mother. The pain in Luna's chest felt as if someone had just smashed her with a rock.

What does Cam's bedroom look like? Is she also in the place where he sleeps – the woman he returns to when he's home? Are her clothes still in the room?

Luna felt like fleeing, but her feet were rooted to the spot. John stopped talking when he noticed Luna's distress. He didn't know what to say to her. When he looked at Luna, he saw that her eyes had become a flowing river.

'Is this Mrs Coal?' Luna asked in sorrow.

'Yes. Cameron's wife, Summer.' The words were followed by a long pause and a slow nod.

Luna's joy disintegrated as reality came crashing into her bubble.

He keeps her alive in his memories and heart. How will I ever fill her shoes?

At that moment, Cam walked in. The look on Luna's face said it all: he had messed up. He hadn't thought about the pictures in the house. All these years, Summer had been the memories that he didn't want to face or let go of. He had been so deep in the clutches of grief that he never had the guts to take down the pictures. Summer was part of this house; she was Mia's mother. How could he just erase her memory? Yet, the pain in Luna's eyes left him in tatters.

Luna looked at Mia, who was oblivious to the charged moment. She was still smiling and chatting away. Cam couldn't speak. All the adults in the room were battling with their emotions.

'Miss Parks! Miss Parks, I know you are there!' Mia spoke as if she were playing hide-and-seek. Luna did not respond, as she was trying to keep her tears at bay. But one betrayed her and slid down her cheek, breaking her rein on her emotions. Cam's eyes misted in grief as he looked on helplessly.

Chapter 21

If my love hurts you, let me bleed instead

'We can fix this; I am sure we can.' John placed his arm around Luna's shoulders.

'Father, is Miss Parks okay?' Mia chimed in with concern. 'Why is Miss Parks so quiet? Did I say something wrong?'

Cam couldn't get over Luna's disappointment. She looked at him in sorrow and complete devastation. Mia pulled her hand away from him; he tried pulling her back, but she got loose and moved towards Luna. Mia felt her way around the furniture until she found Luna.

'Miss Parks, give me your face,' Mia demanded. Luna quickly wiped away the tears. Mia's small, soft hands touched Luna's wet cheeks. They were all watching Mia as she cupped Luna's face in her hands. The quivering in Luna's heated flesh alarmed Mia.

'You are wet; is it tears?' Mia continued to touch Luna's face and traced Luna's thick lips and broad nose. Mia could picture Luna based on how she felt underneath her hands. She knew she probably looked different to Mia and her father because their lips were thinner and their noses more pointed.

'I am just so happy to see you, that's all.' Luna refocused her attention on the little girl. Mia was almost Luna's height; she was a tall girl. But Mia knew something was wrong; it was apparent in Luna's breathing, the tremor in her hands and the shakiness in her voice.

Cam took Mia's arm and led her to her room.

'Just stay here for a minute, Peanut. I will be right back.' He was scared that Luna would run away, and he didn't have time to negotiate with a twelve-year-old.

'Father! Please. Don't take Miss Parks away! Why is she crying? Miss Parks, please don't leave. I love you, Miss Parks,' she protested in tears. Cam tried calming her down, but she kicked and screamed. He had to close her door and lock it. That act alone slit his gut terribly. The rage and fear in his daughter's voice were all his fault. He had not intended to cause so much hurt. How on earth did he not think of this?

Mia's screams almost sent shockwaves through the house; Luna couldn't bear hearing her plead like that. Mia loved her sincerely – she had never before told anyone she loved them. Cam stood by Mia's closed door and just looked at John, begging his father to rescue him.

'I think we should all just breathe and take a moment,' John said. Cam tried stepping towards Luna, but she took two steps back.

'I am sorry, Luna.' He bowed his head.

'Cameron, take all the photographs down. I will take Miss Parks out for a walk. Take them all down now!' John gave Cam a cold eye and guided Luna towards the door. She could still hear Mia's sobs.

'What about Mia?'

'Let her father handle it.'

John took Luna's hand, and they walked off. Despite the tense situation, he was happy that his son had asked him for help. John's chest puffed with pride at being able to be useful again. As they approached the barn, John slowed their steps until they stopped. He looked at Luna with concern.

'Are you all right? I know it's a bit much to take in now because it's not what you expected. Summer was his wife, and we can't take that away or erase it. However, I know my son, and he would never bring you here if he wasn't sure about his feelings for you. Cameron has not brought a single lady home since Summer's passing. Today is meant to be a joyous occasion worthy of celebration. His wife died a catastrophic death, and he has never dealt with it.'

Luna stared blankly at him.

'Let me put it this way ... Summer was his childhood sweetheart. They grew up together right here on this farm. She was orphaned.

Her family was brutally killed; many say it was the Fletchers. Cam took care of her for years until they got married. He was all that she had. The night she died, she had just come from town with two-year-old Mia. My wife was in the fields when the fire broke out.' John gently guided Luna towards a small bench.

'The Fletchers?'

'Yes. I will never forget that night. We tried to save the animals, not realising that Summer had been trapped in the fields. She had little Mia on her back but there was a lot of commotion and a stampede. Summer tried to save my wife, but the fire had taken over the fields. People couldn't see where they were going, and many people died. Cam found Mia wandering in the smoke. He saved Mia and was forced to watch the rest burn to ash.'

John hesitated after his last sentence.

'He didn't save his wife and yours?' Luna looked John dead in the eye.

'He had no time. It was too late. A tree had fallen on Summer, and no one is sure what happened after that.'

'Is that how Mia lost her eyesight?'

'Yes, she could have burnt to death if Cam hadn't found her. He saved her but the heavy smoke had caused severe irritation and damaged her corneas. It affected her greatly because she was only a toddler. But the guilt of not saving his wife has become Cam's silent death.'

John composed his face.

'I didn't know.' Luna felt bewildered at the information John had volunteered.

'Cam's a good man. He just needs to accept his losses; that takes time. He hasn't spent much time at home in a long while. He comes every three months or so just for a day or two. From what I can tell, you bring him so much joy. I have noticed the slight changes in him in these last months. And for that, I should thank you. It also relates to Mia. That child was losing her life, and now that you got her back into school, things have changed for all of us.'

Luna saw the pain in John's eyes; he was a haunted man, only seeking to aid his son. It seemed that Cam's father struggled with more than his son's loss and grief. She saw from his body language that there was something else he wasn't saying. Luna wanted to ask him where he had been during the fire, but the words just couldn't leave her mouth.

Maybe that's why he turns to alcohol for comfort.

'I wish he had told me this himself,' Luna murmured.

'He doesn't talk to anyone; that is his burden. Let him carry it; in time, he will share. I shouldn't even be telling you this but please try to understand. We have much rebuilding to do; we have lost so much.' John rubbed the back of his head. Remembering how he had lost his wife in that fire made him sick all over again.

They started walking again as John showed her around the farm; much needed to be said between Luna and Cam. She worried about Mia, but she still couldn't bear to face Cam. Luna tried to change the topic of conversation. 'Tell me more about the purpose of the farm now.'

'Well, we do a bit of everything but don't have much to produce. This is a tea farm, rooibos, to be specific. In our good years, we supplied many homes. The tea that all families cherish is rooibos tea. Every household has a story about it; it was designed to heal and unite families. Over the years, we lost focus and tried to go into cattle farming. My son's lost interest because of Summer's death.'

Luna noticed that John avoided saying his wife's name. Cam also never mentioned it.

'Why don't you go back to farming rooibos? Everyone loves it; my mother never went a day without it, and my grandmother was the same. I grew up with rooibos tea.'

'The wild rooibos crop grows in the fields high up in Cederberg, but farming occurs on flatter land and especially in the valleys because of the soil texture. The bushy branches must be cut using sickles. It's a long process and requires the assistance of people who know and understand the process. The bundles are transported here for cutting and processing, and drying also takes time. The tea is harvested in the summer to early autumn.'

'I have read up on rooibos farming for a while, but I have never seen the harvesting process.'

'It's fascinating.'

Luna smiled uneasily. Her mind flashed back to the Fletchers; something didn't sit well with her each time someone mentioned them.

'I would imagine it will take years to restore this farm.'

'Not at all. We just need one good harvest, and we will be back in business. I have tried, but I need my sons to help me. Sole hasn't wanted to come back home, and Cameron loves the Navy. I am getting old; I don't have the strength any more.'

'Why don't you just hire people?'

'You can't just trust anyone; besides, everyone with skills works for the Fletchers now. It would be a nightmare trying to get them back.'

The farm was peaceful; Luna digested her surroundings as John continued talking. At some point, she just zoned out. From time to time, she nodded to show that she was still listening. John couldn't see how deeply saddened she was.

Cam observed them from his bedroom window. Seeing his father walk the land with Luna gave him some relief. The pain of removing Summer's memories was like revisiting her death all over again. He had moved everything so fast that he still couldn't process the pain he was in. All he cared about now was getting back to Luna. He went into Mia's room to find her praying on the floor. She begged God that Miss Parks should never leave her and her father. Cam stood by and waited for her to conclude.

'Father.'

'Peanut.'

'Is she gone?' Mia's red cheeks were damp with tears.

'She is not leaving us, Peanut. You shouldn't bother God with such prayers.' He stepped inside and sat down on the floor with her.

'Well, you said He listens to us.'

'That's right.'

'Then why would Miss Parks cry? Who hurt her?'

'She is not feeling well but she is not leaving us.'

'Why did my mother leave us?' The question hit Cam in places where no sound could be measured.

'She passed on; I told you that.' Cam ran his fingers through her hair and remembered he had promised her a month ago to trim it. Another broken promise.

'That's all you ever say.' She folded her hands.

'Can we talk about this a little later? Miss Parks would happily share a cup of tea with you.'

'Yes, Father.' Cam helped Mia up and washed her face. As he waited for Luna and John to return, his phone rang.

'Ryan, thank you—'

'Captain, we need your expertise down at the boarding house. You have an eye for a crime scene.' Ryan's panicked voice cut him off.

'I am not a police officer, Ryan.'

'The cops are here but this is about your partner.'

'Luna?' He rushed to check where John and Luna were and spotted them by the stables.

'Captain, her housemate was burnt to death. You need to bring her down here now.'

'Dead? What? When?'

'Well, your partner is registered as the deceased's next of kin. No other family is noted in her records. We need her here right away.'

The news felt like a poorly written movie script. Cam couldn't imagine the pain that Luna was about to experience. This was not how their weekend was supposed to end. How could he return to work and leave her with this mess?

'I will drive her into town. Keep me posted. See you in a few minutes.'

'Prepare her; it's a horrific scene.'

'Shit!' Cam sighed as he put the phone into his back pocket. He shook his head and called Mia.

'Peanut, I need you to stay here until I come back. Don't leave the house.'

'You just said we're going to have tea with Miss Parks.' Her tiny voice sounded like a desperate plea.

'I know, but I will bring her back.'

He stormed off, not wanting to see the agony in Mia's eyes as another broken promise fell from his lips. He ran across the yard.

'Cameron!' John called out.

'I need Luna,' Cam said.

'Is Mia okay?'

'Yes. We need to go to the boarding house,' Cam said as he approached them.

'Well, catch your breath and tell us what's happening,' John demanded.

'It's your housemate, Luna. We must go!'

'What happened?' Luna asked in a panic.

'Just come with me! Father, please give Mia a bath. I will be back as soon as I can.'

'Luna, let's go to the car,' he commanded.

'You have to tell me what's happening.'

'Just go to the car, Luna!'

With those words, Luna said no more. Something was terribly wrong; she had never seen Cam look so stricken. His face was pale from shock and fear of what was to come. It was like a tornado had hit him. He couldn't breathe but was trying to keep his composure. He would not tell Luna at the farm, as he couldn't risk Mia hearing her cry again. Not for the first time, the angel of death had come to visit and hurt those whom Cam loved.

Chapter 22

Brother, you owe me!

The bakkie raced towards the boarding house; neither Cam nor Luna could put their feelings into words. Mia's cries still rang in Luna's head and now Amora …. It felt as if she had been hit in the gut and was struggling for air. Her face was splashed in sorrow. Cam held Luna's hand gently and drove with the other.

'There are so many cars here. I will have to park down the road. Are you okay, love? Okay, that doesn't deserve an answer, I am not thinking straight.' Cam sighed.

The community had heard of the murder, and everyone had flocked to the street in the hope of seeing something. It was hard to find parking with all the police cars lined up. It boggled Cam's mind that so much in his life was linked to fires. He had met Luna during a fire and now she had lost her colleague in the same modus. His wife and mother had been consumed by a veld fire, which had also robbed his daughter of her eyesight. His losses came in a blaze of fire and there was no explanation for this. It was as if they were cursed. Cam thought about the pain of losing his mother and wife, but he couldn't imagine what Luna was going through.

'You know you can talk to me. I know how you may be feeling. You don't have to go through this alone. You must have been close to Amora; you lived with her.'

Luna knew Cam had good intentions, but what did she know about Amora? She hadn't been that interested in her life. Most of the time, Luna just wanted to be away from her. Amora was too loud, flashy and overtly flirtatious.

Was all this Amora's fault? Did her big mouth rub someone up the wrong way?

'She tried texting me a couple of times, Cam. I didn't respond. I just thought she was being needy and maybe also overworked. I didn't see this coming. I was still working with her two days ago. She called me so many times and I just didn't have the strength to talk to her.' Luna stared at her phone and reread the messages Amora had sent her. She couldn't reveal the content of the texts to anyone without exposing her closely kept secrets.

'Do you know why she texted you?' Cam's hands were clenching the steering wheel tightly.

From the number of people outside, he knew that whatever was waiting for them inside would be hard on Luna. He tried not to think about the boxes he had started packing at home to store Summer's belongings in so that Mia could decide what to do with them once she was older. He had managed to pack away all Summer's photographs and shoes. He needed time to do the rest, but it wasn't on his side.

Luna glanced at Cam, but she could see his mind was elsewhere.

'Do you know Amora's family?' he eventually asked.

'Not in person. I can find her mother's number … I thought this town was safe; I really don't understand.' Luna knew that she shouldn't say much more at this point. She had to keep her distance from Amora's life.

'This is South Africa, after all,' Cam said. 'Killers are always closer than we think. But let's go inside and hear what Ryan has found.'

Guilt engulfed Luna at Cam's words but she quickly composed her expression and nodded.

'We must speak to the police and see if they have found some clues,' Cam said. 'It's a small town; someone must have seen something. People talk and drunks are everywhere. Someone will slip up.'

It's a bad idea to talk to the cops. I should've stayed at the farm and processed the loss. The men could've handled this.

'Do you really think she was killed? This is our home; other nurses also live here. What will happen to them? This is all we have. We don't have families here.'

Luna's tears started falling again. Whoever had killed Amora must be still be lurking in the vicinity.

Seth's timing was impeccable. His truck came racing towards Cam's. The bystanders had to run for safety and were blaspheming and screaming.

'What on earth is he doing here?' Cam said irritably.

'He is speeding; he shouldn't be driving so fast!' Luna wanted to slide down in her seat, but Cam held her hand.

'It's Seth Fourie!' he said. Cam quickly pulled into a vacant spot on the side of the road.

Seth parked in front of them, not caring to switch off his engine, and strode towards Ryan, who was standing outside the boarding house. Seth looked neat enough, but Luna noticed that he was wearing long black leather gloves and that his face seemed flushed. He spoke briefly to Ryan, then jumped back into his car and left without greeting Luna and Cam. Cam gave Seth a look of death; Luna wondered what was going on between them.

'This is bizarre. Maybe Seth saw what had happened. Or is he helping the police? What did Ryan say when he called you?' Luna asked.

'Ryan didn't say much on the phone, but from what I gathered, it's bad. If you want to stay in the car, I'll understand. However, now that this place is a crime scene, I don't think you can stay here. We must find a way to get your things. The place is infested with people; you won't be able to do anything until the crime scene is cleared.'

Luna hadn't thought that far; this was all too much. Where was she going to find a place to stay on such short notice? She couldn't afford to move again. However, if it was true that Amora had been murdered, she, too, could be in trouble.

Is our secret out? What if the police have evidence that Amora killed the doctor in the white coat? And what about Dr Mark? I can't afford to take any risks. Was this a revenge killing by the doctor's family?

Luna tried to quiet her thoughts; entering a room full of policemen was dangerous. There were too many prying eyes. She had to be inconspicuous so that no one paid attention to her. The last thing she needed was people asking her questions. Luna looked at Cam.

Could this be the end of our relationship?

If he ever found out the truth, Cam would likely convince her to turn herself in or report her to the police. The tears that ran down Luna's face were not because of her deep love for Amora; they were induced by panic and shame. Amora had killed the doctor in the white coat to protect her, and Luna had killed Dr Mark to protect their jobs and freedom, and now Amora was dead.

'I am deeply sorry, love,' Cam said. 'I didn't know Amora, but all these people are touched by her death.' He looked at the distraught women and children standing around outside the window.

'I shouldn't have gone away for the weekend, Cam. I should have answered the phone or something.'

'You can't blame yourself; you have a life, and you don't even know what happened. Who knows what she could have been involved in. People get killed for many reasons and we don't know what led to this.'

'Amora was a good person.'

'We all are, love. But death is a frequent guest in our lives.'

'I guess.'

'Think about what I said. We need to get your things out of your room so that people can do their job.'

'Where will I go?'

'You have a husband and a farm. That's also your home.' The thought of going back to Cam's house made Luna anxious. The look on his face also saddened her. He was still grieving for his wife and yet he loved her.

What will I walk into next at the farm?

'For how long?'

'You are not safe here and I don't see you returning to this place.'

'I can't just move in—' Luna wanted to explain, but Ryan was now waiting outside their truck, talking to three police officers. Cam quickly got out and approached him.

'Captain, we have a bad one,' Ryan said. 'This has never happened here before; it is pitiless.'

'Who discovered her body?' Cam asked.

'Mr Fourie found her. He was here to check on the maintenance issues the girls had notified him about.'

Luna remained in the car, unable to imagine what she was about to find.

'Come on, Ryan! Let's get on with it,' Cam said, as he opened Luna's door and helped her out.

'Well, it seems that the victim was severely beaten; she has multiple bruises all over her body, broken ribs, the works. But what killed her will shock you.' Ryan glanced at Luna and then at Cam as if he were asking for permission to continue.

'I am a nurse; I can handle myself,' Luna said. 'I have seen many things, Ryan. Tell me what happened to my friend.'

Ryan admired Luna's strength, but what he had seen had shocked him, even though he was a doctor.

'Her entire head was put in the fire. The person who did this had shoved her head into the fireplace and left her naked body there. The police don't know who did it yet, as some of the evidence had been cleaned up, probably by the murderer.'

'Can we go in?'

'I would have to take you in; the forensic team is still gathering evidence and taking pictures.'

It was hard making their way through the crowds of people, but Cam took the lead. He saw an old friend, Steven Miller, who was now the captain at the local police station. They had a brief conversation and Steven led them into the building. It was a charnel house; the blood-stained trail they followed told the horrific story of Amora's last moments.

'Mind your steps; the blood is still the main clue we have to find out what had happened here,' Steven said.

Amora's body lay turned upwards on the floor. Luna covered her mouth, but her screams erupted like a tidal wave. Cam quickly held her and turned her away.

'I am sorry for your loss,' he whispered to her as he glanced at the body over Luna's shoulder.

'Whoever did this is deranged, an animal that we need to find as soon as possible,' Steven said.

'He cut her legs with that broken wine bottle?' Cam was horrified as he surveyed the scene before him. How could anyone be this cruel?

'Yes, but she was also stabbed in the back with a butcher's knife. The killer wanted to destroy every inch of her body. This was very personal.' As Steven spoke, Ryan approached Amora's body and looked at it closely.

'Her face is almost gone. This person wanted her face to burn away,' Ryan said as he shook his head in revulsion and disbelief.

Luna cried so hard that her entire body went into shock; this was too cruel and evil. She shook in Cam's arms, and he felt the quake in her soul.

Seth, like a deranged animal, had returned to find them in a total state of grief. They hadn't even noticed him standing among them! He was staring right into Cam's back.

'Seth!' Cam almost pushed Luna away. Ryan came over and helped her to the couch. Cam was infuriated.

'Captain.' Seth smiled as if he was greeting his best friend.

'Are you a police officer now?' Cam went to stand toe to toe with him.

'Great marines will always be cops somehow.'

'This is not the place, Seth.'

'Captain, we are all here to serve. Isn't that what we do, Cameron Coal?'

'You're not in the Navy any more,' Cam pushed back.

'That's right. I am just a civilian like all those people outside, is that it? What am I supposed to do now? Clean the streets? Wash horses and fix cars? All these years I have served, and you want me gone? I need my job back, and you will give it to me! Wait, let me calm down, brother. We can fix all of this. Let me help you here,' Seth begged of Cam.

'The police will handle this.' Cam shook his head; he had now seen for himself that Seth was insane.

'Then we can all leave. Let's all go have a drink,' Seth said and gestured towards the door. Cam looked at Seth, surprised by his cockiness. Ryan was observing them as he stood next to Luna. He wanted to stop the two men, but he knew that things had gone too far. Ryan had seen Cam clench his fists.

'Don't do this here,' he said. 'Gentleman, we have a crime scene to process, and anything else can wait.'

'I knew my brothers would be here,' Seth said. 'These nurses pull a crowd; they are always around when tragedy calls. Isn't that funny?' He winked at Luna. She turned her face away, but seeing Amora's body nauseated her.

'Ryan, please take my wife upstairs and help her pack.' Cam kept his eyes on Seth. His anger towards him was mounting.

'Wow! Wife! You move fast; this is not like you, Captain,' Seth exclaimed. 'Well, I have missed a lot. I thought that with your newly found power you wouldn't need a wife. Did you tell her that you let your wife die? Does your new wife know that your little family once enslaved her kind? What chance does she have? What will you offer a slave, Cameron?'

'Seth, you need to leave,' Ryan said as panic filled him. He was still standing beside Luna, who couldn't believe what she was hearing.

'Ryan, take my wife out of here. I can handle this.' He stepped closer to Seth, breathing into his face and biting his lip in fury.

'Am I something to be handled?' Seth asked. 'We are brothers. Can't brothers share secrets? Or is she so pure that you thought you found gold? You must tell me this little marriage is a joke. Better yet, invite me when you marry someone worth your time.'

'Your services won't be needed here, Seth,' Cam said. He tried to hold back but his body moved in ways that made Ryan nervous.

'Well, I can see you have your hands full. Let me not keep you from your *wife*. Does she have a name?' Seth chuckled. His eyes swept over Luna and came to rest on Amora. His work was exemplary and ruthless. Seth looked at Amora's body as if it were a glass of fine wine. Cam was observing him closely – he looked smug, as if he had accomplished something great. Cam knew the look well, as it was the same one that would be on Seth's face whenever they completed a successful mission.

'You will keep away from my wife, do you hear me!'

'She is striking. Something from the bush. What do they call them again? Oh, yes, Bushmen! You have always liked them, so exotic and helpless. From orphans to black girls, Cameron! You have strange taste. You've never liked fresh meat; who eats leftovers?'

A single punch from Cam dropped Seth to the floor. Steven and Ryan tried holding Cam back, but he was relentless. He went for Seth countless times, but Seth just laughed through it all.

'Cam! Cam, stop!' Luna called out, and as if under a spell, he heard her voice and stepped away.

'You sick dog! You owe me, Cameron Coal!' Seth raged.

Cam couldn't look at Luna; he was boiling with anger. Years of grief, anger and heartbreak had finally come to the surface. He was not a man who ever lost his cool and this killed him.

'What do you need from your room?' Cam had his back to Luna and was breathing heavily.

'Everything, I guess.'

'Go to the car and stay there.' Luna didn't dare disobey him.

Chapter 23

The pain in our scars

When they got back to the farm that afternoon, Cam was seething for various reasons. Being a father was demanding enough but loving again was proving to be another major challenge. There were no words to express his agony. Luna kept quiet, too. Both were fighting an inner combat that brooked no expression.

Cam never thought he would have a physical altercation with Seth, especially in front of Luna. Seth had been like a brother to him, but Cam no longer recognised who he had become. Seth was out of control, but he was equally broken. The hateful vitriol Seth's lips had spewed at Luna had sealed his fate. When his first punch had connected with Seth's jaw, Cam knew that their decades-long friendship was over.

When Luna and Cam arrived at the farmstead, they both dreaded entering the house. Cam still wanted to apologise to Luna about the photographs, but he didn't want to steer her in the wrong direction again. She needed him to say something, but silence stretched between them.

John came out to see what was taking them so long. The bakkie was parked outside but he had waited for them to come inside.

'You are back. People are talking; the house phone hasn't stopped ringing,' he said through the car window.

'Just give us a moment, Father.' Cam rubbed his face.

'I understand. I've prepared lunch, and Mia is waiting. I don't think staying in the car will help. Is Luna okay? I have made fresh tea. Come inside.'

Cam glanced at Luna and back at John and sighed. Luna was crying; she couldn't go back to the boarding house. Life as she knew it was over. Although she and Amora had not been particularly close, Amora had been another person Luna could count on in the town. The image of a once-vivacious girl lying on the lounge floor, dead, would not leave her mind. Guilt settled on her and would not give her a moment's peace.

I'm so sorry, Amora. I should've been a better friend to you. I should not have brought you to this forsaken town; you were never happy here and I ignored you.

'Step out, I need to speak to you,' John said, and Cam exited the car. They both moved a bit further away from the bakkie.

'I have cleared Summer's belongings from your room and moved them into the Wendy house for safekeeping. I know it's hard, but you can't let Luna see your grief; you have to move on. I changed your sheets too. I hope you don't mind. I think Luna will appreciate it.' John spoke in hushed tones.

Cam appreciated what his father was saying. He looked back at Luna. He had been a fool, carrying Summer's death like a trophy all these years. Was Luna supposed to live in a house full of memories of his dead wife?

Cam thought of Amora's dead body; he would not put Luna through that pain again. The farm would be her home now, and he had to accept the changes that that would entail. Even if it meant stashing away Summer's things. It was time to let go. He had to be a changed man, a father, a son and a husband. John was trying to stay sober, and Cam took note of his battle. The old man was covered in dust, his hands shaking uncontrollably. He had been working since Cam and Luna left and was doing his best.

'Father, thank you. We will get through this.' Cam reached out and steadied his father's hands. A few words, but John knew what he was trying to say. The rift between them grew smaller.

'Son, we all have our flaws. You have a daughter that's shattered in there and a fiancée in there.' He glanced at the bakkie. 'You have to care for them now.' His face stiffened.

'What about you?' Cam asked.

'I am right here when you need me, but I have to return the farm to its former glory. Chatting to Luna earlier in the day sparked an inexplicable possibility inside me. I will meet with a few people in town in the next few days and see what I can do to restore this place.'

'Thank you.' Cam's voice broke. He had prayed that the veil around his father would lift, and his words gave him hope. Cam had to find it in his heart to trust him again and give him a chance.

'Bring your woman inside and let's have lunch as a family.'

Cam embraced John and did as he was requested. They sat down to lunch together and the brightest light in the room was Mia. She sang and danced around them, her joy pushing out all the darkness.

Luna directed all her focus on Mia. There was still a lot of tension between her and Cam. He spent the late afternoon fixing the windows and making space in his bedroom for her. He moved things around and then went to repair the coal stove. John focused on the taps and patched the outside water tank. By nightfall, they were all exhausted but could not sit idle.

Ryan came over for dinner and filled them in on Amora's case. They had got hold of Amora's mother, who had asked them to just cremate her daughter and send her the ashes.

'This woman was not bothered. She asked me to send her pictures by e-mail so that she could identify the body. Without a second thought, she sent the police her identification documents, and that was it. She didn't even care to ask who had murdered her daughter. She just asked how much her insurance payout would be.'

Ryan couldn't believe how cold Amora's mother had been.

'You are not serious!' John said.

'I have never before had such a response from a mother. She just didn't care. She said she wouldn't waste her time on a deceitful girl. Apparently, she wasn't even aware that Amora lived here. I don't know why, but she was very cold.'

'So, Amora won't have a funeral and a grave?' Luna asked.

'I guess not. Amora's mom said once we are done gathering evidence, we can cremate the body because it has no value anyway. She said we might as well continue burning the body because it was already burnt.'

'Mr Fourie said he would find someone to send her Amora's belongings,' Ryan continued. 'When I leave in two days' time, I will take her ashes with me. The mother is in Cape Town for a few days.'

'So soon?' Luna was shocked.

'We don't have any reason to keep her body. She is gone.'

Cam had withdrawn from the conversation. He was quiet and didn't eat much. No one wanted to talk about Seth, but they all wanted to talk about something. Ryan spoke about Cam's wild childhood on the farm. John had his own stories, but Cam wasn't moved. There was a sadness in his eyes that broke all of them. An anger that had turned him pale yet non-reactive. He was numb.

Once Ryan left, Luna went to read to Mia and John cleared the kitchen. Cam went outside to feed the horses. When Luna was finished, Cam was weeding the garden.

'What do we do when he is like this?' she asked John. 'He hasn't spoken to me since we left the boarding house.'

'Ryan told me what happened. I am deeply sorry for your loss.'

'He hit a man, John. He wouldn't stop.'

'I saw the marks on his hands. He is full of rage, but he hides when he is in pain. He is suffering inside.'

'It has been hours now and it's getting cold out there.'

'We have to let him be. He will come back to us. You have been through so much today; you need to rest and take care of yourself. You are welcome here.'

'My car is still at the boarding house; I need to get it.'

'I will have someone pick it up for you.' John called Ryan from his cell phone and asked him to organise it. John and Luna stood by the kitchen door and watched Cam slave away in the night.

'He is yours now,' John said as he passed her a cup of rooibos tea. Luna sensed the warmth in his heart and was deeply moved.

'Take this to him.'

Luna did as he suggested, but Cam declined the tea.

Entering the house quietly later on, Cam saw Luna fast asleep on the couch. John and Mia had already gone to bed, and the tea Luna had offered him was on the kitchen table. He lifted Luna gently and carried her to bed. She looked so young and beautiful, yet so weary. She was the only reason he still wanted to be home, but it was time to leave. Once in bed, he lay quietly next to her. She was strong at heart, but her mind had taken in too much. Feeling dejected, Cam sat up on the edge of the bed and prayed.

Luna's bags were still unpacked and stored behind the door. He took the first bag and started unpacking her clothes. It was tops on the first shelf and pants on the next. One by one, he took out each item until everything was packed away. It took him a while, but he didn't care to check the time. When he got into bed, all he could think about was the love she had brought into his life, the joy she gave Mia and the bond he was rebuilding with John ... all because of her. He appreciated the blessing her presence had brought.

John hadn't done anything for Cam in years, yet today he had protected his honour and persuaded Luna to stay. Cam couldn't believe how he had almost destroyed what he and Luna had; she needed him, but he needed her more.

'I am sorry, love,' he whispered, gently kissing her. Luna was fast asleep. He ran his fingers over her breasts and back over her face. She stirred. 'Please don't leave us,' he whispered into her neck. 'No one will ever speak to you like that again; I am deeply sorry, love.'

Tears ran unchecked down his face; all the pain and suffering rose from their slumber in his body. Cam felt a rooted desire to connect with Luna again. They could soothe each other's pain with their love as the salve. He kissed her passionately, waking her up.

'Are those tears?'

'I love you,' he whispered.

Luna tasted his tears on her lips. His touch came unexpectedly; his chest expanded with deep breaths. She couldn't deny him. She bit back all the heavy emotions she had felt all day and sought comfort in Cam's love for her.

'Cam ...'

'It's Captain Coal.' He smiled.

She watched him on top of her. What mattered most was his desire for her. She wiped the tears from his face. His hand moved into places she hadn't thought had warmth.

'I thought I was losing you.'

'Don't ever think that.'

'We need you, Luna Coal.'

'Then marry me.'

'It's already done. My father is preparing a letter for your mother in the coming weeks. I am leaving in the morning.'

'So soon?'

'I have to work for you.' His fingers caressed her slowly as Luna clasped his shoulders.

'I know.' She swallowed the anxiety induced by Cam's imminent departure. Luna was not ready for him to go; grief felt heavy in her heart. She would feel alone once Cam left.

He inched closer to her face and kissed the tears leaking from her closed eyes.

'You will stay here and make this house your home. You can make changes as you please. John will be by your side, protecting and supporting you. Take care of Mia for me, because soon she will be yours too. Take care of this land; it will feed us. I hope not to be gone for long and when I return, I will make you, my wife, Luna Parks.'

Luna gasped as his hands traced the contours of her body. Cam disappeared under the sheets and sought her warmth with his tongue. He drank from her like she was the spring of eternal life. He tasted her clenching entrance, teasing and breathing into her. Her body went into vibrations. Her sensitive nub called him in; she felt a heat and need she had not known before. Luna ran her hands through his hair and pulled him closer. Her soles hugged the bed and he had her in his arms. Luna whimpered and craved more. Until she demanded him desperately.

When Cam eventually thrust into her warmth repeatedly, Luna's whimpers filled the room. Cam's answering groans and grunts transported her to unending pleasure waves. It felt like she was surfing on the biggest wave but catching another before the previous one crested.

Cam pleased her long into the night, moving his body against hers in an age-old dance. He professed his love through his body and his words and Luna responded in kind.

'I will be back sooner than you all think.'

Chapter 24

Child of the soil

3 JULY 2005, Clanwilliam, Western Cape

Luna and John worked together to get Mia into a school routine. Cam had not fully disclosed John's problem with alcohol. One night, after they went to sleep, Luna found him outside, searching the big garbage bins for leftover alcohol. It was a heart-wrenching sight; John, wearing only his pyjama pants, was hunched in one of the bins like an animal. He shook violently and tears were running down his chest.

'John!' Luna had come racing.

'Just one tot, just one, my child.'

'You are not allowed to have any alcohol, John.'

'I need to sleep, please. Just one shot,' he cried. 'Please don't tell Cam. I am trying but the things in my head won't let me rest.'

Luna couldn't believe her eyes; she got him out of the bin and covered him with her shawl.

'Mia is sleeping; please calm down.' She took him inside and washed the vomit from his body. It was the hardest thing to endure, but it was her new reality. She had not spoken to Cam in a few weeks.

At the clinic, Luna asked Eve to prescribe sleeping pills and medication to help John deal with his withdrawal symptoms. She had so much on her plate, as the clinic was now one nurse short, and she had to take care of the Coal family and missed Cameron dearly. Negative thoughts about his absence plagued her daily.

Has he abandoned me, like my father did?

On the weekends, Luna went out into the fields with John and Mia to look at the rooibos crop. They had crafted a plan to harvest what was there was from Mia's efforts. Cam's wagon proved to be a great asset to transport the tea. Even though it wasn't the greatest produce, they could package it and sell it to the locals. Eve had allowed Luna to sell the tea from a small stall at the clinic, which worked well. Luna texted Cam to give him updates every night, but she had not received any response.

While John focused on the farm, Luna concentrated on Mia and her work. No one dared mention Amora's death, and Luna grieved for her friend alone. Seth came to the farm periodically, but John chased him away each time. John had also fixed Luna's car, which made things easier for her and Mia. They travelled into town together in the mornings, and John picked Mia up when Luna worked late shifts.

'Has my father called, Miss Parks?'

'Not this week, love. But he will return for your birthday.'

At first, Cam had tried to check in whenever he could, but there were long periods between any contact. They had now gone for weeks without any calls, and they both missed him dearly.

'He has never been around for my birthday; how do you know if he'll come?'

'Well, your birthday is a week away.' Luna tried several times to reassure Mia, but it didn't work.

Mia's birthday came without Cam in sight. Luna baked her a cake, and John roasted some meat. It was bittersweet because Mia cried for her father that Sunday morning. Luna gave Mia some new clothes and a pair of leather boots, which Mia wore on her birthday. They prepared the table and said grace. The coal stove was on, keeping the kitchen warm and cosy. John also had a fire going in the lounge.

As John waited to sing 'Happy birthday' to Mia, he looked up and froze with the cup of tea suspended in mid-air.

'It can't be! My eyes deceive me,' John said.

'What is it?' Luna asked, noticing the shock in his eyes.

'Surely I have died,' he whispered as he stood up from the kitchen table. Luna followed his gaze. A tall man was headed towards the front gate.

'Are you expecting any visitors?'

'Is it my father?' Mia chimed in.

'No, baby. Just a stranger, probably just passing by or seeking directions,' Luna said. She stood up and placed her hands on Mia's shoulders. Her eyes narrowed as she tried to identify the approaching figure; there was something familiar about him that Luna couldn't place.

'It's my son! It's my son! He has returned.' John stumbled out of the kitchen and walked towards the man.

Sole advanced with caution. The house was freshly painted and new saplings had replaced the trees that had died in the fire. There was a big Wendy house on the side of the house and the stables had been extended. The vegetable garden was well kept but he noticed fewer cattle and horses. He saw people standing by the door. One was his father, John. Sole put his hand over his mouth; he couldn't believe how much John had aged. His face was gaunt, and grey hair covered his chin and head. He had also lost a considerable amount of weight over the years.

'Prepare a place for him! It's my son!' John called out.

Sole paused momentarily and admired his surroundings. It had been a long trip; the walk from town had claimed his breath. He hadn't been home in ten years. Everything seemed different. He was nervous; he didn't know how he would be received.

Sole Coal approached John with open arms.

'This can't be!' Luna couldn't believe what she was seeing – he looked just like Cam!

As the two men walked towards her and Mia, Luna grabbed the girl and held onto her.

Twins? Cam has a twin. How is this possible?

'Luna, I want you to meet my son, Sole Coal.' Luna turned towards the door. Sole was the spitting image of Cam.

Sole's eyes were a sparkling bright green, but Cam had brown eyes. His wavy hair was slightly longer than Cam's. Luna tried to say something, but Sole just walked past her and dumped his bags on the floor.

'Sole, this is Luna, Cam's fiancée,' John said, overcome with joy.

'So, he found someone after all,' Sole said in a gentler tone. His voice was a smooth baritone, but it wasn't as deep as Cam's. The words cut into Luna. She didn't know what to make of them.

'Hello,' she said. Just looking at Sole multiplied her yearning for Cam. She missed him and the heavens were playing mind games with her.

'And this little one?' Sole looked at Mia.

'That's Mia; don't you remember Cameron's daughter?' John managed to control the dry look he gave Luna.

'Oh, I see. Well, hello.' Mia held on to Luna and didn't respond. She had felt the tension in Luna's hands and wanted to protect her.

'Does she not speak?' Sole asked.

'She is a little shy, that's all,' Luna shot back.

As if realisation had suddenly struck, Sole crossed his arms and rejected her comment with one long look.

'Aren't you going to show me where I can put my bags?' he said rudely.

'We have a guestroom on your left.' Luna drew Mia closer to her. Besides being tall, Sole was handsome and fierce; his expression was hateful towards her. He seemed very intense.

'Guestroom? You must be joking. I'm no guest.' He walked around the house and opened each door. The first room on his right was Mia's room, and his parents' room, the master bedroom, was further down the hallway. Their pictures were still on the walls, but the master bedroom had better views of the mountain, while the guestroom was dark and only had a single bed. His father's belongings were in Sole's old bedroom, and Cam's childhood room now appeared to be the designated guestroom.

'I guess I'll take this one!' Soal dumped his belongings on Cam's bed. Luna shook her head in John's direction.

'That's our room!' she tried to protest, frustration building in her voice.

This man had just come out of nowhere and he's already making demands.

'That's the one I am taking. That settles it,' Sole ordered. He pulled out a cigarette and lit it in the room. Instead of reprimanding him, John just smiled.

'You can sleep in the maid's room outside,' Sole mocked Luna.

'Sole, please take the guestroom; this is your brother's room,' John pleaded.

'I don't see him around; is he hiding somewhere?' Sole laughed and dismissed John.

Luna said nothing; she was outnumbered, and John was so excited to see his son that he didn't notice her break into pieces. She waited for him to rectify the situation but John and Sole continued talking about Cam's whereabouts. Mia asked to be taken to her room, leaving the birthday cake on the table untouched.

'Lady, while you are at it, remove Cam's things from my room and get us something to drink.' Sole had a strange twinkle in his eye.

'We were celebrating Mia's birthday. There is food on the stove,' John said.

'I need a cold beer; I won't drink this.' Sole pushed the kettle away, placed his jacket over the back of the chair and sat down. Luna knew this was a bad idea; this man was nothing like Cam. He was rude, condescending and racist. John looked at Luna nervously, as if he was unable to do anything about the situation

'Hey, get us some drinks! I am dying of thirst,' Sole called out after Luna as she left the room and rushed into Cam's bedroom and closed the door. She took out her phone and tried calling Cam, but his phone was still off. The door opened and Sole stepped in.

'I said we need beers. How dare you walk away when I am speaking to you.'

'I don't appreciate your tone,' Luna said. She straightened her spine; she wouldn't cower. He looked so much like Cam, and it was distracting. She had to compose herself and calm down. He smelt like hard liquor and cigarettes.

'So, you are my little brother's maid or what?'

'I am his fiancée. Why are you in my house?'

'We will see; get us drinks.' His laugh was low. His disgust said it all.

Appalled, she ignored him. The demands were absurd; Luna would not be spoken to like that.

'I am staying in my husband's bedroom.'

'You are delusional, I see.'

Luna sat down on the bed and just looked at Sole.

'Don't make me shove you out,' Sole said and stormed out, leaving the door open.

Luna panicked; she had nowhere else to go. After Amora's death, the Fouries had closed the boarding house; even Bree and Lucy had moved out.

Why did I agree to move here? How am I going to live with a man like this?

She felt trapped and isolated. John was not coming to her defence. As handsome as Sole was, he was also cold and rude. She wanted to curl up and cry. This was not the life she had imagined.

Where are you, Cam? How could you leave me like this?

There was no point in fighting Sole; she was too exhausted. Luna opened the cupboards; her clothes were packed away neatly and carefully. She had maintained Cam's standard when she started doing the laundry. A shaft of longing for him pierced her heart. She packed and moved her things into the guestroom. It had little space, and some of her clothes had to be stored on the floor.

It will have to be enough; it's not like I'm married to Cam.

The narrow bed she'd had at the boarding house had been better than this one. The single bed had broken springs and the room lacked sunlight. Luna tidied the room and decided that she would stay there for the rest of the day. She thought of Amora; the pain of losing her had finally erupted. As the tears rolled down her eyes, Luna felt a small hand touch her shoulder.

'Miss Parks, can I sit with you?'

'Yes, baby.'

'Is it still my birthday?' Mia sat down next to her.

'Yes, of course.'

'Can we cut my cake?'

'Certainly. Just give me a moment. Go wait in the kitchen; I will be right there.'

When Luna entered the kitchen, she saw that John and Sole had gone out to the stables. Luna couldn't understand why Sole had returned or been so mean towards her. She sat down and sang 'Happy birthday' to Mia, and then they ate some cake and sipped their tea.

'I miss my father, Miss Parks.'

'I miss him too, baby.'

John and Sole were out riding all afternoon, while Luna spent time with Mia, reading to her and cleaning her room. Mia couldn't sleep that night and refused to stay in her room, so Luna allowed her to share her tiny bed.

Luna spent the night thinking, lying in the small bed like a rejected child. No one was protecting her and Mia; no one cared to check on them. When she was about to fall asleep, she heard John open the kitchen door, followed by Sole. They were talking so loudly that Luna could tell they were drunk. John wasn't allowed to drink, and Sole had taken him a million steps back.

Anger consumed Luna in the darkness of night. John was just getting back on his feet. He was on medication, and Cam would never allow him to drink like this. Sole was now singing in the kitchen and Luna knew just how things would turn out if she tried to intervene. She pulled Mia closer to her. John did not need this setback; everything had been perfect without Sole. Luna missed her fiancé and his guidance.

'Cam, we need you.' She wept long into the night.

Chapter 25

The land that was

'Get moving! If you don't get these bags out on time, I will cut your wages; I don't think you will want that right now,' the man shouted from the plantation site.

'Mr Fletcher, we need gloves and water. We have been working all night. The women need a break and some sleep,' a man called out in the field. The others tried to stop him from voicing his concerns, but it was too late.

'You want to sleep? Is that it? You want to sleep on my land?' Joshua Fletcher was a stout, short man with an unforgiving face and a belly that hung over his pants.

'We have moved tons of tea and were not paid last month. We can't continue working like this.' The worker glanced at the other workers and saw the fear in their eyes. He had to retreat; it would not end well.

'Do you think you will find better jobs if you leave this farm? Where will you go?' Mr Fletcher smiled as he sipped on his coffee.

The worker didn't respond. He knew that a number of men and women were killed on this land in the early 1900s. Their remains were ground and used as fertiliser. Blood still ran into the soil; on hot days, they imagined they could smell the stench of rotting flesh. Their mistreatment was not history; it was their reality. They only heard of a democratic South Africa on the radio and read it in the newspapers; nothing had changed for them, even with a black president. They were whipped daily, treating bloodied wounds after hours.

Mr Fletcher watched as Seth's van raced down his driveway. The farm was well maintained, with a massive farmstead and a boutique hotel, a tea-processing area, and shared living quarters for the workers. The lawn was well manicured, watered by automated irrigation systems and a number of large water tanks for periods of drought. Seth hadn't been there in years, but the wealth was evident in the farm's upkeep. Mr Fletcher watched Seth as he approached; he wasn't expecting him.

'You need to go into the fields and bring in all the bagged tea.' Mr Fletcher pointed at an older worker, Hans. He had worked for the Coal family before Mr Fletcher persuaded him to join his farm. Hans knew the tea plant well and was the best man for the job.

'You will find other workers there; ensure that all the tea is packaged right and see what's happening in the grading rooms. I need some of you to gather here in two hours. We must take the packaged tea to town. We have seven hotels waiting for delivery. Don't forget to record the bags so we can pay the correct levy to the Rooibos Council; we must keep the members on our side.'

Mr Fletcher continued talking to Hans as he walked towards Seth's car. 'The new democracy has opened the trading gates again – one good thing about this black government. Once you realise that we don't have all the time in the world, you will respect mine. While you are at it, take Themba to the greenhouse and take the packaged tea there; we need those on a flight to China tonight.'

'If it's not Sly Junior,' Mr Fletcher said as he approached Seth. 'To what do I owe the pleasure? I thought you were out on the waters serving our beloved country.' He extended his hand to greet Seth.

'I would have loved that, but I'm taking a short break.'

'Seth Fourie, you grew up under my nose. I know that Coal boy let you go. I hope you are not here sniffing for a job.'

'I'm taking a break!' Seth reinforced his words. Seth towered over Mr Fletcher; he could see the top of his bald head.

'Well, if that's how you want to keep it, it's fine with me.' Mr Fletcher rolled his eyes and continued sipping his coffee.

'How are things here, Mr Fletcher?' Seth took a deep breath and looked around. The place was like a private heaven; some fields went on for so long that they seemed to go up the hills and over the mountains. The workers moved around like a well-oiled conveyor belt. Mr Fletcher grew rows of roses and sunflowers on either side of the farmstead.

'I am glad you are looking around; we've become the biggest supplier to Rooibos Limited, the distributor here in Clanwilliam. I have taken over most of the Cederberg tea markets, and now we are the biggest tea producers in South Africa, exporting our surplus to external markets. This land keeps on giving. I can't complain; it's good that we are growing. The wine boys make lots of money, but we are right there with them.' Mr Fletcher laughed and rubbed his stomach.

'From what I see, you're still the only man with power in these hills,' Seth said, trying to butter him up.

'That's right! Now, tell me, what brings you here?'

'I come bearing gifts.'

'Well, come out with it, let's see.' Seth opened the back of his truck, pulled out the bags of guns and displayed each one on the bonnet of his bakkie. He explained the makes as a top salesman would. Mr Fletcher noticed the desperation in Seth's body language. He spoke to him without a clue as to what Fletcher already had in his possession. Seth was displaying old stock that Fletcher had bought months ago. He wanted to laugh but let Seth continue for a while.

'Seth … Seth …' Seth looked up to see the Mr Fletcher's disapproval.

'This is just a gift; they do the job.' Seth's voice was meandering. He looked like a street vendor in his faded Navy T-shirt and long pants.

'I don't need these; I have a new supplier in Cape Town, and I had asked your father to service these, but he kept sending me garbage. I don't use second-hand rifles. I will no longer need your family business,' Fletcher said dismissively.

'These are gifts!' Seth beseeched, rubbing his face in confusion.

'Just tell me what you want; these won't cut it for me. Tell me why you are here. Do you need a job?'

Seth stood up straight and shook his head. 'I have information.'

'What kind?'

'The Coals have begun canvassing for clients in town. I hear that they are looking at expanding, and from what I can tell, things are looking up for them.'

'That's it?' The old man didn't look surprised. In fact, he had been keeping an eye on John.

'I thought you should know.'

'You see why I can't use you; I am a smart man, Seth. Your father has been working with me for years, and that's how you got the Navy job. I have built this plantation to become a successful commercialised farm. The Coal family can't touch us now. You are a smart man. Tell me, how do you think we got this place?' Seth didn't understand what Mr Fletcher was alluding to.

'Seth, my boy, you went to school, right?'

'Yes. I did.'

'Your hands look like dried meat; you have been busy. You need to take care of those burns. Do you know how we got rid of the coloured and San people in the Western Cape?'

Fletcher kept his eyes on Seth's hands; something didn't seem right. Seth was sweating and on edge. Fletcher looked at the time – it was barely eight in the morning and yet Seth smelt like a brewery and his eyes were blood-red.

'You see, this entire region was full of them, and then one day, the fields burnt, houses were set alight, schools burnt to the ground, and guess what? People lose hope when the mountains burn and the town goes up in smoke.' Fletcher laughed.

'For decades, we couldn't get our hands on this land; my grandfather tried trading with them, but the San wouldn't leave. We tried putting them into camps, but they still wouldn't leave. So, at harvest time, we cut the water supplies and set the fields alight. They burnt for days and days. The wild animals began disappearing because of the frequent fires. The illustrious rooibos tea trade was cut off at the knees, especially because of the global trade ban due to apartheid. When people starve, you feed them alcohol and drugs. They lose focus, and then you take over their land. Do you see how easy that is? It was a plan that took decades to implement. How do you think the Cape Flats came into existence?'

Fletcher saw that Seth was intrigued. They took a walk across the fields, and Fletcher continued talking.

'The Coal family was powerful in their time, and we had nothing but this land. But, like I said, we have more to offer now, and they have nothing. The little land that they have won't produce what our fields can. When you drove in here, did you see our new irrigation system? It cost millions, and do you think the Coals can match that? Look at all these people who work here; John can't manage the type of farm we have. We are on a journey to control the supply of and markets for rooibos.'

'Mr Fletcher, you burnt the Coal family farm! It was your doing all along!' Seth remembered the night of the fire. He tried to think, but Mr Fletcher kept throwing him bones.

'For a business to survive, you must know your enemies. Isn't that what you do, Mr Sniper?' he grinned.

'You killed all those people; you killed Cam's mother and his wife?'

'I killed that bitch because she refused to marry me! Have you seen John lately? Do you think he is worth a decent woman like Emily? Emily was a doctor and she left me for that loser! I got her into medical school. For years and years, I paid for everything, and she chose that old dog. Do I look like a fool? John took my life, so I took his farm.'

'And killed his wife!' Seth couldn't accept what Fletcher said. He remembered the people he had to pull out of the burning houses. Their flesh falling from their bones. Their screams. It was those memories that fuelled his plans for Amora.

'If a man takes your woman and parades her as his own, what would you do?'

'I don't know.' Seth rubbed the back of his head. For the first time, he understood Cam's pain. Mr Fletcher was unrepentant and didn't care about the innocent people he had killed. He was pleased with himself and oblivious to the carnage his actions had left behind. Seth had come here with a different plan; he wasn't expecting this. Cam had been like a brother to him, even though they were going through a rough patch. Seth loved and loathed Cam in equal measure. Was Seth worthy of this truth? Could he ever be loyal to Cam again?

'You are a young man; use your head. We didn't start the war, they did,' Fletcher said.

'You are just like our forefathers. You began a silent genocide of these people.'

'Your generation is weak and spineless. The British did far more than I could; I just took what was mine and now we are here. Just look at you! Cam fired you and you are here to sell him out. And you think I would reward you for backstabbing your friend? I always knew you people were snakes. Just look at your father and his sister. He left her to wither away slowly. She is a vegetable now, and you, my son, have borne no fruits yourself.

'Where are your wife and kids? What have you built? Yet you stand on my land like a lost sheep judging me? There is a reason Cameron is where he is, and you are here. Go home and think about it. If you dare tell a soul about what I have just told you, your body will fertilise the soil you stand on. Go join the missionaries if you think you can save people.'

Fletcher summoned his guards to escort Seth off his land.

Seth was enraged; Fletcher had no respect for him or his work in the Navy. But most of all, what had he done to a nation of people? Seth realised that Fletcher was no different from Amora or his mother, but neither was he.

'What have I become? I am just like him!'

The morning sun hit his eyes like a call from heaven, and his hands grew hot. His scars hadn't healed properly, and he felt caged in. Nothing he touched worked out for him. Seth was getting desperate. He looked at the petrol gauge in his bakkie; he needed petrol, but he had no money.

Cam had always been better than him in many ways, in school and in the Navy. He was a fast learner and Seth deeply admired how he loved his country and all its people. The only man Seth could call a brother was Cam, but Seth had become a reject. Now that their friendship was soiled, Cam had moved on like Seth had never been there. All Seth felt was pain, sorrow and loss. His father hated him, and he couldn't return to the family home after what he had done. He glanced at the sack full of guns on the seat next to him and cursed Mr Fletcher.

'You live on a hill like a king, and you dare treat me like one of your slaves. Your day will come!' Seth drove through the gates and down the pass, desperately trying to calm himself down.

When he got to town, he went to his father's gun shop. Sly was not there, so he took some money from the cash register and went to the motel bar. Sole and John were seated inside at the bar counter. Seth didn't greet them but sat down at a table near them and observed them from a distance. After a couple of drinks, he went over to the two men.

'If it isn't Sole Coal in the flesh. What brings you to town?'

John just shook his head and continued drinking.

'I'm sorry, and you are?' Sole turned around and saw the poorly dressed man. His boots were spattered in mud and his hands were covered in scabs.

'Seth Fourie. We grew up together.'

'Seth! Man, you have aged! Join us.'

Sole pulled out a barstool for Seth and watched him sit down.

'What do you do now?' Seth asked Sole.

'I am an advocate.'

'Fancy, a lawyer,' Seth said flippantly.

'Advocate! There is a big difference,' Sole shot back arrogantly.

'Well, excuse me. Are you here to clean up your father's mess? Rumour has it he might sell the farm. He is close to bankruptcy and yet here he is, drinking like a fish.'

Sole glanced at his father and gave him a sharp look.

'The farm is doing well, Seth. Leave us alone,' John responded slowly.

'Is this true, father?' Sole asked.

'I said everything is fine!'

'The old man is tired, Sole; that farm won't last another season. Even worse, Cam brought an indigenous mortal onto it. What are the chances? Your brother has lost his mind. Can you believe he wants to marry that Hottentot?'

Sole wasn't impressed with Seth's choice of words but agreed with him about Cam's fiancée. 'I believe I can fix our family affairs. There is nothing for you to worry about.'

'Anyway, if I were you, I'd watch my back. Don't ever trust a drunk man.' Seth winked at John and left the table, avoiding the waitress as he stumbled out.

'Sir, you didn't pay for your beer!' the young girl called out, running after him. Sole found the interaction with Seth strange and unsettling. He didn't know Luna, but he wasn't comfortable with her staying with them.

'Father, is everything okay at the farm?'

'We have challenges like everyone else.'

'What happened to all the cattle?'

'Sold them. Others got poisoned overnight and we had to put them down. Someone did that to them, but I can't prove anything. I have tried talking to Cam about these things, but your brother doesn't believe that we are not liked around here. He doesn't see what I see.'

'Cam doesn't know anything about farming. What did you expect?' Sole rolled his eyes and sipped his beer.

'Well, after your mother died, we had another series of fires. Our water supplies were poisoned, so the crop was lost. The rest of the plants burnt to the ground. Our workers left us, and we couldn't do anything about it,' John sighed heavily.

'And insurance?'

'The insurance company stopped paying because there were too many claims; they thought we were just trying to cash in. And all those fires were not caused by natural disasters.'

'Where is Cameron, Father?'

'He is a captain in the Navy. He left right after you and has been with the Navy ever since.'

'A captain?' Sole couldn't believe it; his brother was too soft and harmless. How did he get into such a profession?

'He loves it.'

'Good for him. Cheers to Cameron Coal!' Sole lifted his glass and laughed. He had always competed with his brother, but this was laughable.

'What are you going to do about that girl? Surely, his maid can't stay with us.'

'He loves her, Sole.'

'Well, let him build her a house away from our land. She doesn't belong there.'

'The child loves her.'

'Even better, she can take that little brat and go live in a motel with her. That child should've died with Summer. Who has the time to look after such a needy thing? If I had it my way, she—' He quickly held his tongue.

'What are you saying, Sole?' John lifted his head.

Sole had assessed the stakes and found them too high. Land claims were piling up since the Land Claims Court was established. He would do everything he could to ensure that his inheritance was not stolen through some bogus marriage.

Chapter 26

My brother's keeper

17 SEPTEMBER 2005, Clanwilliam, Western Cape

Luna's body was stiff and sore when she woke in the mornings. She tried to stretch but her body continued to ache. Her energy levels were low – she had worked herself ragged to keep things going. Life on the farm had become a nightmare for her. Sole controlled John like a puppet. She repeatedly tried to get John to take his medicine, but under Sole's influence, he drank incessantly. Luna detested what Sole was doing to his father. He was abusing the emotions of a despairing father trying to please his once-lost son. John's health was deteriorating. He had a kidney infection, but that didn't stop Sole from bringing him liquor. Luna had fought with Sole daily, so eventually she stopped talking to him.

Luna helped Mia get ready in the mornings, and then they both began working in the fields. Wildflowers were in bloom, carpeting the land with a riot of colours. Luna handled the shovel like a pro. She only felt free when she was in the fields with Mia. Luna heard Cam's voice in the wind and held on to that. She ate from the land, which was thriving despite John's diminished input.

'Miss Parks, did you sleep well last night?' Mia asked. 'I heard you talking to someone.'

Mia was flourishing at school. Her reading from the Braille books Luna had given her had greatly improved. After school, Mia stayed in the library until Luna could pick her up. They interacted as a mother and daughter would.

'My darling girl, it was your father. I didn't want to wake you, but he is in Germany; they are there for the new submarines that the Navy ordered, but I believe he will call again later today.'

Since Cam's departure, they had spoken only three times. Cam had not been home in four months. Mia had stopped talking about him, but in the night, she wailed for him.

'That's wonderful,' Mia grinned.

'Do you want to speak to him if he calls?' Luna looked at her; Mia was kneeling, tasting the soil. They had planted many of the rooibos seeds over winter, and the rains had been good. In eighteen months, Luna hoped they would have their first significant harvest.

'No. You need Father more,' Mia said.

'You are a special one.'

'I know,' Mia giggled. The wind ruffled her dress as she knelt in the soil. Mia refused to wear shoes when they were in the fields. She said she lost her balance and wanted to feel the soil to determine what it needed. Mia had been instrumental in using her senses to direct what they needed to do. Luna trusted Mia, as she had been right each time she advised her on the type of soil in the fields.

'You know he misses you dearly.' Luna tried to channel Cam's love for Mia.

'As long as he comes back to you.'

'What do you mean?'

'Uncle Sole doesn't like you. I heard him talking to someone on the phone.'

'When? What did he say?' Luna placed the shovel on the ground and turned to check if anyone was around. The farmstead was a little further up the hill. She couldn't see where John and Sole were; they hadn't slept at home the night before.

'A couple of days ago. He spoke to this person a lot. When you prepared dinner, I smelt his cigarette. So, I followed him to the barn. He was drunk... I guess. He was shouting at the person; he was talking about you.'

'Mia! What did he say?' Luna stared at her in horror.

'He said he didn't trust you. He told the man to dig deep.' She shrugged her shoulders.

'What else?' Luna pulled Mia up from the ground.

'I don't know ... He said he needs to know who you really are. He also spoke about Father. He said Father was the reason their mother died.'

'That's not true, Mia. You shouldn't listen to that man.'

'He said Father was not innocent.'

'Your father is a good man; Sole is a mean man.'

Mia didn't understand what Luna meant; she knew what she'd heard.

Sole is a well-respected advocate. If he's digging around in my past, he could find out things about me that I'd prefer stayed buried. Amora is dead. Is there a way he could find out what had happened to Dr Mark and the doctor in the interview room?

'What else did Sole say?' Luna's heart was racing as she felt panic rising and threatening to suffocate her in its clasp.

'I can't remember,' Mia said. Luna forced a stiff smile as if Mia could see it, pulled the girl close, and hugged her.

'Miss Parks, you have been overeating Father's bread and meat.' Mia's arms were around her stomach.

'It's the reward of all that birthday cake that we ate for a full week, and you are right; your father made sure that we get fresh bread every morning.' Luna held Mia close and didn't pay much attention to her words.

Luna's appetite had increased in the past few weeks, and she found that eating bread didn't make her feel as weird as eating other things. She had gained weight from cooking every night for the Coals. When she'd lived at the boarding house, she hardly ate or would just have soup and small meals. All she could think about was that Sole was looking for evidence against her.

I know he doesn't like me, but to do a full-on investigation! Why did he even come back? If he was such an important advocate, why did he return to a small farm to live with his father?

Sole was in town; he had been invited to a community meeting chaired by Joshua Fletcher at the community centre. Steven, Eve, Sly and other local farmers were also there. The community was unhappy about the regulations the newly established Rooibos Council wanted to impose. All kinds of matters were discussed which would be tabled at the Rooibos Council by Mr Fletcher: the health of workers, the recent fire in the town and the locals' safety. Farmers in remote regions were being targeted by thieves, who were stealing their cattle and game. Their homes were being invaded at night and their wives were getting beaten and left for dead.

'Ladies and gentlemen, you have to calm down. We are doing everything we can to keep the prices low, but you know the costs of farming tea are increasing. The tax we must pay for exports is beyond us,' Fletcher shouted from the other side of the table.

'Then the council must give us prices that we all agree on! You are exporting the best teas and the rest goes to the restaurants and hotels and the people here don't benefit. Look at our schools. What happened to our donations?' another man across the table called out.

'The clinic is struggling; our nurses don't have supplies. You were supposed to aid us,' Eve chimed in.

'The council is doing its best to return some order to the industry,' Fletcher said placatingly, rising from his seat. 'You all know what happened when the Rooibos Control Board was disbanded eight years ago. There was no control over any of our produce, and we didn't have a unified vision. Give us this harvest season to see if the set prices work for everyone. The set price guarantees your income without worrying about payment.' Fletcher was trying to calm the crowd down, but the more he spoke, the angrier the people became.

'Nonsense! We have heard this story a million times. You have taken control of Cederberg's produce, and we can't even work without your permission in this region. We are all targets of crime, but you sit here and only talk about tea,' Steven said.

'We are supposed to work together but one family takes everything from its people,' Sly Fourie said accusingly. Fletcher stared at him coldly.

'Every family in South Africa lives on that tea, and we don't benefit from it. You sit on the other side of the mountain, and no one knows what you are doing there,' Steven said.

'Steven, your job as a police officer is to ensure that we are safe,' another community member called out. 'How many break-ins have we had in the last year? Have you solved the nurse's murder? When will you find out who set the town on fire? How many homes still need repairs after that fire? *You* must do *your* job!'

'Like I said, we need this council,' Fletcher said. 'We will all benefit if we do our part. Those who don't have jobs must come to us and we will see what we can do.'

Sole tried to provide legal input with the matters that were tabled. After the meeting, he went to the café and reviewed some documents he had received from Cape Town. He read about Luna's education and her mother's background and then noticed something interesting. Luna had left Cape Town on the same day that her boss was murdered. The case was still ongoing, and from what Sole read in the report, she was the nurse on duty that day.

He'd noticed something else in some old court documents. Her family had owned a piece of land around the Cederberg area in the 1960s. He also read the report he'd received from his contacts at the Land Summit Conference that had taken place several days earlier. The conference was reviewing the government's progress since the land reform programme's establishment ten years ago. Sole didn't have time to study the reports and documents in depth, but he was determined that Luna would not lay claim to his inheritance.

When he left the café, it was almost 6 p.m. He picked John up at the motel and headed home. Luna was washing the dishes while Mia was reading in the guest bedroom. John was drunk and went straight to bed. Sole decided to sit in the kitchen; it was time to find out who Luna Parks really was.

'My name is Sole, Luna,' he said softly. She ignored him. 'I think we should start with a clean slate. You are going to be my brother's wife after all.'

'You have been here for a while now, so I don't think we need a formal introduction. I know enough about you.' The smell of beer on his breath made Luna nauseous. She tried drinking water but that didn't help. Sole's hawk-eyed gaze missed nothing.

'I think I was shocked to find you here when I arrived. I wasn't expecting –' Sole couldn't say the words, and Luna glanced at him irritably.

'A black girl in your house, is that it?'

'Call it what you wish. That's not the point here. My brother is a strict man who wouldn't just take anyone from the streets.'

Luna shook her head; Sole was still mocking her.

'Just stop, Sole. Let's call it a night. I'm not in the mood.' After the chat she'd had with Mia, she had become wary of him.

'I hear you crying at night and that's not nice. You clearly love my brother. I hope he loves you back. His first love was Summer, and nothing will change that. However, he has chosen you; we must all live with that. You are a stunning woman but women like you usually have a lot of hidden issues. Those tears come from a dark place. Why do you cry like that when you know your man loves you?' Sole waited for Luna's reaction; he was testing the waters, but she didn't bite.

'Why did you come back?' Luna implored him. 'No one was expecting you, and no one even spoke about you. Did you run away from something? Where are your wife and kids? You have a big mouth, but you are in your father's house here. You should be in the city living it up at your age.'

'Oh, so you can take over *my* home? I knew you had fire in you; tell me more about why I shouldn't be living here, and why you should.' Sole stood up and leant against the fridge. The smirk on his face made Luna sick.

'I don't know why you hate me so much.'

'I don't hate you, Luna; I am just looking out for my family. My brother is clearly grief-stricken; it's created a fog in his judgement. Why would a man like him want to marry a servant?' Luna wanted to walk out of the room, but Sole was standing in her way.

'You can't just run; we all live in the same house. Do you run away from your problems often, Luna?' Sole looked her in the eye; she was in a complete panic.

'I don't know what you're talking about.' Luna didn't want Sole around, but the devil always had a way of arriving uninvited.

'You seem very comfortable here. How did you meet my brother? It seems like he has been feeding you our entire herd of cattle.'

Luna needed to sit down. Her head was spinning, and the kitchen felt too hot.

'You shouldn't be wearing that!' Sole was wearing Cam's black T-shirt and jeans; she wanted to strip the clothes off him.

How dare he go through Cam's belongings! I should've moved Cam's clothes out of that room.

'Oh, you finally noticed. My brother has style. Did you buy these? They fit me so well.' Sole laughed. Luna's frustration was growing rapidly.

'You have no respect for anyone, Sole.' Luna's hands were clenched on her hips.

'If I were you, I would think twice. Do you want to be a part of this family? Mia won't have a sibling if you continue like this! You are growing fast.'

The words blasted Luna into awareness. She looked down at her tummy and back at him with shock.

Could it be? When last did I have my period?

'Oops! You didn't know? That's strange for a nurse. You have been a naughty little pussycat.'

Luna's stomach churned as her mouth filled with saliva. She pushed Sole aside and rushed to the bathroom. Sole followed her; she had her face in the sink.

'I guess this is how you people trap a man. How nice! He can't leave now,' Sole said, pushing the door open.

'Sole, just call it a day. Leave me alone!' Luna's stomach heaved until there was nothing more to expel.

'Imagine what John will say; he's been telling me things about you. You have a wild story. A black city girl finds a new job in a small town, and suddenly, she lives a comfortable life with a white guy who owns a farm, and life is good. Now, we can add a baby to that lousy story. Does Cameron know? Or is it one of your many secrets?' Sole wasn't moved by Luna's obvious discomfort.

'Please, Sole.' She kicked the door closed, leaving him outside. When Sole turned around, he saw Mia in the corridor listening to them.

'Get out of the way, brat!' he said, as he shoved Mia against the wall. 'Your father is a waste of life. Just like you.' He walked outside for a smoke.

Luna was on the floor in tears.

'Miss Parks, are you okay?'

Mia got up, felt her way to the bathroom door and opened it. She walked into the room to sit beside Luna on the floor.

'Yes, I will be.' Luna held her stomach and called Cam from her cell phone.

Baby, please pick up!

'Love, I don't like how your voice sounds.' Cam sounded angelic and calming through the static on the line.

'Your brother is back; he looks just like you,' Luna whispered through the trail of her tears.

'What! That's insane! When? I never told you that I had a twin brother.'

Yes, the evil twin brother …

'Yep, it was a shock to see someone who looks like you but isn't you. It's been a while now. He lives here with us; I wanted to tell you, but I didn't think it was my place. I thought John would have spoken to you. Such a lot has happened. You have to come home. How can I do all this alone? I am so tired.' Luna couldn't go into detail with Mia listening to the conversation.

'You shouldn't cry like this, love. We are almost done here,' Cam said.

'Things are hard now. I just want you to come home.'

'I am trying my best to make plans. Is the bakery sending you bread and cheese as I have asked?' Cam was trying to distract Luna but the pain in her voice made him nervous. He detected that there was a lot she wasn't saying.

'The bread's been great, and you know it's not that we're hungry here.'

'She is pregnant, Father!' Mia called out ecstatically.

'No! No!' Luna said.

'Pregnant?' Cam asked.

'I've been feeling nauseous lately, but I am not sure. I need to take a pregnancy test when I get to work on Monday.'

'Well, if that's the case, it's fantastic news! Get that test done, love. Now I really must come back home! I hope our baby isn't born earlier than expected, like Mia; I'd really want to be there for the birth.' Cam's voice soothed Luna. No one else could make her feel so warm inside.

'You need to be here for the birth. Cam, because I don't think I can stay here any longer. Sole has made my life a living hell!' Luna cried.

Cam knew how cold his brother could be, and he had no doubt that Luna was right. After a brief conversation in which Cam tried to lighten her mood by sharing anecdotes from his trip, Luna gave Mia the phone. Once they'd left the bathroom, Luna texted Cam about what was happening.

Cam, John is sick and Sole keeps feeding him alcohol. The farm is slowly picking up again, but we need manpower and I can't hire anyone. You must come back and manage that process. Sole kicked me out of your room and he's been mean to me. Mia and I miss you so much. Please come back.

When night fell, Luna prayed over Mia's sleeping body. Things were not as they were before. She needed all her strength.

Chapter 27

The sins of a father

18 SEPTEMBER 2005, Clanwilliam, Western Cape

After Luna's conversation with Cam and a night of wet pillows, she wanted to take control of her home. On the Monday morning, she woke up to a delivery of a basket of cheese, bread and biscuits. There was a note with the basket.

> My love,
> I don't like your sunny days to be filled with gloom. We have a wedding to plan. Enjoy these with my little one. Send my love to Mia and John. I will be home soon.
> Yours faithfully,
> Your Captain Husband

The thought of being pregnant gave Luna anxiety. She had only slept with Cam a handful of times, and now she was possibly going to become a mother. Luna rose from her bed, stripped off her night-gown and looked at her tummy in the mirror. Her breasts were fuller and her stomach was rounder. On the other hand, her face seemed pale and her eyes puffy. Mia had been right; she had gained weight. She turned from one side to the other. She couldn't even count the months; Cam had been gone so long that she had forgotten how he felt around her.

How did I get to this place? Is Cam really okay where he is? Why didn't he mention his twin brother to me?

It still bothered Luna that Cam had not shared such crucial information with her. Sole's cold and arrogant personality was the polar opposite of Cam's. He moved around the farm like a king and never cleaned up after himself. Mia disliked him and just stayed in her room when he was around. And from what Luna knew now, he was the enemy.

In those quiet moments Luna had to herself, she would take Cam's wagon and drive into the hills to study the tea. She would look at the plants and taste the soil like Mia did. Mia had told her that most of the soil was sandstone. Luna also compared how the plants were growing with the pictures in the book her mother had given her. If Julie ever visited her, she could explain what the words in the book meant. Wild olive trees and almonds grew on the hills, and the Clanwilliam sugarbush fascinated Luna. It was in bloom and the deep red colours dotted the landscape. Luna wanted to learn about the different species of fynbos vegetation and found a book in the library that listed the indigenous vegetation in the Cederberg. In her free time, she studied it religiously.

That Monday morning, she quickly bathed and prepared breakfast for the family. It was still early, and she heard Sole snoring in her husband's bedroom. He had taken over the sacred space she'd shared with Cam; Luna felt a harsh bitterness come over her.

John found Luna in the barn feeding the animals. She had not joined him and Mia for breakfast.

'Cam will be back soon, Luna,' he said gently.

'I know he will; he promised me.' Luna didn't look at him.

'How are you finding farm life?' John was trying to make polite conversation.

'It's fine.'

'I know I have disappointed you; I didn't defend you against my son. I know it was wrong.'

'It's a little too late now; he walks all over me because you cowered in his presence. You let him destroy your health and Mia has panic attacks at night because she fears him. So, yes, you disappointed me, John.'

Luna hated seeing how much John had deteriorated in the past few months. His cheekbones were more pronounced in his face and his shoulder blades were sticking out because he wasn't eating enough.

'I am deeply sorry, Luna.'

'Sole has been here for a while; what have you been doing in that time, John?' Luna didn't really want an answer. The words weighed on the old man's shoulders like boulders. He tried to explain but the truth was in his actions.

'Sole is also my son. I just didn't know what to do.'

'You don't treat Cam like this. Why is Sole so special?' Luna put the bucket down and turned to observe John's shame.

'Can't you see that Sole is the prodigal son? He was gone for ten years, Luna! Cam is strong and has never needed me,' John said softly.

'Strong? Cameron is suffering because of you! He watched you almost die on the floor countless times, and here comes Sole, and you are all over him like a bad smell. Have you looked at yourself lately? What happened to our efforts to get you off your addiction? You vomit every morning and hardly eat. You were getting better, John! You were happier, but now you've stopped spending time with Mia. How do you think she feels? Her father is not here and now you're also slipping away. She is a child; she can't handle all these changes.'

'I can do better, Luna. Please, my child.'

'You let Sole take Cam's room away like it was a just reward for his rudeness. You watch him treat me like a slave when I am his brother's future wife. Let me tell you this, Ryan tried calling you so you could be part of the wedding arrangements, but from what I've heard, you are always drunk on the phone, and he just gave up. I had to tell Cam what's been happening; what if you die in this house? What will become of us? What about Mia, John? What about the farm? I must still go to work and return to fix the sloppy work you do in the fields if you do any work at all. Then, help Mia with homework and work. Let's not mention cleaning up after Sole. The same son that you love more than your life.'

'Sole is different; you just don't understand him. A lot has happened.'

'He is destroying you; he doesn't want me here! This house is cold, and the tension is unbearable, John. We don't feel safe around him.'

'Just give it time, Luna. Sole has been through so much.'

'Amuse me, John.'

'He is a good guy.' Luna wanted to laugh but it was all so ridiculous.

'I spoke to Cam last night. He'll be back soon. I hope you will have changed this mess by the time he gets back. You and Sole completely messed up Mia's birthday. I don't know how you'll make up for that.'

'Mia is a child; she still has many more birthdays,' John said, and turned around to walk back to the house.

'That's sad to hear,' Luna said, and resumed feeding the animals. She just couldn't see how living here would work with Sole around; he needed to go. The Coals were her family now, and Luna wouldn't let him walk all over her. Just as she was preparing to return to the farmstead, she noticed her car pull out of the parking area next to the house.

'Sole!' Luna screamed at him. 'What do you think you are doing? That's my car! Sole!' She ran towards the car, but he drove off and threw his cigarette out the window. Luna rushed into the house.

'John! What on earth is this? Where is he going with my car! Tell him to come back! I need that car!' Luna screamed at him.

'You are family now, so we all share the little that we have.'

Luna had to take Cam's wagon to work because the bakkie had mechanical issues. John assisted her, but they didn't speak all the way into town. She felt a bitterness she couldn't explain when he dropped her off at the clinic. She just jumped off the wagon and walked straight into the building. Luna's hair had been ruffled by the wind and her uniform was covered in dust; she didn't want to explain herself, but Eve and Bree snickered as she came in.

Am I a joke? A living cartoon?

'Where is Mr Handsome? Trouble in paradise?' Eve asked when she found Luna sitting outside during her lunch break.

'He is at work, like all of us, Eve.'

'You are snappy today; are you okay? You need to take it easy; you look like hell.'

'Thanks for the vote of confidence,' Luna said.

'Mr Fletcher is hosting a big party to celebrate the season's harvest. Are you going? I heard Sly mention that Sole will be going. Such an enigma, that Sole; he disappeared for a decade and then just swaggers back into town!'

'I wasn't invited to the party, and I wouldn't go anyway.' Luna knew that Eve was fishing for information, but she wouldn't tell her anything.

The worst thing Sole could do for our family is attend the Fletcher party. Why would he attend that vile man's event? Cam doesn't hold the Fletchers in high regard, which is another thing the brothers differ on.

'Listen,' Eve said, 'a police officer from Cape Town was here yesterday. She's been coming around frequently, asking questions.'

'What did she want?' Luna quickly stood up and wrung her hands in anxiety.

'She was talking about some doctor. Well, apparently, he is dead or something. She also asked about your work documents. Something about them possibly being fraudulent.'

'Well, that's not true,' Luna said.

'Of course that's not true. I told her to leave because she couldn't look through the personnel files without a valid search warrant or whatever, but she was at the motel afterwards. I don't know if she is still in town.'

This is not good, but what can I do now?

Luna wanted to puke; her head was spinning. She ran inside and into the toilet. Bree followed Luna to check on her.

'Have you eaten?' she shouted outside the door.

'Give me a second!' Luna yelled. She was tired and wrung out; nausea and vomiting usually occurred in the first trimester. Luna felt like she'd be puking until she gave birth to the baby.

When she got back to the farm after work, Sole had still not returned her car. The pregnancy test she'd taken in the toilet that afternoon had confirmed her pregnancy – Luna was in her second trimester. She called Cam to tell him.

'You have brought me so much joy, Luna! Please take care of yourself. I can't wait to be with you,' Cam said. 'Why don't you invite your mother to come and stay with you for a while? It might help you tremendously. And I will write to her immediately to state my intentions. Now that the baby is on the way, we need to set a wedding date.'

As much as Luna didn't want to admit it, not having Amora at work felt lonely. Bree and Lucy worked on alternate days to fill in the gaps. Luna didn't have anyone any more. Her mother would be a great solace to her. Having agreed on the way forward, Luna terminated the call.

Speaking to Cam always calmed her, but after hanging up, she always felt bereft.

You need to come home, Cam. We need you.

Sole didn't come back with her car that day. Luna stayed up most of the night, hoping that Cam would call her. Sending him another long text wouldn't help. She had to take matters into her own hands. It didn't matter if this was her brother-in-law; she hated him more and more with each passing day.

When Julie received Cam's letter stating his intentions, she was surprised, but she wanted her daughter to be happy. Julie requested that Cam send her money, the equivalent of four cows, because after chatting with Luna she understood his diminished circumstances. At Cam's request, Ryan handled the negotiations on his behalf, as he was stationed in Simon's Town, from where he could organise everything. Luna would soon start planning the wedding, even though she didn't have a date for it yet, and Julie would come for a visit to support her daughter.

But how am I going to explain the sleeping arrangements to my mother? And where will she sleep?

The situation made Luna anxious. It was too late to cancel her mom's visit, and Cam wanted Julie to come. And she had spoken so excitedly about the trip that Luna couldn't possibly disappoint her. Sole was still missing in action with Luna's car, and John had also disappeared, so it was only Mia and Luna on the farm. Mia joined Luna in the kitchen while she prepared dinner, chatting excitedly about a friend she had made at school.

'She is so nice, Miss Parks. Her name is Pippa; she is in my class.'

'As long as you are happy, that's all that matters.' Luna sensed that Mia was at peace, a massive change from the restless spirit she had been when they'd first met. Mia was growing up rapidly, and Luna wished Cam could see her in these precious moments.

'How are *you* feeling, Miss Parks?'

'Well, that little thing you said about my tummy was true. I'm going to have a baby.'

'I am going to have a sibling!' Mia said joyfully. Her face turned pink with joy as she clapped loudly. Luna quickly went to her and took her hand.

'Oh, baby! You are going to be a big sister now.'

'I am so happy, Miss Parks. I am going to be a sister! I'll finally have someone to play with at home.' Tears shone in her eyes.

'Don't cry, baby. Don't cry.'

But Mia felt only relief; she had been so lonely all her life. She had prayed for this. All the other kids at school always spoke about their siblings, and some of them even attended the same school. But Mia was an outcast and had no stories to share about her siblings. She hugged Luna so tightly that Luna couldn't contain her tears.

'The baby will love you so much, Mia, just like we do. You are an extraordinary girl, and I am grateful you are with us. You bring me so much joy.' Luna kissed Mia's head.

'My father will love me again, right? I will be a good sister, I promise.'

'Mia, your father already loves you. Nothing will change that.'

'Then why doesn't he ever stay? Why does he make promises that he doesn't keep? He is always in a rush and doesn't even care to listen to me.'

Mia touched her hair; it hadn't been trimmed in months and was reaching her bum. She was extremely uncomfortable, and it affected her self-esteem. Other kids always had something to say about their parents taking them to the salon and sharing crazy hair stories and Mia never had any stories. Mia kept those yearnings to herself because she didn't want to complain and make Miss Parks leave. It was so good to have someone who cared for her, tucked her in at night and read stories to her. Mia was so happy about Miss Parks staying with them.

'Now that you are a big sister, what do you want for dessert?' Luna brushed her hair gently, trying to ease Mia's soft sobs.

'Nothing,' Mia muttered into her chest. Luna realised how much Mia mattered to her. She was more than Cam's wife; she was also Mia's mother figure.

'Well, let me tell you a little secret: My mother is coming to visit soon, and she is so excited to meet you.' Mia pulled back and rested her hands on her thighs. Luna didn't understand her sudden retreat.

'What's wrong, Peanut?'

'My mother is in the graveyard and Father said I should stop going there,' she said softly.

'Where is her grave?' Luna couldn't believe what she was hearing.

'It's down the road.'

'That's not right; you should be able to visit your mother's grave if you want to.' Her voice was tender.

'Miss Parks, is your mother nice?'

'Oh, baby, she is wonderful. She has been wanting to meet you.'

'But Miss Parks ...' she couldn't finish her sentence.

'You can tell me, what's eating you?'

'Can you please trim my hair?'

Luna looked at the girl's hair; it was messy, and her waves needed conditioning and a wash. She wanted to kick herself; the child had been asking for a haircut for a while. Luna didn't know much about white people's hair, but she would learn and be a better parent to Mia.

'Let's do that after dinner. Is that okay?'

Mia's smile quickly returned.

'Miss Parks, what about the sea? My father works there, right? When can I go there?'

Luna felt sad. Cam was supposed to take Mia to the beach, but that promise remained unmet.

'Let's wait for your father so we can go together. It will be so much fun. Things are going to get better, Mia. You have a friend now; you will see how much fun you will have this summer. Don't think so hard, child. You are so precious to all of us.'

The night ended perfectly without John and Sole. Luna could only guess where they were, but she enjoyed the peace for once. She paged through the book her mother had given her, and although it was a challenge to understand the words, the pictures helped her immensely with the tea growing. Living on the farm was the most challenging part of her life; without Cam, it was a nightmare. She resolved to focus on Mia and her pregnancy from then on; Sole and John would have to take a back seat.

Luna remembered Cam's excitement when she'd shared the book with him. He was so invested in teaching her about her heritage. With a baby on the way, she understood why her mother insisted she learn about her ancestors. The child would need a name, and Luna didn't know anything about Khoisan names. She wanted her baby to own a piece of her heritage. Giving birth without having Cam present scared her.

Will Sole help me if I go into labour and we're the only people in the house? Would he even call for help?

It had been Amora's dream to have a husband and kids. Thinking of Amora brought a sharp pang of loss; their last conversation had not been pleasant, and now someone was sniffing around Luna. The truth was that she had lost a friend, and it still hurt like hell.

How can no one tell us what happened to Amora? Who is this police officer sniffing around Clanwilliam? How did she find me? I think Dr Mark's ghost is catching up with me.

Luna had so much more to fight for with her marriage and baby; she could not afford to lose.

Chapter 28

For the enemy is close

Sole returned her car three days later, leaving it with little petrol. Luna found the car keys on the kitchen table that morning. Sole was passed out in the lounge with documents in hand. She was curious about the file on the carpet but didn't need his drama so early in the morning. She got Mia ready for school, and when they got to the car, there were scratches on the driver's door and beer bottles in the back seat; the car's exterior was caked in mud. She drove the car to work, praying that it wouldn't give up on her and she could make it to the petrol station.

He's trying to rile me, but I won't give him the attention.

Sometimes, the best way to deal with an enemy was to stop feeding their ego with responses. After Luna guided Mia to class, she rushed back to the car. Driving slowly to work meant she would be a few minutes late. Luna drove past the boarding house and noticed that Sly and Seth were having a heated argument on the pavement outside. Her face grew hot as she thought about what Seth had said about her and Cam's pain the day they found Amora's body. Luna had not expected Cam to fight for her the way he had; she had fallen even deeper in love with him then. Seth was another man that she didn't want near her.

The clinic was not busy that day, so Luna was caught up in her own thoughts when Eve came to sit with her at reception.

'You've been looking tired lately, Luna. Are you okay?' As Luna had told Cam about her pregnancy, it was probably time to share the news with her boss. Her rounded belly seemed to be expanding each day. Soon, everybody would notice her state.

'Actually, Eve, Cam and I are having a baby.'

'That's wonderful news! Congratulations to you both. When he was here a few months ago, the love I saw between you showed that it wasn't a passing fancy. I must say that you have grown since the day you arrived here. I thought you and your friend would pack up and leave within days.' Eve burst into riotous laughter as she passed Luna a cup of tea.

'We were so determined to prove you wrong. You hated us!' Luna laughed as she rubbed her tummy.

'Amora was a force of nature, and she always had an answer to everything. Running this clinic with just Bree and Lucy was a challenge, and you two came in and allowed me to find myself again. You may not have noticed, but I have also found someone to love. He may not be as handsome as your Cam, but he is a good man,' Eve said shyly.

In the last couple of months, Eve had been coming to work late and went on regular 'work trips'. Luna looked at Eve in wonder. It felt good to have someone to talk to.

'I am happy for you, Eve. Where is he from?'

'He works in Hermanus; he has a restaurant there.'

'Well, I must go and visit for some good old seafood.'

Luna instantly thought of Mia and how badly she wanted to see the sea. Luna also missed surfing; her life had changed so much that she had lost touch with the things she used to do just for herself. She didn't even have time to read a novel or go fishing. Everything was about the farm and Mia, and now, getting ready to have this baby. A part of Luna missed her old life. This new one had too many responsibilities.

'He would love the extra customers. You must bring Captain Hunk; he is like our national treasure,' Eve winked.

'I guess …'

'Child, what is really going on? You walk around like you are dead most of the time and this should be an exhilarating time in your life.'

'I miss my fiancé, Eve. I don't even know where he is now. The last time we spoke, he was in some strange country; I can't even remember the name. He's been sending me gifts but that's not enough.'

'He will be back; they always come back. You need to calm down and focus on your baby.'

Luna dreaded going home most days and preferred to stay at work, which exposed her in many ways. The police were asking questions, and she had to avoid them. Luna couldn't go back to Cape Town just yet. Especially not when people were still talking about Amora's death. It would open old wounds, and she wouldn't have the strength to revisit what she had done.

Amora is better off dead at this point. Otherwise, I'd be accountable for two murders. How much longer can I keep this secret on my own?

When the workday ended, Luna headed to the supermarket to buy a few things. Mia was growing up so fast and Luna had to prepare her for her teens. She bought sanitary pads and bath salts for when Mia's menstrual cycle started; she was thirteen already. She also picked up a few magazines for new mothers and then headed back to the farm.

When she got home, Sole sought to erode the little joy she felt. He stood by the kitchen door, watching her park the car by the side of the house. John was in the garden with Mia. Luna could see that they had just fed the animals and watered the garden. She waved at John and called out to Mia. 'I got you a few things, young lady.' Her voice was filled with delight.

'Miss Parks!' Mia called as she tried finding her way to her. Sole watched them in disgust. Luna glanced at him; he was wearing Cam's white shirt and formal pants. Reading glasses were perched on his nose, and Luna reluctantly had to admit that they made him look attractive. She still couldn't get over how uncanny his resemblance was to Cam.

'Take these bags to your room; I think you will like what's there. And watch out, don't eat too many chocolates.' Luna smiled as she passed Mia the bags.

'Thank you, Miss Parks. The bags feel heavy; are they gifts for me?'

'Yes, I had forgotten to get you something for your birthday.'

'But Miss Parks. You did! My birthday clothes!' Mia laughed.

'Well, you deserve more. You have been such an amazing girl. Moreover, your teacher sent me your report card.'

She glanced at John; he was supposed to have fetched it. Luna was drained, so getting the groceries out of the car felt like she was lugging cows around. John ambled over to assist, but Sole stepped in.

'You have been busy, I see?' he said.

'Hello, Sole.'

'You even got this little car washed; it has seen better days.' He pulled the bags out of the boot. Luna just walked off and ignored him.

'It's Miss Parks, right?' he said as entered the house.

'Sole, just cut it! I am not in the mood.'

'But my dear, you must be! I want us to get to know each other better.'

'I just got home, Sole. Can't all of this wait?' Luna went to the guest bedroom and dropped off her handbag, but Sole followed her.

'Tell me why you left Cape Town.'

Luna leaned against the door and sighed deeply.

'I found a better job ... can't you tell, Mr Advocate? I thought you were smart; such information is free.'

'You only worked there for a short period, right?'

'I wasn't planning to stay until retirement,' Luna said.

'No, you *couldn't*, Miss Parks. There's something I don't understand. Maybe you can enlighten me.' His tone was firm and confident. Luna didn't like his line of questioning.

'I don't have to do anything for you, Sole. I have dinner to prepare and a child to help with homework.'

'If you just give me the facts, I won't take up much of your time,' he smirked.

'What do you really want, Sole?'

'I just want to know where my new sister-in-law comes from. Especially if the records show that a man died just before she got her first nursing job. And when she left the same job, another man was reported dead. Isn't that strange, Miss Parks? And now your friend is also dead, and you are here. Living rent-free. Looks like death follows you. I am trying to get to know you; you can also ask me questions. It's not a one-sided conversation. If you need time to process this, I will give you time.

'But, first, tell me about the dead bodies. That's more fascinating. How does a young little Khoisan nurse get all these jobs? Why are you now a farm girl? While you are thinking, tell me why you have a book under your bed that belongs to the Fletchers, Miss Parks? And just across that very mountain, the Fletchers reside. Do you see why I'm interested? I've tried to fill in the missing pieces, but it still doesn't make sense.'

Shock waves went through Luna's legs and straight into her soul. She instantly panicked and couldn't move or say a word. Sole watched her struggle to find her tongue. Her face had turned pale, and her hands were trembling. As she tried to compose herself, Sole watched her like prey. If her wide eyes and rapid breathing were anything to go by, he must be onto something, he thought to himself. Luna pushed him out of the way and went into the bathroom and heaved.

'Miss Parks!' Mia came into the bathroom. 'Are you okay? Is the baby okay?'

Luna felt like stuffing Mia's mouth with her foot, but Mia couldn't see her gestures.

'Well, well, well ... So, you *are* pregnant!' Sole said triumphantly. 'You are something else, Luna Parks. A baby? Does Cam know? Hell, we live with you, and you didn't confirm my suspicions. You're very secretive. Is this even my brother's child?'

He laughed out loud as John came rushing down the corridor.

'Luna, is that true? Are you pregnant?'

'Yes, grandpa. I am going to be a sister!' Mia called out. Luna just wanted to hide and scream.

'We'll help her; is something wrong with the child?' John asked tensely.

'I just need some fresh air.'

'Yes, Father, let's allow Miss Parks to rest. I think I can still make a mean ox liver or steak. Miss Parks, can you eat that?' Sole was mocking her.

'Just give me a moment.' Luna closed the door, shutting all of them out, and sat down on the cold floor.

Fuck! Fuck! How did Sole get all this information? Why is he so fixated on me? He's crossed the line – if only I could get rid of him ... And what does my book have to do with the Fletchers?

Chapter 29

Sweet joy

10 FEBRUARY 2006, Clanwilliam, Western Cape

As the months passed, Luna worried that Cam would not return in time for the child's birth. She was busy at work, but her tummy had grown ever bigger, and she had to waddle everywhere. Her mother had visited the previous month, and Luna had booked her into a guesthouse. She didn't want her to be in Sole's debauched presence. Luna feared her mother would convince her not to proceed with the wedding if she saw her living conditions. Sole continued to pester and pepper her with questions she wouldn't answer. It seemed he got closer and closer to the truth whenever he confronted her with his questions. Luna wanted her mother to meet Cameron first, not the evil twin brother. She needed to keep the Coal family drama away from Julie.

Cam texted weekly and ensured that Ryan popped in whenever he was in town to examine Luna. Cam's gifts never stopped coming, and Sole would sneer every time one was delivered. He called Luna all sorts of names – his favourite was 'opportunist'. There were no words to describe how much Luna missed Cam. Things were tense in the house, but at least John tried to help with the chores.

Then Sole started travelling to Cape Town on Mondays, returning on Thursdays; those were the most peaceful days for Luna and Mia. Luna had overhead Sole telling John that he had been roped in on one of the most significant land claim cases in the Cederberg region.

John took Luna's advice and stayed off alcohol on the days Sole wasn't around. Yet the moment he came back, John would revert to his drinking sprees. It seemed as if he could not refuse Sole, as if he was overcompensating for something. The good news was that the police had stopped sniffing around Luna's place of work.

'You are looking radiant, Luna. You are a beautiful bride-to-be,' Eve said as they filed away the day's work.

'You mean I look like I'm ready to pop!'

'When is your due date? It should be close.'

'In three weeks. I am so scared, Eve; we've spent so much time without Cam and couldn't even celebrate Christmas as a family. The festive season passed without fanfare because celebrating without him just felt wrong. My father-in-law went out drinking, and I was left with Mia. I had never felt so lost in my life. We don't even acknowledge family holidays because we don't know what to do without Cam. I don't know the Coals' customs and traditions; Cam and I are not married yet.'

'Haven't you set a wedding date?' Eve raised her eyebrows in surprise.

'No, we haven't.' Luna looked at her swollen feet, trying to avoid making eye contact with Eve. She carried the shame of being pregnant and unmarried according to Western customs. Luna heard the whispers when she walked around town; some would even spit in disgust as she walked past. It wasn't only Sole who thought her an opportunist.

'I think you will get there soon. After you have your baby, things will be clearer. But what you have done with the school and this clinic should be celebrated. Luna, you have done so much for this community; we are so grateful to you.'

'Oh, Eve! I really enjoy what I do. This work gives me great joy. I have met wonderful people and I still have so much to learn.'

'Just don't leave us and decide to become a farm girl after you get married,' Eve joked. Her comment unsettled Luna. She loved being on the farm and was learning a lot. Something about being on the land made her feel at home. The weekend rides into the fields with Mia and the days she spent learning about rooibos tea gave her great joy. She just wished Cam was there with her and that Sole was not.

'I can do both; I've been doing it all these months.'

'Well, Amora's death made me wonder. I didn't think you would still want to hang around. A young person like you still has so much to offer. Amora died in such a horrible way; I can't imagine the pain you still carry. We all miss her. Bree and Lucy talk about her a bit, and I still can't bring myself to accept her death.'

'We all have different ways of dealing with grief.' Luna tried standing but the weight of her tummy held her down. She was also weighed down by guilt. It had been a year since she and Amora had arrived in Clanwilliam with hearts full of hope.

If I had known that Amora would die here, would I have made a different decision?

Luna's phone vibrated, and she reacted in surprise. 'Mother! Where? Are you sure?' Luna cried as she answered her phone.

'Yes. Open the door. I am here,' Julie responded.

'My mother is here, Eve. She is outside! Please help me up.'

Eve beat Luna to the door, as she was lighter on her feet. Julie had multiple bags with her.

'Mother?' Luna finally reached her. A sense of calm came over her when she saw her mother. Julie Parks always knew how to make things better. Luna needed her prayers.

'Help me, my child, the heat is killing me. If you hug me one more time, that child will melt out of you.'

'I wasn't expecting you,' Luna said joyfully, holding back her sudden tears.

'I got sick of waiting for my grandchild. I am here now. I don't want to miss anything. Don't you dare chase me away as you have before; I want to meet these Coals. If they think they can enjoy this pregnancy without me, they must think again. I am tired of waiting for that man. What type of son-in-law keeps an old woman waiting like this. What if I die?'

Luna started laughing and Eve joined in.

'I am so glad you are here, Mrs Parks. Your daughter has been overeating, and I don't mean good food,' Eve said as she side-eyed Luna.

'All of that nonsense will stop from now on. That's why Luna's got so big. I will cook for her tonight. She needs to rest. How have you been?' Julie asked as she sat down in the reception area. She was wearing her best dress and looked just like Luna. Her hair was pulled back into a bun, and she didn't seem to smile much or take anyone's nonsense.

'We are doing well.'

'I am glad; I need you to let my child go, Eve. She should be on maternity leave by now. She can't work in her condition. And besides, I want her to show me around town, so I know how things work around here. Once the baby is born, she won't have time for anything else. But first, a cup of tea would be lovely.'

'I couldn't agree with you more; I've been telling her to slow down but she refuses,' Eve smiled.

'Mother!' Luna called out in protest from the kitchenette, where she was making Julie's tea.

'I am not leaving until this child is born,' Julie said firmly.

'We will miss her,' Eve said. 'I will struggle to keep this place going without her. We don't have enough nurses around here. And we haven't managed to replace her late friend.'

'Who is her late friend? Luna doesn't have any friends.' Julie turned to take her cup of tea from Luna. She sniffed it and gave it back. 'I didn't teach you to make tea like that. Why does it have a white layer?'

'I used the microwave to boil the water. Our kettle stopped working.'

Julie shook her head and rejected the tea.

'Amora Grootboom; she was murdered,' Eve continued.

'I don't know anyone by that name.' Julie stared at Luna, who busied herself by returning the teacup to the kitchenette; the lies she and Amora had told Eve were about to be exposed.

'That's strange. Luna's long-time friend, Amora. Maybe you forgot her? They arrived here together and were as close as sisters. She was found dead at the boarding house. From what I know, Luna worked with her in Cape Town, and they were transferred here. I wasn't expecting them, but here we are.' Eve watched as Luna stumbled out the door with Julie's bags.

'I know everything about my child, and I don't know that girl. Luna was headhunted. I know nothing about a dead girl. Luna always only focused on her education; friends are the last thing she should have, especially now that she is getting married. There is no time for that.'

Eve didn't want to argue with Julie, but something was off. Luna was never headhunted.

'Eve! Let me call it a day. I believe my mother is tired; let me take her home. I think you will be fine here.'

Luna rushed to her locker and collected her things. Julie was already standing by the car when she returned. Eve was confused by Luna's sudden panic.

Luna had no more excuses to keep her mother away from the farm, not if she was visiting long term. And wary of being caught out in the lies she'd told Eve, she knew had to get out of there. Luna was excited to show her mother the farm and all the work she had done in the garden.

But how will Sole receive us?

They had a light meal in town and then took a brief walk so that Luna could show Julie around. Julie didn't care much for the local shops, though she did pick up more tea and restocked some toiletries. Luna pointed out the boarding house as they drove by, and then they picked Mia up from school. As they drove towards the farm, Julie asked her to stop near a small bridge.

'Is something wrong?' Luna looked around; Mia was giggling at the stories Julie had been sharing along the way.

'That signboard and the number on it ... Look at the erf number and logo, Luna.'

'Oh, that's the gravel road to the Fletcher farm; it's quite far. That's an old board, Mother. I doubt it means anything.'

Julie exited the car and pulled a piece of paper from her bag. She stared at the paper and then at the board in disbelief.

'The gods must be crazy!' she called out. Julie glanced at Luna and back at the board.

'What is it?' Luna was bewildered.

Is my mother going senile? What's going on?

'That book I gave you has the same logo on the back cover. Haven't you noticed?'

'Mother, get back in the car. It's just a board. I don't want to get into trouble. The Fletchers are not nice people.'

I don't know what she's saying. My back is killing me, and I want to get home and take a nap. My mother's fascination with an old, rickety, rusted sign will not help me right now.

'My child, I told you to read your ancestors' book! Where is it? I need it back.' Julie returned to the car and observed the fields. 'We are on old land, Luna.'

Luna had zoned out, as she was fretting about bringing her mother to the farm. She didn't know what she would find there. Sole was unwelcoming and John's drinking got out of hand at times. Mia had stumbled over his passed-out body in the bathroom once.

What if John is naked and drunk on the floor?

'Mother, please remember that these people are my family now. Please be kind,' Luna pleaded as they approached the gates to the farm.

'Is this the farm? It's huge. Just look at the mountains surrounding it. Luna, this is wonderful. I am so happy for you. I can see why you decided to move here. I don't like that you moved in with this man, but I like this area.'

'His name is Cameron,' she reminded her mother as she parked the car.

'I would hardly know, would I, Luna? This man paid *lobola* for you, but I haven't even met him yet.'

'Miss Parks, I need the bathroom,' Mia said from the back seat.

'Oh, sorry, baby. You can quickly go inside.'

Mia got out of the car with her backpack. As she approached the door, Sole stepped out.

'Watch your step, brat,' he said as Mia passed. Just the sight of him made Luna freeze.

'Is that him? Your darling Cameron?' Julie looked at the white man in confusion and wonder. Out of all the men her daughter could've chosen, she had chosen a white man. Julie had tried to educate Luna as much as possible about her heritage. Still, they all lived in a democratic South Africa, where interracial relationships could be explored without fear of persecution. Change was still a difficult thing to accept.

'That's his twin brother.'

'So, he also looks like a returned sailor?' Julie couldn't hide her disappointment; she didn't think she would feel this way. Reality was hard to accept.

'Mother, please,' Luna said as she opened the door.

Sole watched them unload the car.

'You brought another one of your kind,' Sole sneered. 'What's the story now? Are you opening a safe house for black women on our farm? Did she flee from the townships?'

Luna felt her stomach drop as Julie turned to study Sole. The look in her eyes could have frozen hell to its core.

Chapter 30

The Bridge

'If that's how you speak to my daughter, let it be the last time!' Rage shot through Julie.

'It's fine, Mother. This is Sole Coal, Cam's brother.' Luna attempted to cut through the tension.

'I didn't think you would have a mother,' Sole chimed in with a smirk. 'What is this now? Are we not good enough? You had to call the entire village to live in my house?' He was unmoved by Julie's rage.

'Show me your beautiful home, my child?' Julie ignored Sole and ushered Luna inside.

As they entered the house, Luna thought of the shameful bedroom she slept in.

I must ask Mia to return to her room so my mother can sleep with me. I hope it won't hurt Mia's feelings.

This was not what she had ever imagined. Her mother would have to take the bed and she would sleep on the floor.

'This is cosy,' Julie said as she observed the kitchen.

'Cam was busy renovating. We still have to do a few touch-ups, but this is home. I am so glad you are here.'

'Touch-ups? Right!' Sole said from a distance. 'Where is she from with all these bags?' he added. Julie and Sole stared at each other, neither willing to relent.

'Where will I sleep? Is the little girl okay?'

'Mia? She is probably listening to music or reading; those are her favourite pastimes. We are in here.'

Luna guided Julie to the guestroom, opening the door slowly, as if expecting a brand-new room.

'Luna! You sleep here? With your husband? On this makeshift bed with blankets? With a child?' Julie was stupefied. Luna entered the room and placed Julie's bags on the floor. The room felt cold and eerie. The single bed had no headboard, there were no carpets on the floor and most of Luna's clothes were folded on the floor on top of newspapers. Sole laughed as he passed them in the hallway and opened the door to Cam's bedroom.

'Luna, is this where you sleep? In this storeroom? It feels like a fridge. You can't sleep in here in your condition!'

'Mother, this is all we have right now,' Luna said, ashamed, as she sat down on the bed.

'So, you left a perfectly comfortable home with me to come and live like a homeless person in Clanwilliam! I understand now why you didn't want me to come to the farm when I was here last time. I don't understand why you subject yourself to this, Luna! I might not be wealthy, but I raised you with dignity and pride. What is this? We can just go home, Luna. You have a home, you know. Cameron had better get back fast; he needs to explain this to me. Do you love this Cameron of yours?'

Luna wanted to tell her the truth, but it would just cause another fight. She averted her eyes so that she could not see the disappointment on her mother's face.

'Yes, I do, Mother. He is a good man. I just have to wait out this period. Things will be better when he returns.' Luna's face looked like she was in pain, but Julie continued talking.

Luna noticed Sole stepping out of the house. His gaze brushed hers as he walked past their door. John was back; she could hear his drunken ruckus from inside their room.

'This town is so small, and the farm is not that close to town. Luna, love can be so debilitating. You are here caring for his child and rude brother, yet you sleep on this dilapidated, makeshift bed? Is it really worth it? Men will use you and then leave you, Luna. You know what happened with that father of yours – here one day and gone the next. Are you even sure that this Cameron is coming back?'

'Mother, please.'

'Marriage is no joke, my child. You won't be able to leave when you want. You have to think about this. You can't just be happy because you want a wedding. You are giving these people every-thing. What about your job? Will this man take care of you when you can't work? What do you really know about these people?' Julie looked around in distress.

'I am fine, Mother. All these questions right now won't help me. I have a baby on the way; this is all we have now. Please, there are people here and I don't want any more trouble. I need to check on Mia. Please settle in; I will be back.'

As Luna left the room, Braxton Hicks contractions seared her abdomen momentarily. She breathed through them to hide her dis-comfort from her mother.

'Luna, this is not how you treat guests. Come back here!'

But Luna continued walking to escape her mother's chastisement. She did not want Julie's drama to add to her problems.

I'm an adult, for goodness' sake! She can't speak to me as if I'm still a teenager.

John and Sole were outside, at the back of the house, whispering. Luna followed the sound of their voices, but something told her to keep her distance. The darkness of night helped to conceal her pres-ence. Her intention was to find a quiet place to sit and just breathe. As she drew nearer to them, she heard John say something in his inebriated state. She wanted to check on him, but it was getting late, and she hadn't even begun cooking. Luna heard her mother talking to Mia in the house, but that was not her concern.

'I am sorry I told you to leave, but I thought what you did to Cam would destroy all of us,' Luna heard John say. 'He was going to find out; he always does. What were you going to say? How were you going to live with him in this house? You know how he gets when he is angry. I wasn't going to allow him to kill you. Asking you to leave was the only solution. I have always dreaded this day, Sole;

I knew it would come and here you are. What will I ever tell Mia? How will they accept this? Cameron is going to marry Luna; you must leave them alone. You have taken so much from Cameron already. You are a grown man now; just find your own peace and let this go.'

'Father, if he marries that girl, I will be left with nothing. Do you understand that?'

'Cam lives here, and you don't.'

'Cam doesn't care about this farm. I have the means and I know people who can help us rebuild it. But this girl can't have my inheritance.'

'You worry about things that don't serve us. You have been here for a few weeks and you haven't helped us with anything. Luna cooks, cleans and buys food. Hell, she is way better than you, and your brother is not even here to see how you treat your own child and his wife. Have you no shame, Sole?'

'Mia is no child of mine. She was supposed to die! You were there; it's your fault Cam saved Mia from the fire. You changed the plan, Father. She was supposed to burn with Summer. Then all of this wouldn't have happened.'

'You wanted me to kill a child? Is that it? Are you sick in the head? You are spoilt and I keep protecting you. I thought you would change, maybe grow up a little, but you are still the same. You killed Summer, Sole. It was a mistake to sleep with her, but what you did after that to keep your secret is all on you.'

'How many times should I tell you this? I went into a room; I didn't know it was her inside. We were at a party, and she thought I was Cameron. I was drunk; I didn't stop her. The child was conceived that night and I never touched Summer again. She wanted to tell Cam, but I couldn't allow that. But what you did to me was harsh and evil. You forced me to leave, Father! You chose Cameron over me!' Sole said in a plaintive tone. Luna pressed herself against the wall and held her breath.

'You slept with Summer, Sole! You soiled her and let Cam believe that this child was his. You were not man enough to face your brother and you dragged me into your secret. You were there that night; you could have saved Summer, but you wanted her to die so that your secret could stay safe. I had to let you go. What did you think would happen? Did you think Summer would have left Cam for you? You were just a one-night stand; she didn't even know it was you who came into her room that night. How would you let Cam know all of this without destroying this family? Now you want to come back because you want this land?'

'Father, it was a mistake! We were young and drunk.'

'No, Sole. Knowing you could have saved Summer has killed me all these years. You saw she was in trouble; you removed Mia from her back. You uprooted that tree that fell on her. I saw you, Sole. I tried to protect this family. All you keep doing is mess it up for everyone and blame others for your mistakes.'

My poor Cam. All these years he had tried to build a relationship with Mia but struggled to connect with her. All this time, he had thought that he was a lousy father, but his own father and brother were the cause of his anguish.

'You promised me that you would never say anything,' Sole pleaded.

'I am tired of keeping your secrets. My actions weigh heavily on me, Sole, and what we did ten years ago has been the biggest yoke. Do you know how hard Cole has tried in the past decade to care for this family while you were out there living your best life as a hot-shot lawyer? I am sick of it. Just look at how you are treating Mia and Luna now! Why are you so full of hate? Your brother has raised your child, and this is the thanks he gets?'

'You are drunk; let's go inside!'

'You are a fine one to speak. I drink because of the sin you let me carry all these years. I have watched Cam mourn Summer to no end. You broke him. You killed his wife! Summer was pure and innocent, but you took advantage of her youth. You saw her try to save your mother, but you sabotaged her. The memory of those flames has stayed in my mind ever since. Why are you back, Sole? You have been in the wild all these years, and when your brother tries to build his life, you come back?'

'This is my home too, Father. Have you not missed me?'

John was both devasted and full of remorse. Something in him had changed; seeing Luna suffer broke his heart. He had not kept his promises to his son, and he couldn't live with himself any more. Drinking was the only way he could escape his conscience, because with Sole's return, the reminder of what he had done stared him in the face daily.

'I missed you, like any father would long for his son, but you have your own motives. Now, you call me a drunk? Do you know how much I suffered when my wife died? Do you know that this farm is in debt? We can lose it any day now, and here you are, standing over me like a king! You are not remorseful, Sole.'

Luna was shaking with rage and fear. The fabric of this family would unravel if what she'd just heard was ever revealed. It would obliterate the lives Cam and Mia had carved out for themselves – a life built on a foundation of hurtful lies.

Sole is dangerous. He killed Cam's wife, and he has no remorse, and he wanted the same fate for his own flesh and blood. What chance do I have against that kind of evil?

When Luna slipped back into the house, her mother was preparing supper in the kitchen. She wouldn't look at Luna, but Julie was aware of her tears.

'Where have you been? Are you okay, my child? Why are you crying?'

'I am just tired, Mother. I miss my fiancé, and all of this is overwhelming. Maybe you're right; we should have gone home. You shouldn't have come here, Mother. When will you let me be? You can't control my life forever.'

'Watch your tone, Luna. I understand that this is not ideal, but just look at you; your child will arrive any day now. I have to be here for you.'

'Thank you, but please have some boundaries.' Luna stood next to the fridge, feeling breathless. She tried to calm down; the stress was not good for the baby. Mia was in the lounge reading one of her Braille books. Luna's heart broke for her.

'I am here to make sure you are well, my child,' Julie said.' I don't want to mess up your plans. You will have this baby, and after that, I can leave. I have things to sort out. I am retiring soon, and I thought you needed me here. I don't mean to overstep, but you are my only child. I can't let you go through childbirth alone. We also need to sort out your wedding plans. Have you been learning from that book I gave you?' Julie sensed that something was amiss, but Luna pushed her away.

'Mom, you know I can't read that language. I have tried but I just can't. It's a wonderful book but I don't have the energy right now.'

'That book is the backbone of your ancestors. Your child will be mixed, but they must also know their origins. As much as you live on this farm, your ancestors also lived like this at some point. That book will help you. It was written over many years, and it contains valuable information, Luna. Don't take it lightly. Didn't you look at that signboard near the bridge?'

'Mother, those boards are old. They mean nothing.'

'You can be foolish at times, my child.'

Julie glanced at the family picture on the wall and noticed something familiar. The photo was not taken on the Coal farm, but something about the building the family stood in front of niggled at her. She had seen that building somewhere.

'I need a shower,' Luna said. 'John and Sole are outside. John is Cam's father, so don't be alarmed when you see him. I just need a moment to myself. Thank you for cooking.'

'You need to get off your feet and stop crying. These people will think you are weak. Pull yourself together. We need to discuss baby names and a birthing plan too. That clinic is too far; I think a home birth will be better. We just need some supplies. Call your boss tomorrow and ask for some. I think she will help you.'

Luna couldn't keep up; it was just too much information. Everyone seemed to have something to say, and she just couldn't take it any more.

Chapter 31

The Tea Merchant

John did not sleep well that night; he was up for most it, pondering the state of his family. He worried deeply about his conversation with Sole. Sole's behaviour made John rethink his actions over the years. If Cam ever found out the truth, he would surely go mad. Sole's lack of remorse and arrogance irked John; what kind of son had he raised?

Mia's attachment to Luna was a concern, because what would happen if Luna decided to leave? It sounded like her mother wasn't happy with her daughter's living conditions. John had heard snippets of their conversation in his drunken haze. He also heard Mia cry at night, and Luna would always wake up to comfort her. Mia had rarely slept alone since Luna moved in.

He peeked into Mia's bedroom and found Luna and Mia sleeping on the floor. Mia's bed wouldn't fit them both. Seeing a pregnant woman on the floor tore at his heart; Luna was sacrificing so much for Mia. Sole's arrival had changed the way they lived. There was no more harmony or happiness. Mia adored Luna, and John could understand why. She had taken the place of the mother Mia had had for such a short time, and all because of Sole. Mia had opened her heart to Luna, something she had never done with anyone else. John closed Mia's door to find Julie cleaning the guest bedroom.

'Mrs Parks, we finally meet. My apologies that I couldn't welcome you last night.'

'John, good to meet you. I was about to make some tea.'

'I will be happy to make it. Continue doing what you do; you'll find me in the kitchen. The cattle need to be taken out to graze, and the horses need a bit of exercise. Afterwards, I was thinking we could go to town. I need a few things. We are preparing for harvest. I think this will be a good time for us to get to know each other.'

'Thank you for the invitation, I will join you. I must pass by the clinic and get some supplies and medication for Luna and Mia.'

'Is everything all right?'

'Mia didn't sleep well, and Luna complained about back pain. I just want to prepare things for her. Children can sense when a new child is on the way, and Mia is getting anxious, so that might be why. She is a wonderful child.'

'We can take the wagon; I must also pass by the market.'

'Wonderful! I will see you shortly.'

As she went about her business, Julie spotted Sole smoking outside. She sorted Luna and Mia's clothes and did their laundry. It wasn't much, but Julie wanted to relieve Luna of some of the load she carried. John had fed the animals and was ready to leave. Sole didn't bother speaking to them throughout the morning, and Luna and Mia were still sleeping.

John and Julie rode into town, chatting throughout the journey. They both knew so much about rooibos, and Julie was so curious about what she had seen on the bridge the day before. She asked John to drive closer to the Fletcher land. John didn't protest; Julie was a fountain of information. She knew her history well and he found her fascinating.

When Luna woke up, the weather had cleared, and the sun was on top of the mountains. She went outside and found Sole tending to the garden. He carried a shovel and was still disrespectfully clothed in Cam's farming attire.

Luna walked to her car and opened the boot. She'd forgotten to remove some items the day before. She peered inside and noticed the uniform she'd worn when she'd left Cape Town; her name tag was still on it.

Why is this still here? When did I last see it?

'Can I play in the fields for a bit, Miss Parks?' Mia asked.

'Mia, be careful out there. Take something to eat,' Luna called out. She felt nervous, but Mia was fearless and brave.

'Let her go; nothing will happen to her,' Sole called out, watching Mia. 'She's lived here all her life and knows her way around.'. His daughter had grown into a tall and beautiful girl. Even acknowledging her in the silent chamber of his heart brought feelings of regret and shame. He could've raised and loved her, even as an uncle, yet all of it was taken away. Sole couldn't claim her now; she didn't even know him, and she loved Luna more than she did him.

Sole walked towards Luna. She didn't notice how close he'd come because she was watching Mia navigate the footpath with her stick.

'Charles and Robertson Private Clinic!' he called out.

Pale and tight-lipped, Luna continued clearing her boot. She found Mia's school shoes and books. When she remembered what she had overheard the night before, she wanted to hurt Sole. He made her sick to her stomach.

'You must be an actress,' Sole whispered in Luna's ear as he squeezed her shoulders.

'Living with you can turn one into an animal, but I choose not to be like you,' Luna replied.

'Do you even like it here?'

'I actually belong here. This is my family because of Cameron.'

'You speak highly of Cam; he is not an idol.'

'And you are?' Luna snapped back.

'I am way better than him, that's for sure.'

'Right!' Luna laughed.

'Don't marry him, Luna. For your own sake.'

'I will marry whomever I please, Sole.'

'Everyone is fooled by your innocent and caring act. I thought you would have taken your bags and left us alone, but you are still here. Your acting skills have the entire town in thrall. How do you do it?'

'Get your hands off me, Sole.'

'And if I don't, will you kill me? Is that it?'

Luna tried shaking him off, but he just squeezed harder. His words frightened her.

'I found out something interesting,' Sole hissed. 'There are some court documents that I can't explain. What's your connection with the Fletchers? Are you an informer?'

'You always work too hard, don't you?' Luna said scornfully.

'The book you have belongs to the Fletchers. I searched for the logo and the erf number on the back of that book. Your darling mother must know something. Is she here to help you take over our land? What do you people know about rooibos tea? You aren't just consumers.'

'You need to stay away from my belongings, Sole! What do you want?'

'Well, you seem to forget that you are in my house, and this is my land. Tell me, why are you in possession of documents that belong to the Fletchers?'

'I don't know what you are talking about!' Luna was both exasperated and frightened. John and her mother weren't around; no one could protect her.

'If you say so ... Let's go back to the man you killed at your previous employment. What happened there, Luna? You were not transferred here; no one signed your papers. Only Dr Mark Rivers could do that, and he is dead. How did you get the job at the clinic? Did *you* kill your friend Amora?'

'I did no such thing!' Luna stiffened as her baby kicked. She bit her lip so hard that she could taste blood.

'You keep lying, but remember when I took your little car for a joy ride? I saw your uniform and the tiny blood splatters on it. These led me back to the dead man. Is it his blood on that uniform, Luna? You have to tell me the truth; we are family now.'

'I have nothing to tell you; get off me!' Luna pushed him away.

'No, come here.' Sole grabbed her by the hand and dragged her into the house. He didn't care if he was hurting her; he tightened his arm around her like barbed wire. Luna huffed, trying to wrestle away from his grip. When they got to Sole's bedroom, she noticed that papers were scattered all over the bed. Sole pushed her inside the room and closed the door.

'Tell me who Calextina Sarah Parks is?' Sole's piercing green gaze bored into her.

'I don't know.'

'Rubbish!'

Luna tried to think of a way out, but she was in a panic.

'I won't ask you again.'

'She was my great-grandmother!'

'What? That's impossible!' Sole was pacing the room, both shocked and confused. 'You people own Fletcher's land! How is that possible?'

Luna was dumbfounded, but realisation dawned as she recalled her mother's stories about their family history. Luna picked up the papers on the bed and started reading them. Her eyes couldn't comprehend what she was seeing.

'What do you know about this?' Sole demanded.

'I promise, I know nothing, Sole. I didn't know anything about this! I haven't even met the Fletchers.'

'Why do you have that wooden box with their tea branding on it?'

'It was a gift from my mother.'

'Your mother knows the Fletchers?'

'No ... I don't know ... I mean, I'm not sure.'

'That land was registered in your family name in 1934. Is that why you came here? You want that land?'

'I don't want anyone's land! I am here because my fiancé asked me to be here, Sole. Please believe me!'

The documents were shaking in her hands as she tried to make sense of her altered reality. These proved that her family had once owned the Fletcher land. At the bottom of the page, she saw her grandmother's printed name, but there was no signature. Someone had replaced her name with 'J. S. Fletcher' in 1985.

'What will you do about this?' Sole asked.

'I don't know, Sole.' Luna was trembling.

'If you love my brother as much as you say you do, you will get that land and share it with him. And you will leave ours alone.'

Luna couldn't believe what she was hearing.

Does he hate Cam that much? Is Sole so selfish that he doesn't want his twin brother to share in their family's land?

'What will you do with this farm?' Luna asked Sole. 'You haven't set foot on it in years and now you think you can just walk in and kick everyone out.'

'John will die soon; he is old. Cameron is marrying you, and you will have to build your own home. This farm belongs to the family; you can't raise your kids here. I'm the eldest, so the land will become mine when John passes.' Sole looked at Luna's tummy in disgust. She felt the sudden urge to protect her unborn child from his evil gaze.

'You are a monster and a liar!' Luna shouted.

'You know nothing about me!' Sole drew closer to her face.

'What do you want to do?'

'You have no clue what I can do, Luna. Don't test me.'

'Are you going to kill me the way you killed Summer? Is that it? You think you are better than Cameron, don't you? Why are you suddenly so quiet?' Luna pushed him away.

Her heart felt as if it would beat right out of her chest. Confronting Sole with what she knew could be the last thing she ever did. Luna knew the lengths that Sole had taken to cover up his secrets. The darkness in his eyes was apparent. He was shaking his head in disbelief.

Sole is close to discovering my secret, but I know his. If we strike a deal, maybe I can save my life. I don't have to tell him the whole truth, but just enough for him to believe me.

'You want the truth, Sole ... I killed Dr Mark Rivers because he wanted to have sex with me. I was a virgin and I had to protect myself. That man had harassed me at work for weeks on end. He begged me day and night, but I refused. I killed him in self-defence. What you did to Summer, though, was pure evil, and you lost your mother in the process. What you did to your brother is unforgivable. You can't even look at Mia, and she is *your* child. You are a coward! You came here and turned John into a drunk. That man was trying to change; he was depressed and isolated all these years and you think you are better? He lied for you, and you still don't care. You can't blackmail me, Sole. You have a child that lives in this house and that's proof enough of your deceit and betrayal towards your own brother.'

'You are delusional!' Sole screamed.

'I heard your little talk with your father! Don't you dare try to lie!'

'You better close your mouth if you want this marriage to happen. Otherwise, you will raise that child alone or in jail.'

'Checkmate, Sole. Do you want me to leave that badly? How do I know you didn't forge these documents?'

'You can go to the Title Deeds Office, but you won't find this document. But in my involvement with Land Claims the past few months, I've learnt about how people have concealed their actions to steal land from the indigenous people. The case I'm working on with the Ebenhauser community is a clear example. Just because something is not documented doesn't negate its validity. Most Khoisan in the Cederberg region are landless while white farmers control more than ninety per cent of the land under rooibos cultivation.'

Luna looked at him – Sole was serious.

'It's the lasting impact of colonisation on the indigenous people of South Africa. Unfortunately, the wheels of justice move very slowly, even under the new dispensation. I just can't believe all of this!' Luna said.

'You said you don't know the Fletchers.' Sole was trying to calm himself down. He still needed to understand what the connection was between Luna and the Fletchers.

'No, I don't.' Luna sighed with relief; she finally had some power over him. The fighting had to stop. The truth was bitter and could destroy everything they both wanted. It would be a secret that bound them.

'John has told me things about the Fletchers,' Sole said. 'They are dangerous. I have been trying to find out what's happening there, so I went to Fletcher's harvest party. I couldn't snoop around because he's got surveillance cameras everywhere. I need to help my father with our farm and Seth did something that bothered me.'

'What did he do?'

'I saw him talk to someone and there were guns in his car. What bothered me the most was the way he sounded; he's mentally unstable.'

'Seth is a drunk. I don't think we should worry about him,' Luna said dismissively.

'Do you really love Cam?' Sole came to sit down next to Luna and sighed deeply. He felt tired and defeated. And scared that Luna would tell Cam the truth. He wasn't ready to fight with his brother, and he also didn't want the responsibility of being a father.

'Your brother is an honourable man; he has lost so much. Please don't take Mia away from him.'

'I have no desire to. We all do stupid things in life, and they come back to bite us.'

Sole looked at Luna. She was pale, yet her love for his family made her solid. He wished his family could love him the way they loved Luna. Sole felt a heaviness in his heart that he couldn't explain.

Luna observed him closely. This was the first time they were having a civilised conversation. Peace could prevail. Sole sat with his head bowed, his hands covering his face. Luna didn't know what to do, but eventually she touched his shoulder.

'We are family, Sole; we can't live with so much hate. You have to forgive yourself.'

'I've tried, Luna, but I just can't forget. My father is losing his mind and it's all my fault. I don't know what he will say when Cam comes back. I miss my family, Luna. It has been hard. I have no family of my own and I just can't seem to move on.'

'Everybody deserves love, Sole, and with you being an advocate, I'm sure women are throwing themselves at you.'

'I have wronged so many people to get to where I am, Luna. The courtroom is a cold battlefield.' He stood up and walked to the window.

'Try to fix your family,' Luna said. 'That's where you will find peace. This land is big enough for all of us.'

'I hear you,' Sole said as he nodded in dismay.

Sole and Luna sat in the bedroom and read through all the documents he had collected. Sole believed they had a strong case to reclaim the Fletcher land but that they would have to wait for the right time. Luna's baby was due soon and she needed to focus on that.

When John and Julie returned, Luna and Sole shared their discovery with them. Julie was shocked that her mother's stories and the family heirloom had been the key to what was rightfully theirs. If Julie passed the land on as her inheritance, Luna would be the owner. Not only was Luna a well-respected nurse in the Clanwilliam community, but she was also The Tea Merchant.

Chapter 32

The beginning of the end

Cam entered the house, tiptoeing to minimise the sound of his footsteps echoing in the still night. He dropped his backpack in the lounge and looked around in the dark; everything was still in place. New school photos of Mia hung on the walls. The sneakers left near the fireplace gave him pause; it didn't look like something John would wear. Various documents, the Coal family photo taken at the Fletcher farm and Luna's ancestors' book were scattered on the coffee table; Cam didn't have time to peruse them because he was eager to be reunited with his love.

He drank a glass of water in the kitchen and then went to his bedroom, where he was surprised to find a man sleeping in his bed. Cam couldn't make out the man's features as his face was hidden in the pillows. Anger rose within him, but he didn't let it overwhelm him before he could understand what was happening. Cam opened the guest bedroom door slowly. A heavily pregnant woman lay on the floor on a makeshift mattress, and with the help of the hallway light, Cam realised it was Luna. An elderly woman was sleeping on a single bed covered in blankets.

Luna lay there like an abandoned child; this was no place for her to sleep, especially in her condition. How long had she been sleeping there? Her petite body was carrying so much weight. He wanted to pick her up but didn't want to startle her.

'Why is she on the floor? How long has she been sleeping here? How could Father allow this?' Cam muttered to himself. It hurt his soul.

'My Love ... Sweets.' Luna opened her eyes slowly, fighting the cobwebs of sleep.

Cam stooped down and gently touched her belly. Happiness and a frisson of excitement filled him as he felt the baby move under his touch. He was going to have a child. Cam kissed Luna repeatedly, reacquainting himself with her skin and lips. She felt warm and soft.

'Luna Coal.' He dropped down and lay next to her. Their eyes locked. 'Hello, mother of my child,' he whispered. Cam's eyes were hot with love and desire; his gaze touched on her everywhere.

Luna touched his face in disbelief. He was in his uniform, clean-shaven, and he had a new haircut. Luna thought she was dreaming. His familiar scent, of the ocean and burnt leather, confirmed that her husband-to-be had returned. She couldn't breathe past the joy she felt.

'Cameron!' she teared up. Months of longing were expressed through her tears. 'You are here!' She cried so hard that Julie woke up.

'Luna!' she called out. 'Is the baby okay?' Julie jumped out of bed and switched on the light. She was wearing a long night dress, but her breasts were slightly visible. Her eyes flashed with anger at the scene before her.

'Sole, what are you doing in here? Leave us at once!' She pulled a blanket off the bed and covered herself.

'Mother!' Luna called out. 'It's Cameron! My husband is back.'

He had kept his promise and come home in time for the birth. Luna thought of her mother's lost love, her father who had left and never returned. Luna's voracious gaze took Cam in; he was just like she had imagined him on all those lonely, cold nights. Cam helped Luna up and introduced himself to Julie.

'Mrs Parks, I apologise for disturbing your sleep. I needed to see my wife.' He placed his hand on Luna's shoulders.

'It is lovely to finally meet you. We have been praying for your safe return.' Julie couldn't believe her eyes. Sole and Cam were the same person. She couldn't get past how handsome Cam was, but he was also so much more substantial than Sole. Cam's deep voice was the defining factor, as was his uniform, which made him look distinguished and dignified.

As he was speaking, John and Sole came rushing in after having heard Luna's cries. When John saw Cameron, he froze with joy. Sole was right behind him.

'Father. Sole.' Cam shook their hands. 'Why is my wife sleeping on the floor?' he asked. Cam looked at them all, but for a long moment, no one said anything. 'Luna, why are you on the floor in your condition? Why is Mrs Parks sleeping in that decrepit bed?'

'Cam, it was just for one night,' Luna lied.

'Don't lie to me, Luna. Why are your clothes on the floor? It's clear you have moved into this room. Why is that? I prepared our room for you, and now you are on the floor.'

His tone was changing; John knew that Cam was struggling to contain his anger.

'Son, we can fix that in the morning. Let's not wake Mia up. It's really late. We are happy that you are home.' John gave Cam an awkward smile.

'I don't care! I want her back in her own room now. Luna, please bring my daughter.' Cam's tone brooked no argument. Luna went to Mia's room and woke her up.

'Peanut, your father is here,' she whispered. Luna led Mia out of the bed and to the guestroom.

'Peanut,' Cam said, taking Mia into his arms and kissing her. She cried into his chest, which brought Julie and Luna to tears.

'I am here, sweet baby. I am here,' Cam soothed her.

'Sole, I think it's time to give your brother his space; he must be tired.' John looked meaningfully at Sole; they both knew what he wasn't saying. This wasn't about the bedroom – Sole feared his father would tell Cam everything.

'I will get the bedroom ready. Luna, I am deeply sorry.' Remorse overwhelmed Sole; he wasn't expecting to feel like this. When he saw Mia in Cam's arms, he knew he couldn't break the bond that they had. Sole wasn't as gentle and patient as Cam. It hurt to see Mia's love for Cam when she didn't even care to acknowledge him. And as Luna knew the truth, Sole would have to ensure that she stayed happy. This was his family and breaking it up would be unforgivable.

Luna was not his enemy – the enemy was within. Sole sighed heavily and walked off.

Luna could see how terrified Sole was of Cam and she accepted his apology with a curt nod. She had waited for Cam for this very moment. She needed his love to protect her. She was so tired of fighting, fearing and feeling out of place. Cam's presence conveyed so much without him having to say anything. That's why she loved him; he didn't have to exert any power or express mere words. His presence and his eyes did all the talking.

John helped Sole clear the main bedroom and John offered Julie his room. He and Sole would have to take the guest bedroom. Cam and Luna returned to their rightful place, and as she closed her eyes, surrounded by Cam's warmth, she thanked God.

In the dead of night, all the stars aligned, and the moon danced. Luna could finally sleep in peace. The last couple of months had been hard.

'Cameron!' Luna called out in her sleep. She was soaking wet; sweat covered her face. 'It's the baby! Call my mother!' All the tension was released in her body, and she cried out in both joy and panic. Baby Emily Coal was born that night. Joy filled the house like angels in the skies.

The next day, Julie baked and cooked for everyone, and they spoke about family traditions and Julie's love for rooibos tea. Knowing the truth was bittersweet for all of them. Julie and Cam seemed to get along well. Luna was on bed rest and Sole was trying to obtain more information to strengthen the land claim they would soon lodge.

That week, Cam learnt that Seth had been arrested for illegal possession of unlicensed firearms. When Cam reached the holding cells at the police station, Sole was also there, trying to obtain documents from the police. He asked Cam to stay with him while he spoke to Seth.

'Brother,' Cam said as he looked at him through the bars.

'Cameron.' Seth stood up to greet him.

'This is no place for you.' Cameron held out his hand through the bars and noticed the scars on Seth's hands.

'I belong here, Cam. You can't help me this time around.'

'We will get you out, brother. It's just a matter of time.' Cam was saddened; things had turned out for the worse for Seth. Cam and Seth had once understood each other deeply; they had lived with one another for years in the Navy, been on missions together, even eaten from the same plate in the wild. Seth was an intelligent sniper and the Navy had lost his skills. Though they still needed him, his arrest and the investigation into his previous conduct would hinder his return.

'What do you need?' Cam asked.

'I need you, my brother. You're all I have. I'm sorry for what I said about your wife; I don't know what's wrong with me, Cam,' he said pitifully, gazing at Cam with endless sorrow.

'Why did you have those guns? Where were you going?' Sole asked Seth.

'At first, I was going to kill myself. But that would have been too easy. Then I wanted to go hunting, but that would not have been the same without Ryan and Cam. Then I went to the motel and had some drinks. After that, I don't remember much. I blacked out.'

'You need to get off the alcohol, Seth. How did you burn your hands?'

'I cooked a bitch!' Seth said and abruptly pulled away from Cam's touch.

'A bitch, you say?' Sole raised his eyebrows in shock.

'Fish, not bitch! That's an old story. I have news for you, Cameron.' Seth was rubbing the scars on his hands. He still smelt of alcohol. Cam and Sole didn't know that they were facing a cold-blooded killer. Seth was playing them; he knew Cam had a soft spot for him, and he would use the information he had to escape. Amora would soon be a distant memory – just another dead black girl.

'We don't have time; what is it?' Cam stood side by side with Sole.

'The Fletchers are behind the killings happening in the region;

they have been burning your land for years. That old man told me to my face. I thought he was crazy, but he is a killer.'

'Seth, are you sure?'

'Yes. Have I ever lied to you?'

Cameron looked at Sole. Raged filled his face. Death would come upon the Fletcher land. Sole asked Seth for more details, and he told them about the voice recorder in his car with which he had recorded his conversation with Fletcher. Cam felt an uncontrollable rage build up inside him. A yearning filled with hate. With everything else he knew about the Fletcher land, this pushed him to the very edge.

'Let's get my wife's land back!' Cam said to Sole.

A war had been declared, and the devil watched them from behind the steel cage.

In life, we choose our battles. We choose family. We choose love.

Sole had chosen his battle. He kept the police at bay to protect Luna so that they could bring the mighty Fletchers down. Steven played his role as Sole's friend and together they managed to conceal who had murdered Dr Mark Rivers. Luna and Cam got married on the beach in Hermanus in a beautiful white wedding as per Mia's request. The reception was held at Eve's boyfriend's restaurant. It was a joyous celebration of redemption. Their families and all their community friends came to witness the event.

A family was restored with love, but the fight had just begun.

THE END

COMING SOON

The Advocate

Find out what happens to Sole, Cameron and Luna in Book II of this two-part series!

OTHER TITLES BY JACKIE PHAMOTSE

Fiction

BARE: The Blessers Game
BARE II: The Cradle of the Hockey Club
BARE III: Ego
BARE IV: Mercy
BARE V: Curtain Call

Liwa – Always on their Minds

Kids' Series

Liwa, Oh Mama it's Red Apples
Liwa and Noel
Chasing Sunsets

Non-Fiction

I Tweet What I Like

Author's Note

The Tea Merchant is a new world steeped in history; may it remind you of who you are and what you desire from life. Luna Parks and Cameron Coal will teach you a few things about standing up for those you love. It's a story full of suspense with love at its centre. Paul and Rita Thomas from the *BARE* series inspired this book. Their love was unconditional and forgiving – the type of love you want to sacrifice your life for.

May you open your heart to mend those relationships that you long for. I believe we are all capable of loving and receiving genuine love.

Thank you to the few friends who stayed with me throughout this turbulent journey. I still have no words to explain what I am going through, but we are all fighting to stay true to ourselves and live out our deepest desires. I've overcome my fear of not wanting to write a romance – well, I've given it my spin.

To Kim Woolf and Mary Kganyago, thank you for reading the manuscript. I truly appreciate your feedback and encouragement.

To Tumi Mofokeng, please don't forget your dreams – they matter. P.S. I stole your daughter's name, sending you my love.

To my dearest friend and editor, Thembi Mazibuko, I am nothing without you. This season of my life has been full of challenges, and you have lifted me in so many ways that words can't express. I love you.

To my supporters: the mighty BARE NATION. May you continue anchoring me. You have given me hope when there was none. I love you all.

GOD IS STILL KING.